Frontier Resistance

Leonie Rogers

FRONTIER RESISTANCE
Book 2 of the FRONTIER series

Hague Publishing
PO Box 451
Bassendean Western Australia 6934
Email: contact@haguepublishing.com
Web: www.haguepublishing.com

ISBN 978-0-9925437-0-9

Cover Art: *Frontier Resistance* by Emma Llewelyn
Typography cover design by The Scarlett Rugers Design Agency

Typeset Garamond 11/12
Printed in the USA by CreateSpace

Dedication

To Mal. For all of your patience as I've sat writing, thinking and staring into space. Thank you from the bottom of my heart. Once again, I have to say thank you to Briana, who reads every chapter as I write it, and tells me very honestly if it's working or not. Love you Grubsy.

To Lach, whose drumming, marimba playing and general percussive noise have formed the background to so much of this story. It pains me to admit it, but sometimes it helps me think. Weird eh?

Much love to you all.

Chapter 1

SHANNA ran. Insectoid limbs scythed through the vegetation behind her, and red beams slashed past on either side, scorching as they grazed her skin. Her feet seemed mired in mud, and her pack dragged her backwards, overbalancing her towards the six-limbed creatures that dogged her steps. She flung her head frantically from side to side, desperately seeking her starcats. Where were Storm and Twister?

Ahead of her, she saw Allad stumble and fall, the tall scout's body a smoking ruin as the beams sliced across him. Satin snarled and leapt at the invaders, only to perish in turn. Where were the others? What had happened to them?

Still alone, Shanna struggled on, forcing one leaden leg after the other. She tried to discard her pack, but the straps refused to loosen, and then she stumbled over the first body. Storm. His fur was burnt and his eyes staring, and she burst into tears, sobbing as she ran, wanting to do nothing more than stop and cradle him, yet unable to do so for fear of the aliens hunting her. The tears threatened to blind her, but a voice, screaming from ahead, spurred her on.

Her breath was like fire in her throat, and now she could hear the sounds of offworld footsteps only seconds behind her, while a mound in the vegetation ahead told the tale of another body. Frantically she tried to change her course, but her heavy legs refused to turn and she almost fell as she tried to hurdle the still form. A plaintive "No!" burst from her lips as she recognised the familiar cadet insignia and name on the sleeve of Verren's bloodstained uniform.

The first clutch of an alien limb on her pack almost threw her backwards. Sobbing to breathe, she forced the words out. "Get away! No!" Drawing a ragged breath she tried to turn, but chitinous limbs restrained her. She fought them, but they dragged her back inexorably until she was stranded on her back, held down by the hard alien carapaces, unable to move. She flailed her arms desperately, but they were too heavy. And then she woke, disorientated, lathered in sweat, and panting.

For a moment she panicked, still unable to move and not understanding where she was until a plaintive hum jerked her into the present, and the weight upon her resolved into the anxious faces of two starcats, tidemarks glowing dimly in the darkness. Her muscles lost their terrified tension and she let her head collapse back against the unfamiliar softness of a pillow.

"Storm? Twister?" Relief flooded over her, and one of the feline bodies moved, and then she was able to lift her arms to caress the silky heads. Soft purrs sounded, and she felt the huge cat bodies curl gently around her, providing sorely needed comfort.

For a few moments she just lay there, but the vivid images from her nightmare remained - or rather, the real images of the last year replaced them, devastating in their rawness. Arad's tear streaked face as he sat with Breeze's still form vied with the sound of the alien vehicles destroying the beauty of her home world, grinding relentlessly towards the plateau that housed her people. Images of sliders, swarming towards her as their sensitive antennae quested for living flesh, mixed with a jumbled montage of cliff faces scarred by alien aircraft and flashes of the fear she'd experienced when they'd rescued the human slaves from their Garsal captors.

Then came more images - her brother, Kaidan, standing on the front lines with his bow; Verren binding gaping wounds in the aftermath of the battle; Ragar and Zandany sending their starcats to stand guard on the alien prisoners, and Taya and Amma, standing as stunned as she had, before the glowing Starlyne she'd thought was only an animal but had now proved to be so much more.

Her breath caught in her throat once more. She was inside a Starlyne habitation - she'd gone willingly, because of two images sent by the creatures as they'd communicated with the human beings of Frontier. The first image had shown her the origins of her starcat friends. Within the Starlyne memories, she'd seen a tiny feline creature, newly arrived on a crashed starship and accompanied by a human child, yet frolicking in friendship with a Starlyne youngling in a sunlit glade. The second image had featured Storm, Twister and herself as the hope of both human and Starlyne, and it had engendered a burning desire within her to know more about their intentions and her place within their plans. Surely the fate of colliding worlds could not rest with her and her two starcats? The sweat on her body chilled suddenly, and she convulsively grabbed at the two huge heads next to her. Ear tip tidemarks cycled soothingly as if her cats knew what she was feeling, and slowly the overwhelming emotions were submerged once again by physical exhaustion, and she descended back into the blackness of sleep.

***

A soft chime sounded and Shanna raised her head, rubbing her eyes. Two warm, furry bodies rumbled, purring as she rolled over on the unfamiliarly soft bed and pushed herself upright. As she did her recent bruises made themselves painfully evident. A dim light emanated from the smooth walls around the room, and she could see her classmates stirring sleepily around her, their starcats stretching and chirping, tousled heads slowly appearing.

After she'd gone back to sleep, her dreams had continued to be full of confused nightmares and disjointed emotions, cycling from one to another in a constant whirl, but she suppressed the lingering fears born of her unconscious mind ruthlessly in case they overwhelmed her ability to function. Storm turned knowing eyes on her, but she distracted herself by scratching his head and hoping that her nightmares hadn't disturbed anyone else.

As she lay there, she remembered the moment from the day before, after they had left the pungo grove and followed the Starlyne into the wilderness of Below, when Teacher had paused after several hundred metres of silent travel to speak to them all.

"Your fellows will join us," had come the silent words, along with an image of Nelson, Perri and Barron. The group had exchanged startled glances, and the Starlyne spoke again. "We can speed their healing, and you are needed as a complete unit. Barron will bring a starcat cub for Arad. He has already been chosen." With that startling comment, Teacher turned again and began to glide silently through the trees, her glow illuminating the vegetation.

The patrol had followed almost automatically. Their subsequent trek through the vegetation of Below had been completely free from predator encounters, which Shanna had found oddly eerie. After several hours of walking, the Starlyne had led them into what appeared to be a natural cave. Twenty metres into the winding tunnel, the rough granite walls had become smooth, then after an S-shaped curve the walls began to glow softly, providing a dim illumination that enabled the Patrol to see where they were walking. The starcats padded softly beside their human companions completely unperturbed, while their partners walked wide-eyed, glancing warily around them. Shanna had run a hand down each cat's silky head, and tried to avoid the sudden tremble of apprehension that ran through her body. Teacher had conveyed them without words through the tunnels, winding through a complex maze of many branchings that had made Shanna so dizzy she wondered if she'd ever find her way out again, before showing the Scouts and cadets to their current quarters – two large sleeping rooms, each with an adjacent bathing facility, and a large communal room between, furnished with long low tables and a yielding floor dotted with large cushions. They'd all washed rapidly in the bathing pool, before falling exhausted into the large beds provided. There had been little conversation, and Shanna had felt as if she were in a strange and alien dream.

Now, as she stretched luxuriously, wriggling from side to side, Shanna took another look around the sleeping room. The bed was low and fashioned from what appeared to be a solid piece of polished wood, which was topped with a vaguely organic looking mattress. The bedding looked bizarrely normal and smelt faintly of something freshly aromatic. As she moved around, easing herself out from under her cats, she noticed that the surface under her was oddly yielding, almost conforming to the contours of her body. She yawned widely again, scrubbing her eyes with her hands before running them over her hair, feeling oily wisps sticking out everywhere. Looking around for her pack, Shanna noticed for the first time that there appeared to be small storage compartments built into the walls of the room, and that while she had slept, somehow her pack had ended up tucked neatly into one of them. With a sigh, she swung her legs over the edge of the bed and stood, noticing that she'd apparently taken the time to change into a singlet top and shorts before falling asleep. She must have been exhausted not to remember changing.

"What do you think we're meant to be doing?" asked Amma through a yawn, as she climbed out of the bed next to Shanna. "I think I need to bathe again – I was so tired last night that I seem to have missed a few bits, and I think I might have bled on the pillow." She rubbed at a bloodstain with distaste. Shanna smiled stiffly, feeling the puffy side of her face crinkle uncomfortably, and investigated with a careful fingertip.

"I wouldn't mind another scrub myself, and then perhaps we can get Verren to stick our damaged bits back together."

"Did someone say my name?" Verren lifted a tousled head from under his bedding and yawned widely at the two girls.

"Yes, that was us," laughed Amma, "we're a bit battered still. Can you do a bit of a repair job when we're clean and dressed?"

Verren struggled to a sitting position and stretched stiffly, before swinging his legs gingerly over the edge of the bed and leaning his elbows heavily onto his knees.

"I suppose so." He yawned again. "Give me a few more minutes." He waved a sleepy hand at the two girls, who busied themselves in their packs.

"We'll grab the bathroom then," said Amma. "Shan, do you want to give Taya a poke? We'll get the three of us out of the way, and then they can have it." Shanna grimaced slightly, but rounded Verren's bed and approached Taya, who was sitting up in bed and examining her now grossly swollen left ankle.

"Bath Taya? Amma and I thought the three of us might snaffle the bathing room first, and then Verren's going to patch us up." The other girl looked up and nodded tiredly.

"Can you give me a hand up?" Surprised, Shanna nodded and hauled the other girl to her feet. Taya winced as she placed weight on the leg and hobbled a few steps with Shanna's support. From her bed, Spinner watched carefully and then poured himself off it, easing his large body under Taya's other side with loving gentleness.

"That looks nasty!" Shanna dropped to her haunches, and ran an eye over the swelling and the purpling bruise. "How on earth did you walk on that yesterday? Verren, I think you need to take a look at this now!"

She and Spinner carefully eased Taya back onto her bed as Verren pushed himself resignedly to his feet and, squatting down, gently eased the swollen ankle onto his knee.

"Show me how much you can move it, Taya." He frowned as Taya slowly moved the ankle up and down, then side to side, wincing as the movements pushed into pain. He gently probed the ankle with his fingertips, then grasped the heel and tested the ligaments. Taya gasped in pain as he drew it forward. "Well, that's good," he said, and gently placed her foot back on the floor.

"Good?" gasped Taya, "that nearly killed me!" She narrowed her eyes at Verren.

"It means you still have some ligaments attached," replied Verren. "If it hadn't hurt, you would've been in much more trouble! It'll take a little while to settle down, but if we strap it, it'll feel a lot better, and then you'll need to do some specific exercises. It'll be some weeks until it's properly right, but once you get over the next few days, you should be on the mend. When you've had a chance to get clean, I'll strap it. Shan, help her to the bathing room, and Taya, make sure there's not too much hot water on the ankle or the swelling will get worse." He yawned again, and began rummaging through his pack.

Shanna supported Taya over to the bathing room while Amma sifted through the other girl's pack for some clean clothing. Their four cats purred their way towards the warm bath, dipping their paws into the water with pleased hums. Multicoloured tidemarks rippled in happy rhythms. Shanna supported Taya while she shed her clothing.

"Can you just slide in Taya? And then we'll prop your foot on the edge." Shanna and Amma lowered the injured girl to the edge of the pool, and she slid gracefully into the water at the shallow end, flipping around and propping her foot on the raised edge, before sinking back into the water gratefully.

"Thanks, guys," she even smiled briefly at Shanna, which made her more uneasy, and the three of them began a thorough scrub, shaking out their hair and using handfuls of soapleaves to lather themselves thoroughly.

"So what do you think will be happening today?" asked Shanna. Amma shook her head and shrugged her shoulders.

"After the last few months, I'm not sure anything would surprise me."

Taya wrung out her hair, and tossing it back, began to lift herself out of the warm water, wriggling her toes carefully.

"Who'd know? Two days ago, we thought Starlynes were animals – special animals but still animals, and now we're having a bath inside, I suppose you'd call it one of their houses ... " She shook her head dazedly, and Shanna found herself nodding in agreement. "Well, time to get dressed, and let the others in to get clean, although I think I could stay here all day. Spinner!" Taya called her cat who had been happily lounging on the edge of the pool, paddling his paws in the warm water. The other three stirred themselves, padding over to Taya and after allowing her to use them to balance on while she dressed, assisted her out of the bathing room - Spinner and Spider on each side, while Storm and Twister carefully pushed the door open and held it back.

"Finally!" Ragar greeted the three girls as they exited the bathing room. "Zandany's just about gone back to sleep waiting for you!" Zandany stretched and yawned as he levered himself off his bed.

"You all smell much better,' he grinned, standing back to let Taya hobble to her bed again. She lay down, elevating her ankle with a sigh of relief, and carefully began to comb her long dark hair.

The three girls exchanged smiles, even though Shanna felt slightly awkward about Taya's sudden camaraderie. Picking up her own comb she ran it carefully through the snags in her hair, wincing as the comb stuck in a particularly large tangle. As she tugged the comb through the strands, she resolutely decided it was time to find out what had caused the sudden change of heart.

"Taya?" Shanna's tone was hesitant, and the dark haired girl lifted her head and looked up with a raised eyebrow. Shanna pulled the comb out of her hair, placed it on her bed and gathered her courage. "Why are you being nice to me?" Across the room, Amma's head lifted with a sudden jerk, and she dropped the sock she was putting on.

There was a long silence, while emotions chased themselves one by one across Taya's face. Some of the old hatred flickered briefly, followed by a dull rising flush, then her shoulders sagged and her face crumpled, while a surprising tear slid down one cheek. Taya ducked her head and scrubbed at her face. There was complete silence in the room; Amma sitting statue-like on her bed. Shanna slowly dragged her comb through another tangle while holding her breath, and the four cats were uncharacteristically silent.

The tableau was broken as Spinner gently nudged Taya's hands with his nose, ruby tidemarks glinting softly. She raised her face, and Shanna was horrified to see a torrent of tears pouring down the other girl's face. She made an involuntary movement towards Taya, but stopped mid-movement as Taya cleared her throat noisily and scrubbed her hand across her face again, drying the tears on her trouser leg.

Clearing her throat, Taya set her shoulders back, and turned to look over her shoulder at Amma.

"Come and sit over here. I'm only going through this once. It may as well be now, and then you can tell the others." She sniffed, looking much younger than Shanna had ever imagined that she could. Amma wasted no time, and carrying her boots and socks over to where Taya sat on her bed, settled herself on the floor next to Shanna. The four cats settled down at their partners' feet, as Amma and Shanna exchanged puzzled glances.

"It was two years ago that it began," said Taya. She wiped a final tear from her cheek and shook her dark hair back. "My father is a stone mason, and my mother works as an artificer for the council. I was with my father at a quarry east of Watchtower, waiting for him to arrange delivery of an order of stone for one of his projects." She paused, and deliberately pushed her hair off her face again. "The owner had a starcat – a large male called Phantom, with deep violet ear tip tidemarks." She raised a hand as Shanna leaned forward, stopping the younger girl's sudden exclamation. "I know — he's one of the cats bred by your parents." Shanna went to speak again, and Taya impatiently hushed her, some of the animosity returning to her face. "He was the first starcat that I'd met up close, and I found him absolutely fascinating. For an hour he allowed me to stroke him, and I was flattered that he seemed to like me so much. Well, Dad finished up his business, and we hopped back into our wagon and headed off home to Watchtower." She paused and cleared her throat, tears glinting in her eyes again, but defiantly rubbed her hand across her face and continued.

"We were only on the road for about fifteen minutes, and I was telling Dad all about Phantom, when it happened. We'd been laughing and chatting about how great it would be if we could have our own cat, when Dad stopped laughing. His face went white and he was staring at me." Taya paused, her eyes looking into the distance. "He couldn't even speak, and I was looking around frantically, wondering if some predator was about to pounce. I was saying: 'Dad, Dad, what's wrong?' But he just kept looking at me, and then he reached forward with one hand, and it was shaking so much that I thought he was ill." Taya's face was crumpled, and her voice was quivering when she finally managed to continue. "He, he, f-finally managed to hook one f-finger into m-my hair, and pulled it over my sh-shoulder so that I could see it. And there it was…glowing. Exactly the same shade and pattern of Phantom's tidemarks."

Taya paused, and then deliberately pulled a lock of hair forward over her shoulder, and before Shanna and Ammas' astounded eyes, the lock of hair began to glow in the familiar rippling patterns of a starcat's coat. As they watched, the rest of her hair took on the pattern, gently twinkling and shining iridescent ruby against the background of brown so dark it was almost black. As Shanna and Amma sat, silently astounded, Taya went on.

"My father was horrified. He kept telling me to stop, and eventually he began to shake me, and shout at me. He became more and more angry when I couldn't make my hair stop glowing. Eventually I had to climb out of the wagon because he was hurting me." Her eyes were haunted. "I ran in the end, and hid in the bush. He shouted and shouted for what seemed like hours, but I stayed hidden deep in a patch of pungo trees, until eventually he stopped shouting, and began to plead for me to come out. I was frightened. I'd never seen my father like that. He was so angry with me!" Again Taya wiped tears from her eyes, hair glowing incongruously brightly, reflecting off the drops rolling down her cheeks.

"When I finally crawled out of the bush, he was sobbing, down on his knees at the edge of the road, begging me to come out and come home. Even then, he could barely look at me. When I finally came back to the wagon, he made me wrap my hair up in an old cloth, and then run from the wagon into the house when we got home. He wouldn't look at me or talk to me the whole way there. I ran into my room, and looked into the mirror. My hair was like this," she held up a strand, "glowing in Phantom's patterns, except that now, it glows in Spinner's patterns."

"But Taya, how come we've never seen your hair do that before?" Amma broke in.

Taya looked at the two of them.

"When my mother found out, she was furious with my father. She came into my room, and just looked at me, then after covering my hair with a scarf, she took me to see Master Cerren. In her position as an artificer, she'd heard enough about him to know that he might be able to help. I felt like a freak, and I was sure that if people found out about my hair they'd react like my father had." She looked around then, and nodded sadly to herself. "We've all spoken about the physical changes in the population. No-one worries about the little ones, but it's different when things are so obvious, and it wasn't only the visible changes with me. When we reached Master Cerren's office, my mother ushered me inside and pulled the scarf off my hair. By that time, I was exhausted and shaking. I just stood there, while Master Cerren looked up at me." Amma put a hand on Taya's arm, and Shanna found that her own hand had involuntarily risen to her mouth.

"For a few moments he said nothing, and then asked the two of us to sit down. His old cat, Prince, strolled over to me, and nudged me with his head. My hair immediately changed colour to match his tidemarks, and then the clock over the mantelpiece stopped ticking. It was quite loud, so the sudden silence was very obvious, and then, to make things worse, all the lamps went out."

"But, but ... " Amma was unable to get any further.

"Amma, it was me. Master Cerren was calm, as was my mother, and after the initial surprise, they tested me with a number of devices in the Masters' offices. I was a freak. Lamps went out, mechanical devices ceased working around me, and my hair kept changing colour and pattern – I literally glowed in the dark."

Shanna took a deep breath.

"But you must have learned to control it, because none of us had any idea!"

Taya nodded.

"Master Cerren worked with me for several days before I was able to change my hair back to its original colour. He talked me through what was going on, and tried to convince me that it was just a simple change, in fact perhaps an enhancement of our genes as a result of our time here on Frontier – you know what I'm talking about – we've been over it time after time since we first found the Garsal aircraft. And now, we find out that the Starlynes have been tampering with us the whole time we've been there – and it's probable that I'm not really a freak. It took me months to get everything under control properly, and then I began Scout training." Taya's hair dimmed to its natural colour, and then the walls around them began to pulse in Spinner's tidemark patterns. Shanna blinked several times in disbelief.

"Taya, was it because of Phantom that you hated me so much?" Shanna's voice trembled, and she had trouble meeting the other girl's eyes.

The dark haired girl grimaced.

"Partly — I'd spent so much time trying to learn to control myself and stop glowing in the dark, or extinguishing lights and seizing mechanical equipment, and then, all of a sudden, there was the possibility of ending up with one of your family's starcats — and one of those had provided the catalyst for my abnormalities to make themselves known. The truth be told that it wasn't just the starcat that bothered me, but that you were so much younger than the rest of us — and so normal! And then you turned up with two cats, and every time I was near you and those two cats, it became harder and harder to stop my hair changing. There was something about the combination of Storm, Twister, and yourself, and the constant nearness of Spinner, that seemed to erode my self control. I was continually struggling to avoid showing everyone how different I was, and the closer I got to Spinner, the harder the struggle became. Shanna, you were everything I wanted to be, and you were way too young! And way too normal! Every time I turned around you were there, doing it better Even now, it's easier to change the wall colours just because you're near me. Even one of your cats near me makes me edge closer to losing control!" A trace of the old resentment flashed across Taya's face.

"But Taya, I didn't know! I didn't mean to make anything difficult for you — and I wouldn't have a clue why the boys and I make things tougher!" Shanna was almost crying, and she cleared her throat, frantically trying to control her emotions.

Amma put her other hand on the younger girl's arm, and gripped it gently.

"Shan, this isn't your fault, and Taya, your abilities are not your fault either — like you said, they're most likely to be one of the changes that the Starlynes have facilitated." She looked grimly at the other two girls. "And who knows what they've done to the rest of us? I, for one, intend to ask some very direct questions!" She tied her bootlace with a firm tug, and looked firmly at the other two. "And one more thing Taya, are you sure that you can only fade with the assistance of Spinner?" Amma's voice was accusing.

The other girl looked slightly guilty.

"Every time I tried without Spinner I could feel my control slipping, and I knew that you'd all find out about me, so I pretended that I needed Spinner to help me — that way I could stop my hair glowing, but still fade. It made me so angry that everyone thought that learning to fade was such a great thing, but that I still needed to hide what I was." Her voice trailed off. Shanna looked at the ground as she wondered what to say.

"Well, that was interesting!" Ragar's voice startled the three girls, and they realised that he and the other two young men had probably been listening for some time. "Do we really need the new wall decorations Tay?"

Taya gave a start, and the walls returned to their previous soft glow.

"Sorry, forgot I'd done that." She ducked her head, looking at the floor in some embarrassment.

"You know," said Verren thoughtfully. "Here we are — in quarters provided by an alien race, knowing they've been fiddling with our genetic makeup in ways we don't understand, but ready to learn whatever they teach us, to deal with yet another alien race ... and one of us has learnt to vanish, another glows in the dark and turns off equipment, so who knows what they've done to the rest of us? It's not really what I signed on to Scout training for! I think my head's about to explode!" He flopped heavily on to his bed. "Someone tell me if I start growing tentacles!"

There was a collective laugh at the bizarre nature of their predicament, and some of the emotion in the room eased to a more manageable level as the cadets went back to finishing their dressing, and tidying away their belongings, just as if what they'd heard was an everyday occurrence.

Shanna's head buzzed with Taya's revelations. The root of all of the older girl's animosity was now bare for her to see, and there was a small hope that their relationship might really begin to change for the better. After all the frustrations of the last months, Shanna wasn't quite sure how to proceed though, and as she tied her bootlace and tucked her trouser leg back down, she sighed internally yet again. A thought struck her.

"If Master Cerren knew about you, Taya, and how to help you learn to control things, there must be others who have changed and required help! Who and where are they?"

"Part of the answer is here." Spiron's deep voice caused a sudden cessation of activity in the room, and the cadets turned as one to the adjoining door where the Patrol First was standing. He opened one hand and a soft glow, similar to Taya's hair, outlined it and radiated from his palm, finally appearing to hover like a ball of light above it.

Chapter 2

THERE was a stunned silence as Spiron, apparently clutching a ball of light, strolled into their room. He was followed by the rest of the Patrol, all fully dressed and ready for the day. Apart from Spiron's glowing ball, Challon appeared to be causing a small spark to sizzle from one fingertip to another, Karri and Kalli each had glowing hair just like Taya's. Arad, still with red rimmed eyes, was mirroring Spiron's efforts, and Sandar appeared to be balancing a small flame over his fingertips. Allad brought up the rear, nonchalantly gesturing with one fingertip at the door, which promptly slammed shut and then opened again to allow seven, slightly affronted starcats inside.

"It's time for a few more explanations," said the Patrol First, grinning at the cadets with an amused twinkle in his eyes. "But let's sit in the other room. Someone appears to have left breakfast for us, and I'm hungry." He exited the cadets' sleeping quarters, followed by his amused patrol, and the six speechless cadets. The tables in the other room were covered in a variety of fruits and hot cereal, and there was a line of bowls along one wall, obviously intended for the starcats. Steaming pitchers of tea sat on the tables' polished surfaces, and the group eagerly filled plates, bowls, and mugs before seating themselves slightly awkwardly either on the yielding floor surface, or on the cushions scattered around the room. The sight of familiar human crockery and cutlery seemed out of place in the oddly alien surroundings.

Shanna opened her mouth to ask a question as the Patrol First seated himself, but he forestalled her with an upraised palm. "Eat, and we will explain." He spooned a mouthful of porridge himself, and waved the spoon at Allad while his mouth was full. The tall Scout smiled briefly and began.

"So, Taya, you've finally come clean?" Allad's moustached face was compassionate as he looked at Taya, who had propped her injured ankle up on one of the cushions and was slowly spooning warm porridge into her mouth. Her face was surprised but she nodded hesitantly, then looked down. There was a glint of red playing across her hair. "As you all know, it takes many and varied skills to become a Scout. You need to be bright, practical, and most of all, flexible. You need to be acceptable to starcats, and in addition, we look for a small spark of something else." Allad paused briefly, bit into a juicy sorplum, chewed a moment and went on.

"The conversation that we began up on the plateau when we discovered the first piece of that Garsal craft was the first step in sounding you out about the 'differences' that occur in the human population here on Frontier. Until now, we've never been precisely sure why nearly all Scouts demonstrate some kind of extra talent, and it's not something that we talk about except in general terms, until a cadet has demonstrated that spark."

"But no one said anything when I faded…" Shanna was confused.

"We were a little distracted at the time," replied Allad with a wry grin. "It was really the last thing on anyone's mind right then as we were still coming to grips with the revelations about the Garsal and the threat of imminent invasion. Fortunately your fellow cadets didn't seem too perturbed, and of course we already knew about Taya, so we just let it ride – to sort out at a later date. In the Scout Corps, such gifts are expected and are very welcome. It's not widely known outside the Corps, of course, and there are those who are not Scouts who demonstrate those same gifts as well. Most are identified early, like Taya, and if they appear suitable, are subtly directed towards us as a career option."

"So, does that mean that all of us are likely to start glowing in the dark?" said Verren incredulously.

"Well, no," replied Allad. "Actually, we've no idea what you're capable of – but we're fairly certain that all of you will have that special spark, as that's actually part of my talent – sensing that spark – and if that first cyclone clean-up hadn't fortuitously placed you all under our patrol's supervision, then the first trip Below would have done so – deliberately. I can usually tell whether a cadet has the spark, and I think that you all do. However, it remains to be seen just what form that spark will take. There are several of us with my talent."

"So this 'spark' you're talking about – do you think it relates to what the Starlynes have done to humanity since we've been here?" asked Zandany.

Allad nodded. "We originally thought that it was the planet changing us, but we've had to revise all of our preconceptions in the last two days. We also suspect that we've only just scratched the surface of what the Starlynes may have done to us."

Spiron nodded his head emphatically at Allad's statement, and there was a murmur of agreement from the rest of the Patrol.

"In fact we're hoping that they explain precisely what they've done, rather than leaving us with the rather vague information imparted a couple of days ago. That's one of the reasons we're here." The Patrol First scraped the last spoonful from his bowl, and then placed it on the table in front of him. Levering himself to his feet he looked around the room, eyeing each Scout and Cadet individually, face contemplative. "That's one of the first things we need to address with Teacher. We don't want to be blindly following instructions without understanding what's really going on – it's not our way. We've spent over three hundred years learning how to live on this planet and working towards regaining the stars. To simply do everything an alien race suggests, just because they've been clandestinely altering us to suit their aims, does not seem either reasonable or sensible. The council would also like to know why, if one Starlyne can stop a convoy of Garsal vehicles in its tracks, then why can't they do the same thing to anything mechanical?"

There was a flurry of nods around the room. Ragar spoke up. "Yes, I'd wondered that too. It seems like a much simpler response than altering an entire race!"

Shanna nodded emphatically, agreeing with her fellow cadet and wondering what else the Starlynes might have done to the human population living on Frontier, and what forms that 'spark' the older Scouts talked about might take in her friends. As if sensing her disquiet, Storm bumped her hand with his large head and purred gently as she ran her hand over his silky fur.

"What do you think might happen today?" asked Amma, with some uncertainty. "Keeper talked as if time was a premium."

"Yes, he did," replied Spiron. "I suggest we clean up and meet back in here shortly. I'm sure that our hosts will be along very soon — they woke us and have given us time to clean up and eat, and if there were no reason for that they wouldn't have done so." He turned, called Fury, and exited the central room, followed by the rest of the patrol. The cadets filed out one by one trailed by their cats, and without talking began to tidy their sleeping room.

Shanna carefully stowed her belongings in her pack, separating her filthy, damaged clothes into a separate pile, and hoping that she might have the opportunity to wash and repair them at some point in the future. She carefully tucked her glowstone into the neck of her uniform shirt, feeling a pang of homesickness as she handled its smoothness. She firmly pushed the homesickness back down, trying to concentrate on pulling herself together so that she would be able to cope with whatever the day might bring. Twister gave her a gentle nudge with his nose and she absently scratched his head before tightening her belt and firming up her boot laces. She wondered what Kaidan was up to, whether he was home, whether her parents really had any idea what their daughter was doing, and if they did, what they thought. She absently pulled her bedding together, and smoothed the soft quilt with her hand. She scratched her cats again. Contented purring resonated from both of them.

Shanna swiped each soft coat with a loving hand and looked around the sleeping room. Verren was just taking a roll of strapping out of his pack, and Ragar was tightening a boot lace. Across the room, Taya was sitting on her bed waiting for Verren to strap her ankle, and as Shanna watched she could see the odd glint of red chasing across her hair. Amma was sitting, scratching a purring Spider, and Zandany was staring thoughtfully at nothing much while rubbing Punch's ears.

"What are you thinking, Zan?" asked Shanna curiously.

Zandany smiled at her and stood. "I was just wondering what kind of strange thing that I might be about to start doing, actually. I haven't started glowing or vanishing, have I?" He grinned again, and pulled one of Punch's ears, and the big cat hummed happily at him.

"No glowing, no vanishing – I think that's my speciality – and so far no other weird stuff either," replied Shanna grinning back at him, feeling slightly less apprehensive about the days ahead, realising that she wasn't alone in all of the uncertainty. It was comforting to understand that the other cadets were probably feeling exactly as she was, and with a rush of compassion she looked across again at Taya. Resolutely, she decided that she needed to speak to Taya privately when the next opportunity arose. Despite the older girl's startling confessions she knew there were still unresolved issues between them, and that the enmity they'd felt had run too deep to simply begin a new relationship immediately.

"Shall we go out then?" asked Ragar, "Verren's strapped Taya's ankle up, everything's tidy, and there's a whole new pile of experiences just around the corner. Mind you, I think I'm a little scared – Tay, you can lean on me if you need to." He walked around the end of his bed and helped Taya up, letting her lean on him as she tested how her ankle felt in the strapping. "How does it feel?" he asked

"Better, thanks to Verren!" Taya limped a couple of careful steps, nodded to Ragar and removed her arm from his shoulder, while Spinner paced within easy reach of his partner.

Back in the communal room, they found the rest of the Patrol seated on cushions on the floor. Shanna was startled to realise that all the debris of breakfast had vanished and the tables moved over to the far wall, leaving nothing on their polished surfaces except for some pitchers of water and tall jugs containing a variety of juices. Some cups, apparently fashioned from tree knots, were placed next to them. The cadets sat down with the Patrol members, their Starcats lazily couching themselves next to their partners, completely at ease. They all looked around bemusedly at each other, and then Karri said. "So, what's next?"

***

Anjo looked out of the window over the rooftops of Watchtower. The sun lit the light coloured stone buildings of the town, built to withstand the violent cyclonic storms that regularly spiralled in from the ocean to devastate the continent. The storm season was now nearly over, and Anjo wondered what the insectoid Garsal would do next, and what their response to the loss of their vehicles would be. Two days previously, Master Erilla had been suddenly summoned from her questioning of Anjo and he'd not seen her since. The quarters to which he'd been assigned were comfortable and were next to those allocated to Semba. There had been no requirement for either of the offworlders to remain sequestered in their quarters, and they had been encouraged to join in the communal eating in the Scout Compound, had they so wished. Anjo's stomach rumbled, and he decided to venture into the eatery. Leaving his room, he tapped on Semba's door. "Semba, are you coming to eat?" There was a short silence while Anjo waited patiently.

"I-I'll stay here again this morning, but come in and chat when you're back." Semba's voice was quavery, and Anjo sighed. The woman had been emotionally fragile since their rescue, and Anjo worried about how slow she'd been to recover. He'd felt nothing but enormous relief since his arrival on the plateau along with a desire to make the most of whatever this new world might offer, and hoped fervently that he would never need to go Below again.

"All right, I'll see you after breakfast."

Anjo descended the two flights of stairs down to the ground floor and walked along the wider corridor to the dining hall. There were several Scouts still eating their breakfasts, and Anjo recognised Master Cerren sitting with a boy who looked oddly familiar. He looked up as Anjo walked through the door and beckoned him over to the table.

"When you've filled your plate, please join Kaidan and myself. "I've a few things to talk over with you."

"Of course Master Cerren," Anjo replied, returning the young man's welcoming smile. He filled his plate with food, enjoying having hot, freshly cooked food every day; it was such a contrast to his time as a Garsal slave.

"Anjo," Master Cerren said, as Anjo sat down next to them. "This is Kaidan, you know his sister, Shanna – the girl with the two cats." Anjo nodded, eyebrows lifted with surprise as the pieces clicked into place – the familiarity of Kaiden's features now made sense.

Swallowing his mouthful, Anjo replied, "She's quite a remarkable young lady, Kaidan. She saved my life." Kaidan smiled at him.

"Yes she's certainly one of a kind," Kaidan said.

Master Cerren raised an eyebrow at Kaidan, and the young man blushed a fiery red. "And she's also quite nice," he said hurriedly, "Actually I really do like her – most of the time."

Master Cerren's cat roused herself from her relaxed position near his feet and nudged Kaidan with her large head, and Kaidan absently scratched her along the line of her jaw. She purred thunderously. Even after almost three weeks with these people, Anjo still had difficulty reacting calmly to the enormous felines that strolled so casually and seemingly everywhere on this planet. The large, dark grey cat looked at him and slowly blinked her violet eyes, the glowing tidemarks rippling across her coat in slow, rhythmic patterns, and he had a feeling that she knew exactly what he was thinking. He forked up another mouthful of food slightly nervously, and chewed slowly, trying to relax his suddenly tense muscles.

"I'd like you to spend some time with Kaidan each day, Anjo. He'll be teaching you about this planet, and how to avoid some of the more common hazards you'll encounter as you learn to live here. It's something all children here learn as a matter of course, and it's essential you learn the basics so that you can move around safely when you finally leave Scout Compound." The Master smiled, "And you will eventually, when this is over." There was quiet confidence in his voice, the confidence that made the people of this planet so unusual in Anjo's experience. Of course, he reminded himself, they had never known subjugation under the Garsal, had never had their independence compromised, living only under their own laws. As far as he could tell, from his limited experience of less than three weeks, the society was egalitarian and very ordered. Everyone seemed to have some kind of place or purpose to their existence.

"When will I start?" he asked.

"Kaidan has time after breakfast each day. He can work with you for two hours each morning, but then he has other tasks. I need to resume discussing the Garsal with you each day after lunch. There have been a number of changes in the situation that require some rethinking, and you may still have more information that will allow us to rescue the other humans on their ship, and then rid the planet of the Garsal. When you return to your room after breakfast, you'll find some more suitable clothing. Kaidan will go with you now and when you've changed, he'll get your education started."

"What about Semba?" Anjo asked. "She'll be expecting me to drop in."

"I'll make sure she's fine. I think she still needs some more time to adjust to her change of circumstances." Master Cerren hesitated slightly. "Anjo, did you know she was actually born in captivity to the Garsal? She's never known anything else. You at least remember living free, and were always thinking of escape. Semba was born in an experimental breeding colony in a Garsal hive, and transferred onto your ship directly from there." Master Cerren's face was grave, and Anjo realised he'd never talked to Semba about her past. He'd always assumed that she'd been taken from a human colony that had been overtaken by the Garsal like he had. Life had been hard, but there was always the small hope of freedom, and rumours that 'somewhere' members of the federation were still resisting the Garsal invasion. He'd never met a resistance member, or even known anyone who had, but there were enough rumours that nearly everyone believed there were those who resisted, no matter how futile that seemed. He realised that Semba had no concept of life free of the insectoid invaders, and no foundation for living except under Garsal rule.

"I had no idea. We didn't speak much on the ship, because of the informers. And on the vehicle, there was no time..." He broke off, ashamed that he'd never thought to ask Semba about her previous life but had simply made assumptions, which he now discovered were not based in reality. "I'll try and spend some time with her each day, help her to adjust. It must be almost impossible for her to understand your society." Anjo pushed out his chair and stood. "I'll go and change now. If you'll join me in a few minutes, Kaidan?"

***

Kaidan watched the offworlder leave the dining room and then turned back to Master Cerren. "Master, when will I be able to go home to see Mum and Dad?"

Master Cerren's face was compassionate. "Not yet, Kaidan. I'm sorry, but this is an important task I've set you to, and it's essential that we explain a few things to your family before you speak to them yourself. I've sent messages to them and they know you're fine, and that Shanna's on an extended trip Below." He hesitated briefly, then nodded decisively to himself. "They'll be in Watchtower in about five days' time, as I've asked them to meet with myself and the council here. We'll be explaining to them, and the other starcat breeders, exactly what's happened in the last few weeks." He looked gravely at Kaidan. "From our discussions with the Starlynes, it appears that our cats may have more of a role to play in maintaining our freedom than we imagined. At that time, we'll also explain what your part in all of this will be." He stood up decisively. "In the meantime, you can start familiarising Anjo with this world. Remember that he knows nothing of how to survive here — not a thing, and I expect you to bring him home each morning relatively unscathed! And if you encounter anyone except Scouts or your archery group, explain that he is visiting from Starfall, and is unfamiliar with our local hazards. Hopefully that will keep most people from inquiring too deeply about his origin until we're ready to explain everything. Which we will very shortly." He looked at Kaidan with an earnest expression, "It's essential that Anjo's identity as an offworlder is kept quiet until the right time. Can I trust you with this?"

Kaidan nodded gravely to the Master, who looked at him for a moment more. Socks purred and he nodded decisively to himself. "Off you go now, then and get started." He made a shooing motion with his hands and Kaidan, sighing internally, turned away and left the dining room.

He was still very unsettled, very homesick, and missing his family in a way that he'd never expected. In the days since his part in the battle against the Garsal, and after the Starlyne revelations, he'd felt unmoored from his foundations, adrift in uncertainties and isolation. When the greying Master Cerren had approached him about educating the offworlder, he'd been flattered and jumped at the chance to do something other than mope about, confined as he'd been to Scout Compound, but it didn't change the fact that he missed his family. His group of archers were also still in the compound, but he was so much younger than the others and missed having friends his own age.

Sighing again, he climbed the stairs to the second level and waited outside the quarters assigned to Anjo. The offworlder had been pleasant but he had a very strange accent, and Kaidan hoped he'd be able to understand him.

Chapter 3

FOR thirty minutes, the Patrol and the cadets had sat uneasily on the floor of the communal living area, all looking a little uncertainly at each other, slightly unsettled, and all wondering what might happen next. The waiting was a bit anticlimactic. Shanna finally resorted to scratching Storm and Twister, running her hands over their scrapes and missing fur. Unlike their human counterparts, both were completely relaxed in the unfamiliar surroundings and purred loudly as they draped their long lengths around her, tidemarks softly glowing in the colours and patterns of the completely unconcerned starcat. She ran her hands over Storm's head, and the blue marked cat melted himself luxuriously into her lap. His brother wriggled slightly and leaned himself more comfortably against Shanna's back, rumbling with contented purring.

The room was oddly quiet, and Shanna could see the other cadets sneaking nervous glances at each other. She attempted a nervous grin as Ragar wiggled his eyebrows at her across the room, and sighed internally as she resigned herself to waiting. Idly, she wondered what Challon did with his sparks, or how useful glowing hair really was. Balls of light and little flames had obvious uses, and Allad had already demonstrated his ability to close and open doors; and his ability to determine whether others had the "spark" that the Scouts seem to value so highly was obviously quite useful. She pondered her fading ability, and made her hands fade. She decided to see if she could make them vanish alternately to while away the time while she waited. It took a little concerted concentration, but she finally managed it and amused herself by fading them in alternating patterns, counting under her breath as she experimented.

"Shan!" There was a furious whisper from Taya, "Can you stop that?" Shanna looked up, startled, to see Taya frowning at her, brows lowered, as her hair pulsed in Spinner's tidemark patterns.

"Sorry, Taya, I wasn't thinking!" Shanna was apologetic. She hastily made her right hand reappear and tucked her hands away in her lap, wondering if she'd managed to alienate Taya just when they'd made some progress on repairing their relationship. Storm grunted, slightly affronted, as she disturbed his slumbers. She watched curiously as Taya's hair slowly settled back into its normal colour, noticing that the wall behind the other girl showed faint tidemark patterns for a few moments after her hair had stopped glowing.

Abruptly the door into the outer corridor opened and Teacher glided in, coiling her large body into concentric circles so quickly that Shanna was startled that such a large ... personage ... (she had to quickly replace the word 'beast' in her mind) was able to move so rapidly. There was a flurry of movement and Teacher was suddenly surrounded by the group's starcats, all gently rubbing their long lengths against her coils in an ecstasy of greeting, and the room was momentarily filled with hums and purrs. Storm had almost catapulted out of Shanna's lap in his hurry to greet Teacher. The Starlyne lowered her head and unfolded her hands to run them over the shining bodies.

The Scouts and Cadets came to their feet in a group, and Spiron stepped forward towards Teacher. She raised her head and the group again experienced the almost overwhelming communication without words that sufficed for Starlyne speech. This time, Shanna wasn't quite as disoriented by the flow of information.

"Welcome to our abode," came the quiet voice, accompanied by images of the entry to the underground dwelling, the quarters where the humans had been accommodated, and what Shanna imagined must be other areas where the Starlynes dwelt. "This is just one of our places of residence here Below. We will use it as your training base for some time then we will move on. There are many facilities like this across this planet you have named Frontier. We call it differently – for us this world is called 'Haven' – the only place of safety we found in our flight from the Garsal threat so long ago." Along with the last statement came a flood of emotion, sorrow for safety now lost, mixed with hope for a possible final resolution of an ages old conflict. The two emotions warred, and Shanna felt slightly unsteady with the level of their intensity and she almost staggered physically as they ceased.

"My apologies, students." Teacher ducked her head. "You are unaccustomed to our way of speaking, and I neglected to temper my feelings. I did not mean to overwhelm you."

"Teacher," said Spiron. "As you said, we aren't yet accustomed to the way you communicate but I am sure we will learn to adjust. Might we ask what you plan for this time we have with you?"

"Of course," she replied. "We have waited to allow you to sleep and refresh yourselves, so that you might be ready to understand what we have to tell you." She finished stroking the starcats, and rearranged herself slightly as they returned to their partners. "We know that you have many questions, and there is much to explain about what we have done to your species, over many years, without your knowledge." There was a brief wave of discomfort from the Starlyne. "When we made the first choice to begin to assist the changes within your species, it was a time of much uncertainty for our people." Quickly flowing images of Starlynes conferring in groups, with traces of confusion, concern, and, oddly, guilt, wafting through the montages, flitted across the minds of the assembled humans, before Teacher went on. "We feared that when one day we had to tell you what we had done, you would withdraw from us, or even turn against us. We felt guilt for accelerating the natural changes that without doubt would set you apart from the rest of your race, and even now there is still no consensus that we have done the right thing. Most of us believe you to be the best hope for both species, but there is a small group that fears what you might become if your people become resentful of the changes."

"You've talked frequently of these changes," said Spiron. "That is our first question – what do you mean by changes?"

Teacher folded her hands beneath her neck, apparently somehow drawing her arms into the flesh of her body, leaving only the tips of her fingers visible. Her glowing sides rippled in muddy patterns, and there was a silent pause for a few minutes. Shanna held her breath, then let it out in a rush as Teacher continued. The image of the small feline, the child, and the Starlyne youngling hovered in the air between the Starlyne and the humans.

"You know from your own records that the survivors of the crash struggled to live on this world. Every year since the first one was held, we have listened in on your Day of Remembrance Ceremonies, and each year we have grieved with you. The survivors of the crash still had many of the tools of high technology at their disposal in those early years, so when they had secured the first interlude of peace from the denizens of this world, they began to record and observe the symbiotic viruses and spores that they realised had already begun to blend with humanity. Right from the beginning, the leaders of the colony decided to restrict the information in order to avoid panic. Wisely, they felt that this information would only add to the fears of the involuntary settlers, particularly since they knew that the remains of their original high technology equipment would last only for a short while. Stored away in your records at Starfall are the original projections of the changes that humanity might undergo – or as much as your ancestors were able to understand and extrapolate with the technology that they had left to them."

"I have seen a little of what you are talking about," interjected Spiron. "It is part of the information a Patrol Leader is made privy to, but some of our records have deteriorated over time, and for some we now lack the technology to access it. We have records of some of the technology our ancestors were unable to maintain and have slowly begun to rebuild our civilisation, but we are still a long way from being able to reclaim what we once had. We know so much, and understand so much, but for us, surviving the challenges of this planet has taken so much of our available resources that only recently have we begun to attempt to reconstruct some of the more basic pieces of technology our ancestors took for granted. We have the theory, but lack both the human and material resources for construction." He broke off as Teacher inclined her head to him.

"Patrol Leader, this is known to us. It is not a failing of your people that this is so. From afar we have admired your perseverance. The creatures and vegetation of this world almost destroyed you in the beginning – that your ancestors preserved so much and that you have valued the education of your children almost above all, is to the credit of your race. We have watched your struggles, and we made that one, now irreversible, choice to change your species' development." She gently eased her narrow tail on the floor. Bizarrely, Shanna noticed that the very end of her tail was tipped in a gently glowing silky tassel.

"As your species became gradually infected with the symbiotic viruses that make their home on this world we, in turn, chose to make some adjustments of our own that would accelerate those changes, and also give you conscious control over those changes. We also chose to do the same to the feline companions that had come with you from your home world. With them, and yourselves, we facilitated the incorporation of the symbiotic viruses into your tissues, but added our own technological expertise to enable complete integration of the changes. We arranged things so that those of you compatible with the newly developed starcats would change faster. To a certain extent, they have acted as our catalysts." There was a start from Taya. "Since many of you ended up in the Scout Corps, there began to be an acceptance of what you now call the 'spark' of ability within that body. With each generation that 'spark' has intensified, so that now we have not only those with the 'spark', but their catalyst companions, who you call starcats, approaching the pinnacle of development." Again Teacher paused, and Shanna tried to understand what the Starlyne had told them. Once again, the group was overwhelmed with a series of images. Some seemed familiar from her studies of biology, some seemed to relate to even more complex concepts than those she had studied, and some were of various humans and starcats. With a start, Shanna recognised some she knew – Master Cerren and Prince, her mother and Sabre, Josen and his starcat, Master Yendy, Master Peron, and then that same image of herself and her two cats, this time ringed with both her cadet group and Patrol Ten, prominent amongst them Satin and Allad.

"You are the first humans who will learn to fully control and use your talents. Some of you have discovered the beginnings of what you might do, others as yet have no idea. But within this group is the catalyst for even more rapid change." The Scouts and cadets all looked a little uneasily at each other.

"What do you mean 'only the beginnings'?" asked Allad. His moustache bristled slightly, and Satin rubbed her sleek head gently against his hand. She began a deep rumbling purr.

"You have learnt a few tricks, Allad, and your ability to detect the spark is well developed, but there is much more to learn, even for you." There was a hint of a smile in the silent voice and, Shanna thought, underlying amusement. "Follow me now and we will begin. There is much you have to learn, and the sooner you begin the better. But first the injured amongst you must be healed." The Starlyne abruptly uncoiled herself and glided towards the door in a fluid, sinuous movement. Slightly startled at the sudden movement, the normally athletic group was slow to regain their feet. The door to the outer hallway opened smoothly to allow Teacher's passage, and the human contingent filed out slowly, accompanied by their feline companions.

Verren nudged Shanna. "So what do you think we'll end up being able to do? As far as I know, I've never demonstrated any kind of weird ability!"

Shanna rolled her eyes at him. "Verren, you learnt to fade!"

"Oh yes ... but I meant something that you can't do."

"Well, that means you'll probably never be able to cook then," replied Ragar with a quiet snicker as they paced after the Starlyne. The other cadets smiled, even Taya, who was limping slightly despite Zandany's supporting elbow, and they followed Patrol Ten and the Starlyne down the dimly lit corridor.

Many twists and turns later, the Starlyne paused outside another sliding door. "Please enter, and your injuries will be treated. When you are healed, we will begin to explore what you can do." With that cryptic statement the door opened, and Teacher gestured for them to enter. There were a number of Starlynes gliding across the cushioned floor, and a number of raised platforms dotted here and there across the room. As the group entered, the sinuous creatures paused in their activities and turned towards them, fanning out towards individuals.

Several hours later, Shanna touched the side of her face incredulously for what must have been the tenth time, marvelling at the lack of pain and swelling. Just in front of her she could see Taya rotating her ankle and smiling up at the Starlyne who was gently running her fingers down the outside of the girl's leg. There was an immense feeling of satisfaction emanating from the creatures in the room. Shanna had sat enthralled on one of the platforms, watching as the Starlyne healers gently probed each injury with their fingertips, their bodies glowing and flickering in complex patterns. After several moments of simply sitting curled in one spot, they would abruptly uncoil and hasten towards the outer edge of the room. At a touch, a drawer or bench would appear from the apparently seamless wall and the Starlyne would remove either equipment or vial from the surface, before gliding back to their human patient and applying whatever equipment or medication they had determined would help. Despite the alien environment, Shanna had found it difficult to feel fearful of the huge gliding Starlynes and their novel methods of treatment. Watching her friends' bruises and cuts fade, and seeing Taya's swollen ankle gradually resume its normal size and shape was almost miraculous.

Across the room, she could see Verren following one of the Starlyne healers around the room, almost jogging in his haste to look at everything that the creature was doing. He noticed her watching him.

"My family won't believe what these people can do!" he exclaimed, "The equipment, the knowledge! How they can look, touch, and diagnose, then treat so quickly!" The Starlyne he was following stopped suddenly and Verren actually cannoned into its glowing side, bouncing backwards and apologising profusely, before rejoining his now mostly healed classmates.

"Verren!" Ragar grabbed his fellow cadet and sat him forcibly on the nearest platform. "You're going to break something, or worse, re-injure one of us!" Cirrus came and carefully leaned her bulk across Verren's legs, effectively pinning him down, as the other cadets laughed at his expression.

***

Kaidan took a deep breath, and squatted down next to Anjo, carefully indicating the leaves of the 'wait a while' trees. "If you look carefully Anjo, you'll see the sap oozing to the surface of the leaves. If you get any of it on you, it's really sticky and everything sticks to you." He smiled slightly, recalling his last encounter with the plant. "See the leaf patterns? You'll notice that the leaves are only about a centimetre long and a few millimetres wide, and are quite a dusky green – which is really different to most of the other plants around here. That's your clue to identification if you're in a hurry." Too late, Kaidan made a grab for Anjo's hand as the offworlder closed his hand around the frond Kaidan was indicating. "Oh dear."

"You're right about the stickiness!" said Anjo ruefully, flicking his hand to try and detach the sticky leaves from his skin.

"Careful!" admonished Kaidan, "You need to scrape as much as possible off with a stick first, then rinse your hand in water as soon as you can. When the sap sets, you need hot water to soften it, and in the time it takes to set you can get all kinds of stuff stuck to you." He handed Anjo a clean stick and Anjo began to clean the leaves and stem off his hand.

"Yuck!" Anjo stuck and unstuck his thumb and forefinger, watching the tacky sap form golden brown strings which gradually began to solidify. He hastily recommenced scraping as much of the residue off his hand as possible. "Hmm, think I'm going to have to use some hot water later!"

"Yep, you will," Kaidan said smiling, "Now, don't touch anything else before I have time to explain it! You could get yourself into some serious trouble if you touch the wrong thing." He gestured to Anjo to follow him.

"Kaidan," Anjo's voice was hesitant. "How old are you?" Kaidan stopped abruptly and turned to face the offworlder, eyebrows drawing down in puzzlement.

"Didn't Master Cerren tell you? I'm thirteen."

"Thirteen?" Anjo's voice was slightly startled. "I thought you were sixteen or seventeen! So how old is your sister?"

"Shanna? Oh, she's just turned sixteen." He turned towards the vegetation in front. "Now come and check this out – I can see a marmal track here, and once you're out and about you need to know about them – they're delicious!"

Anjo swallowed slightly, feeling confronted by the fact that one day he might have to kill and butcher his own food should he continue wishing to eat meat, and slightly bemused that his teacher was all of thirteen years old. Before his Garsal captivity, he'd come from a city on his home planet – a city where meat was sold neatly packaged in sterile containers, not still walking around on its own legs. There would be more to get used to on Frontier than just the local flora and fauna.

***

The Garsal Overlord surveyed the hive entrance. Despite the recent loss of the exploratory vehicles, he felt some small satisfaction. This world was his to win or lose. The feeling was slightly dampened as he watched the slaves struggling to set the archway capstone into place. His supply of labour had been severely reduced by the hazards found on this planet.

On the other hand, this planet had yielded some wonderful stone for the hive. He refused to allow the loss of the exploratory vehicles to spoil the thought of showing the Matriarch images of the finished archway. The pale grey stone showed up well against the thick greenery around the entrance, and other slaves had already begun work on the ground paving. There was still the pressing need for certain minerals, and he toyed with the idea of establishing an external mining camp on the sites that the vehicles had already located. Clicking his manipulator arms irritably, he decided that the security of the hive was more important. His limited vehicle supply and slave labour pool must be used carefully, and venture nowhere near the humans until he could be certain of defeating them and adding them to the labour pool. How technologically limited humans had overcome the Garsal sent to locate them was a nagging problem. The limited and grainy images sent back to the mother ship had shown that they were generally taller than the human stock he was accustomed to, but still nowhere had any of the images shown high tech weapons, equipment, or anything that might mark these human beings as significantly different to the enslaved ones in his ship.

Irritably, he motioned with one manipulator arm and Zoash hurried forward. "Overlord?" he queried.

"Prepare a montage of the archway for the Matriarch."

"It will be done as you wish." Zoash motioned in turn to an aide who began to record the images. "Overlord, will you be pursuing the humans?" The Overlord swung to face his hatching sib, quelling his irritation. Zoash's posture was all correct obedience, and the Overlord knew that he would have asked the same question had their positions been reversed – it was the Garsal way. Rankings had been determined in the creche through ruthless competition, and those most likely to gain the right to breed were often paired with a subservient sibling. That sibling's sole purpose was to challenge and drive the higher ranked brother. Early rankings did not determine the limits of ambition however, and many a higher ranked warrior had been displaced by a crafty undersib. Already several of the Overlord's hatching had risen high within the Garsal hierarchy, and more than one was close to earning breeding privileges. Assuming that Zoash had no such ambition of his own could be tantamount to suicide – they shared the same genes after all. Still, he was correct to challenge the Overlord, and he was correct to provoke him with doubts and insecurities. Only the strong deserved to breed.

"At this stage, I will not be pursuing them. We will bide our time, Zoash, and obtain more information before committing ourselves to battle. You will detail two of the remaining vehicles south to explore for the most needed minerals." His hatching sib nodded and made a small notation on his tablet. "And you will select troopers to begin the task of camouflaging the ship and hive."

"You would hide from the humans, Overlord?" Zoash's tone was properly respectful but the Overlord assayed a sharp look. His irritation climbed.

"We are not hiding, Zosh. Simply being cautious until we have more information. There is little likelihood of such a primitive culture locating us, however it is wise not to be unprepared." Zoash bowed his head.

"Of course, Overlord."

Chapter 4

IT HAD been a strange kind of day, and Shanna wasn't yet quite sure what to make of it. After leaving the medical facility, she and the others had followed Teacher into another of the large rooms where a further group of somewhat larger Starlynes had gathered. She felt very small and very young, dwarfed by the creatures, and she could see the same feelings on her fellow cadets' faces. The older Scouts seemed more self possessed but still uncertain. The day had become surreal rather than educational.

"Please just relax," Teacher had stated, indicating the couches and cushions positioned around the room. "We would spend some time with your cats." With that somewhat cryptic comment, she had made a small gesture, and all of the starcats simultaneously turned their heads towards her, then to their companions for permission, before grouping themselves around the Starlyne educator. Shanna and her fellows propped themselves on the cushions and simply watched.

"What do you think they're doing?" asked Amma, quietly.

"Wish I knew," replied Zandany, grimacing slightly. "While it's nice not to hurt every time I move, I'd still really like to know exactly what's going on."

"Watch and listen, cadets," Spiron said. "We'll learn by observation if necessary." The Patrol Leader frowned slightly as he followed his own advice. The Starlynes had joined the starcats grouped around Teacher. Fury and Satin had advanced themselves slightly in front of the others, almost as if they were mimicking the rank structure of the Patrol. Intrigued, they all watched as Satin lifted her face towards Teacher, accepting the caress of the Starlyne's small hands. She dipped her head momentarily and looked at Fury, who in turn swept a look across the grouped cats. They immediately divided themselves between the assembled Starlynes, each cat pairing up with one of the gently glowing creatures. Except for Storm and Twister, who together approached a Starlyne coiled on the perimeter of the group.

Shanna watched, intrigued, as Storm and Twister wound their lengths along the Starlyne, allowing it to run its hands across their heads and through the silkiness of their fur. Twister was purring loudly enough that she could hear him across the room. Storm, ever the more self possessed of the two cats, was leaning into the Starlyne's caress with a look of bliss on his face. After about ten minutes of effusive caresses, the two had followed the Starlyne across the room, lying down near its coils. She noticed that the Starlyne was unusually patterned, its tidemarks glowing in spirals rather than the more vertical wave that usually characterised both Starlyne and starcat markings. As the Starlyne and cats communed, she noticed that the Starlyne's tidemarks began to show both blue and indigo hues, matching those of her cats.

"Look at the Starlyne's tidemarks," she whispered to Amma. "Is the same thing happening with Spider?"

Amma nodded. The Starlyne with Spider was showing tidemarks tinged with the deep blue of Spider's own glowing patterns.

"Wonder what that means?" mused Amma, "Look at the Starlyne with Satin!" Satin was sitting regally with her Starlyne companion, both pulsing with emerald green tones as their tidemarks chased each other across their bodies. Occasionally the Starlyne would incline its head, and Satin would gently dip hers in return. "Looks like we're in for a bit of a wait." She settled herself back against the couch she was reclining on, and patted the seat companionably. "I reckon we can just relax for a while." Shanna nodded and joined Amma on the couch, punching a cushion into a more comfortable shape.

An hour later, Shanna was nudged awake by Storm. She roused herself hurriedly, rubbing her eyes and looking around to see what was happening. The blue marked cat purred at her and nudged her hand with his head, entreating for a scratch. She obliged as Twister pushed in towards her other hand.

"What's been going on?" Shanna asked Amma.

"More of the same until the cats returned to us just then. You looked so relaxed, I didn't bother waking you."

"Did you know you sleep with your mouth open, Shan?" asked Verren. "I was so tempted to stick something in it, but Amma wouldn't let me."

"Verren!" Amma gave the other cadet a poke in the ribs, as Shanna blushed. "You're so mean!"

Teacher glided over to the seated group. They scrambled to their feet, cats leaning comfortably against their partners, tidemarks rippling gently. She coiled herself gracefully and folded her small hands against her chest.

"Students, you will be divided into smaller groups this afternoon and then we will begin your training. Please follow me back to your quarters. You will need to eat before we begin. You will find that we have supplied you with a coloured armband which will be awaiting you on your bed. The colour will indicate your group. There will be an hour for eating, please be ready to proceed when the chime sounds." She turned sinuously and glided out of the door, and the humans, with mute glances at each other, followed silently.

Back at their quarters, Teacher silently indicated that they should enter, and glided off without a backward glance. They entered the rooms bemusedly and there was a buzz of conversation as everyone speculated on what "groups" actually meant. The table in the main room was again loaded with food, and they began filling plates and cups.

"Mmmm, not sure what this is, but it's really good," mumbled Ragar around a mouthful of what appeared to be some sort of heavily spiced stew.

"So, did you all notice the tidemark changes on the Starlynes?" There was general nodding as Scouts and cadets found seats on the cushions scattered around the room.

"I've never seen that happen in any other cat and Starlyne encounter," offered Allad.

"No, me neither," replied Spiron. "I've no idea what it means – perhaps the Starlynes have ways of communicating with our starcats that we don't understand. Of course, we all know that they understand more than the average animal – the complex commands, the ability to understand what we mean from just a few signals." He paused and took a bite out of the flatbread he'd been dipping in his stew.

"My mum used to joke that I talked to them when I was small," said Shanna. "Perhaps she was right." At her feet, Twister twinkled his earmarks as if replying, and the group laughed. The buzz of conversation continued throughout the meal.

"Well, we'd better go and see what these armbands are like," said Spiron, placing his bowl back on the tabletop, and heaving himself to his feet. "Meet back here in ten minutes and we'll see how they've grouped us. Perhaps that will tell us."

When Shanna entered the sleeping room, she could see Verren waving an armband. "Looks like I'm in blue group." Shanna picked up the armband on the end of her bed. There were three stripes of colour on it: blue, emerald green, and indigo. She frowned at it, puzzled.

"I'm blue group too, Verren!" Amma's voice was excited.

"I'm emerald," came Ragar's voice,

"Me too." That was Zandany.

"I'm indigo," said Taya.

"Shan, what group are you?" asked Amma. Shanna turned around slowly, holding the armband.

"Apparently I'm all three – not sure how that works." There was a sudden silence in the room. "Maybe it's just a 'multicolour' group." She felt suddenly uncomfortable again, just when she'd finally thought she was finding some acceptance amongst her peers. Amma hastened to agree with her, however.

"Yes, probably 'rainbow' group." She giggled slightly. "So, two blue, two emerald, one indigo, and one rainbow. Wonder what the others are in."

"Speaking of which," said Ragar, "We'd better join the others!"

The six of them filed into the common room, glancing around at the assembled Scouts, and surreptitiously noting the colour on each person's sleeve. "Divide into colour groups," commanded Spiron.

After a bit of shuffling, they all looked at each other, assembled in their various groups. Grouped with Amma and Verren, were Arad and Challon. Taya was standing with Karri and Kalli, and Ragar and Zandany were standing next to Sandar. Spiron and Allad were standing together, dual bands of blue and green on their left arms, and Shanna, yet again, was alone, the three bands of colour on her left arm setting her apart. She was uncomfortably aware of the stares of the rest of the group. Group 'rainbow' indeed, she thought grimly.

"So," said Spiron, "we can already see that there appears to be some similarity of groupings based on known gifts. It remains to see what else we might discover." He broke off as Teacher entered the room, and they turned as one to face her.

"I see you are already grouped." Her voice was pleased. "As you may have already surmised, we are grouping you by gifts. Shanna has taught you all to fade, however some of you are able to do this only with the assistance of your cats. In your group sessions, you will discover skills that you can master without needing physical contact with your cats. When you work together, you will all learn to do what your friends can do, however for some of these skills, you will need the assistance of your starcats. Yes, Spiron."

"Teacher, what do the multiple bands mean?" The Starlyne uncoiled and recoiled herself, and then replied, her thoughts amused.

"The multiple bands mean that you will be learning multiple skills – skills that you can learn to use without your cat's physical presence. There will be some differences between you all, and some will be more or less proficient. When the others arrive, they will join their respective groups. And Arad, you will again have a new companion. She will arrive with your friends." With that startling statement, she turned and glided out the door. "Follow please."

Again feeling like schoolchildren, the humans followed their Starlyne mentor. Taking a different direction than the morning, she moved swiftly down the passage that Shanna vaguely remembered entering the facility through. After taking a side passage, Teacher paused outside another door.

"Blue group, and today Spiron, Allad and Shanna, please enter. One of my fellows will be waiting." The designated people broke from the main group and entered the room to find yet another of the Starlynes awaiting them. Shanna recognised the spiral patterned tidemarks on its side and wondered at seeing the same creature again. She noticed the far wall contained a large double door, and that there were cushions scattered across the other half of the room.

As they walked into the room, a deep 'voice' rumbled through Shanna's mind, almost tickling with overtones of amusement and interest; and she caught a suppressed sense of satisfaction and a fleeting picture of Storm and Twister. She frowned slightly and the voice rumbled again.

"Welcome students, I am Fractus." The spiral patterns twinkled on the Starlyne's sides. "There is much to learn and little time, so we will begin immediately. Be seated with your cats please, and demonstrate your ability to fade." Shanna and Amma exchanged quizzical glances, then followed the Starlyne's instructions. Shanna smiled slightly as she faded from view, feeling that at least there would be one thing she could achieve without too much trouble. Around the room she could see Amma, Verren, Allad and Spiron fading with ease. Challon put a hand on Dipper and faded slowly, but Arad, cat-less, stood stricken, and Shanna's eyes welled with tears in sudden sympathy as his face blanched and then began to crumple.

Before anyone could react, Cirrus had slid her sleek length underneath his hand, purring softly and blinking her great violet eyes. Shanna saw him swallow, collect himself visibly, and determinedly begin to fade. Arad's tall form wavered once or twice, then vanished, leaving only a trace of the heat shimmer of a faded starcat. Shanna realised that her throat was hurting with the force of shared grief, and placed a hand on each of her cats, breathing deeply to ease the tightness.

"Well done, students." The Starlyne's deep voice echoed in Shanna's head, "Please relax your fade and listen." Allowing herself to reappear, Shanna turned her attention to the Starlyne. "When you fade, you do many complex things. Put simply, you manipulate light waves, forcing them to flow around you. Your cats also have this ability, and for those whose instinct is less developed, they reinforce the ability. Arad and Challon will not need the presence of a starcat in time. This is just one of the simplest things you will be able to do. There is much more to learn. We will begin now with Amma."

Shanna felt Amma startle slightly next to her, but sighed in relief to realise that for once, she would not be immediately in the spotlight. There was another faint feeling of amusement that she knew was only for her.

"Amma, your family predicts the weather – not only predicts it in general terms, but understands specifics of what is to come. And you are currently the most accurate of your family."

Amma nodded, and Shanna recalled with a grin the amount of money she'd won betting on Amma's accuracy.

"You do this because you are sensitive to changes in air pressure and currents, humidity, and electromagnetic fields. Your mind processes the information and consequently you understand the weather. This is the least of your abilities. You, Amma, will learn to fly, and when you have learnt, we will see who you might teach."

"Learn to fly? Are you serious?" Amma leapt abruptly to her feet, gesticulating wildly with her arms. "How on earth will I fly? You might not have noticed, but I don't have wings." The normally calm cadet was almost hysterical, and Shanna reached up to lay a hand on her arm.

"I had no idea I could vanish either Amma – and now I discover that apparently I can manipulate light waves! I mean, really!" There was a small sound of hastily stifled laughter from Verren. "Fractus, exactly what do you mean by 'fly'?"

The Starlyne gestured gracefully with its small hands and indicated the door in the wall. "I shall show you." The door opened of its own accord, and they followed the Starlyne into a small cavern. Shanna smelt the freshness of Below, mixed with the pungent odour of pungo, as a small air current stirred the wisps escaping from her braids. There were a number of strange looking suits, which appeared to have oddly elongated extensions on the arms and legs. She frowned at them, thinking they looked remarkably like the kites her father had made when she was a small child.

"The Garsal are a high technology race. They conquer because their defence and detection technologies are second to none, and their sheer numbers then allow them to overwhelm other species. Approaching them using high tech equipment is unfeasible – we learnt that at the expense of almost all of our race." A sensation of sadness floated over the room. "These glider suits will allow Amma, and perhaps a few more of you, to fly. Amma will learn to read the air currents, she will learn to launch and fly and she, and you, will travel more swiftly than you have ever dreamed. She will be able to search for the Garsal ship from the air, locating in a short time what might otherwise take you months."

Shanna turned her head to watch Amma and almost laughed out loud as she saw that the older girl was standing stunned, mouth hanging open. She took the opportunity to nudge her gently in the ribs.

She grinned as Amma shut her mouth with a snap, then opened and shut it again, completely speechless. She shook her head.

The Starlyne beckoned them back into the other room, and when they had seated themselves, nodded to Challon. "Challon, you will learn to create lightning."

"I'll what?" The dark, lean man nearly fell off his cushion. Dipper nudged him with his head, and he re-seated himself.

"You have the ability to draw electromagnetic charge from the ambient atmosphere. This will prove most useful as an offensive weapon. And for sabotage." Shanna felt slightly evil to be enjoying everyone else's discomfiture so much. But she was finding it a nice change not to be the centre of attention for once.

Fractus turned to Arad, whose red rimmed eyes still spoke of sadness. "Your new companion will be here tomorrow. Be comforted, this time of sadness will pass and you will eventually be able to think of Breeze without undue pain. Arad, you will learn to make light to illuminate the darkness, and to create warmth and heat. You will learn to adjust your light to dazzle, or to find a safe path in the night. You will be a comfort to your friends."

The Starlyne turned again, spiral tidemarks pulsing gently as Arad blinked against tears. Shanna's throat had tightened again.

"Verren, you have within you the ability to see into the infrared and ultraviolet spectrum, and perhaps even further with training. In addition, you will never be lost. You will always know precisely where you are." There was a strangled noise from Verren's corner and Shanna almost laughed out loud.

"Allad, you have already learnt to identify the spark within a person. But there is much more that you can learn. You will learn to identify what lies ahead, lurking in the bush or around the corner. Instead of small tricks with doors, you will learn to move boulders." Fractus moved on. "Spiron, you will learn to expand your light, to superheat metals or to freeze and cool as required. Both of you will learn more about your other gifts from my compatriot. These are simply the things you will learn here." Finally Fractus turned to Shanna, and his tidemarks began to pulse with blue and violet tints. She swallowed slightly apprehensively.

"Shanna, you have demonstrated your ability to fade. You have already hidden one other. Here you will learn to hide the whole patrol, and you, like Amma, will learn to fly. You will also learn how many of the gifts of your friends you are able to emulate. You will attend the two other class groups in turn, in order to explore the whole spectrum of your gifts." Shanna blushed bright red. "You and your starcats will have many new skills to explore, and the time is short." The Starlyne uncoiled abruptly. "We will begin. Amma, and indeed all of you — we will begin with understanding how you will sense air currents."

***

The Garsal Commander waited at the sealed door to the female quarters. He placed his manipulator limb on the annunciator and as the offering receptacle extruded itself, lowered the recordings of the hive entrance carefully onto its surface, along with a selection of the local fruits that had tested safe and were delicious to the Garsal palate. As the offering was withdrawn into the sequestered female's quarters, he inclined his thorax towards the external monitors. The Matriarch would indicate her approval or otherwise in her own time.

Chapter 5

KAIDAN beckoned to Anjo, and indicated that he should take a seat on a granite rock on a small knoll near the edge of the trees. Teaching the offworlder about life on Frontier was proving to be more difficult than he'd initially imagined. After returning Anjo to his quarters the previous day, covered in dirt and sticky sap, he'd decided that he needed to know more about the man's previous life and what, if any, skills he might already have.

"Anjo, if I'm to help you learn about my world, I think I need to know more about yours. What your life was like before the Garsal took you?" he asked.

Anjo looked briefly stricken and Kaidan was worried that he'd asked the wrong thing, but Anjo visibly pulled himself together, looked into the distance and cleared his throat before nodding to himself.

"My home world is called Delicata – it's one of the most beautiful worlds in the inner systems of what used to be called the Federation. Or it was." He paused, looking at the greenery surrounding him. "It was green like this world, when humanity first settled it. Green, with breathtaking mountains and amazing crystal caverns. Nothing on Delicata was particularly dangerous to humanity and we spread out rapidly, building in harmony with the environment and quickly constructing the most spectacular cities the galaxy had ever seen. Humanity and its allies turned Delicata into one of the greatest centres of learning and art that the Galaxy had ever known." He turned his head to regard Kaidan, eyes sad, and expression distant with remembrance.

"We were far from the original Garsal incursions, and it took many years for the population of Delicata to understand the reality of the Garsal threat. First the outlying worlds fell – in our arrogance at the centre and pinnacle of civilisation, we didn't think much of them – they were the wild fringes of the Federation's borders. Humanity and its allies in the inner worlds had become complacent. The war was unpopular, but distant – something that was happening far away, and only occasionally impacting on families who had sons or daughters in the military or exploratory services." Anjo grimaced slightly. "There weren't many of those on Delicata – our world was 'above' military or frontier service." He stood abruptly and paced, and Kaidan held himself still, trying to reconcile the history that every child on Frontier had been taught, with the image of a civilisation so sheltered that it ignored a life and death struggle on its fringes simply because it was distant. He wrestled with the concept, reminding himself that Anjo was thinking of galactic distances, not the kilometres between towns that he was accustomed to. On Frontier, each new settlement was eagerly awaited, and despite the time it took for information to percolate across the plateau, every minute scrap of information was absorbed and discussed in detail.

"But how could they not recognise the Garsal as a threat?" he finally asked. Anjo stopped pacing and regarded Kaidan with haunted eyes.

"The Federation was enormous – it numbered thousands of worlds, spread across thousands of light years. Those of us who lived on central worlds were isolated in our settled and pampered lives of comfort. Delicata was a world of beauty and academia. People visited Delicata to be inspired by its extraordinary natural grandeur, and nowhere else in the known galaxy were there more knowledgeable or clever philosophers and scientists. We were the jewel in the crown of the Federation. Six races living together in harmony, yet blinded to the reality of the Garsal threat. We were warned. The outlying worlds sent emissaries to the central worlds, but their entreaties were fobbed off with empty promises, and limited support was offered. Complacency, peace, and folly meant that the Garsal gained an early foothold on a wide front. They established breeding colonies, aided by the unwilling slaves of their conquered worlds, and continued to expand. Within fifty years, they were no longer a remote threat. They were knocking on the doors of long established colonies, and the alarm bells began to ring." Anjo shook his head. "I was a child when the central worlds finally took the Garsal threat seriously. I remember the announcement on the NetNews. But more than that, I remember my parents' expressions. They were academics who knew much of theory, but little of practicality. For the first time in their cocooned world, a tangible threat was on their doorstep." He turned away abruptly, and looked towards the walls of Watchtower, faintly visible through the trees. Kaidan looked down at the ground, not really knowing how to cope with the intensity of emotion displayed by Anjo. Almost not daring to breathe, he raised his eyes from the ground. Hesitantly, he posed a query.

"Anjo, you keep speaking of your parents in the past tense?"

The offworlder avoided Kaidan's eyes. "The Garsal invaded Delicata not quite three years after that NetNews broadcast, and my father was killed by them when they purged the university in which he worked. My mother tried so hard to resist the Garsal. After my father's death, she joined a guerrilla resistance cell, and we lived on the run in the city for several years." Anjo paused slightly, and sat back down on the rock next to Kaidan. "She was killed in a Garsal raid on the building we were hiding in, and I ended up as a slave. I was eighteen by then, a veteran urban fighter and the possessor of a basic Delicatan education – heavily reliant on technology no longer available to me, and quite accomplished in a number of artistic fields." His tone was wry. Kaidan felt his heart almost stop as he imagined losing both his parents, but Anjo continued. "I was caught by the Garsal in the raid that killed my mother, and until your sister's Patrol rescued me I've been their slave. I spent four years labouring on a hive construction on Delicata, having to participate in the destruction of one of the most beautiful crystal caves near the capital, and watching the surrounding vegetation sacrificed so that the hive could be furnished with rare woods. The Garsal care nothing for the surface of a planet, and everything for the construction of their hives. They use a planet until there is nothing but multiple hives." Anjo paused and sighed heavily. "My immediate family is gone and my beautiful planet is now half destroyed. And here I am, hundreds of light years away on the most dangerous planet I've ever seen - an urban fighter trying to learn how to survive in the wilderness - to learn what you've grown up knowing. Kaidan, before I came here, I'd never really been out of a city except for school excursions! I struggle to see the simplest differences in the colour of a leaf that you take for granted as obvious, and where you see animal tracks, I just see scuffed earth."

Kaidan nodded slowly at Anjo, struggling to deal with the depth of sorrow that must have marked Anjo's life. "Anjo, I had no idea about your previous life – or your losses."

Kaidan dropped his eyes and focused on a piece of grass at his feet, unsure of how to proceed; in his relatively short life, personal loss had yet to make an appearance. He had parents and a sister, along with friends and colleagues who were healthy and happy, although after listening to Anjo's story, he wondered how long his planet would be able to resist the Garsal threat. Anjo's people had had access to technology that the settlers of Frontier had only read or dreamed about. Kaidan reflected on the difficulties they'd experienced simply breaching the vehicles the Garsal had sent against them. And the casualties they'd suffered. He'd visited Gwen, one of his fellow archers who'd been injured in the battle, now settled in the infirmary in the Scout Corps basement. She was still gravely unwell, despite the care lavished upon her. He'd spent some time just sitting, watching her sleep until he'd realised she was awake. She'd smiled at him, briefly, then lapsed back into either sleep or unconsciousness, and he'd left confused. He knew her slightly, as a member of his squad, and he wondered with a sudden pang, whether she had a husband, or children.

Anjo put a hand on Kaidan's shoulder. "Let's get back to it Kaidan. My history is years old, and I need to learn to live here. And if I don't learn, it's pretty obvious I'll never be able to move around outside a town. Start from the absolute basics, and I'll do my best." Kaidan smiled at the offworlder.

"How about we take a sample of everything I show you, and next time I'll bring a notebook for you. And there are a few beginner texts that might be useful. I'll ask Master Cerren."

Anjo smiled back. "I think that would help."

***

Shanna jumped, then jumped again, teetering before she located a safe place to land. Sweat coated her body and ran down her face, as she pushed herself harder and harder, ducking and winding through the dimness of the maze of obstacles the Starlyne teacher had provided for the morning's activity. She could hear the others panting both in front and behind her, and feel the comfortable presence of Storm and Twister pacing her easily.

"Faster!" came Teacher's strident thought. "Push harder and faster, *feel* where the obstacles are, and then avoid them! This is something that you should all be able to master." Shanna tried to follow the instructions, but the sweat dripping into her eyes in burning droplets broke her concentration. She shook her head, spraying sweat onto the immaculate coats of her feline companions eliciting a grumpy hum from the pacing Storm. There was a sudden shout of surprise ahead, and dimly through the limited light Shanna realised that Verren was way ahead, hurtling through the final obstacles while Cirrus bounced eagerly ahead of him, her ever present exuberance evident in every bound. As she watched, Verren tripped and fell spectacularly off the last platform. There was a pleased feeling from Teacher, and then Shanna cannoned off a soft pillar she'd not seen.

"Well done, Verren," came Teacher's thought. "We will begin again in a moment, after you have regained your breath. Next time, you will try not to panic when you realise that you can see and feel the obstacles. That way you won't fall when you jump. Simply remain calm and land normally." She glided swiftly away.

"Remain calm?" The last word emerged from Verren's mouth in a squeak. "That scared the living daylights out of me. And the landing just reinforced that feeling." As Shanna finally attained the finishing line, she could see him struggle slowly to a sitting position. He propped himself on his elbows and took a few, slow, deep breaths.

"What did you actually do?" asked Spiron, standing with his hands propped on his hips. He frowned slightly at Verren.

"I did what Teacher said to do," replied Verren, "and then, suddenly, I could see and feel everything – well not actually see," he wrinkled his forehead in concentration and looked up at the ring around him. "Then I was here, on the ground. Everything looked really weird!" He put out a hand and Ragar pulled him to his feet.

"Return to your starting positions," came Teacher's voice again, amusement colouring her words.

The group hastily jogged back to the beginning of the course; Shanna caught Verren wincing slightly as he jogged, but noticed he forbore any further complaints. She lined up with everyone else, and wiped a last bit of sweat from her face as she leaned forward.

The morning continued, and gradually as the time progressed, each of the Scouts and Cadets had their own episode of unforeseen enhanced vision or a sudden 'feeling' of where an obstacle was going to be. She'd suddenly 'felt' Storm and Twister — recognising the feeling from the battle with the Garsal, when she had somehow been able to know where her cats and the other faded Scouts were.

Most of them were bruised, and Allad was sporting a fairly spectacular black eye. Shanna was convinced her cats were secretly amused at her gracelessness, as she'd caught the flicker of amused tidemarks from the corner of her eye several times during the moments of enhanced sensation. She'd found that as the extra sense had shut down she'd become suddenly disoriented, and had several times run full tilt into obstacles or fallen off padded beams. As the group returned to their quarters, the buzz of conversation was loud and upbeat.

"I wonder how many others might be able to do this?" speculated Spiron. Allad gently touched his puffy eye.

"Yes, but how long is it going to take us to learn to control not only this, but everything else Teacher expects us to learn?"

Shanna nodded, already feeling exhausted. And the day was only halfway through. That afternoon she was scheduled to join Taya, Kalli and Karri as they worked on their talents. Apparently Taya's talent should extend beyond stopping not only clocks but nearly any mechanical device, and Karri and Kalli were to learn the same skills.

Everything seemed to be happening so quickly, and yet still not fast enough. Despite the passing of less than three weeks, Sandar had already demonstrated his ability to make small flames, and their Starlyne teacher, Radiant, had explained that with training he would go beyond flames, to fireballs. Ragar and Zandany's talents apparently mirrored Sandar's. Both had already progressed to fingertip flames, and Shanna could see the two of them playing with their new-found ability, making flames dance from one finger to another. She wondered how they stopped themselves from being burnt. And then amended the thought: How was she going to stop her fingertips from being burnt, since she was apparently meant to learn how to do that as well

Amma threaded her arm through Shanna's companionably as they walked towards their quarters. "How weird was that? Every day, in fact just about every hour since we've been with the Starlynes, I learn something ridiculous that I'm expected to be able to do. Flying, for example. If my lack of grace just then was anything to go by, the first time I try to fly one of those things Fractus showed us will probably be my last!"

"Try being me," sighed Shanna. "Apparently I'm going to learn to do nearly everything, plus some extras, and all I could do this morning was to run into a pole." Amma smiled at her, not at all bothered that her friend was apparently remarkably talented.

"Yes, well, I wonder how on earth we'll have enough time to do all of that before the Garsal move against us again. And really, how much difference will just the sixteen of us, if you count Barron and Nelson and Perri as well, actually make? There must be hundreds, perhaps thousands of them on that ship, if they're here to start a colony."

"Maybe the Starlynes will disable them, the way Keeper did when he disabled the vehicles," replied Shanna. "I've been wondering why they need us, when they can do something like that."

The Scouts ahead of them suddenly came to a halt outside their door. Teacher was waiting for them, her small hands folded at her chest.

"Your question is well timed, Shanna." There was a sadness in her eyes, and her tidemarks were dimmed. "Come with me now, to observe the passing of Keeper of the Knowledge. When one such as Keeper expends his energy in that way, it presages his passing from this world. Keeper is many of your centuries old. He is one of the last who fled from our home world in search of safety. And he chose to end his days here, saving you all from the Garsal, so that one day both our peoples might live, free and safe from the Garsal predation. We have great power, but we are very limited; one great expenditure of ability, and we die. This was Keeper's choice. Please follow me."

Suddenly sobered, the Cadets and Scouts turned and followed the Starlyne, exchanging startled glances. Shanna had wondered why they hadn't seen Keeper since their arrival at the habitat. They emerged from the Starlyne habitation into a glade ringed by pungo trees, their distinctive aroma wafting on the warm breeze. Sunlight glinted through the leafy canopy onto the immense shape of Keeper of the Knowledge. He was coiled in the centre of the glade, while hundreds of other Starlynes of all shapes and sizes were emerging from the vegetation around him. Teacher motioned with her hands, and beckoned the humans forwards to stand with the front row of Starlynes. Self-consciously, Shanna fidgeted, unsure whether Keeper was actually dead, or just dying. She had no idea where to look, or what to do. Storm insinuated himself under one of her hands and Twister the other, and she occupied herself by stroking each silky head.

There was a sudden silence in the glade, and all that could be heard was the soft whisper of the wind through the leaves. They stood in silence for some time, Starlynes glowing gently violet in a myriad of patterns, and the starcats adding their multitoned hues to the gathering. "We are here to stand with Keeper of the Knowledge, for the time of his passing." The silent voice of an unknown Starlyne reverberated in their minds. Images of Keeper flickered past, too fast for the humans to process, and then all fell silent and still again as Keeper's voice spoke.

"Finally we are together, and there is hope for all of our peoples. Starlyne, Humanity, their Federation friends, and perhaps one day even our old enemy." Again silence fell, but even the humans were able to feel the undercurrent of shock amongst the Starlynes assembled. It was quickly stifled, and the atmosphere took on an almost anticipatory air.

Keeper's familiar tones sounded. "I would have Fractus and Teacher stand with me." The two named Starlynes glided out of the assembled crowd, each positioning themselves to either side of the coiled Starlyne. "And the six young humans, their starcats, and the one named Allad, with Satin."

The cadets looked apprehensively at each other but followed as their starcats glided forward, ringing the Starlyne. Shanna looked at Storm and Twister as they tucked themselves against the slowly fading tidemarks on the Starlyne's side. She followed suit, hesitantly extending a hand to the great creature's soft side. He was satiny and smooth. On either side, she could see Verren and Amma mirroring her actions, and out of the corner of her eye she noticed Fractus and Teacher extending their hands.

A soft sound issued from the assembled Starlynes; the first audible sound that Shanna had heard the creatures make. It was a song floating ethereally above them, multiple harmonies in otherworldly patterns, expressing grief at a loved one's parting, love of the one passing, joy in the promise of more to come, and stirring in the hope of a future not yet realised. It soared through dizzying octaves, both heard and unheard, and wrenched the hearts of all of those who heard its lilting tones. Tears streaked the human faces, and Shanna was struck with the sorrow of the passing of a being known only briefly, yet one who had changed her entire life with its touch. She saw through tears, the sudden brightening of Keeper's tidemarks, felt an immense yet fleeting touch of astounding love, heard an echo of words in her mind, and saw the Starlyne rejoice in that astounding love. Then he was gone. And his last words echoed in her mind again.

"Remember. Compassion, love and hope will always defeat hatred."

The blaze of Keeper's tidemarks abruptly vanished, and the glade was suddenly shadowed. The Starlyne congregation slowly diminished until only the human beings, their cats, Fractus, and Teacher remained. Fractus turned slowly, uncoiling himself and turning his head to regard the cadets and Allad, grouped around Keeper's now lifeless coils.

"You have been greatly honoured. Keeper of the Knowledge was our greatest elder. He truly believed that our paths must be as one on this journey to rid our world of the Garsal threat. There will be some meaning in those last words, but I worry that our people will misunderstand his compassion for even the Garsal. Too long have we hidden, too fearful of their numbers for very many of us to look at them with compassion. Yet they too may have some greater purpose in this universe, strange though that might seem, and at odds with their threat to our shared world. Please return to your quarters. There will be no further classes today and you will wish to reunite with your other companions."

Fractus turned back to Keeper's body, lowering himself into a position of repose and folding his small hands into his neck; even as the humans grouped themselves around Spiron.

"Let us return to our quarters, then," Spiron said. "We have much to discuss." The others nodded and still saddened, they turned away and re-entered the underground haven.

Chapter 6

AS THEY entered their quarters, there was an exclamation of surprise. "Barron! Perri! Nelson!" The group crowded into the room, their sadness at Keeper's passing briefly forgotten in the joy of reunion with their previously injured companions. Their injuries were obviously much improved, and Barron was sporting both blue and indigo stripes, while Nelson was wearing indigo, and Perri emerald. The noise increased rapidly as everyone tried to talk at once.

There was a sudden loud squeak from amongst the cushions on the floor, which stopped the noise in its tracks, and a young, blue-toned starcat cub emerged, padded across to Arad and sat firmly on his foot. Hunter made what Shanna could only describe as a relieved noise as the Scout looked quizzically down at the cub. She was barely old enough to have left her mother.

"And this is Nosey." Barron sighed heavily. "She's one of Gem's cubs. We met her before we left the access tunnel, and I found her in my backpack two hours out. I couldn't figure out why my pack felt so uncomfortable. At first I put it down to the arm pain distracting me, but then it began to wriggle." The small cub squeaked again and looked entreatingly up at Arad. Shanna noticed that she had particularly large violet eyes, and her blue tidemarks twinkled fetchingly as she unashamedly batted her eyelashes at the Scout whose foot she was occupying. "My pack doesn't normally wriggle, so I ditched it pretty quickly, wondering what I'd managed to pick up. It kept wriggling until I opened it, and there she was, squeezed in on top of my gear. I still have no idea why Hunter didn't alert me." He turned a frown on his cat, who had the grace to look slightly sheepish. "By that time, it was too late to take her back so we brought her along with us. She's a handful!" Nosey squeaked plaintively at Arad, and poked him with one blue tipped paw.

The Scout, his eyes still reddened, looked down at the round bellied cub and sighed heavily, grimacing. "This is unexpected, to say the least. Teacher did say that my new starcat would arrive today, but I was not expecting such a … teeny weeny monster." He squatted down, and Nosey nudged his hand gently and batted her eyelashes again. He scratched the side of Nosey's cheek. "I was expecting something at least a little larger." Nosey leaned into his hand and wriggled her bottom closer to Arad, "with perhaps a little training," the little starcat squeaked plaintively again, "and maybe even a different colour." He gave in and picked the pudgy little cat up, and she purred loudly and snuggled into his arms. "She's really rather engaging, though." The corners of his mouth turned up in the beginnings of his first smile since Breeze had died in the battle with the Garsal, and then turned to a quizzical frown. "And there's usually choice involved."

"Engaging?" Barron rolled his eyes, and Perri chuckled.

"Nelson and I had to be carried here on stretchers, and she spent some time riding with each of us. I can tell you that there wasn't much peace and quiet to be had when she was. She's got huge paws, and she's not very graceful when she's crawling all over your injured knee." Shanna noticed that Perri's knee was encased in what looked like a brace made from some kind of dark grey material. "Which is now much better, but I've got to wear this thing for a few weeks. Show them your scars, Barron and Nelson!"

Barron rolled a sleeve up to expose a neat, smooth scar from his shoulder to his elbow, and Nelson unbuttoned his shirt to expose the same kind of smooth scarring across his chest and side. It was somewhat pinker than Barron's scar, but Shanna, remembering the injuries she'd seen after the vehicle battle, gasped in astonishment. As the group drew in around their three companions to examine their much improved injuries, Shanna hesitantly approached Arad and Nosey. Arad had moved over to one of the floor cushions and Nosey was sprawled in his lap, luxuriating with her feet in the air as he scratched her belly. The tall Scout's face was indulgent, and he smiled fondly at the cub as Shanna approached. She was startled to see that Arad's whole body emitting a soft glow.

"Arad!" Arad looked up at Shanna's exclamation, and the yellow white glow flickered briefly before steadying again. She held a hand up, almost disbelieving. "And you're warm!" The group quickly reformed around Arad, while Nosey lay purring under the Scout's suddenly still hand. The light flickered again and Nosey gave a small chirrup and batted Arad's hand. He looked down at her, smiled properly and resumed scratching the cub's upturned belly. Again the warm light steadied, and warmth radiated outwards. The rest of the starcats hummed approvingly and nudged their human partners aside to better access Arad's warmth, basking in it and humming gently at Nosey.

"Well, that's not quite what I expected." Arad looked again at Nosey. "How much training did you say she's had, Barron?"

Barron snorted softly. "I didn't – she's only just weaned. As far as we could tell, she's had the normal amount of handling for a weanling and knows the absolute basics, but there's a reason her name is Nosey, and she was quite selective about the commands she obeyed on the way here! She comes to the food call and sits when she feels like it! I wish you luck!" He grinned. "Better you than me! Anyway, let's eat, there's food getting cold on the table." Arad's glow faded as he gently rolled Nosey off his lap and joined his fellow humans while they moved as one to the table, talking and gesturing, catching up on the last few days in a cloud of chatter.

Shanna helped herself to a bowl of stew and tucked herself away in a corner of the room, Storm and Twister curled on either side. She was suddenly tired, saddened by Keeper's death, and the anxiety she kept trying to suppress resurfaced. The first few days of learning from the Starlynes had been difficult as she attempted to expand her ability to fade to encompass other things. She wondered suddenly how Kaidan was faring, and what the reaction of her parents might be when they learned where she was and what she was doing. It seemed an eon since she'd last spoken to them. So much had occurred in the last few months, so many things had changed, and here she was sitting on a cushion, eating lunch in the habitat of an alien race, and about to challenge another alien race for possession of her world. She put the bowl aside, suddenly full despite eating only a few mouthfuls, and leaned her head back against the wall, closing her eyes against the sudden prickling of tears. Storm laid his head across her lap and Twister nudged one of her hands gently with his cool, damp nose. Shanna vigorously blinked her eyes, trying to surreptitiously remove the suspicious wetness from her lashes. She looked around quickly to see if anyone had noticed her momentary weakness and resolutely picked her bowl up again, knowing that she needed to eat something.

After the meal ended, the group slowly dispersed. For the first time in months, Shanna found herself with nothing to do. She briefly contemplated bathing, but the bathroom was occupied, and then she found herself longing for a moment of solitude, preferably outside. Calling Storm and Twister, she quietly left the common room and wound her way through the maze of tunnels to the training room that Fractus usually occupied. She pushed open the door and then exited the room on its other side through the large double doors. Again she felt the freshness of a breeze against her face and smelt the familiar odour of a pungo tree. She followed the air current to another door with a small grille at the top, and hesitantly pushed at it. The door swung open, revealing a small glade with a gentle slope topped by a number of flat rocks. With Storm and Twister by her side, she reasoned, she should be safe if she climbed the slope to the rocks. And she suspected that the Starlynes had some way of keeping most of Frontier's more aggressive predators away.

Carefully skirting a clump of barbed palms, Shanna climbed the slope and was rewarded by the sight of a steep, yet beautiful valley below her. She set Twister to watch. Unusually, there were many soothall berry plants evident on the slope below, and Shanna quickly scanned around her for any spooner spider nests. Finding none nearby, she perched herself on one of the rocks and sat quietly, just enjoying the view, the company of her cats, and the relief of being outside by herself. Again the sense of fatigue washed over her and, finally knowing herself to be alone, Shanna allowed the tears to flow unchecked. She cried for the sadness of Arad's loss, and the joy of his new found friend, and for those Scouts and archers who had perished, even if she hadn't known them. She cried because she missed her brother and her parents, and the familiar surrounds of her home at Hillview. And for the loss of Keeper, a being who had thought humanity so important that he'd given his life for the hope of an alliance between his people and hers. Finally she cried for herself, for the fear of failing her friends, and for the possibility of losing her world.

The shadows had lengthened when Shanna's tears finally stopped falling. The odour of the pungo trees was even more pungent, and she could hear the calls of birds echoing faintly on the breeze wafting up from the valley. Storm nudged her hand gently and looked pointedly at his brother sitting vigilantly on guard next to her, and Shanna indicated that the two cats should swap places. Twister hummed quietly at her and relaxed. Again the three of them sat quietly, listening, looking, and allowing the natural sounds of Below to refresh them.

Storm's ears twitched suddenly behind him and his posture straightened, then relaxed again. Behind her Shanna heard a quiet footfall, then Verren and Cirrus crested the rise just to Shanna's left. She scrubbed her face furtively with one hand, aware that her eyes were probably red and puffy, and that when she cried her nose glowed like a beacon. Verren saw her, walked over quietly and sat next to Shanna on her rock.

"Are you OK, Shan?" his voice was concerned, "I saw you leave after lunch, and you've been gone for hours." Shanna felt the tears threaten again and tried to clear her throat enough to reply, but gave up and simply waved a hand helplessly and shook her head. The tears started again, and Verren simply sat a bit closer, and put an arm around her shoulders. She leaned on him gratefully and just let the tears fall, thankful now for the warmth of another human being. Twister edged a little closer and leaned his head in her lap again. When she'd finally regained control of her emotions once more, Shanna became aware that she'd leaked tears all over Verren's shoulder and sat bolt upright, brushing at the damp patch on his sleeve.

"Sorry! I didn't mean to drip all over you."

"It's fine, Shan, it's been a really bizarre time, hasn't it?" His voice was tired too, and Shanna realised that she was not the only one struggling with all of the changes. Verren had a family too, as did all of the other cadets. She knew some of the Scouts in Patrol Ten were married and had children, and were away from their families as well.

"It's been really strange, Verren. Each day has so many new things to learn, and sometimes I just don't think I'll be able to learn enough, fast enough."

"I know what you mean, Shan, I keep thinking about what the Garsal might be doing on that ship of theirs – what if more arrive? With more flight-capable craft? What's going to happen to the plateau? To our families? I feel like there's so little time to do everything, and then, what are we actually going to do to stop them enslaving our world too? The Starlynes seem to think we can, but I can't in my wildest dreams imagine how." He withdrew his arm from Shanna's shoulders as he spoke, gesticulating with both hands, and she realised that she missed its warm presence. "I guess there's a plan, and I suppose they've now talked with our Council. I wonder when we'll know what they really want us to do?"

Shanna nodded her agreement. "We don't even know where the colony ship is. Perhaps the Starlynes do, although Fractus did say that they detect technology easily, so perhaps that'll be our task — we've little technology, and they didn't seem to be able to detect us when we were watching that vehicle."

"True, true ... " Verren's tone was pensive. The two of them sat quietly for a few moments, watching the horizon change colour as the sun gradually set. "We'd better go back inside I suppose, it'll be dinner time shortly, and you didn't eat much lunch." Shanna raised her eyebrows at him. "You were sitting so quietly in that corner that I was a bit worried." Verren stood and held out a hand. "Come on, let's go and find the others." Shanna let him pull her to her feet, called Storm and Twister, and followed Verren off the hillside, back into the Starlyne habitation. Her hand felt slightly tingly, and she felt a warmth inside her that hadn't been there before. Shaking her head, she took a couple of quick steps, caught up to Verren, and cocked an eyebrow at him.

"At least you don't have to cook, so it should be pretty edible!" she said.

Verren sniffed. "I'm really a very good cook, you know."

***

There was a missive from the Matriach sitting on the Overlords's desk in his living quarters. It requested his presence in her reception chamber the following day. He stalked backwards and forwards as he considered the request. The language was plain, and there were none of the flowery phrases of praise he had hoped for, but neither was there any language of condemnation in the few lines on the archaic paper. At the very least, he would be able to enter the sequestered portion of the colony ship for the first time since their arrival on this planet. He chose to take that as a sign of approval. He tapped his console and Zoash appeared promptly.

"Prepare an offering for the Matriarch immediately. Include samples of the hive stone, some of the new fruits and the appropriate blossoms from the hydroponics section," the Commander said, pausing for a moment to consider. "Then attend me when you're finished. We will discuss the issues with the predator beasts and the humans."

Chapter 7

MASTER Cerren glanced at the clock on the mantel and pushed his chair back, getting to his feet as he did so. He strode over to the window of his office, now relocated to the Scout precinct, watching as Janna, Adlan and Josen approached the double story building. The morning sun slanted through the window, illuminating the stack of leather folders on his desk. He tapped his long fingers on the window sill briefly before running them through what remained of his hair. From the couch on the other side of the room, Socks yawned and hummed a query at the greying Master.

"It's all right for you, lady cat." Master Cerren frowned down at the three figures, now about to enter the building. "You're not the one who has to explain what you've done with someone else's children."

The grey starcat uncurled her length from its position of comfort and poured her body off the couch, nosing up to the Master's hand on the window sill. He obliged and ran his hand over her sleek head, and her tidemarks glowed steadily as she leaned her warm length companionably on his leg. He scratched Socks' upturned head and she responded with a purr, claws gently flexing in the rug spread across the stone floor. Master Cerren turned his head and looked out across the town wall towards the greenly vegetated slope where Kaidan was tutoring Anjo in the joys and dangers of survival on Frontier, and then looked back at the pile of folders on the desk.

There was a sudden clatter from the door at the end of the hallway outside his office, and Cerren tapped one last time on the windowsill and moved decisively back to his desk. He sat down, shuffled through the folders and selected one, depositing it on the polished wooden surface of the desktop. There was the sound of approaching feet before a tap at the door.

"Enter please," he called, rising, as Master Peron ushered Josen, followed by Janna and Adlan into his office. All were accompanied by starcats. Socks hummed a greeting to Boots, Sabre, and Moshi, and politely touched her nose to Josen's red-toned Anvil. Master Peron's new cub, Thunder, entered last and rolled over as Socks strolled across to him. He was a large cub, with chunky legs and wide violet tidemarks splashed across his dark grey flanks. Receiving permission from Socks, he rolled back onto his feet and trotting over to Master Peron sat neatly at his feet.

"Thank you for coming Josen, Janna, Adlan," said Master Cerren, "please, take a seat. We have much to talk about, and it may take some time."

"Thank you," replied Janna. "And might we be able to see Kaidan while we're here? Peron has explained that Shanna's out with a Patrol, but I would assume that Kaidan might be available, when he's finished whatever training you've assigned him today?"

"I believe Kaidan will be some time yet," said Master Cerren, flashing a glance at Peron, who nodded,. "So, if we might discuss a few things first?" Janna looked slightly unsettled, but nodded and sat on the couch next to her husband. Adlan signalled, and the Hillview starcats settled themselves comfortably on the large rug with Socks and Anvil. Little Thunder remained sitting at Master Peron's feet while the Scout Master leaned against the mantelpiece.

The two Masters looked at each other grimly, then as Peron nodded slightly, Cerren opened the folder in front of him and began the story of the Garsal incursion, and the startling discoveries about the Starlyne people.

***

Anjo wrote furiously in his notebook as Kaidan pointed out the defining characteristics of the broadleaved oil root plant they were studying. Using the pencil supplied by his young tutor, he quickly sketched the deep green leaf before filling in the fine detail of the tuberous root with its multitude of fine, hairlike protrusions. The two had spent the day moving carefully through the archery course area, with Kaidan encouraging Anjo to demonstrate what he'd learnt over the previous few days. Although Anjo had struggled with noting the presence of any wildlife, Kaidan had been pleased to see that he had an eye for the more dangerous plants.

"Let's lunch over here," called Kaidan. "There's nothing around here that's going to cause any problems for us." He settled down on the ground in the shade of a pungo tree and unpacked food from the small backpack he'd been wearing. "Got your water bottle?" Anjo produced the water bottle from its pocket attached to the back of his belt, and Kaidan handed him a chunk of cheese, several pieces of fruit, and a pile of nuts that they'd harvested earlier from a patch of roundnut bushes. As they ate, Kaidan quizzed Anjo about the oil root plant.

"We'll have to get you to practice your identification every day, I think," said Kaidan. "You've a good memory, but it always takes you a while to distinguish the different colours of green." He grinned at the older man, and went on. "Fortunately we've nothing else to do at the moment, and this is much better than sitting around waiting for something to happen at Scout HQ." Anjo grinned back companionably. Kaidan smiled again as Anjo wriggled slightly, adjusting the long sleeved shirt he was wearing. The offworlder was still adapting to the local clothing customs. Nearly everyone on Frontier wore shirts and trousers or shorts, depending on the weather. Masters of any profession were entitled to wear robes indicating their rank, but in practice, teachers were the only ones who wore them regularly. Boots were the standard footwear for most people, although sturdy shoes were also worn in towns. Anjo asked why there was little clothing variety, apart from colour and the occasional embroidery.

"Well, you never know what the weather will do in storm season, and most of us need to wear practical clothing for our day to day activities."

"But what about when you're relaxing after the day's work? Or for celebrations? I take it you do have celebrations?"

Kaidan chuckled. "Of course we do, but when this kind of clothing is so comfortable, why would we bother with anything else much?" His voice was slightly teasing, but then he relented. "Anjo, on special days when we celebrate, everyone wears something special. You should see my Dad's fancy boots!" He smiled again at the other man.

"Hopefully I will, one day. You must be missing your family." Anjo's voice trailed off as Kaidan ducked his head slightly.

"I am, but I do understand why I've not been allowed to go home yet. And it's not really been that long. Hopefully Master Cerren will be explaining a few things to them sometime soon so I don't have to pretend that I've just been training a bit more."

Anjo thought Kaidan sounded considerably more mature than he would have at his age.

"I still can't believe that they took kids like you to face the Garsal," said Anjo, frowning at the boy. Kaidan looked up at him again, idly shelling another nut.

"Anjo, there's not really that many of us living here on Frontier. Your population on Delicata was much larger than ours is, but you still fought when you were only a few years older than me." He looked Anjo straight in the eyes. "You have to remember that we started from just one colony ship, and many of the people on that ship either died in the crash or shortly after. Until the first town wall was complete, our forebears lived day to day not knowing if they'd even survive to the end of that day – and even now we've only just reached the point where we can afford to explore off the plateau – and all of this has taken us three hundred years. Your people had an entirely explored and populated planet. We have three major settlements on one plateau, and if we lose this we lose everything. As far as I'm concerned, it doesn't matter how young I am if they need me." He swallowed his last piece of cheese and brushed his hands down his pants, flicking the last crumbs off onto the ground.

"And your parents will think the same?" asked Anjo, quizzically. He popped a nut in his mouth, and chewed reflectively. "These are pretty good!"

"They're my favourites, and no, I'm not sure Mum and Dad will think the same thing, at least to start with, but when they understand what's at stake they'll come around. At least I hope so, or I'll never get to do anything interesting ever again." He frowned slightly, "And now Shan's somewhere Below and I don't know when I might see her again, so I need to keep being involved. Mum and Dad will be involved because they breed starcats, and we know that they're even more important now. I'm not going to sit at home or here and be left out." Kaidan's voice was impassioned but then his expression changed to mischievous. "And don't ever tell Shan that I said anything nice about her." He grinned and pointed to the crumbs on the ground. "And always make sure you're careful about what you do with any food scraps." As the two watched, a small rodent-like creature with a fluffy fringe of fur on each paw, darted out and ran its rubbery snout across the cheese crumbs, causing them to vanish. As it moved, it left a little blob of white slime after each crumb was ingested. "Those little blobs get on everything, and they stink when they're dried. The little beast is called a stinkrat — as you can see, they're not really bothered by humans, but if we had a starcat with us, we'd not see one." He shooed the little animal away and it growled in an oddly squeaky way. "Just stay away from the blobs and you'll be fine." He motioned to Anjo to join him as he moved towards the trees. Anjo carefully skirted the drying blobs, wrinkling his nose as an unpleasant stench wafted towards him.

***

Master Cerren closed the leather folder and placed it on his desk. He was sweating as he flicked a slightly apprehensive look at Peron who was gently teasing Thunder with a piece of string. Both Masters looked at Janna and Adlan. Adlan was eyeing his wife warily. Janna's face was like a thundercloud. On the mat, the three Hillview starcats had lifted their heads and their eyes were focused alertly on their human partners. Josen looked carefully at the floor.

"You mean to say that both of our children were involved in that battle you've just described?" Janna's voice was almost a hiss. "And you've left Shanna down Below? With a group of apparently sentient Starlynes who have been genetically engineering us? Without consulting us? And you sent our thirteen year old into battle against hostile insectoid aliens?" Her voice rose on each question, and Adlan carefully placed a hand on her arm as she seemed about to explode out of her chair. His eyebrows were drawn down into a frown as he turned his gaze on the apprehensive Scout Master.

"You have some explaining to do, Master Cerren." Adlan's voice was flat. Josen looked slightly embarrassed but nodded firmly in agreement.

"Please understand that this was not at all premeditated," protested Master Peron. "When Shanna joined the Scout Corps, we had no idea that she'd be caught up in anything like this. By chance, her group located the remains of the flying craft after the cyclone, and she ended up on that first trip Below. Despite searching diligently, we failed to discover any evidence of further alien life here and thought that perhaps it was an isolated contact, so we decided to go ahead with the cadets' first formal excursion Below. Then they inadvertently stumbled on the exploratory vehicle and rescued the captive human slaves. By then, she and the other cadets were so obviously desperately needed that we had little choice. There are so few of us really equipped to survive and explore Below." Janna's expression softened slightly as the reality of the Master's words sank in.

"But there's still Kaidan." The hard tone returned to her voice.

Master Cerren's face was troubled. "It is true that in Kaidan's case, our acts, or more correctly my acts, were deliberate. I alone made the choice to send him with the archers as the Garsal vehicles approached. There is no one else for you to blame except for me." He bowed his head, and Socks got to her feet and thrust her grey head under his hand. "I took the risk of sending Kaidan, because I feared that without all the archers we had available, the Garsal might overcome us, and because, young though he is, he had the requisite skill level and had practiced with the explosive arrowheads. It was a joint decision to leave the cadets and Patrol Ten with the Starlynes, but I stand by it as necessary for the future of all of our peoples on this planet. The cadets were not compelled to go - we allowed them the choice, and your Shanna chose to go with them. And you have heard how important our feline companions are." He stopped talking abruptly, and there was an uncomfortable silence in the room. The clock on the mantel ticked loudly in the quiet.

"This really is about our survival, isn't it?" asked Adlan. "You're really convinced that if we don't meet the Garsal with every available resource, that we will be enslaved?" Janna leaned forward as her husband spoke, and Master Peron nodded gravely but allowed Cerren to answer.

"We are convinced that this is the case." Cerren said, his voice firm. "And we are certain that allying with the Starlyne people is our only chance for freedom, but that is not to say that we trust them completely. They did hide themselves from us for three hundred years when we desperately needed their help, but we do need each other at this time. And it appears we need our starcats just as much." As one, Moshi, Boots, Sabre and Anvil returned to their human friends, humming tones that Cerren was only able to describe as affirming. He wondered privately just how much contact the Starlynes had had with the cats during the last three hundred years.

"In that case, we would like to see our son," replied Janna, exchanging glances with Adlan, "And then we will discuss this further. I for one need time to think. And to settle down." Her face was still angry. Peron nodded at Master Cerren, and gestured with one hand.

"Please follow me. You are welcome to discuss anything you've heard in here with Kaidan, but we would ask you not to talk to anyone else at this time. Josen, perhaps you would like to discuss any questions you might have with Cerren while you wait." He opened the door politely.

***

"Let's head back to Scout HQ," suggested Kaidan. "I've probably shown you enough plants and tracks for the day, and you'll want to have a rest and clean up before dinner." Anjo nodded and stretched, and the two of them headed companionably towards the outskirts of Watchtower.

As they entered Scout Compound, one of the third year cadets approached them. "Kaidan, Master Peron would like you to go straight to his office please, and Anjo, Master Erilla would like to speak to you again after you're washed and changed. She will be in the conference room."

Kaidan nodded, said his farewells to Anjo and took the stairs to Master Peron's first floor office two at a time. When he knocked at the door it was opened almost immediately by the Master. As Kaidan entered, he was enveloped in hugs from both his mother and father. Surprised to have had no warning of their presence, he hugged them back vigorously, startled to see that his mother had tears in her eyes. Janna stepped back briefly, looked him over, then hugged him again.

"Kaidan, are you all right?" asked Adlan, concern colouring his voice.

"I'm fine, Dad," he replied, voice slightly muffled as his mother hugged him yet again. "Mum, what's going on?"

"Master Cerren's just told us what he's had you doing over the last few weeks!" replied Janna, finally stepping back slightly but keeping one of her hands on Kaidan's shoulder. "And I'm astounded that they sent you, a child, into such danger!" Her eyes flashed suddenly as she pushed her son out to arm's length to examine him better, her eyes raking him up and down.

"But Mum," began Kaidan as Janna ignored his protests and continued to speak, faster and faster, the words pouring out of her in a torrent.

"Are you sure you're alright? How is your sister? Master Cerren said she stayed Below after the battle, to go and 'study'" — she drew the word out incredulously — "with the Starlynes, but that you'd been with her right up until then." She finally drew a breath. "I want to know everything, and then your father and I need to discuss a few more things with the Masters." She frowned ominously.

"I'll leave you for a while then." Master Peron finally spoke up. "Your parents know exactly what has happened Kaidan, so you may speak freely with them." He stood, called Thunder to heel and left the office, the little starcat padding his oversized feet diligently after the tall Master.

"Now, sit and tell us exactly what you've been up to young man," Adlan said, drawing them over to the large couch under the window ledge. As Kaidan sat down, his mother by his side, still running her eyes over him, Boots strolled over and laid his large head heavily in Kaidan's lap. Where did he begin?

***

As the door closed behind Josen and the third year cadet, Master Cerren raised his eyebrows at Peron and indicated the comfortable chair next to his desk. Peron sighed heavily, and nodded a 'yes' as Cerren lifted the steaming teapot from the tray on the end of the desk.

"I'm afraid Janna's rather angry at us." He steepled his fingers, then picked up the mug of tea and took a sip, sighing again at the hot liquid.

"And justifiably too," Cerren said. "If we'd had a mite more warning, we might have avoided this situation. As it was we used the resources we had on hand at the time, and they were barely adequate." Peron nodded, his eyebrows drawn together and his face set into lines of concern.

"Without every last archer, we would not have managed to hold those vehicles for as long as we did. And when I think of the casualties we took ... " Peron shook his head. "Our Starlyne allies have offered medical assistance, which we have accepted, but I can't stop thinking about the aid they could have provided in those early days when the colony hung on by a thread. When I think of the lives they might have saved, the technology we might not have lost, and the population we might now have had, it's very hard not to be angry with them."

Cerren nodded again. "It's a dilemma. The general public will be angry I'm sure, when the information is released. And it will need to be made public very soon. Our population is at risk and there is much to do in very little time." Socks made an encouraging hum and he went on. "And I've yet to talk to the families of the other cadets left Below. At least they're a bit older; hopefully that might make a difference." His voice trailed off. There was silence for some minutes before Peron spoke up again.

"I truly believe that we have little choice. It is very obvious that we cannot face the Garsal alone. When I sit and really think, I do understand the Starlyne position. They live very long lives, but they breed very, very slowly. They believe they're the last of their race, and we humans caused the death of many of them when we arrived on this planet. I can understand their reluctance to expose themselves. But now we discover that they have surreptitiously manipulated our genetic code for the last three hundred years. Yes, they claim it's to provide both races with the best chance of survival against a common foe. And yes, I believe them, but I suspect many won't. They've not yet seen the Garsal, and until our population is directly impacted they will not understand the issues. Have you received any word from the Council in Starfall?"

Cerren put down his cup and shook his head slowly. "Not yet. I'm sure they've now met with the Starlynes themselves, and I expect to hear from them within the next few days. They will want to meet with Anjo and Semba too, I'm sure, so I'm expecting not just a messenger but most likely a small delegation. Erilla will be talking to Anjo again each day, and then she hopes to try and encourage Semba to be more forthcoming. The poor woman is extremely traumatised, however, and I'm not sure how much more information she'll be able to provide. She is living proof of the Garsal crime, though. And before then, we have two unhappy parents to deal with, some negotiations to conclude with said unhappy parents, not to mention Josen who obviously feels as though he's between a rock and a hard place, and the new half-yearly intake of cadets arrives tomorrow. And they are very badly needed indeed, yet under the current circumstances we'll have to pull in our retired Scouts so that they can begin their training. I believe Master Yendy has that under control?"

Peron nodded absently.

"And you've been liaising with the plateau Starlynes in regard to the training they can offer our Scouts?" Cerren said.

Peron nodded again and produced a file. "This is the list Cally's prepared for us. She's suggested that those who were precocious as cadets should be our priority. I agree, given what we've seen with our latest recruits." He laid the file on the desk and Cerren leafed through it, nodding as he noted particular names.

"I agree. We'll leave that to Cally and Yendy. In the meantime, you and I can begin some preliminary planning for the arrival of the expected delegation. They may think we've been somewhat presumptuous, and the Senior Councillor is likely to be difficult unless we have the answers to all of her questions at our fingertips. Where do you suggest we start?" The two Masters began planning, Peron taking notes, swiftly jotting down points as they talked.

***

Kaidan finished his recitation of the recent events, then scrubbed his hands on his trousers and looked anxiously at his parents. Adlan's face was drawn into a somewhat perturbed expression, not quite a scowl, but he was certainly not happy. Janna's face had relaxed slightly during Kaidan's tale and she was tapping one finger thoughtfully on her jawbone. Boots in his normal fashion, had used the time to sneak his body onto the couch and across Kaidan's lap. Kaidan absently scratched the big cat's cheek as Boots rumbled a purr through his legs.

"So you are really completely unhurt?" asked Adlan.

"Yes, Dad, I'm fine."

"And you've been teaching this 'Anjo', the dangers of this planet?" Kaidan nodded.

"And you're certain that Shanna made her own choice?"

"Dad, Shanna's wherever she is because she chose to go there. She was fine when I left Below. Until now I didn't realise she was actually going with the Starlynes, but — you remember how I told you about the picture of her and the boys at the end of the images? There's got to be something in that, and I think she needed to find out what that meant. Actually, *I'd* really like to know what that meant." Kaidan nodded his head vigorously, disturbing Boots, who rumbled his displeasure and nudged Kaidan's hand to keep him scratching.

Janna interrupted. "I still don't think they should have sent you. I understand Shanna's presence – she's at least training to be a Scout, but you're only thirteen. And no matter how much Cerren goes on about your talents, you're still too young!" She emphasised her point with a waving index finger, causing Kaidan to lean back from it somewhat warily.

"Mum, they didn't have any choice, there wasn't anyone else!" Kaidan said defensively. "There's not that many of us who can reliably hit what we aim at. Look, initially I was here just to learn how to use the explosive tipped arrows, but everything moved so fast. There was no choice but to use all of us, and if they hadn't you'd probably all be learning about the Garsal the really hard way right now." His face grew even more serious, and for once there was no hint of a blush as he went on. "Shan's important, Mum, and so am I – we're both really good at what we do. You should have seen her, she was amazing! And you and Dad bred Storm and Twister, and our starcats are going to be really important to our survival. We have to help, whether you're angry or not." Kaidan held his ground stubbornly and all of a sudden the fight seemed to leave Janna. Leaning back into the couch she shook her head. Sabre appeared at her left hand, violet eyes glowing and looked unblinkingly at her partner. Janna looked back at her consideringly, holding the starcat's gaze, then nodded at her son.

"For once you're right Kaidan, we need to help. However," she raised one finger warningly, "There will be conditions, won't there, Adlan?" Kaidan's father nodded slowly, and got to his feet.

"In that case, we need to go and discuss a few more things with the Masters." He held out his hand to Janna, flicked a finger at Boots, who slid his long length onto the floor, then pulled his wife to her feet. "There will be conditions, but when our freedom is at stake we can do no more than rise to the occasion, all of us. Let's begin."

Kaidan breathed a silent thank you and bounced to his feet, relieved at his parents' apparent acquiescence, and joined them as they exited Master Peron's office.

Chapter 8

FOR another four weeks, day after day, Shanna and her fellow cadets and Scouts laboured at exploring and perfecting their new-found abilities. Shanna reeled from one day into the next exhausted, frantically trying to consolidate each new discovery about her abilities. Surprisingly, it had been Amma and Taya who had seemed most comfortable with their skills. Amma had gone from incredulous to determined, and was almost effortlessly making the most enormous strides in understanding how her talent worked. Taya, finally released from the fear of being considered abnormal, had begun to function as an integral part of the Scout team. After the other girl's revelations, Shanna had realised that the Masters had all known about Taya's issues and the precocious ability she'd shown on that day she'd accompanied her father to the quarry, which went a long way to explaining their forbearance with her difficult behaviour.

One night as she lay drowsily in her bed, Shanna had realised that if she herself had not been inducted into the Scout Corps as early as she had, she might very well have demonstrated her fading ability in a group that would not have understood or anticipated such a thing. It sobered her enough to make her rethink some of the issues she'd had with the older girl. They were still not really friends — not in the way she was with Amma for example - but at least they were no longer enemies.

The starcats had spent most of their time over the last four weeks either assisting their companions or snuggling (Shanna had been unable to think of a better word) up to whichever Starlyne was providing the teaching for that day. They seemed completely besotted with the Starlynes, taking every opportunity to swipe their sleek lengths along any Starlyne who might be passing. Initially Shanna had thought that perhaps such attentions might annoy the great creatures, but the Starlynes apparently looked forward to the encounters with as much enthusiasm as the starcats.

As Shanna entered the common room for breakfast, yawning and rubbing one eye, Arad hurried over to her looking worried. There was no one else in the room as she'd woken early, and she smiled at him as he approached.

"Have you seen Nosey this morning?" he asked. Shanna shook her head and lifted a querying eyebrow at the Scout.

"What do you mean? Have you lost her?" It was an odd question — no one ever lost a starcat.

"Not exactly," Arad looked slightly embarrassed. "She was on my bed as normal when I went to sleep, but she wasn't there when I woke up. Actually, would you send Storm or Twister to search the place for her, please? I've looked everywhere I can think of." Shanna took pity on Arad, and called Twister to her.

"Twister, find Nosey!" Twister blinked his tidemarks once, and immediately shot out of the common room door and vanished up the corridor. "Well, there's one answer, Arad. You couldn't find her in here, because she isn't in here."

"But where on earth would she have gone without me?" asked Arad in a puzzled tone. "If she needs to go out in the night, she always wakes me." He smiled ruefully. "And everyone else as well." Shanna shared a companionable grimace with him. The whole group had experienced Nosey's boisterous rousing of her companion.

Storm hummed quietly at them and looked pointedly at the door, and the two of them followed him as he took the path his brother had taken, but at a more sedate pace. For ten minutes, Storm wound them through the maze of underground corridors of the Starlyne habitat. After more than four weeks, Shanna could now usually recognise where she was, but this time Storm led them into a completely new area of the complex. Abruptly, Twister was with them again. He hummed quietly, and winked his tidemarks at his brother in a pattern that Shanna had learned to recognise as quiet amusement. Intrigued she shared a look with Arad as the two of them followed the two cats. Two more corners and through a sliding door, and then the corridor sloped upwards and exited into a tiny sheltered valley hemmed about by sheer rock walls. In the midst of the open space was Nosey, surrounded by ten tiny Starlynes, the eleven of them gambolling and playing, rolling over and over each other. The pudgy little starcat was bouncing and leaping, and tapping the tiny Starlynes as she leapt up and over them. *Would you call them children?* wondered Shanna.

Arad watched with his mouth open, eyes wide as his starcat and the Starlyne younglings played. They were exuberant and both Shanna and Arad could feel the enjoyment wafting in waves off the group. An adult Starlyne glided up to them as they stood there, watching the merriment. "She arrived as the younglings did this morning. They think she's wonderful." The tone of the creature's voice was fond.

"She's rather naughty, actually," said Arad, firmly, "She shouldn't have wandered off like that." His eyes continued to reflect the enjoyment so obviously being had by the small group gambolling together despite his stern tone, as Nosey swarmed up a small tree and then launched herself over the little Starlynes, bouncing on her paws behind them as they turned to chase her down.

"There is no harm," came the Starlyne's thought. "She is still very young, despite her precocious nature. She is welcome to play with our young each day if you wish. She brings them much joy." Her tone was indulgent, and

Shanna noticed her tidemarks were mirroring the little starcat's blue toned ones. Storm and Twister hummed approvingly as Nosey finally left the Starlyne younglings and bounded over to Arad and sat to attention on his foot.

"You're a problem, Nosey." He shook his head, then bent down and with a grunt hefted her growing weight. He turned her to face him, suspended by her armpits, and she had the grace to look slightly embarrassed yet unrepentant at the same time. She tried a small purr and batted her eyelashes at him. "So, you want to play?" She purred more loudly, and Arad sighed. "I'll bring her each day before we breakfast, and then hopefully she'll stay out of trouble for the rest of it!" The Starlyne emitted a feeling of pleased amusement and dipped her head before gliding away. Shanna giggled.

"Maybe it'll keep her out of trouble Arad, but maybe not." The older Scout snorted in agreement and put Nosey back on the ground with a rub on her head.

"Come on, Trouble!" He hand-signalled Nosey and he and Shanna began the trek back to the common room. "Wonder what we've got happening today?"

"Maybe Spiron will know," Shanna said.

Two hours later, Shanna joined the other cadets on top of the small slope outside Fractus' teaching room. Patrol Ten was nowhere to be seen. Below them, the steep slope into the valley dropped away, soothall berry plants dotting its sides. Teacher slid her bulk around one of the granite outcrops and joined them.

"Today we wish to assess how you might work as a group, now that you have begun to learn some of your new skills. Your task is to navigate your way across this valley to the light you can now see flashing on the far horizon." A blue light appeared amongst the foliage, far away on the other side of the valley. The cadets nodded. *That doesn't seem too hard*, thought Shanna, before Teacher went on. "We have prepared a number of surprises. There will be obstacles, and there will be mechanical devices designed to mimic the Garsal technology. There will be the normal creatures of Below. And as you can see, this valley is home to many spooner spiders amongst the soothall bushes so you will need to be careful. You have until midnight to complete your task." She glided away and vanished into the habitat.

"Just like that?" said Zandany.

"Apparently," replied Taya, wiggling her eyebrows at him. "I'm wondering if we need to go and get our packs."

"No." Came a firm thought from the direction of the habitat.

"Well, I guess that answers that question – looks like it's just the six of us then, with what we have in our pockets," said Verren. "I wonder what the others are doing."

"I guess we'd better stop wondering about the others and get down to doing something ourselves," replied Shanna. "It's what? Mid-morning?" She squinted at the sun, visible to the east.

"Actually it's 10.15am," said Amma, grinning at the others, "And it's going to rain just around midnight, so if we don't want to get wet we'd better get a move on, but perhaps we need to plan a little first." She indicated to Spider to take the watch, and Shanna sent Twister to assist. The group sat themselves on the granite rocks, leaning their heads together.

"I think we should begin in a standard Patrol formation, even though there are only six of us," said Ragar, "It's something we know how to do, and it'll cover all the basics. What do you reckon?" There were nods from around the group.

"In that case," Verren said, "you're Patrol First, and Amma's your deputy. I assume you'll want Shanna on point? With me backing her as guide, since I'm now theoretically the super navigator?"

"Are you sure you don't want to lead, Verren?" grinned Ragar, "You've got all the ideas!"

"Nope! You know me," replied the other cadet, "Not that great at making tough decisions - you can have that job."

Planning took less than ten minutes and as the group began to descend the slope, Shanna was on point with Storm and Twister ranging ahead, followed by Verren, who had Cirrus swing left and right as required. Amma and Zandany flanked Taya in the middle with Ragar acting as rear guard. It was the first time the cadets had been alone as a group Below, and Shanna felt a shiver of excitement. She smiled at Verren, then turned her attention forward as he indicated that she should proceed as directly as possible towards the light that Teacher had shown them. Shanna hoped fervently that Verren's location sense was as good as Fractus had suggested it would become. He'd certainly become adept at leading them through the mazes prepared by the spiral patterned Starlyne.

She pulled her attention back and began to glide as silently as possible through the thick bush. Locating the first soothall bush she gave it a wide berth, signalling back to the others, and the cadet patrol began to work its way into the vegetation on the slope.

Thirty minutes later Storm appeared next to her, tidemarks flaring, and she raised a hand to signal the group to stop. Faintly through the vegetation, she could see the outline of Twister's form, frozen in a position of watch. Leaving point position to Verren, she glided softly towards Twister, sliding silently around a barbed palm, and joined him under the fragrant fronds of a pungo tree. They were positioned on the slope of the valley, about half of the way down to the valley floor, and Twister had his eyes fixed on an odd protuberance amongst a clump of bushes flanked by grey granite rocks. The rocks formed a barrier to either side, funnelling the clearest path downwards towards the lump standing slightly above the bushes. To either side of the rocks two wings of soothall bushes stood, and Shanna could clearly see spooner spider nests at the base of each one. Beyond them the slope dropped off into a sheer face on either side.

She followed Twister's gaze to the protuberance, trying to see why he had stopped rather than investigating, and then realised. There was a small glow coming from one edge of it. It was faint, and dimly green, blending in well with the surrounding vegetation, and mildly ominous. Carefully she picked up a small stone, and lobbed it towards the dimly seen glow. There was a bright flash and the pebble bounced back towards her, a small spark hovering mid-air for a split second to show where the pebble had struck whatever the Star-lynes had erected there. Shanna slid back to the Patrol, dropped through it to Ragar, and quietly informed him of the dilemma. He nodded and waved Taya forward. Shanna explained the issue in a few quick words and the group, maintaining its formation, quietly moved up to Twister's location.

Shanna picked up another pebble and lobbed it gently towards the dim green glow, to show Taya what occurred. "Wonder what that'd do to us if we blundered into it?" she whispered quietly to Shanna. The dark haired girl gave a quick hand signal to Spinner, and he dropped to his belly and faded. Shanna realised that the other girl's hair was now glowing very softly in Spinner's tidemark patterns, and her face was screwed up in concentration. There was a sudden snapping sound from in front of them and the dim green glow abruptly went out. "Try another pebble, Shan," Taya whispered.

Shanna carefully lobbed another pebble towards the protuberance and shared a grin with Taya as it passed the lump with no spark or bounce. She repeated the action with a small stick and another pebble, then hand signalled Twister to approach cautiously. The big cat stalked forward noiselessly, sniffed, then relaxed, allowing his tidemarks to sparkle on the tips of his ears. Spinner appeared by Taya's side and she dropped back into the centre of the patrol again. Ragar indicated that they should move forward. Shanna - taking a deep breath - followed Twister, Storm by her side, and approached the clump of bushes, heart racing. At the last moment she lobbed another pebble, and reassured, passed through them to examine the odd gadget concealed behind it.

She sent Storm on a wide sweep down the slope, while ever vigilant Twister, took up a post on one of the barrier rocks. There was nothing much to see, simply a lumpy brown metal object roughly disguised to look like a tree limb. It would have succeeded too, except for the green glow that had given it away.

Ragar promptly reformed the patrol after they had cleared the barrier. Shanna resumed point, and Verren indicated in which direction they should go with concise hand signals.

Two long hours later, they finally reached the bottom of the valley. There had been a number of obstacles and several close encounters with wildlife. Shanna was hot, dirty, and thirsty. They all had water bottles, but hers was starting to get low. She raised a hand and, leaving Storm on guard, dropped back to Ragar.

"I think we need some water, Ragar. I'd like to send Twister ahead to look."

"If you see anything edible, collect it as well. We've nothing to eat with us, and midnight is looking like a much harder deadline than I first thought. Are you OK on point still?" Shanna nodded at him and returned to her position. For the first time that day, she thought about the lessons they'd had in 'feeling' where things were. She attempted to relax and concentrated on locating Storm and Twister by feel, and then attempted to search out anything else ahead. Her cats were easy to locate; it was as if they were extensions of her own body. She could feel Twister blurring through the trees at top speed, while Storm was like a steadfast seeking beacon, directly ahead. She 'felt' as he glided from side to side in front of the patrol, 'felt' the moment when Twister stopped abruptly, and knew he'd found water.

The rest of the vegetation remained obstinately blank and Shanna wondered if she'd ever learn to feel what might be ahead. Fractus had insisted that she would, but apart from her cats nothing seemed to be stirring her senses. Behind her she could vaguely 'feel' her fellow cadets – or more correctly – her fellow cadets' starcats. Twister appeared from a clump of pungo trees directly ahead, and she turned and nodded slightly to Ragar. He nosed up to Shanna, and she patted his sleek coat, noting the dampness on his face.

The vegetation slowly became thicker as the noise of the running creek began to seep through the trees. It became more and more difficult to skirt dangerous plants and the soothall berry bushes with their spooner spider nests appeared in even thicker patches, the blue berries dangling temptingly and lushly all around them. Shanna had both Storm and Twister weaving ahead of the patrol, and they led the group on a winding circuitous route through the dense greenness. Quite suddenly the trees thinned, and the creek came into view, lightly obscured by hanging branches.

The two starcats had led the cadets to a deep pool, with a small waterfall on the upstream side. It was flanked by a small cliff that Shanna could now see formed a ridge extending some way on either side of the river. There were a double series of rocky rapids immediately downstream. With some dismay, Shanna realised that the creek was more like a small river, over five metres wide, deep, and with no obvious way across. She paused just before reaching the bank, signalled the rest of the patrol, and squatted quietly behind a bush, just watching. She 'felt' the rest of the patrol sink into quietness as they reached the line of trees, then sent Storm and Twister to check the river bank. The two cats faded quietly, and she felt them drift silently up the bank in either direction. There was a twinkle of violet ear tidemarks from Twister on the upstream bank, but nothing from Storm. Next to Shanna, Ragar raised an eyebrow silently in question. Shanna shook her head and signalled a wait request. He nodded and passed the hand signal down the line. They sat in silence for a number of minutes, and then Storm reappeared abruptly at

Shanna's side, ears flattened and the fur on his neck standing stiff above his leather harness.

He blinked at Shanna, and she signalled a 'stay here' at Ragar, then faded herself. Placing one hand on her cat as he faded again, she followed him silently out of the trees and down the riverbank to the head of the rapids. Storm stopped behind a large rock and Shanna followed his lead in concealment, despite the two of them being faded. She cautiously inched her head around it so that she could get a good view of whatever was downriver.

There was a family group of plungers basking on the riverbank, lazily trailing their clawed front flippers in the water. Shanna had never seen a plunger in the flesh before, but their large furred forms and flippers with retractable claws were unmistakeable. The aquatic mammals were crafty hunters, deadly in the water and surprisingly fast on their four flippered feet out of it. There were five in the family group. The two patterned parents and three adolescents, their uniformly brown fur not yet differentiating them into male and female. Shanna and Storm watched for several minutes, hoping that the group might show signs of wanting to move on. They lolled unconcernedly on the muddy bank, however, and Shanna realised that this section of river was most likely their territory. She touched Storm, and the two of them glided soundlessly up the riverbank into the concealing trees. She let the fade subside as she joined the others.

Carefully keeping her voice low, Shanna whispered to Ragar her findings. He signalled to Amma and Verren, and the four of them formed a small grouping.

"I think we have no option but to travel upstream and look for a crossing point. There's five plungers and only six of us, along with seven cats," said Ragar resignedly. "Amma, what's the time now? And Verren, give us your best estimate of how much further we've got to go to reach the finish point."

Shanna could feel Storm and Twister sitting alertly on watch, and realised how thirsty she now was as Amma cocked her head briefly and considered. She opened her water bottle and sipped quietly.

"I think it's about mid-afternoon. There's something interfering with my time sense at the moment." Amma trailed off and frowned. "I'm not sure what, but it's like trying to feel through a smothering blanket." Verren nodded his agreement.

"The further we've dropped into the valley, the harder it's been to navigate. I've been relying on a combination of my location sense and standard navigating techniques, so I'm not as certain as I was a couple of hours ago, but I'm fairly sure we're about a third of the way to where we need to be. We're going to be pushing the time limit as we are, but I can't see a way across here that won't alert the plungers. Although we could set half the cats to seeing them off, they're territorial and would probably defend their ground. There's no point risking an injury on a training exercise."

"Right then," said Ragar quietly, but decisively. "We move upstream, which gives us two options — back into the bush and back up the slope we've just come down and around, or we try and stay closer to the riverbank, which means a really steep but brief climb, followed by hopefully a safer crossing." He deliberated for a moment. "We need the shorter option. Shan, we're going to need you to climb first, faded, and then fade Taya and Zandany while they climb. We three can manage our fades without our cats, but they can't yet. Are you up to it?" Shanna nodded nervously, her stomach suddenly twisting itself into knots. Despite Taya having confessed that she could fade without Spinner, she seemed to have developed a bit of a block in actually doing it.

Right, she thought, Climb steep, slippery cliff, faded, then stay faded and fade two others, while avoiding alerting plunger family downstream … and all without ever having tried to climb and fade at the same time.

"Sure you're OK, Shan?" Verren's voice was slightly concerned, and Shanna swallowed and nodded quickly to cover her nervousness.

"Yep, I'll send Twister up first, and keep Storm below until I'm up. He'll flick his earmarks when I'm up, and then you can send Zandany. Can you send one of the other cats to watch the plungers while we're ascending?"

Ragar nodded and motioned to Verren, who sent Cirrus off with the flick of a finger. Ragar put a hand on Shanna's shoulder. "You'll be fine. You've faded all of us at some point or other in the last few weeks."

Yes, thought Shanna, but it wasn't potentially life or death then! Resolutely, she signalled Twister to fade, and to climb the cliff face. He vanished from view, and from her place in the trees, she saw a small piece of vegetation float off the side of the cliff face. Within a few moments, there was a twinkle of violet marks from the top of the rock face and Shanna determinedly faded herself. She sent Storm off to the base of the cliff and followed him, moving as silently as possible and feeling the slight breeze wafting through the valley. She felt grateful that it was blowing across the river so that her scent would not alert the plungers.

At the base of the cliff, Shanna took several minutes to scout the easiest route to the top. She noted a barbed palm halfway up the face concealed amongst the ferns drooping from the rocks. It was near the most likely path up the rock face. She wondered what else might be concealed in the damp greenery.

To her right, the cliff face extended into the tree line but it was overhanging for as far as she was able to see, and completely unclimbable. Her heart thudded as she moved closer to the cliff face and placed her right hand carefully on the damp ledge above her. Gripping it tightly, she took the first step off the river bank and began to inch her way upwards. Each handhold had to be carefully sought, each rock tested with foot or hand before she entrusted her body weight to it. Half way up the face, she looked above, seeking the next handhold, and remembered the barbed palm. She paused, and there it was, sitting just above her, its characteristic foliage almost invisible from directly below. She looked around to her right, searching for the way around that she'd scouted from the riverbank below.

A combination of sweat and spray from the small waterfall dripped into her left eye, and she blinked furiously to regain her vision, her eye stinging briefly from the salt. She located the next ledge and realised that she would be at maximum stretch to reach it, and the next foothold. She placed her foot, then inching sideways as far as she was able, she transferred her weight off her right arm, launched it out and up towards the small ledge, grasping just the edge of it. She checked her fade, uncomfortably awkward at full stretch, pulled at the rock with her hand to check its stability, then shifted her weight onto her right foot a little more and thrust her hand fully onto the small ledge.

Hot needles of pain lanced into her fingertips, and Shanna was momentarily overwhelmed by it. Instinct kicked in and she maintained her hold on the rock face despite the pain, but the observers concealed amongst the trees saw a brief flicker of her form appear. Sweat poured from her face as she frantically tried to imagine what she'd put her fingers on, and her muscles quivered with strain as she hung at full stretch on the cliff face. The fear of falling prevented her from withdrawing her hand, yet the fear of what might have caused the pain screamed at her to let go. She felt her fingers throb and imagined them bloating with the swelling caused by any of the hundreds of toxic plants and animals she'd studied in the last few months. A small whimper tried to force itself through her gritted teeth but she pushed it back, the image of the plunger family fresh in her mind.

With a titanic effort Shanna kept her right hand where it was, and as fast as possible, trying not to panic, scrabbled several footholds higher on the damp rocks. When she was high enough to look over the small ledge, she could see that she'd placed her hand into a patch of fire lichen. Its normally fiery tones had been concealed by the ledge. Fortunately fire lichen, although extremely painful, would leave her with only blisters and swelling and nothing more serious. She gritted her teeth again, pulled her hand out of the patch and climbed far enough up the cliff for her to carefully kick the lichen off the ledge, to float down onto the river bank where its bright red foliage lay as a warning to the others.

Finally reaching the top, Shanna hauled herself up and over trying to avoid brushing the erupting blisters on anything. Her right hand throbbed and burned, and she could feel that several of the blisters had burst, leaking watery fluid which dripped off her hand. She cradled it, desperately wishing she could stick it immediately into the river. She flicked her eyes across the landscape, noting Twister's earmarks twinkling briefly at her as he patrolled the area at the top of the cliff face. Apart from a few soothall bushes further upstream, Shanna could see nothing immediately threatening in the immediate vicinity. She pulled her silent whistle, fumbling awkwardly with her left hand, and blew to call

Storm to her. While he climbed, she awkwardly penned a brief note with her left hand to Ragar on a scrap of stained paper from her thigh pocket, describing the hazards of the climb, and then sent it back down with Storm.

She had a moment of respite as the big cat vanished, lying on the cliff top panting and trying to gently flex her hand, before she saw the telltale twinkle of Storm's tidemarks, and felt the cat's reassuring presence by her side again. Closing her eyes briefly, she 'felt' for Zandany's presence as he moved towards the cliff face. He was faded but she could tell he was touching Punch, then 'pushed' her fade towards him. She had no idea how she did it, but she imagined it like a balloon, or bubble, radiating out from her. She 'felt' the fade incorporate him and then concentrated. Fading herself was second nature, fading someone else took a good deal more concentration and effort. It also seemed to take a lot more energy, and Shanna had been extremely hungry after the practice sessions in the Starlyne habitat.

About fifteen minutes later, she 'felt' Zandany arrive at the cliff top, then his arrival over the edge. She maintained her balloon until Punch arrived, and Zandany had placed his hand back on the ever reliable red-toned cat.

"Are you OK, Shan? I saw the fire lichen on the ground and we all saw you flicker on the way up the cliff." His whisper was concerned, and Punch nosed her so gently she could feel the sympathy in the normally imperturbable cat's touch.

"I'm OK. Lots of blisters, but OK. Can you and Punch check out the surroundings? I can't see much that's a problem, but I've only had a few moments to check." She felt the other cadet crawl quietly away and returned her attention to the riverbank below.

As Storm twinkled his ears again, she extended her balloon to encompass Taya. She 'felt' the other girl pause at the red patch on the mud then begin to climb. Shanna was beginning to feel the strain of maintaining the fade. Her right hand throbbed and burned and sweat was again trickling into her eyes, as she 'felt' the other girl move slowly up the rock face. She was beginning to tremble with tiredness by the time Taya rolled her body over the top. She kept the fade going though her jaw was clenched with effort and her cheeks were aching with fatigue, and as soon as Spinner arrived and Taya had placed her hand on his neck, relaxed the balloon, almost gasping with effort. She kept herself faded and 'felt' Taya move away with her cat. The other three ascended relatively quickly but the waiting seemed to go on forever, and Shanna didn't dare move away from her cliff top watch until Verren and Cirrus had attained the top. The plunger family had remained in their relaxed posture, undisturbed on the muddy bank the whole time.

As she pushed herself to her feet, Shanna felt suddenly lightheaded and had to steady herself on Storm's suddenly present body. She leaned on him for support and proceeded slowly to where she could feel the others gathered in a patch of pungo trees about fifty metres up from the cliff line.

Her hand dripped serous fluid and throbbed with every step, and there was a querying twinkle from Storm's ears. Joining the other, now visible cadets inside the grove, she let her fade go with a quiet sigh of relief and sat suddenly on the ground, legs feeling like rubber and an aching hunger in her belly. Verren dropped to one knee next to her. "Shan, what's happened to your hand?"

"Fire lichen," she sighed tiredly. She looked at the hand. Her middle to little fingers had taken the brunt of the lichen and were almost solid blisters. The index finger and thumb were speckled with tiny blisters – painful, but not debilitating.

"You climbed with your hand like that?" exclaimed Ragar quietly. "Was that when we saw you flicker?" Shanna nodded.

"Well, it was either climb or fall and I didn't feel like dying, so there weren't a lot of other options."

"We need some water to clean these, Ragar, and I need whatever you all have in your pockets that might help me make some kind of dressing." Verren's hands were very gentle as he carefully pried Shanna's fingers apart to see the extent of the damage.

"Zan, go and tell Amma she's to continue sentry. You get some water and we'll make this our food break. We'll pool what we've collected." He sucked in a breath as Verren turned Shanna's hand over to expose the blistered palm and fingertips. "Still can't believe you climbed with that hand!" Storm eased his body behind Shanna as she felt suddenly faint. With her left hand, she fumbled in one of her thigh pockets and pulled out the nuts she'd harvested earlier.

"Here's my contribution. It's not much I'm afraid." She drew in a hissing breath as Verren poured cool water over her hand. The relief was enormous. He carefully turned her hand, allowing the water to cascade between her fingers, and wash away some of the fire lichen that was still sitting on the webbing between her fingers. "Thanks, Verren." Her tone was heartfelt, and he smiled briefly at her before returning his attention to her hand. She suddenly felt better.

Chapter 9

THE cadets had struggled to cross the river. Even with the barrier of the waterfall protecting them from the plunger family basking on the bank downstream, they had hesitated to swim the river. While fetching water to clean Shanna's blistered hand, Zandany had seen large shadowy shapes swimming ominously in the dim depths. Warily, the group had continued to move upstream, searching for a narrow or shallow area to cross the water. As the hours wore on, Shanna had struggled more and more with fatigue. Storm and Twister alternated between ranging ahead, and subtly assisting her around and over some of the more difficult obstacles.

Finally, Twister located a large tree which had fallen across the narrowest section of the river they'd seen and the group had crossed, faded, and melted into the trees on the opposite shore. The light slanting through the trees was the fading colour of late afternoon, and Ragar called a quick halt. Shanna sank onto a rock while Verren sent Cirrus out to circle the group. "How long have we left until midnight, Amma?" he asked.

"About six hours, I think," replied Amma. She pushed her hair back off her face, smearing more streaks of dirt across her left cheek. "That river's really slowed us down. Are we far off track, Verren?"

Verren creased his forehead in thought. "We're now a long way north of the finish point. The problem is, I don't have a map, so apart from knowing we've got to head uphill as soon as we can, I can't really guide us around any obstacles. Sure, I can keep us pointed towards the finish point – I know where that is in relation to where we started, and where we are now – but the bits in between I've never seen." He shrugged. "I think we've just figured out my limitations. I know where we are in relation to where we've been, and I know where we're going, but without a map I could easily lead us into a dead end." The others nodded.

"So we need to go uphill, and we need to go south." Ragar tapped a finger on his cheek. "The question is, how do we make sure we take the fastest and safest route? I'm sure we can guarantee that there'll be more obstacles – and those obstacles will be just where the best route is. And judging from the first half of this trip, we may well be funnelled into them. It's about to get dark, and there's no moon for the first few hours."

Zandany raised a hand. "Shan, you and Amma have your glowstones, don't you?" The girls both nodded. "And Ragar and I can make flames, so we'll have some form of light. The question is, will it attract predators?" There were nods of agreement around the group, coupled with some of concern.

"At this stage I think we need to keep moving, and if we end up funnelled into any traps, we'll just have to deal with them." Amma's voice was firm. "And I'll take point for a bit. In case the rest of you haven't noticed, Shan's about to collapse." Shanna pushed herself to her feet with her left hand, standing unsteadily.

"I'm OK." She belied the phrase by wobbling again, and put out her uninjured hand to steady herself on Twister. The big cat hummed at her, concern rippling his tidemarks. "Just a bit tired. That fade really took it out of me." She sat on the rock before her legs could give way, as Ragar shook his head.

"I hadn't even considered what that might do to you. Verren, what do you think?" Verren tilted Shanna's head up, and looked at her eyes, and then checked her heart rate. He sighed quietly.

"You're right, Amma. She needs to eat and rest. Anyone collect any more food?" He held out a hand. Zandany pulled a handful of berries out of a chest pocket.

"Sorry about the sweat."

Verren pushed them into Shanna's hand. "Eat, Shan. Oh thanks, Taya." He passed over half a dozen nuts. "Come on, eat them, Shan."

"I'm sorry guys," Shanna put the first of the sweet berries into her mouth, savouring the taste and feeling relief course through her body. She resolutely tried to hand the food back to the others. "I'll be OK, I just need a little more rest, and you all need food too." Verren closed her hand over the berries.

"Eat! We'll be in all kinds of trouble – actually in more kinds of trouble – if you flake on us now. None of us want to have to haul your carcass up the hill!"

Shanna nodded tiredly and chewed one of the nuts, washing it down with some water. Her hand throbbed under its makeshift dressing, and she looked ahead to the upcoming climb with some trepidation. She forced a few more nuts down, chewing grimly as she contemplated how difficult it would be for her friends to carry her up the hillside. She could see Ragar tapping one finger thoughtfully on the rock, and determinedly swallowed more of the berries. The faintness began to slowly subside and she sat a little straighter before swallowing the last of the food.

"Right, new plan," said Ragar, "We're going to become unpredictable." He looked around grimly at the others. "The Starlynes know us well. They know our strengths and they know our weaknesses, or they think they do. We're going to avoid the easy path. Anything useful we come across we'll collect. Things like plybrush if we see it, or any kind of food. Verren, the next soothall we come across, we'll harvest. Shan needs to be in less pain in case we need to fade again, so we'll use the raw fruit on those blisters." He held a hand up as Verren opened his mouth to protest. "I know it's a risk, but we need her ready to conceal us at any moment, and you can sort the rest out later. Shan, until your hand is settled you travel in the middle. Can you ask Storm or Twister to Scout ahead though? Verren will take the point."

Shanna nodded. She was impressed by Ragar's decisiveness. He outlined the rest of his plan for the ascent towards the finishing point, quietly tasking each of the cadets. Pleased and surprised smiles appeared on their grubby faces. They began their ascent.

Within the hour, Verren brought the patrol to a halt. The obvious path took them rapidly upwards through a narrow declivity in the steepening valley wall. "Send Twister out for us, Shan," requested Ragar. At Shanna's quick hand signal, Twister vanished quickly ahead. Beside her, Ragar sent Sparks in a different direction. She saw his tidemarks twinkle briefly before his form faded into the vegetation on the southern side of the narrow passage.

The sun had now completely set and the brief twilight was fading quickly. Small rustles made by the stirring night-time creatures were beginning to sound in the greenery around them, and Shanna sent Storm to circle the group as they waited. Her fatigue had lessened after she'd eaten and she no longer felt light headed, but the steady upward gradient was already taking its toll, and she hoped desperately that she wouldn't have to hold a sustained fade.

Twister reappeared silently by her side, several pieces of vegetation in his mouth and a dismayed pattern of flickering tidemarks on his coat. Shanna and Ragar sorted quickly through the vegetation as Sparks nosed to Ragar's side, dropping a mouthful of his own. "We'll go south," said Ragar, and Shanna nodded slowly in the deepening dusk. Around them the others were quietly watchful, eyes focused on the gathering darkness and ears alert for any threatening sound. Seven starcats glided silently around their human companions, guarding, as Ragar signalled quietly, and the group slid silently through the trees, parallel with the steepening terrain.

As the last of the twilight vanished, Shanna saw a pale glow gradually illuminate the surrounds as Amma uncovered her glowstone. She awkwardly fished her own out from under her shirt and let its cool light provide much needed visibility. She felt a sudden pang of homesickness, so strong that she almost stumbled, but resolutely pulled her focus back into the here and now.

Again Verren signalled a halt and they settled quietly, ears searching for any malign sound. Shanna could see Amma's pool of light moving forward towards Verren, then it stopped and she could see that the two of them were crouched low over something in front of the group. Several moments later, Verren's shape appeared against the pool of light and he arrived at Shanna's side, quietly motioning for her to remove her hand dressings. She unwound the now less than pristine cloth wrappings, trying to hold the throbbing hand steady for Verren's view.

"Hold still Shan. This will hurt briefly, and then hopefully you'll feel better." He poised the halved soothall berry, now grasped carefully between thumb and finger, and at her nod gently squeezed it as he drew the dark flesh across the worst of the blistered and swollen skin. Sharp pain throbbed viciously, and

Shanna nearly pulled her hand away, but it was immediately replaced by an abrupt, sudden cool ebbing of the pain, as if Verren was washing the malign sensation from her hand.

"Thank you!" she gasped. Verren rewrapped the injured hand and shook his head slightly.

"It'll feel good, but it's not fixed. Don't remove the dressing, and be careful what you do with it, or you'll have all the skin off! This is just a stopgap." He went to move away, but paused. "Can I borrow your stone, Shan? I nearly stumbled into the spooner nest before Cirrus stopped me!"

Shanna nodded "If I'm travelling in the middle, you need it more than I do!" she said, pulling the chain over her head. It snagged in her tangled braids briefly before she could tug it free and drop it into his waiting hand.

They resumed their travel across the valley wall, and Shanna marvelled thankfully at the relief from the pain of her injured hand. She began actively scanning the vegetation in the dim light provided by the widely spaced glowstones. By the time the group stopped again, she'd managed to harvest quite a number of nuts. She set Storm to circling, as Ragar softly called the group in.

"Pool your food again," he asked, and Taya quickly divided it equally into six portions, taking one to Zandany, who remained vigilantly on watch with Punch. "Are you sure this is the spot to turn, Verren?" Verren nodded.

"The finish point is immediately above us. A straight line between here and there should take us about two hours, assuming we meet no obstacles."

"Great, so we'll turn straight up the side here. We'll try and 'feel' our way as much as possible. Verren, you'll stay up the front, but try not to use the glowstone if you can avoid it. Shan, you'll travel behind him. If there's a threat, fade us – don't hesitate, just do it until we sort out what's going on. Amma, how long do we have?"

Amma screwed her face up slightly, "About four hours I think, but the rain'll be here in less than that."

"OK then, we all know what to do. Let's go."

The light from the glowstones was extinguished and the dark descended like a blanket. Shanna was briefly blinded before her night vision began to reassert itself. She relaxed slightly and tried to 'feel' the others. Their familiar presences surrounded her and she gradually extended her 'feel' around her. It was very much like the bubble she imagined when she faded. A brief moment of dislocation occurred and then she had it; the landscape was suddenly 'there', in odd but strangely familiar shapes and feelings. She knew exactly where Verren was, the lurking barbed palm behind the frondan, and the small marmal cowering in the entrance to its burrow, frozen in the presence of so many starcats. There was a pleased hum from her elbow and Storm eased his body underneath her uninjured hand, wriggling luxuriously. As she signalled, he and Twister began their sweeps in front of the now moving group of cadets.

The gradient beneath her feet steepened and Shanna leant forward and started up the hill, making use of every piece of cover that she could now 'feel' and see. Absently, she chewed her share of the rations they'd pooled, concentrating on what was in front and to each side of the humans and their cats. Her leg muscles tightened, each step now an almost vertical lift of her body, senses alert to sounds and feelings and the oddly altered vision. There was a sharp crack from ahead and she stopped in her tracks half crouched, listening, alert to any message from her cats or from Verren. A sudden soft slithering alerted her to his presence, and Verren's hand grasped her elbow urgently.

"Fade us Shan, now!" She didn't hesitate but faded herself, and pushed her bubble out around the whole group of human beings, knowing that the cats would take their cue from her.

"What's going on?" her whisper was barely audible.

"There's a small staureg camped in the trees just above us, where the valley wall flattens out. I've sent Cirrus to circle around for a safe path, but we're up wind of it ...." his whisper broke off, and Shanna was struck with a sudden chill of fear. They'd faced stauregs before, but always with Patrol Ten, and always before the staureg knew they were there. Most likely, this spiky reptile was already alert to their presence, and its wily intelligence would be preparing to ambush them. She dropped back to alert Ragar, detecting him by 'feel', feeling herself slowly begin to wilt again from holding the fade over so many, and whispered the information.

"OK, drop the group fade in two minutes. The others will know by then." Shanna resumed her place behind Verren's position, thankfully reducing her bubble of fade at the allotted time to include only herself. She crunched a handful of nuts as quietly as possible, hoping to forestall the exhaustion that had so overwhelmed her previously, and at Verren's low whistle slowly crept forward. Storm and Twister slid under each hand and the sense of strain eased slightly. There was a faint echo of discomfort from her injured hand, but she ignored it and followed their guiding bodies as quietly as possible up the last slope, and into the trees on the flat ground above.

The two cats angled her obliquely across through the trees, moving silently with their hackles raised and their bodies faded. Shanna strained her senses, trying to 'feel' ahead far enough to discover any obstacles. Abruptly she 'felt' to her right a huge cold-blooded bulk lurking in the cover of a thick grove.

Goosebumps walked across her skin and she tried to move even more silently, wishing that the exertions of the day had not made her sweat so much. To her ears came the faint sounds of the creature scenting the air and she crouched even lower despite the fade, and she and her two cats slunk through the vegetation. As they skulked past, the wind changed and began to blow gently but steadily from the beast, and Shanna allowed herself to relax slightly as the staureg began to settle as the scents that so troubled it vanished.

The group continued upwards on the deviated route, and ten minutes later Shanna finally allowed the fade to vanish, exhaling in an excess of relief. Storm and Twister recommenced their arcing patrols.

Ragar's plan of unpredictability continued. The easy option was avoided, and the more difficult route taken each time an opportunity presented itself. Their path was constantly upward, the steepness causing legs to burn, and hearts to pound. Tiredness became their constant companion, and Shanna's fatigue began to seep into her bones. There were several predator encounters - fortunately none the size or danger of the staureg - and several times they'd had to divert to skirt patches of dangerous vegetation. Constant vigilance was essential Below, and now there was the added strain of trying to 'feel' ahead.

They paused at last to assess their location and plan for the last surge to the top. Shanna was finding it more and more difficult to think. Her attention kept straying as Verren estimated how much further they had to go, and a miserable, chilly, drizzle began as they gathered under the shelter of a large weeping pungo.

"We've about an hour left," said Amma, "and the rain is only going to get worse."

"I'd say we're close to an hour from our destination," replied Verren. "I'm keen to use the glowstone from now on; I'm struggling to keep focus the other way, and I keep flicking into dizziness when I lose it." He pulled Shanna's glowstone from inside his shirt, illuminating the ring of filthy faces. Shanna could see bloody parallel scratches across Verren's face, and Taya's trousers were holed through at the knee. The others looked like she felt, utterly exhausted.

"Come on," said Ragar, "We're almost there, just one more push! We'll try and move as fast as possible, and this time Verren, we'll take the direct route – it's the only chance we'll have to make it in time." He tapped his jaw thoughtfully with one finger. "When we're fifteen minutes out, Verren, you'll flash the stone three times, and then we'll travel in complete darkness, faded and navigating by 'feel'. Shan, can you take the lead? I want you and Verren travelling together, so that we have maximum protection up front."

Shanna struggled for a moment, then nodded tiredly, finally making sense of Ragar's words. Her stomach tied itself in knots and she wondered whether she'd be able to keep the pace required. Fumbling in her pocket, she pulled out the last few nuts she'd scrounged and crunched them tiredly. Her right hand gave a tingling throb and she felt the soggy dampness of her dressing, and realised that most of the blisters had ruptured during the trek.

The rain steadily increased as the cadet group forged their way upwards. The ground turned to soggy slush under their feet and the grade steepened again. Storm, Twister and Cirrus alternated ahead of the group and the glowstone, now returned to Shanna, illuminated the dripping vegetation. By the time that Verren motioned to Shanna to flash her glowstone three times, her hand had begun to throb again. She dropped the stone back into the neck of her wet shirt and, gritting her teeth, faded. Concentrating, Shanna extended her bubble of 'feel', locating her fellow cadets, placing all the cats, and trying to pierce the darkness as the Starlyne tutors had taught her.

As they moved forward they struck yet another steep slope. The throbbing in Shanna's hand accelerated to a crescendo as they struggled up the slope, senses extended, still faded and trying desperately to make the finish before the deadline. She could almost feel Amma counting the seconds down with each struggling step she took.

Fatigue flooded her body as she struggled to maintain the fade. Storm bounded back to her through the rain, and flashed his tidemarks at her, and she stared stupidly at him until she realised that they were patterns of welcome and homecoming, and that the finish must be almost dead ahead. She struggled up a final steep slope, calves and thighs burning, complete darkness around her, struggling to maintain a sense of where she was and what might be between her and their final destination.

She narrowly avoided a nest of spooner spiders below the soothall bush in front of her at the last moment, the presence of the lurking danger flaring in her oddly doubled vision like a glow of poisonous green malevolence. She stumbled sideways and wrenched her ankle as she skated on a greasy patch of mud. The ankle added its throb to the screaming pain from her blistered hand. Struggling upwards, Shanna felt her senses begin to dislocate as tiredness siphoned the strength from her limbs. She gritted her teeth, and maintaining her fade, felt Storm slide under her left hand. His presence spurred her to one last effort, and she pushed herself up and over the lip of the valley. There was a painful flood of light and everything blurred abruptly, then she was powerless to prevent her fall as her fade departed and her body folded in a blur of light and sound.

Chapter 10

AS THE door closed behind the three from Hillview, Master Cerren sank into his chair with a sigh of exhaustion. Socks padded over to him and rubbed her head comfortingly on his leg, regarding him steadily with her violet eyes. He rubbed the back of his neck, easing it side to side to try and reduce some of the tension the interview had produced. Peron echoed his stretch and wriggled slightly so that the sleeping Thunder was more comfortably cushioned on his lap.

"So, do you think that went well?" he asked.

"Time will tell, Peron, time will tell. I think it went as well as it could under the circumstances."

There was a knock at the door. One of the retired Scouts recently returned to duty peered in, an expression of urgency on his wrinkled face.

"Master Cerren, the council delegation has arrived at the gate, and the senior Councillor has come in person. I've had the guest quarters prepared and refreshments will be waiting in the conference room. They'll arrive within the quarter hour."

"Thank you Romon, could you notify Erilla and the other Masters, please? And make sure that Anjo is available if required." The grey haired old man nodded and withdrew his head.

Peron eased himself from under Thunder's relaxed body, and stood.

"Sooner than expected, and the senior herself. Time to brace ourselves, I'd say."

Master Cerren levered himself to his feet, set Socks to keep an eye on Thunder, and opened the door. "After you, old friend." Peron gathered the sheaf of notes he'd made earlier, and preceded Cerren from the room.

***

The walk home from Watchtower was unusually quiet. The normal cheerful chatter had been replaced with a brooding silence, and Kaidan flicked his eyes anxiously from parent to parent as they walked. The three starcats paced in an equilateral triangle around the small family. The walk seemed longer than normal, and Kaidan worried that his parents' anger might bubble over into argument. They never argued. Or at least he'd never seen them argue. The idea of a full blown argument between his parents made him extremely uneasy.

The discussion with the two Masters had been an uncomfortable one. Kaidan had sat quietly in one corner of the room as Janna had harangued the two men again over their decision to send Kaidan to face the Garsal. He'd been utterly embarrassed. His father had been quietly conciliatory, reminding his wife of the stakes involved, and there had been a moment when Janna had turned a hurt, frosty stare on her husband. The image was burned into Kaidan's brain and he replayed the expression as they walked, anxiety increasing each time.

One of the conditions of Kaidan's further involvement had been a return home to Hillview. Adlan had agreed to walk him into town each day so that he could continue Anjo's education, and had extracted a promise from the Masters that when circumstances allowed, Anjo would spend some time at Hillview. Cerren had agreed that Kaidan would not be used on the front line of defence without prior consultation with his parents.

The pay-off was that Shanna would continue to make her own choices. Kaidan was both envious and annoyed at what he felt was 'babying' and over protective behaviour on the part of his mother. As the distance from Watch-tower increased, Kaidan felt more and more as if the last few weeks had been something he and his friends had dreamt up as a playtime adventure. And then the expression on his mother's face would rise up to haunt him again. His emotions began to bubble quietly.

The road slowly rose and shortly Hillview appeared, sitting securely into the hillside, and on the breeze came the welcome sounds of the starcats greeting them. Boots, Moshi and Sabre replied, tidemarks flickering in relaxed colours.

After dinner the three sat quietly and still uncomfortably, together by the fire. The lack of conversation was a gaping void in the room as all three stared fixedly into the fire. "The Garsal killed some of us, Mum! And they killed Anjo's parents," burst out Kaidan, after the silence had stretched him to breaking point. "Why are you so angry? And so angry with Dad?" The last came out in almost a whimper, and to his horror he felt tears brimming in his eyes. He turned his head to one side and looked into the fire, surreptitiously brushing at his eyes with the hand furthest away from his parents. Boots wasn't fooled, however, and bumped Kaidan with his large head, so much love in his large eyes that Kaidan almost dissolved completely.

"I know that Kai, really I do, but you could have died!" Janna's voice seemed to break on the last word. "And now Shanna's Below, and who knows if we'll ever see her again." She broke down completely. Adlan leaned towards her and pulled her to his side, and she sobbed as if her heart might break. Kaidan gave in then, tears falling in slow drops down his face, and joined his parents, and the three of them huddled together in shared misery. Finally, Janna wound down, and pushing her hair back she sat dishevelled, tucked into her husband's comforting side with Kaidan curled against them both while three starcats joined them, large bodies pulsing in tones of shared love.

"Kai, both your Mum and I wish you'd never become so involved in something like this," said Adlan as he tightened his arm around his wife. "You're so young." He was silent for a few moments. "This is not how things were meant to go. But this is how it is. We can't change it. For better or worse, our world is at a crossroads. We either join with our new allies to fight the Garsal, or we become yet another source of slaves and watch them destroy our world. I don't see any other choices." Janna made a small sound and shook her head, while Sabre purred gently and comfortingly.

"Mum, I'm here," Kaidan said. "And Shanna's got the boys. They'll look after her." He'd never seen his mother look so helpless, or so lost.

"Kai, you need to give us a little time to get used to all this," his father said. "Our whole world has changed completely in a single afternoon. You've had a few weeks to get used to it. You've seen these Garsal – fought them. You've even spoken to a human from another world." Adlan shook his head wonderingly. "We're still coming to grips with it all. This morning we were just a family of starcat breeders. And now apparently we, our children, and our starcats are completely essential to the defence of our planet. Plus we have to face the reality that we might not survive that defence. Or not all of us ... " He broke off, face reddened, and Kaidan realised his father was struggling to keep his emotions in check as well. They sat tucked together for some hours, staring into the fire. Kaidan wondering yet again what Shanna was doing.

***

Shanna woke in a confused blur. The light was too bright and she was dizzy, and her right hand throbbed violently. The room whirled. Suddenly nausea overwhelmed her and she vomited, heaving with the spasms, barely aware of the gentle hands supporting her to one side. She was faintly aware of the anxious hums of two starcats. She subsided finally, gasping, and closed her eyes against the light. Around her she could hear muffled voices.

"Only exhausted, I think ... " the voice faded, and everything went black again.

When she awoke again, she was somewhere else. Somewhere with a soft bed and the familiar comforting warmth of two starcat bodies tucked around her.

"You've decided to join us in the land of the living again, then?" Amma's voice was soft in her ear. Shanna blinked her eyes; they felt sticky and grainy, and there was a foul taste in her mouth. "Here, drink this. Verren dropped it off – he said one of the Starlynes left it."

Shanna forced her eyes open, rubbing the crustiness of sleep from them with one hand, and slowly levering herself upright. She was back in the sleeping quarters. Amma tucked an extra pillow behind her, and she leaned her exhausted body back against it, gratefully taking the proffered cup. She sipped and felt the tangy sweetness of the liquid dissolve the foul taste in her mouth, and send a surge of strength through her limbs. She pushed herself off the pillows slightly and reached forward to stroke the two cats sharing her bed, only then realising that her right hand was softly bandaged, with only a faint stretchy ache when she moved it, rather than the throbbing burn she recalled all too clearly.

"How did I get back here?" she asked Amma.

"The Starlynes carried you in a litter slung between two of them the next morning. That was yesterday. We walked, but not the way we came, up and down the valley. There's a network of tunnels that we came through. It only took about four hours." Amma grimaced, twisting her lips wryly. "They carted you off to the infirmary and popped you back into bed here about two hours later. Apparently you're exhausted."

"You reckon?" replied Shanna. "I feel like I've been trampled by a herd of horgals. My hand feels better though." She poked the dressing gingerly. "Do you know when this can come off?"

"I think Verren's going to take it off later. In the meantime, do you think you can get up? There's more food outside — you must be hungry." Shanna nodded and pushed the covers back. After a shaky start she managed to stagger out to the communal room, collapsing onto the soft cushions in one corner, while Storm and Twister nudged her gently with their cold noses and purred thunderously. The other cadets and Scouts were scattered around the room with their cats, and Spiron hastened over to Shanna where she sat propped against the wall.

"How are you feeling, Shanna?"

"Like I've been trampled by something very heavy!" She had one hand on each of her cats.

"The Starlynes said you were just exhausted, but you've been asleep for over a day." He frowned. "It appears we've discovered some limitations to our new abilities. You might be able to hide others, but the fatigue it generates is a problem. Here, eat something." Verren pushed a plate at Shanna. "You have to be hungry." Shanna took the plate as her belly grumbled loudly in agreement, and began to pick at the fruit piled on it. The sweetness seemed to fill a need she hadn't realised was there.

"So, did we make it?" Shanna asked as the other cadets settled around her with their cats.

"Make what?" replied Amma, puzzled. She was teasing Spider, ruffling the starcat's immaculately groomed fur each time she finished a section. Spider growled slightly and gently nibbled her partner's hand before going back to her fastidious washing.

"You know, the other side of the valley, in time." Shanna picked up another piece of the fruit and stuffed it into her mouth.

"Oh that!" replied Ragar, "Just, apparently. The Starlynes haven't said much; actually they don't seem to have foreseen the exhaustion problem, and it's got them all in a tizz." He smiled. "Now that you're up and about, maybe we'll hear a bit more."

Shanna sat back and continued to eat, comfortable in the company of her fellow cadets. The conversation continued as they rehashed the struggle across the valley, discussing where they might have been able to reduce the time it had taken, and exploring different ideas about getting around the obstacles they'd encountered. Shanna felt a warmth in the group, something that hadn't been there previously even though they'd fought the Garsal together not so long ago. The group exercise, no matter how it had ended, had shown them how to rely on each other in a way they'd never had to previously. They were friends, she realised suddenly, feeling warmed by the easy companionship of her classmates and their concern for her illness and injury. Even Taya had asked about her hand. Their starcats sprawled relaxed about them, tidemarks slowly flickering in the patterns of laziness and comfort.

A day later, Shanna sat with the other cadets and Scouts in the living area waiting for Teacher. They'd had twenty four hours of further rest, and her hand had appeared to be almost completely healed when Verren had removed the dressing. The newly healed skin was still red and shiny in patches, but it only felt tight rather than painful, and the more she moved it the better it felt. Every now and then she relived the moment when she'd placed her hand into the fire moss, and occasionally found herself flexing and extending her fingers reflexively before she realised that the discomfort was only a memory. Several huge meals later she'd finally felt like herself again, and began to practice some of her new skills. She'd found the exercises surprisingly draining though. It seemed that she hadn't recovered quite as much as she'd thought she had.

The door opened, and Teacher glided into the room, coiling her sinuous body neatly, her tidemarks dimmer than usual. "Your performances on your exercises were a revelation to us." She untucked her hands and gestured as her voice resounded in their minds. "There was much to ponder, and much to revise." She paused and Shanna could sense a hesitant feeling from the Starlyne. She looked around her at her fellow humans, and saw expressions of puzzlement on their faces.

"What do you mean, 'a revelation' and 'revise'," asked Spiron. He got to his feet and moved closer to Teacher.

Teacher ducked her head in a slightly embarrassed fashion — the first time Shanna had seen anything really perturb the dignified creature. "Firstly, we did not expect either group to complete their objective at this stage." There was a flurry of confused head shaking from the Scout group.

"But ... " said Spiron, and then ceased as Teacher went on.

"We expected the exercises to be beyond your current capabilities and that they would simply point out areas of weakness."

"But both groups did complete their objectives!" exclaimed Barron. "Even if only just." It was news to Shanna that the experienced Scouts had also been toiling away at the same time they'd been struggling across the valley. She looked at Amma, who raised one eyebrow and shrugged to indicate her confusion.

"They've not said a word to us," she whispered.

"Secondly, we were not prepared for the exhaustive drain prolonged use of your gifts would place upon your bodies. Although Shanna was the only one to collapse," Shanna looked at the floor, embarrassed, "the rest of you were fatigued well beyond normal." She paused as Spiron raised one hand.

"Teacher, with all respect, none of us were carrying food with us. Anything we ate, we collected along the way."

"We have taken that into account, Spiron, but Shanna can tell you herself – she is still not recovered completely, even with a full day's rest and plenty of food." Teacher gestured gracefully towards Shanna. Spiron looked at her with one eyebrow raised, an enquiring look on his face.

She ducked her head again, embarrassed. "She's right, Spiron. I've started to practice again, but although it's easy to fade, holding the fade makes me really tired. And then I'm starving again."

"It seems that extending the use of your abilities increases the energy required to use them. You have proved adept pupils, learning quickly and applying your learning in very practical and sometimes surprising ways, but your bodies struggle to cope with the energy drain when using your gifts for extended times. For Shanna to fade herself the output is negligible, but when she extended the fade to include others at a distance, the effort required was much more significant. This has left her very drained – in a similar fashion to exercising at a peak performance level for hours. The resources remain depleted until enough food has been consumed to allow the body to replace its stores, and even now she is still in deficit. It is a problem that we have discussed at length for the last day." There was an air of determination now emanating from Teacher, and she folded her small hands neatly below her neck region.

"Have you come up with any solutions yet?" asked Barron. "Otherwise it seems the simplest answer is for us to eat more. But that would be rather difficult on an extended trip, here Below." He looked up at Teacher consideringly. "And I am sure that the question of the Garsal ship's location somewhere here Below, is a priority."

"You are correct, Barron. The location of the Garsal ship is a priority. It will not be too far from here, but we have been very cautious. The Garsal do not yet realise that we are on this planet. We believe that we are the only Starlyne people left anywhere in this galaxy, and premature revelation of our presence might jeopardise the survival of our whole race."

"With respect, Teacher, our people are already at risk!" exclaimed Allad. "We need to locate that ship to ensure that our people are safe."

"Allad, this is something we understand all too well," replied Teacher, and she radiated earnestness, "but we must prepare well, or the Garsal will take both of our peoples for their slave pool. Keeper was one of our greatest elders and he is no longer here with his wisdom and vision. As a people, we are determined to unite with humanity to confront the Garsal threat, but if we rush in unprepared, it may all be for naught.

Our priority, and your peoples' as well, is the location of the Garsal ship, but before we can do this the problem of the energy drain must be solved. We have some ideas, but it will be a few days before we can trial them. In the meantime, we would ask that you continue to learn with the assistance of your teachers. For the rest of today, you will continue to rest, eat more," there was a wash of amusement above the concerned tone of her thoughts. "And share your experiences from the exercises." With barely a sound she uncoiled her bulk and exited the room.

The group sat slightly stunned, each person looking around at the others, before Spiron got to his feet again. "Well, let's get into it then, shall we? In the light of what we've learnt, let's eat again, and then we'll discuss our exercises. I can see you cadets are bursting to know what we've been up to!" He smiled slightly, and led the way to the table.

***

The Garsal Commander scrolled through the list that the Matriarch had provided him. It detailed her requirements for living quarters for herself and the rest of the sequestered females, along with her timing expectations. His meeting with her, in the isolated female living quarters, had been very formal, hedged about by etiquette and ceremony. She had found favour with a number of the local fruit samples that he had supplied her with, but had conveyed her displeasure at the time taken for the construction of the hive. He had pleaded the excuses of inclement weather and shown her images of the fearsome monsters that so populated this planet, but she had heard his excuses with an expression of subtle disdain and a flick of displeasure from her manipulator arms.

He had responded with samples of the stone used for the hive construction and images of the completed entry arch. She had again flicked her arms and asked bluntly when she might see some further progress. Behind her had stood the rank of senior females all watching him attempt to maintain his dignity and worth and all, he felt, assessing whether he might make a worthy suitor should the matriarch agree that he would be worthy of offspring.

He looked again at the scrolling list and flicked his faceted eyes across the timeline that the Matriarch had outlined. He turned towards Zoash in dissatisfaction. "She makes unreasonable demands."

"She is the Matriarch," replied his sib, disapprovingly. The Overlord flicked a manipulator arm in frustration. His sib was correct.

On a second screen sat his incomplete plans for the location of the human settlement. He was certain that the enormous plateau was where they were hidden, as no further traces had been found by the exploratory teams as they had moved further south. The enigma of their existence puzzled him. "And why are there humans here?" he said irritably. "High Command declared the Federation completely conquered before sending colony ships towards this arm of the galaxy. Yet here they are."

"And humans who somehow eliminated four of our armoured exploratory vehicles," Zoash pointed out. "I have good news in that respect, however." He tapped the screen and a new list appeared. It detailed resources newly located that might allow the Garsal to start the slow process of manufacturing replacement aircraft.

"This at least pleases me, Zoash. In this, you have done well." The Overlord's hatching sib bowed obsequiously. The Overlord tapped again, decisively, and closed the screens down. "You will arrange a meeting with the Construction Supervisor and another meeting with the Senior Officers. It is essential that we locate a way onto the plateau and begin the process of subjugating the humans on this planet."

Chapter 11

"CAN you believe it?" giggled Amma. "That must have really blown the Starlyne's little socks off." The cadets were all wiping tears of laughter from their eyes as they filed into their sleeping room. Zandany collapsed backwards onto his bed, still laughing, while he tickled Punch's ears.

"I know, I know! I can just see it in my mind – the isolated building perched on a knoll, overhung by a cliff face, apparently impregnable. Sentries on guard everywhere looking out over all of the approaches, but not one of them considered looking up!"

Ragar guffawed loudly. "And then Sandar starts sending fireballs zipping around the place to distract everyone a bit further, while Allad gets the rock going!"

"And then the rock pops over the edge of the cliff, and all the sentries have to bolt, or slither, I suppose!" Shanna snickered, and bounced onto her bed. "And then the ropes pop over the cliff edge and the cats go down!" Twister purred loudly, and Storm twinkled his ear tips.

"And that's it! They're in and the sentries are out, and it only took them four hours!" Taya's eyes gleamed with amusement. "And there we were slogging our way down and up that valley, avoiding plungers and traps, and scaling cliffs – why couldn't we have had the building assault?"

"I reckon!" replied Verren, "They didn't even get a scratch, get wet or dirty, and they didn't even miss lunch!"

The group had spent the day discussing their individual exercises. While the cadets had slogged through Below, the Scouts had assaulted an isolated building. Initially it had seemed that the Scouts had had the easier task, although as they'd analysed the tasks, Shanna had been able to see that each of the two groups had been ideally suited to the one they'd been assigned. The timing differences were more about inexperience and experience, rather than expertise. After explaining the methods each group had used to achieve their objectives, they'd then discussed the decisions made, the reasons behind them, and whether there had been alternate ways of getting the jobs done. They'd then spent some time discussing methods that might have been useful had the tasks been reversed, and who they'd have placed where if they'd been able to choose the groups themselves.

It had been fascinating and Shanna had developed fresh respect for her companions, particularly the experience of the older Scouts which allowed them to consider all kinds of alternative ways of achieving the same aim.

"We're in the bathroom first!" Verren grabbed his sleeping shorts and vanished into the bathing room followed by Ragar and Zandany, their three cats padding behind. There was an almighty splash followed by Verren's out-raged voice. "Cirrus! Did you have to?"

The door closed on the muted sounds of starcat and human bathing, and Shanna leaned back on her bed tiredly, idly stroking Storm's large head. Although the day had been physically restful, she was beginning to wonder how long it would take for her to replenish her 'depleted energy stores' and start to feel normal again. She lay for a time, wondering what form the Starlyne's solution might take as her cats stealthily squirmed their way further onto her bed, which was fortunately large enough to take them all. She'd stuffed herself with food to the point of feeling uncomfortable, while the others had all urged her to eat more until she'd threatened that one more mouthful would cause the whole lot to come back up again. They'd finally desisted, laughing as she lay back feeling bloated.

The next morning, Shanna frowned with concentration, trying to see just how Taya did her trick with machinery. Under the guidance of Radiant, one of the other teaching Starlynes, she'd been attempting to stop a clock ticking, a task that Taya was able to do with ease. Finally, Spinner leaned his long length against her leg and the ticking ceased. Storm and Twister had watched with great interest, mirroring Spinner's tidemark shifts and then added their assistance to Shanna's other side. Abruptly, all the mechanisms in the room ceased their various activities, and the lights went out.

"Shanna," came Radiant's thought. "Could you restore the lighting please?" Shanna withdrew her leg from Spinner and the lights came up again, and as Storm and Twister eased away from her body the machines all recommenced their varied activities. "Interesting," came the Starlyne's thought, "Taya, I'd like to see what you can do with Storm and Twister assisting." Taya looked puzzled as she'd had no need of contact with a starcat to work her mechanical control, but shrugged and asked Shanna to send the cats over.

"Stop this room first Taya, without any cat contact, and then see how far you can push yourself. First with Spinner and then with the addition of Storm and Twister." The dark haired girl nodded and the room went dark, lit only by the glowing tidemarks of five starcats and the Starlyne instructor. Shanna saw one of Spinner's tidemarks dim as Taya placed her hand on him. She could almost feel the effort exerted by the other girl, then spontaneously decided to add her touch to her own cats as they pressed into Taya. A moment later, there was the loudest flurry of Starlyne conversation Shanna had ever experienced. She had the impression of shock, alarm, and then through the confusion, Radiant's firm tones. And then the lights came back on.

"Even more interesting," came his voice. "Taya, how do you feel?" Taya looked at him uncertainly.

"Fine, I suppose. It was hard work at first, but when I touched Spinner it became easier, and then with the addition of Storm, Twister, and Shanna, it was almost easy. I only stopped because I ran out of things to stop, if you know what I mean." She paled slightly, "I hope I didn't stop anything essential!" There was a brief feeling of amusement from Radiant.

"Nothing stayed stopped, Taya, but I think that it might be wise to provide a warning next time we try expanding someone's abilities." There was a quiet sound at the door and Teacher appeared.

"Shanna, I have something for you to try." She handed Shanna a small blue patch. It seemed to have some kind of paper backing. Shanna looked uncertainly up at the Starlyne.

"What is this?"

"It's a trial energy supplement," replied the Starlyne, "We hope that it might be part of the answer to your fatigue issues. Just pull off the backing and stick it onto your arm." Shanna took a cautious sniff as she pulled the backing off. The strip smelt sweetly of fruit. Shanna looked at it again, shrugged, and stuck it on the exposed skin of her forearm. Her eyes popped as her body tingled strongly. Strangely, she felt her fatigue lessen and energy course through her limbs.

"Wow! That was just weird! And I feel heaps better already." She smiled, faded herself, and experimentally faded the whole group. The flooding exhaustion was no longer there and she let the fade go with a sigh of pleasure. "Well, it worked."

Teacher's thought was tinged with satisfaction. "It's a high energy supplement on a micro needle patch, which we hope will be effective and easy for you to carry. And it appears that Radiant has discovered yet another method of enhancing your skills – but as he said, some warning might be in order next time." She glided from the room, the feeling of satisfaction, layered with amusement, clear in her wake.

Shanna returned to her lesson with enthusiasm.

***

Master Cerren finally leaned back in his chair at the council table. Around the room, the assembled councillors were variously tapping fingers, frowning at note pads, or sitting staring blankly into space. Senior Councillor Tamazine was studying them carefully. Several of her senior aides were whispering quietly in one corner, while her personal scribe sat attentively at her elbow, occasionally notating at her dictation.

He was sweating, he noted, and Socks' tidemarks were slightly muted, reflecting his anxiety, although she appeared relaxed enough to the casual observer. Late afternoon sunlight slanted through the windows and he sighed, tired after the hours of deliberation with both the Senior Councillor and the Watchtower Council.

Councillor Tamazine was a stubborn woman, he reflected. His initial discussions with her had been heated. She had felt he'd overstepped his authority by committing to an alliance with the Starlyne people without prior consultation with Starfall's senior council. Patiently he had reminded her of the autonomy clauses in each major town's settlement charter, but after a full day's discussions he'd finally lost his temper.

"In that case, Tamazine, what would you have had us do? We were Below and the Starlynes had just ended a dangerous situation by siding with us - and saving us I might add. They are vastly more powerful than we are, technologically adept, and familiar with the Garsal threat!" His voice had grown louder on each sentence, and eventually he'd stood and thumped the table with his fist. "We were there – you were not! There were few choices available at the time, and we made the best ones we could!"

Councillor Tamazine had pushed her seat back deliberately and stood slowly, her brilliant violet eyes boring into his blue ones. Seconds had passed, before she'd dropped her gaze and resumed her seat. "Sit, Cerren. You are correct. Faced with the same choices, I would have chosen as you did. However, sending the cadet class?" She had shaken her head slowly. "Enough. We need to plan, and discuss how to save ourselves from these Garsal. Call the Watchtower Council to meet tomorrow. We must decide how to break the news to the general populace," she said, concluding the meeting.

The next day's Council meeting proved acrimonious, and it was obvious that the councillors were divided. Not about the threat of the Garsal incursion, but about the methods proposed to inform the community and the subsequent emergency measures.

Tamazine had proposed that all non-essential community members would be evacuated from Watchtower and that she would establish an operations command centre in the town. In her eyes, that meant that Watchtower would host the Senior Council of Frontier until the safety of Frontier's population could be assured, and that she, personally, would lead the response, with Watchtower's Council providing auxiliary support. This was the main reason for the discord. Watchtower's councillors felt that they had managed the early response well, and that at least initially, Tamazine's staff should watch and learn. They were resistant to a sudden change of control, and some were taking it personally.

Cerren himself had mixed feelings. As a long serving councillor he was more familiar with the "big picture" that Tamazine was working from, yet he felt that she needed to give credence to the significant skill level already demonstrated by Watchtower's Council. During his long career he had learnt that central though the senior Council in Starfall was, they did not have a monopoly on skill and wisdom.

He had argued long and hard for a more integrative approach, but Tamazine had (somewhat arrogantly Cerren felt) decided that the Senior Council should take direct control immediately. Her reasoning had been that the people of Frontier needed to see strong leadership from the beginning, and that the Senior Council should provide it. Cerren had replied that Watchtower's Council had already been leading effectively, and that Watchtower's location on the southern edge of the plateau made its citizens more familiar with the hazards of Below. Tamazine had simply shaken her head and when Cerren had pointed out the risks of placing all of the leadership in one place, forestalled further comment with a curt order to cease and desist.

Tamazine stood. "Call a public meeting for tomorrow in the Old Storm Shelter." she looked around at the assembled councillors. "Use the storm warning system to alert everyone." Tamazine was referring to the signal flags that all the towns used to alert the population to the current storm status, but which also included a number of more general signals to alert the populace to town meetings and other events. The Senior Councillor replaced her chair, collected her entourage with a gesture, and left the room.

Cerren sighed heavily again, and flicking a finger at Socks, made his way out of the room and back to Scout Headquarters, pondering the advisability of some of Tamazine's decisions. She'd swept into Watchtower like a small cyclone, with the backing of the majority of Skyfall's council, and he was concerned that the comfortable safety now enjoyed by the inhabitants of Skyfall had blinded her eyes to some of the realities of the alien incursion.

Socks brushed against him, rubbing her head under his hand, and he scratched the softness of her fur, before shrugging his shoulders and striding off. It was essential that the Scout hierarchy had the latest information regarding Tamazine's decisions as soon as possible. As Frontier's first line of defence, its Scout Corps would need to plan and prepare, and unlike Skyfall's Council he had no doubt that the Scout Council would be fully up to the task. He wondered how much mediation he'd have to do in the coming days and weeks in order to achieve a streamlined command group. And then there were the fourteen captured Garsal troopers he had stowed in the cells under the old Storm Shelter. He wondered what Tamazine would say when she saw them?

He sighed again and wished he could somehow get the creatures to speak. Anjo had assured him that they spoke the common tongue but they showed no desire to demonstrate that skill.

***

The Garsal Overlord surveyed the vehicles arrayed in the hold of the colony ship. He refused to look at the vacant spaces left by the three lost aircraft. The cargomaster had carefully spaced the remaining crawlers across the area allocated to their type, the wider spaces between vehicles cleverly disguising the loss of four of them. He allowed his eyes to count the heavily armoured vehicles one by one, added the two still exploring south of the ship, and came to his conclusion.

The Matriarch would be displeased if the hive did not progress to her expected timetable and the depleted vehicle ranks must not be reduced even further at this stage. First priority would be given to hive construction. Second priority would be manufacturing replacement aircraft, which would allow easy location of the human presence on the plateau. In the meantime, sentries around the hive site would be doubled and guard towers built. He tapped a manipulator arm across the tablet held in front of him, allowing his claw tipped digits to add the guard towers to the hive design.

Visually they appeared pleasing, merely decorative elevations of the already begun building. He gestured peremptorily to Zoash, and his aide took the tablet. "You will arrange for the appropriate defence weapons to be installed as soon as the towers are complete, and I would have the sensor array begun immediately."

"You are concerned the humans might locate us?" asked Zoash. His voice was carefully neutral but the Overlord heard the unspoken criticism.

"You will also dedicate ten of the slaves to scour the area inside the perimeter. They are to remove any of the dangerous vegetation that so plagues this planet."

"Are they to be supplied with protective equipment, Overlord?"

The Overlord debated with himself for a few moments. "Until we have subjugated the native humans, our current slave resources are limited. Of course you will issue them with protective equipment!" He allowed himself to savour a small moment of revenge for Zoash's previous comment. He had spoken loudly enough that all would hear. "The Matriarch will require well trained servants when she relocates to the hive. New slaves take time to train and humans are often stubborn. We will draw them from our well trained pool and not sully her presence with untrained servitors."

"As you have said, Overlord, so shall I do." Zoash withdrew as the Overlord once again ran his eyes over the neat lines of vehicles.

***

The Storm Shelter was packed, with latecomers now lining both the side walls and the back of the room. Fortunately Kaidan and his parents had arrived early and were seated towards the front of the massive hall. Behind the podium, Kaidan could see Masters Cerren, Peron and Erilla from the Scout Corps, and Payne, Senior Councillor of Watchtower, sitting in high backed chairs. The familiar faces of Watchtower's Council were seated on one side of the raised platform, facing a second group on the other side. Kaidan was startled to see that sprinkled amongst them were the formal robes of Skyfall councillors. Next to Councillor Payne, a tall, violet-eyed woman in formal robes sat surveying those who continued to file into the hall. Kaidan watched her curiously. She seemed completely self-contained, ignoring Councillor Payne sitting next to her.

Kaidan nudged his father and indicated the woman at the front of the room.

"That would be Tamazine, the Senior Councillor," Adlan whispered. "She's been Senior for the last five years. A tough woman but generally fair, according to what I've heard."

Kaidan nodded. Even without the subject matter, this could be an interesting meeting.

Payne stood and tapped the podium firmly, and the chatter in the room gradually diminished into silence. "Today I stand not as the bearer of good news, but to tell you of the greatest threat to our survival on Frontier." He paused, and the silence grew thick. "Please bear with me as I explain the series of events that have led to this moment." Kaidan flicked a glance at his parents. They were sitting, hand in hand, all their attention focused on Councillor Payne. Payne began to speak, outlining the events that had occurred since the first storm of the season. Kaidan hadn't thought that the hall could grow any quieter, but as the councillor spoke, even the restless shifting of bodies ceased and it was as if the collective was holding its breath.

The councillor's voice rolled on and despite knowing nearly all of the story already, and having participated in some of it, Kaidan was caught up in the emotion of the events yet again. Payne was a skilled orator, and he felt as though he was there as Patrol Ten located the alien craft and removed the body of the Garsal from inside it. He felt his heart pound when Payne described the first view of the alien ground vehicle, then the astonishment when the two human slaves appeared and were maltreated by their alien oppressors. He caught his breath when Anjo and Semba were rescued, and felt again the thrill of excitement then fear, when he realised that he was about to go into battle against the alien intruders.

As Payne described the Starlyne encounter, Kaidan relived the enormity of the revelation imparted by Keeper of the Knowledge, tinged with the sadness of remembered loss, and pictures of those Scouts, starcats and archers lost in the battle to stop the vehicles drifted across his mind.

As the councillor spoke, Kaidan saw a dim glow begin to illuminate the hall, and realised that their Starlyne allies had decided to make their presence known in person. Heavens knew how the creature had managed to navigate the stairs.

The crowd murmured, the sound moving forward like a wave from the back of the hall , as the glowing form of the Starlyne ambassador made its way down the centre aisle. Each row turned to view the creature as it made its way onto the dais with a lithe undulation. The murmuring ceased, and Kaidan was again swept up in the wordless communication from the creature. This time he was more prepared, and as the creature communicated its history in vast images and sensations, he managed to remain a little more separate from the experience. Again the episode ended with a montage of images of humans and starcats – slightly different this time he noted: it included Janna and Adlan, and Josen, and various Scout Masters. But the final image was again of his sister, accompanied by Storm and Twister, and this time, surrounded by her fellow cadets and Patrol Ten.

As the final image faded, Kaidan regained his equilibrium much faster, and looking around was able to see that his parents were slowly straightening themselves in their seats, looking dazed. All over the room, people were shaking their heads and pushing themselves upright.

Senior Councillor Tamazine stood and moved forward on the dais to stand next to the Starlyne. She was dwarfed by its size, but not diminished. Cerren and Payne stood and joined her.

"This is 'Speaker for Law', one of our Starlyne allies and the liaison between our peoples on the plateau. I will now outline the actions we find necessary to take to deal with this Garsal Incursion." She swept her gaze around the crowded hall, and Kaidan felt the first shiver of unease. Her expression was unyielding and her tone hard. She began to speak and his dismay deepened.

Two hours later, Kaidan walked through the gates of Watchtower, accompanied by his parents and their three starcats. They walked in silence for several minutes before Janna finally let out a sigh of exasperation. "So, we're to relocate to Watchtower immediately? Complete with all cats. And Hillview is to be mothballed until the Senior Councillor decides otherwise." She shook her head in disgust. "And all without even the smallest hint that these Garsal even know where we are!"

"Mum," asked Kaidan anxiously, "I'll be with you in Watchtower, won't I? They won't send me away with the other kids?" His two concerns; of being pushed away from either the centre of activity or his family, were vying with each other for prominence.

Adlan pulled his son close and put his arm around Kaidan's shoulders. "If we're in Watchtower, then there's no way you'll be anywhere else. If Tamazine decides she needs to break the family up any further, she might find that this family and its starcats will not be cooperating with her plans."

"There's no need to vacate Watchtower at this stage," Janna agreed. "Or for us to leave Hillview. If the Garsal are detected closing in on the plateau, then I'll be happy to relocate. But why do we have to leave our home now? Is there really an urgent need for us to be living in Watchtower or more correctly, living below Watchtower, right now?"

Kaidan felt a sense of relief, realising that his parents would not allow him to be evacuated straight away. Janna and Adlan continued to discuss the actions that Tamazine had outlined as the three of them walked. Kaidan noticed that the three cats accompanying them had their tidemarks dimmed, flickering in tones of disquiet. As they approached Hillview and the sounds of greeting from the breeding cats drifted through the air, the sun dropped towards the horizon and once again Kaidan wondered what Shanna was doing.

Chapter 12

SHANNA was sitting, one foot up, perched on the rocks overlooking the valley again. Storm lay at her feet while Twister sat on watch in the early dusk. Marra, the largest of the three moons, was slowly rising above the horizon, spreading its pearly glow across the landscape. She was tired but her mind had drifted to her family again, and feeling homesick she'd quietly left the noise of the common room to seek the solitude of the outdoors. The Starlyne habitat was comfortable and fascinating, but it wasn't home. She enjoyed the friendship of her fellow cadets and Scouts, but sometimes the constant companionship became wearing and Shanna had taken to slipping away quietly after the evening meal to sit alone with her thoughts. The air felt cool and fresh after the fan driven air of the underground habitat.

Her thoughts drifted to her family. She was tired, physically fatigued after yet another obstacle course and the constant practice of exploring her gifts. Shanna's ability to hide her fellow Scouts with the aid of her cats had grown rapidly. With Storm and Twister's help she had finally mastered the basics of nearly all of the other abilities demonstrated amongst the group of sixteen, but she was quick to admit that it was only the basics.

It seemed that if there was an inborn skill, that person had an innate understanding of how it worked, and using it was simple. Shanna appeared to have the ability to learn nearly anything, but it wasn't easy and she remained in awe of Taya's skill with mechanical objects, or Allad's casual ability to move things. Sometimes her brain buzzed so hard with all of the new skills she was attempting to pack away inside her head that it felt like it might explode right out of her skull. She leaned her chin on her knee and clasped her hands around her leg. Storm bumped her dangling foot gently with his head and she tickled his chest with the toe of her boot as he leaned into it. His rumbling purr was comforting.

Time had passed quickly while the human beings struggled to consolidate their skills and to learn new ones. Ever present in everyone's minds was the Garsal ship somewhere to the south, possibly calling for reinforcements, already possibly searching for the plateau and their settlements. The thought of those insectoid creatures overrunning her planet chilled Shanna. Their callous disregard for the vegetation and wildlife of Below remained etched in Shanna's mind, and the maltreatment of the human slaves never failed to send shivers down her spine.

Twister hummed quietly and Shanna lifted her head, looking behind her. Fractus was gliding almost noiselessly up the hill toward the rocks where she perched.

"Good evening, Shanna," came the Starlyne's greeting. He glided up to the outcrop, winding his length dexterously through the obstacles and came to a halt next to her rock. Storm smooched his body against the Starlyne's long length, purring, and the Starlyne unfolded his small hands to rub the blue tidemarked cat's face. He coiled himself amongst the rocks and turned his head towards the moonrise. "Sometimes I like to sit here and just watch," he said. "It helps to clear the mind and refresh the spirit." They sat in silence companionably for a while, each comfortable with their own thoughts.

"Fractus, do you really think we can save ourselves from the Garsal?" Shanna asked after a while.

The Starlyne turned its head from the vista spread out below them. "Shanna, I truly hope so. I know that Keeper was certain that together we could. He was such a steadfast believer in that possibility, but sometimes when I miss him most, it's hard to imagine that we might finally be free from our greatest fear." Shanna could feel the grief emanating from the Starlyne — almost the feel of tears — and she stretched out a hand towards the creature, gently touching the softness of the Starlyne's flank, much as she would have rested her hand upon a fellow human in need of comfort.

"Fractus, we've made so much progress, but I keep on thinking about what might be happening here Below, with the Garsal at the ship." Storm pressed against her dangling leg comfortingly and she dropped her hand to his head.

"I know, Shanna, and the location of that ship is our biggest priority." He issued a mental sigh. "I'm afraid we may well have to begin the search before you are all completely competent with your gifts. As we've told you before, the Garsal are able to detect high technology equipment. Your level of low technology but high personal skill, is the key to locating them. We will have to leave soon, and there is still much you have to explore."

"Will you be coming with us?"

The Starlyne turned his head back, watching Marra rising slowly above the horizon. "Some of us must. I will be one. But we are fearful of what might happen should the Garsal realise that we, their old enemy, are here. We are so few."

"There are few of us, too," said Shanna, and she felt agreement tinged with renewed determination waft from the Starlyne next to her, and his tidemarks began to pulse gently. The two of them turned back towards Marra and they sat there quietly until Mutta and Murru joined the first moon in the sky, and then the Starlyne slid noiselessly away. Shanna sat on her rock for a few more minutes until the three moons slowly separated to trace their individual routes across the night sky, dropping their odd shadows across the landscape. She called her two cats and they walked pensively back to the habitat.

The next morning, Fractus took his group of students back into the large cavern with the fliers. For a few moments there was silence, and then Fractus' calm voice sounded.

"You've trained on the suspended model, but now is the time to try without a safety line." He turned gracefully through a half circle and looked at the group of human beings behind him. Amma, Shanna, Allad and Spiron were all carrying the helmets and goggles supplied by their Starlyne trainer. "Amma, you will be first."

With a guilty feeling of relief, Shanna saw her friend swallow convulsively. But with a shrug, she stepped forward from the group and approached the glider suits. The four of them had practiced with the suits in a huge piece of equipment that Fractus had referred to as a wind chamber, but there had been a safety line and any mishaps had been quickly rectified without major injury, although the bruising had been spectacular on occasion. Shanna hurried to assist Amma to don the suit, carefully checking the fasteners as she'd been taught. The suit moulded itself to Amma's clothed form. There had been some discussion about aerodynamics and whether removing all clothing but underwear might improve flying ability. The very real dangers of stripping while Below, in a hurry, had negated this. Trials with normal clothing under the suit versus underwear had shown very little difference in the wind chamber, as the suit moulded itself firmly to the body once it was on.

Fractus nodded to the other three as well, and they collected their suits. Shanna felt suddenly hot and cold all at once, and repressed a shiver of half fear, half anticipation. Every time she'd practiced in the wind chamber, the initial drop off required at the beginning of the flight had scared her witless. The first time she'd just plummeted, not breathing, until the safety rope had scooped her up, absorbing the impact into a gentle pendulum, and she'd been left breathless, hanging in the air and shaking. She firmly put that memory as far away as possible. Her other flights had been much more successful.

An hour later, the group was at the pinnacle of a small outcrop overlooking the valley that they'd slogged through on that first team exercise. All of them now carried a small supply of patches in thigh and shirt pockets, but the Starlynes had cautioned them against overuse. The patches weren't a drug, but they were a sudden boost of usable energy and the Starlyne were wary about long term usage of an energy source that wasn't consumed in the normal fashion. There was also the problem that they were quite difficult to make in quantity. They were hopeful that with practice, the energy stores required by the scouts would reduce, and so far it seemed that they were correct. As Shanna had expanded her skills it had become easier; however, using them for extended periods of time was still problematic.

There was little discussion as Fractus nodded to Amma. He was apparently talking privately to her, as she nodded back to him, her face serious and pale, before she walked to Spiron, Allad and Shanna for one last check. Spider rubbed her head reassuringly across Amma's leg, then went and sat on the very edge of the outcrop, looking into the distance. "Can you just tighten the back strap, Allad?" she asked. There was a hint of a quiver in her voice and the older Scout complied quickly, finishing with a brief squeeze to her shoulder.

"You'll be OK, Amma, you see those currents so easily," said Shanna, trying to keep the quiver out of her own voice. Although she could feel the air currents when she concentrated, it still seemed to take a lot more energy from her than it did from Amma, and the glider suits didn't take into account her wish to be touching a starcat for assistance. Neither Storm nor Twister seemed unduly concerned about the day's activities, though.

The final check over, Amma turned resolutely to the cliff edge. She rested one hand briefly on Spider's head, studied the air briefly, then flicked out the arm extensions and leapt forward. As she left the outcrop, Shanna saw the leg extensions slide past Amma's boots. Then the wingsuit's membranes caught the wind and Amma soared. She looked like a strange parody of a flying marsupial, but was much more graceful. Belatedly, Shanna extended her own senses, trying to track the air currents that Amma was so easily reading. The group watched her swoop and glide, circling higher in the thermals that spiralled above the valley, then slipping sideways to catch yet another current. Shanna exchanged a glance with Allad and Spiron. Allad grinned at her.

"That looks fantastic! What do you reckon, Shan, Spiron?" Shanna gulped a little and attempted to smile back at her mentor.

"Well, it looks fantastic, but I'm not sure I'm ready!" Her voice quivered slightly despite her resolve. "Allad, what if it all goes wrong?" Allad turned to her.

"If our hosts had any doubts about your abilities, Shan, you wouldn't be here trying this today. You're important to them. There's no way they'd risk you." Spiron nodded his agreement but Shanna was guiltily glad to see that his normally unflappable calm was belied by a slight pallor. The group stood watching Amma; she seemed at home in the sky, easily twisting and soaring. Finally she glided in towards them and brought herself to a graceful halt, almost hovering in the air before dropping to the rock. She was glowing and Spider rippled her tidemarks in satisfaction, greeting her friend rapturously. The group on the outcrop broke into cheers and applause.

"That was amazing! Just amazing!" she exclaimed. "You'll have so much fun!"

"Now the three of you, one at a time. Allad, you first," came Fractus' thought.

Each of the others was checked over after donning their wingsuit. Shanna found that her hands were trembling slightly as she pulled the fasteners tight, firming the mottled fabric around her body. She checked the extensor tabs, making sure that they were positioned correctly. On the outcrop, Allad jumped gleefully into the air and Shanna felt a sudden urge to vomit as she imagined plummeting straight down, and swallowed convulsively. The older Scout was rapidly gaining height however, and testing his ability to steer. He didn't have Amma's grace, but he was steady and confident, and a few minutes later he swooped in to land competently.

Fractus turned his head to Shanna. "You will go next, Shanna." There was a feeling of comfort from the Starlyne, his spiralling tidemarks pulsing gently. Shanna called Storm and Twister, and ran her hands over each head. Her hands were shaking. There were a few encouraging comments from the Scouts and cadets, and she took the few steps necessary to perch on the edge. It felt strange to stand on the edge of a drop without being tied on to something. There was an encouraging touch of comfort from Fractus, and Shanna took a deep breath, then another. Part of her wanted to leap, but the other part wanted to run and hide in some deep burrow and never come out.

"Go on, Shan!" Amma's voice was encouraging. "Just look really hard, and you'll see them! You know you can!" Her voice was encouraging, and Shanna took one final breath and lengthened the arm extenders. She bent her shaky knees and jumped forward, training taking over so that she assumed the correct position.

Five seconds later when she wobbled and plummeted, she frantically flicked the leg extensions out. As she felt the wing membranes fill with a jerk she was suddenly shooting forwards, not down. Her brain screamed panicked thoughts at her as she wobbled through the air, but deliberately she forced herself to relax and concentrate. Her oddly enhanced vision became reality and dead ahead she saw a small thermal and shot towards it. Then, as the wingsuit began to rise, leaned slightly to bring herself into a spiralling lift.

As she lifted on the thermal, she overcompensated and tightened the spiral so much that she became momentarily dizzy before relaxing again and allowing her turn to widen. The feeling was exhilarating, exciting, and terrifying all at once. Concentration was essential she discovered, as she played gently with the wingsuit. If she relaxed too much, she lost the ability to detect the changes in the air currents and quickly slipped out of control. If she became overly nervous, the same thing happened. It was like balancing on a knife edge. She practiced gently changing her orientation, carefully adjusting her arms and legs, and then practiced speeding up and slowing down.

Shanna relished the freedom given by the skies, and looked down to see her classmates only dots on the outcrop below. Momentarily disoriented by the change in perspective, she lost control briefly and had to wrestle a little to regain it. Her arms and legs began to feel the strain, and finally Shanna decided it was time to head in and land. Carefully checking the wind direction, she circled gently then dropped altitude, heading into the wind to slow her speed. As she approached the rocky outcrop, she realised she was going too fast and too low. She pulled up, just missed the edge, and ploughed straight into the group of humans, eventually thumping onto the ground in a tangle of arms and legs.

There was a moment of silence and then, "Shan, can you get off my head?" Ragar's voice was plaintive.

"Sorry!" Shanna wriggled her foot out from underneath Zandany's leg, eased her body off Ragar's head and attempted to untangle her limbs. She was going to have some good bruises later. She retracted the extended portions of her wingsuit and rolled awkwardly to one side of the pile of bodies. "Sorry," she said again, when she accidentally whacked Taya with a flailing arm as she struggled to a sitting position.

"Well, not the most graceful landing," Amma giggled, "But you looked pretty happy in the sky after you got past the wobbles." Shanna grimaced slightly.

"Yes, well, once I remembered to concentrate on what I was doing it was a bit easier, but I think I need to work on my landings." Her voice trailed off as the others laughed.

"Let's see if I can do any better, then," smiled Spiron, although Shanna noticed he still looked a little pale. He approached the edge with Fury pacing beside him, frowned once as he flicked his extenders out, then leapt. His initial flight was only slightly less graceful than Amma's, and Shanna felt a bit embarrassed that she'd been the only really clumsy one. She felt a great sense of relief at having come through the flight safely, along with a scared sneaking desire to do it again. Oddly drained, Shanna stood with the others to watch, absently nibbling on a handful of dried fruit suggested by the Starlyne physicians as a high energy snack. Spiron's flight was surprisingly graceful, at odds with his strong physique, and his landing was pinpoint. Shanna blushed again, remembering her crash landing. After Spiron landed, Fractus turned to the assembled humans.

"After your noon meal, please wait for us in the communal room. There will be a planning meeting." He glided away without any further instructions, vanishing back into the underground complex.

Lunch was a flurry of discussion, and Shanna was treated to a re-enactment of her landing to the non-fliers of the group, complete with facial expressions and limb tangles. Storm and Twister lay relaxed across the floor, amusement in every tidemark glint. After she'd recovered from the embarrassment yet again, she had to admit that it must have looked remarkably funny.

Their laughter was brought to an abrupt halt as Fractus, Teacher, Radiant, and an unknown Starlyne entered the room. The newcomer was easily the largest Starlyne they'd seen. He (Shanna somehow knew the creature was male) glided in, coiled himself and regarded the group of humans.

"We lack time," the new Starlyne said. "The Garsal threat grows daily, and we have still not located their colony ship, or cut their communication lines. We believe that the Garsal commander has for one reason or another decided not to notify his central command of the human presence here. If he had, they would already be here in force. Therefore we have a small window of opportunity to locate and destroy their communication equipment. The Starlyne Elders have decided that this is the course of action we should take now, even though you are not yet ready. We have spoken to your fellows on the plateau and your Senior Council is in agreement with this plan. If for any reason, the Garsal Commander changes his mind and notifies his central command, our chance will be lost." There was such a sense of age and weariness pouring from the enormous creature in front of her that Shanna felt both uneasy and oddly perturbed. He went on. "All of you here are to go – tomorrow. It may take some weeks, but now that you have flown perhaps the locating may go more quickly." The Starlyne uncoiled rapidly and exited the room before anyone could speak. There was a blank silence for some moments before Fractus spoke.

"Please excuse the rudeness of our Eldest. He is the oldest of us here on Haven that you call Frontier. He is old beyond measure, and the reappearance of the Garsal threat has affected him greatly. His offspring perished in the escape and his mate passed into eternity many years ago now. He has mourned greatly and struggles to see the hope that Keeper of the Law believed in so deeply. He is worn, and grieves still for the loss of his family and the majority of our people."

Spiron nodded. "So, we are to venture deeper Below, locate the Garsal colony ship and destroy its communications. It makes sense, and it is something that we've already discussed." He paced as he talked, and Shanna felt a thrill that she would finally be able to venture beyond the Starlyne enclave into the vast and fascinating wilderness of Below again. Despite the time she'd spent with the Starlynes, she felt that she hadn't really been Below in the real sense of the word. Below meant danger, life, exhilaration, beauty and peril all wrapped up in each moment, but more and more it seemed to mean 'home' to Shanna.

All her experiences Below had been tied up in the discovery of the Garsal threat, but it was still the most amazing, enticing, place she'd ever been. The thrill was followed almost immediately by a chill of pure fear. She exchanged a worried glance with Amma, seated next to her on one of the large cushions strewn around the room. Storm nudged her hand with his head, tidemarks twinkling reassuringly, and Shanna flicked another glance around the room. Her fellow humans were wearing varied expressions: anticipation, apprehension, concern, and trepidation. Teacher's tidemarks were cycling faster than normal and the spiralling patterns on Fractus brightened and dimmed uncharacteristically fast. Radiant appeared his normal imperturbable self, but Shanna's attention was drawn to his tail tassel which was flicking distractedly.

"So, apparently we just up and leave tomorrow sometime," said Barron, musingly, "no warning, no preparation, just leave."

Fractus uncoiled suddenly, tidemarks flashing with amusement. His voice sounded wryly. "Not completely without preparation. We three have made quite a few preparations. You will find supplies of easily carried food and some new equipment in your sleeping rooms. We will be carrying our own supplies, but those of you who are fliers will need to carry your wingsuits in your packs.

All Starlyne technology will be left behind. Part of our downfall was the ease with which the Garsal detected our equipment, and despite advances in the years since our escape, we are fearful that if the Garsal detect us now before we locate their ship, they might call immediately for reinforcements."

"But where will we be heading?" asked Allad.

"The vehicles have left wide tracks," Teacher said. "Inclement weather further south may well have washed them away by the time we arrive there, but we are hopeful that there will still be enough to follow, and with the use of the wingsuits, and Shanna's ability to fade others, that we will be able to locate the Garsal compound without being detected ourselves."

"You want me to fade while flying," said Shanna incredulously, "And fade others as well? Didn't you see my crash landing?" There were a few snickers from her fellow cadets.

"By the time we reach the Garsal encampment you will be well practiced Shanna, as will your fellows. We expect to be travelling for many days," came Teacher's thought, and a feeling of relief wafted over Shanna. She'd had a sudden fear that she would be put to the test immediately, and a vision of her plummeting from the sky and landing in the middle of the Garsal colony, leaving her fellows exposed, had flashed in her mind.

"Verren, you should have a thorough look at the maps we have of the area of Below that we suspect the Garsal are located within," said Radiant. "We have provided you with all of the information we have accumulated over our years on this planet. Unfortunately with so few of us that far south, they are not complete, but they are more than you already have."

The planning session continued and the cadets were sent to check the new equipment supplied by their Starlyne allies. There were supplies of the energy patches placed by each bed, along with packages of concentrated foodstuffs and synthetic water containers. Verren located neatly rolled maps packaged in a cylinder on his bed and spent several hours poring over them, Arad joining him after the planning session had come to an end. It appeared that though Arad's direction sense was not as well developed as Verren's, it was still remarkably accurate and was improving the longer that Nosey was around.

The chubby starcat cub was still constantly getting herself into hot water. She appeared at the most inopportune moments, bouncing from place to place, hiding in packs and sneaking under blankets. Shanna removed the cub's head from inside her pack for what felt like the millionth time and growled gently at her.

"I don't know how you cope with this one, Arad!" Shanna's tone was exasperated but fond, as the little starcat batted her eyelashes at her. Twister levered himself up to mock growl at Nosey. She bounced again and attacked him, all wildly waving paws and huge eyes, and the now fully grown starcat rolled over on his back and allowed her to jump all over him, batting her gently with his paws.

"Well, she's still a handful, but her behaviour's improving and she learns very fast," replied Arad, looking up from his study of one of the maps rolled out on Verren's bed. Nosey looked up at Arad's voice and left her wrestle with Twister to gallop over to Arad and rub her head on his hand. The tall Scout scratched Nosey's cheek and she closed her eyes and leaned into his hand, emitting a high pitched purr.

Shanna smiled at Arad and began to repack the belongings that Nosey had scattered across her bed. "What will you do with her tomorrow, Arad?" she asked. Arad looked up, surprised.

"What do you mean?"

"Well, she's so little, Arad. She's much younger than our cats were the first time we came Below," she broke off as Arad began to shake his head, eyes dancing.

"Do you really think that she'd stay behind? After the lengths she went to get here? And I'm needed in my capacity as medic and navigator. Spiron, Barron and I have already discussed this. She and I will be in the centre of the Patrol at all times, and she will learn along the way. She will not slow us down – not nearly as much as she would by escaping and following. And I'm sure she would if we tried to leave her here." He returned his attention to the map.

Shanna shook her head slightly. The idea of a starcat cub accompanying the group on a dangerous expedition through unknown territory in search of invading alien intruders seemed absurd to her, but then again she mused, she herself had been no more than a 'cub' on her first expedition Below. She shook her head again. She assumed that the Starlynes knew, shrugged to herself and resumed packing. There were more important things to consider at the moment. Like how to fit her wingsuit into her pack. She picked it up again and attempted to fold it yet another way.

***

The Overlord paced through the hive. Beside him stalked the Matriarch, three senior females trailing in her wake. He had awoken to a demanding missive delivered by the orderly of the day. The wafer of parchment was finely lettered in delicate brushstrokes, but the words contained within were imperative. He had scrambled from his bedding, hurriedly sending the orderly for the appropriate gifts and offerings, then hastened to meet the Matriarch as she exited the sealed section of the ship for the first time.

Although much progress had been made on the construction of the hive, it was not at the stage that the Matriarch had requested. She stalked imperiously through the debris of partially finished stonework, apparently ignoring the fine designs on the completed portions. He hastened to show her the female quarters, designed and laid out to her specifications. She walked slowly through them with no sign of emotion or approval evident. Her silence grew daunting. The three female followers walked behind her, heads turning from side to side and flimsy robes fluttering. They mirrored the lack of expression from the Matriarch.

The inspection went on for the entire morning with never a sound of approval or disapproval from the four females. The entire inspection was done in silence, with no stop for the proffered refreshments. Only once did the Matriarch pause in her inspection. At the end of the inspection, they passed through the cavern where the engineers laboured at manufacturing replacement aircraft frames. There she had stopped, surveyed the industry, then turned abruptly and returned to her quarters.

The Overlord sat heavily in his chair. He was certain that the Matriarch was displeased with the progress of the hive, and he expected to hear of her displeasure in detail. Resolutely, he finalised the plan to infiltrate the plateau and begin the process of adding to his slave pool. Again he toyed with the idea of requesting reinforcements, but vanity and hope of offspring won out. He called for Zoash.

Chapter 13

IT FELT odd to venturing Below without actually having to 'go Below,' thought Shanna as the sixteen humans, three Starlynes, 16 grown starcats, and one cub began their trek through the thick vegetation below the plateau. Two hours after leaving the Starlyne habitation, the patrol encountered the first of the devastation left by the Garsal vehicles. The felled trees and wheel ruts had left deep scars on the formerly pristine environment. Shanna felt an almost physical pain at the damage. Perched on fallen tree trunks, the group surveyed the crushed greenery and tracks left by alien invaders.

"It will repair," came Teacher's soothing voice. "See the new shoots?" Shanna's heart lifted slightly as she saw that nearly all of the stumps were sprouting new growth, but she felt the impact of the Garsal incursion deep in her bones. Reality came flooding back, and she could see from the expressions on her fellow cadets' faces that the exciting prospect of their trek through Below had suddenly been submerged into the reality of seeking out the invaders and disabling their communications – a dangerous and possibly fatal task.

They resumed their steady progress, paralleling the Garsal vehicle tracks in standard patrol formation, with the three Starlynes in a triangular pattern at the head and either side of the patrol. Shanna and Allad were in their customary position at the front of the Patrol - Storm, Twister and Satin weaving ahead of the group. They had encountered rather less wildlife than normal, which the scouts attributed to the presence of their Starlyne friends. As Shanna mused on that, she felt faint amusement with a flavour she attributed to Fractus, touch her briefly. She turned her attention to the vegetation ahead and glided silently through the bush. She wondered how far away the Garsal ship might be. Perhaps it might not be as difficult to locate as they'd thought. The devastation wrought by the mechanical vehicles was proving to be easy to follow, and there was no evidence that the insectoid creatures were close by. Remembering the lack of bushcraft demonstrated by those in the original vehicle, Shanna felt the first stirrings of hope again. She looked ahead through the dimness generated by the dense canopy, catching a glimpse of Storm's blue tidemarks ahead, and concentrated on route finding.

*****

Master Cerren shook his head again, frustrated. He caught Peron and Yendy's eyes across the table and raised an eyebrow at them. Peron nodded and quietly left the room, Thunder padding noiselessly behind him, while Yendy sighed visibly and nodded as well.

"Tamazine, if we persist with a complete centralisation of control, we make ourselves a sitting target should the Garsal have any more of those flying craft. The old storm caverns and the plateau tunnels do not have the capacity to hold all those you have designated to move into Watchtower." His voice was firm, and he tried very hard not to show his irritation with the senior councillor. Tamazine got to her feet, summoning an aide, who handed her a file. She opened it, slowly running her eyes down the list.

"For effective communication, everyone must be in the same place, Cerren. You must understand this."

"As I've explained, Councillor, the Scout Corps can arrange a rapid communication network using our retirees and their starcats, and of course there are always the signal flags. Surely we can adapt the storm and danger codes for this emergency!" Cerren tried hard to keep his voice even but allowed himself to stand, leaning across the conference table towards the Senior Councillor. "And production of food and animal husbandry must continue, or our folk will face famine as well as alien invaders! I would urge you to reconsider removing the farmers from the outlying villages at the very least. It would be more prudent to make the most of this part of the growing season. If the Garsal are detected approaching the plateau we can signal the villagers to take refuge – here if you feel it's absolutely necessary, but they do have their own underground shelters. And the starcat breeders – they are essential to our defence, yet you wish them to take their cats away from their familiar surroundings!" He was unable to keep a tinge of frustration from colouring his tone and sat down abruptly, hoping he hadn't alienated Tamazine entirely.

He'd always known her as a reasonable person, an able administrator, supremely self confident and competent at her job, and was perplexed as to why she had become so intractable and so determined to tightly control the response to the Garsal threat.

Tamazine spoke again. "Cerren, I will take your thoughts under advisement. We will meet again at this time tomorrow." She rose and left the room followed by her troupe of aides. Cerren stayed seated at the conference table and regarded the others seated around it. Payne was tapping a pencil rhythmically on the polished wood, Yendy was scowling at his notes, and Erilla, who had sat silently through the proceedings, met his gaze squarely.

"Peron has gone to set the wheels in motion?" she asked.

Cerren nodded in reply, twisting his mouth in a rueful grimace. "I wish I knew why she is so bent on such a destructive strategy. She's alienating the people we need most."

Erilla straightened in her chair and snorted. "Our Senior Councillor has been an excellent administrator. Until now, she has been precisely what our community has needed: stability. She has been a planner for effective government and a bringer of order and justice. But in this situation she is completely out of her depth. You must remember, Cerren, Tamazine has spent her entire life in Starfall. She was a member of the judiciary before she was a councillor. Her life has been very, very predictable. Of course she's had to deal with cyclones, but those procedures were established years ago, and apart from the odd refinement, we are well practiced at storm damage. As our first settlement, Starfall and its surrounds are the most secure places we have on the plateau, and indeed the planet." Erilla looked up as Peron returned and joined the group at the table. "It's done?" she asked.

"Yes, I've given the orders and sent messages to those who need to know." He pulled the water jug across the table and poured himself a glass and then pushed himself back into his chair with a heavy sigh.

"Good," she replied. "At least we'll have a buffer if reason fails."

She returned her attention to the rest of the group. "Back to Tamazine. I think she's out of her depth. She's able as we all know, but she's never had to deal with the unpredictable. Her career has fitted her to deal with administrative and legal issues and policies across the plateau, but an unknown and completely unpredictable emergency is beyond her scope of experience." She snorted suddenly. "Alien invasion is beyond all of our scopes of experience, but a career in the Scout Corps or Militia is at least some kind of preparation for dealing with the unexpected." There were various nods around the table.

"And she is fairly unimaginative as well. Clever and well versed in the law, normally a good mediator and facilitator, she's probably fearful of the future so she grasps the reins more tightly to increase her sense of control," replied Cerren. "Your words are, as ever Erilla, enlightening. Perhaps I should listen more and talk less, and I might approach your insights." He motioned to Peron, who poured another glass of water from the jug and pushed it across the table to him. Sipping thoughtfully he added, "I'll try and reason with her again tomorrow. We have several Patrols sweeping the base of the plateau and our Starlyne allies are assisting. They have ways of communicating that the Garsal cannot detect, although apparently they are relatively short range and must be relayed. I hope to discuss this as another means of bringing sense to the argument." He pushed his chair back and Socks strolled over to him, her blue tidemarks rippling soothingly as she brushed his leg.

"Peron will keep you informed of the other matters, Payne. Do I have your support tomorrow when I talk with Tamazine again, though?"

"Of course," Watchtower's senior Councillor said. "And I hope you can get her to see sense. My staff are currently dealing with hordes of very unhappy people. Watchtower's a large town, and Tamazine's plan calls for fully half of the population to relocate to settlements closer to Starfall. It's a logistical nightmare if nothing else, but my concerns are the same as yours. We need much better planning, and much less concentration of our people in large groups." He shook his head and sighed heavily. "Most of the people understand the urgency of preparing to deal with the Garsal threat, but it's not real to them yet. Many are reluctant to leave their homes – understandably so – and crops, or businesses, and others fear family separation." Peron put a hand on the man's shoulder.

"We understand. I'll see you tonight. Please leave word with your secretary to admit me." The Scouts watched silently as Payne gathered his notes and left the room.

Cerren rubbed his hand down Socks's head and she leaned into it, her purring rumbling through the room so loudly that Thunder looked around, startled.

"Do our Starlyne allies understand the issues, Peron?" he asked.

Master Peron nodded. "They do. Speaker has been very understanding. Apparently the Starlynes have had some dissent in their ranks as well, but the majority are united in their desire to deal with this threat. I'm encouraged to hear that they're not perfect. In fact it reassures me." He went on. "I have two of the third-years stationed with Speaker at all times on a rotating roster. They are available as messengers. We've accelerated the training program for the second-years and the new first-years, and I've placed Toman in charge of the buffer activities. She's well seasoned for the task, and has a nice devious mind."

Erilla laughed. "You're right there. She was my mentor when I became a cadet. I was never able to outsmart her."

"So we'll meet tomorrow again, after the meeting with Tamazine?" asked Peron.

Cerren nodded. "I'll do my best, but I'm not sure if I'll be able to get her to change her mind. Payne will help, but if she's determined to keep personal control of this emergency then we may be in for a great deal of trouble. Erilla, I'll need your insights as to the best way to approach each point. Will you walk with me to my office?" The four of them left the meeting room and began the short walk to Scout Headquarters, starcats pacing around them, deep in conversation.

The meeting began smoothly the next day. Tamazine agreed to relent on the matter of the farmers and Payne dispatched messengers to the outlying settlements immediately, hoping to halt the evacuation before it became too advanced. On the matter of starcat breeders though, she was immovable.

"You have said many times, Cerren, that our allies see the starcats as essential to our survival!" Tamazine's voice echoed through the chamber. "You will message them immediately and inform them that they will relocate here, today!" Her cheeks were red, and her normally controlled face was set into hard lines. "And you will tell them to present their prepared cats to myself and my staff. We will choose later today."

"You want to choose a starcat?" asked Erilla, her eyes narrowing. "And all of your staff as well?" She swept her eyes around the room, at the senior

Councillor's staff, and the other Councillors from Starfall. "The last time I spoke to our local breeders, they had only a few cubs available, and only one mature, ready-trained cat. Our new cadet class will need to choose very shortly as well." She shuffled a few of the pages in front of her. "I understand you've never had a cat of your own." She paused and fixed her eyes on the Senior Councillor. Tamazine dropped her eyes slightly before the Scout's piercing green gaze.

"No, I've never had a starcat of my own. Until now, there hasn't been the need."

"You do realise the demands a starcat cub will make on your time?" asked Cerren incredulously.

"I will take the trained cat," replied Tamazine.

"Even *I* know that cat choosing is a mutual affair," said Payne, looking around at the Scouts sitting around the conference table. He glanced at the starcats relaxing around the room. Despite their relaxed postures, they were all alert, eyes and ears following the conversation, and he wondered exactly how much they really understood. "Are you sure you've thought this through?"

"Tamazine, why have you decided that you need a starcat?" Peron broke in. Shanna's mentor's face was troubled.

"It is essential that our government is protected and remains stable. I have decided to lead the way by choosing a starcat, and my associates have decided to follow suit," replied Tamazine. Cerren noted that she avoided meeting anyone's eyes after this extraordinary statement. He began to shake his head but caught himself quickly.

"But why you?" he asked. "There are plenty of us with starcats to protect the government. In my eyes, there is no need for you to 'lead the way' as you've put it." He held her gaze, refusing to let her drop her eyes. The silence grew uncomfortably long as the Senior Councillor's face slowly reddened. A sneaking suspicion entered Cerren's mind. He dismissed it initially, discounting it as unworthy of the woman before him with her reputation for upright honesty and even-handedness, but as the silence extended and the red stain deepened across her face, he was forced to reconsider. He risked a quick glance at Erilla. She was watching the interplay thoughtfully, one finger tapping her chin, and an eyebrow quirked upward above her green eyes.

"Enough!" snapped Tamazine finally. "My reasons are my own. You will inform the breeders immediately." She snapped the folder in front of her shut and without looking, gestured imperiously to the aide behind her. The aide placed another folder in her open hand. Cerren held her gaze for a moment longer.

"I will send the messengers, but I believe you're making a significant mistake, Councillor. The people of Watchtower are used to their independence. I suspect that you may have a cold reception this afternoon." He turned to

Peron and nodded briefly. The other Master left the room quietly with Thunder at his heels. Socks strolled over to her partner and sat slightly to one side and just behind him, violet eyes on Tamazine. Her blue tidemarks cycled in a pattern that Cerren interpreted as watchful. The Councillor seemed slightly unsettled by the deep grey cat's steady regard.

She opened the new folder. "We will move to the next point on the agenda. The disposition of the militia." She tapped the map spread out on the table before them and rested a fingertip on one of the small wooden tokens that represented the various Scout Patrols and Militia units tasked around Watchtower and Below. "Is there any word from Spiron, Master Cerren?"

"We've had word from our Starlyne allies that they've just begun the trek to locate the Garsal Colony ship. They plan to disable the communications systems on the ship and provide us with further information on just how many Garsal there might be, as well as any information on the human slave situation. Unfortunately we'll be out of touch with them for some time until they can begin to relay through the Starlyne network again." He looked up as Peron re-entered the room, catching the other Master's quick nod, and took several steps from his chair to bend over the map across from Tamazine. Payne was neatly moving the Militia tokens into position, consulting a notepad from time to time to make sure they were positioned correctly. Erilla stepped up to the map as well and carefully moved the Patrol tokens into their current positions.

In the back of his mind, Cerren turned Tamazine's comments over and over, replaying her expressions and statements. He was uneasy at the Councillor's adamant stance on the starcat breeders, and suspicious of her sudden desire for a starcat companion. The uncomfortable thought that had crossed his mind during the discussion presented itself again, and he was forced to reconsider it. At his side, Socks thrust her large head under his hand, and startled, he looked down at her. She swiped her head on his hand again and flickered her tidemarks gently in patterns of encouragement and reassurance. Surprised, he sat back in his seat, the better to observe the interaction between Tamazine and Erilla. The Scout Master was patiently explaining why the various patrols were in each location, indicating with gestures the terrain demonstrated by the map contours. On the other side of the Senior Councillor, Payne was indicating unit strengths and travel times, and colour coding each token to show each unit's capabilities.

Peron took a seat next to the Scout Master. "I've sent the messengers," he said quietly. "As requested." His face took on a grave expression, and he lowered his voice even more. "I have more to tell you after this meeting." He turned his face forward politely as Erilla asked him a question regarding one of the patrols.

By the end of the meeting, Cerren was convinced his first thought about the Councillor's motivations was correct. The thoughts had continued to intrude during the discussion and he hoped that his distraction hadn't showed. He gathered Erilla and Peron with his eyes as they left the conference room, and the three Masters walked silently together to his office. A thoughtful staff member had left a tray of lunch, complete with a pot of hot tea, sitting on his desk. Cerren made a mental note to thank the provider.

"So, what do you make of this sudden desire of Tamazine's?" asked Peron with a quizzical lift of his eyebrows. Erilla snorted slightly and took a sip of her tea. Cerren sighed heavily, sipped, and then placed his mug back on the table.

"I think she's running scared to be quite frank, and I think she wants a cat because she thinks having one might keep her safe."

"I thought the same thing, Cerren," replied Erilla. She placed her mug carefully on the table. "Unfortunately, she has no idea what starcat partnership is really about." Her cat, Nimbus, paced over to her and laid his head in her lap. His indigo tidemarks flickered in complex patterns and he hummed at her. She looked down. "Nimbus agrees." She paused briefly. "Has anyone ever been left at a choosing?"

Peron steepled his fingertips and leaned back in his chair, thoughtfully. "Actually, yes," he replied. "You remember, Cerren?"

Master Cerren nodded, recalling the incident to mind. "It was a few years back. The man in question attempted to choose one of Josen's cubs, but none chose him — in fact none would even approach him. He tried again with a selection of ready trained cats out at Hillview. Again, no success. It caused quite a stir at the time. There were several instances during my time at Starfall as well. It appears that if someone is unsuitable, the cats know."

"I'm concerned that self-interest is driving Tamazine, whether she is honest enough with herself to admit it or not. We have such a need of our cats, now more than ever before, and it's essential that they go to the right people!" said Peron vehemently. "What happens if her people take all of the young cats?"

"That would be a problem. I think that the new cadets should be present this afternoon as well. It would be a little early in the normal scheme of things, but on the accelerated schedule we're following, it will be entirely appropriate," replied Peron. "I'll make the arrangements immediately."

He placed his mug on the table and stood to leave the room. "Tamazine may not be pleased, but the cadets must have the opportunity, and we all know that there's no changing a starcat's mind once they've decided who they want. As the current head of training, I will take responsibility for their presence if she decides to object."

"Peron, would you also arrange for Anjo and Semba to observe this afternoon?" asked Erilla. "Anjo is reasonably comfortable around the cats now, but Semba is still uneasy. I'm hopeful that if she watches the cubs playing she might feel less frightened of them. She is still struggling to adapt and I'm becoming more than a little concerned."

"That's an excellent idea," replied Cerren., "And yet another reminder for Tamazine and her staff of the very real issues of the Garsal." He drank the dregs from his cup and placed it back on the table. Socks gave an approving hum and little Thunder purred from behind Peron's foot. "And Peron, could you also schedule a session with the Garsal captives immediately after the choosing?"

"I'll notify Yendy and Lonish and ask them to brief the cadets, and I'll send a message to Toman." Peron shut the door quietly behind him. Cerren and Erilla sat quietly for some time.

"I truly hope we can talk some sense into Tamazine," sighed Erilla finally.

"If we don't, I fear that our struggle against the Garsal may well become even more difficult," replied Cerren. "I also wish there was a faster way of communicating with our people Below. Their input would be extraordinarily valuable right now. Sometimes I still wonder if we did the right thing with those cadets."

"Nonsense," Erilla said. "You made the correct choice. There was nothing else to do at the time. Whether everyone on the plateau realises it or not, we've been at war since the rescue of the offworlders. Whatever those cadets and Patrol Ten can learn can only be to our benefit. Rest assured, however, that I pray daily for their safety on this current mission." She pushed herself to her feet and called Nimbus. "I'll see you in the arena this afternoon."

After his office had emptied, Cerren sat quietly for some time. His eyes drifted frequently towards the south facing window as he reflected on the group travelling so far Below. There was a reassuring hum from Socks, and he pushed himself to his feet with a sigh as the blue-toned cat slid her head under his hand. There were too many things to do for him to sit idle.

Several hours later, he sat on the seating at the edge of the arena as Janna, Adlan and Josen sent not only their own cubs through their paces, but Gem's. Damar and Feeny had appeared at the tunnel access only an hour before, and as Gem's cubs were of the appropriate age Feeny had agreed to allow them to participate in the imminent choosing. She and Gem had happily handed them over to the experienced breeders to show them off while she sat back beside Cerren, Gem leaning on her legs.

"Did you receive the message I sent regarding Nosey?" she asked.

"Yes," he replied. "She's now with Arad, I believe."

"Little monster. He'll have his hands full with that one. Reminds me of Satin, actually." Cerren laughed at her droll tone. "When a starcat decides who she wants, who are we to get in her way?"

Cerren looked across the arena. The six new cadets were standing in one group watching the display avidly, while the Senior Councillor and her aides were standing in a second group. The one fully trained youngster was first put through his paces by Josen, the red-toned starcat demonstrating his athleticism as he circled the arena and swarmed up the poles at either end.

"Nice cat," commented Yendy.

"He certainly is," replied Erilla. "In some ways it's a pity we start our cadets with cubs. That one's ready and able for anything. All he needs is a partner, and we'd have another cat ready for action." At her words, Cerren looked around the group of Masters. Masters were often assigned to head-quarters when they were catless or their cats were ageing. It allowed them time to work with a new partner, time to develop the proper relationship, and to work on those specialised skills that a Scout's starcat partner needed. The group of Masters had a variety of cats sitting with them, from Master Lonish's aged Samson to little Thunder, now beginning to grow into his huge paws. None were catless.

Sitting on a bench a little further down were Anjo, Semba and young Kaidan from Hillview. He'd travelled into Watchtower with his parents and their cats, and was chatting avidly with Anjo. Every time Cerren looked at him, he was haunted by the decision he'd made to send Kaidan with the archers, and he feared that if worst came to worst in the struggle against the Garsal, he'd choose to do the same thing again. Janna's accusing look flashed across his mind again. Even now when he spoke to her, he could see the echoes of anger in her eyes. Josen concluded his display by encouraging the ruby-toned youngster to one last display of agility before the cat blurred back to his side.

"And if you'll all come forward now, we'll introduce you to the cubs and the choosing can begin." He beckoned to the six cadets, then somewhat belatedly to Tamazine's group. They shuffled forward looking slightly hesitant, and Cerren leant forward to watch the unfolding events. The young starcats were as engaging as ever. Janna and Adlan had brought in five blue and violet-toned youngsters, and Josen had another four in addition to the fully trained youngster, while Gem's five made fourteen. The fourteen young cats pounced and bounced around the arena. The cadets needed no urging to play with the youngsters, and as normal the cadets experienced with starcats managed to avoid the pitfalls of tumbles and lace tying, while two of them ended up sprawled in the dirt. One wide-eyed cub was happily bounding from cadet to cadet, looking earnestly into each face, then running in rapid spirals around the shortest cadet before snuggling into her legs possessively.

The Councillor's group was more hesitant before Tamazine strode forward towards the cubs, and Cerren was amused to see them scurrying in her wake like a small group of marmal younglings hurrying after their mother. He settled in to watch what might happen.

As Tamazine strode through the chaos of the starcat cubs, he could see that she was heading in a straight line for the ruby-toned youngster. The young male cat looked at the figure of the Senior Councillor striding towards him and looked up at Josen. The trainer flicked his fingers in a hand signal, releasing him to move at his own will, and suddenly the youngster blurred into movement. In a flash, he was gone from Josen's side and Tamazine came to a confused halt. Cerren swung his head from side to side, hoping to catch the mirage like shimmer of a faded starcat, when all the Masters' cats came to sudden attention. Beside Cerren, Socks was abruptly upright, head turned to the left, facing Kaidan, Anjo and Semba on the bench to the side. He followed her gaze.

A startled Anjo was sitting on his bottom in the dust of the arena, having toppled backwards off the bench. The young cat was standing astride him, purring enthusiastically and rubbing the startled offworlder's face alternately with each side of his cheeks. Kaidan was giggling while attempting to reassure Semba, and Anjo was just sitting there on his backside, looking stunned. Cerren's surprise broke into a pleased grin as he contemplated the starcat's choice and the Senior Councillor's annoyance.

In the midst of the arena, each cadet was now playing ecstatically with a young cub – three of Hillview's, two of Josen's, and one of Gem's. The other eight cubs were trotting around the Councillor's group. Two returned to Janna and Adlan, and one of the red-toned cubs butted his head at a young aide standing by Tamazine's side. As the little cat twined his body around the aide's legs, the young man looked down surprised, then knelt to stroke the soft fur of the cub's head. The little cub's tidemarks flickered in patterns of pleased excitement. Gem's cubs returned to their mother and Cerren nodded approvingly; they really were a little young yet and he wondered fleetingly how Arad was getting on with Nosey.

He looked across at Tamazine. Her face was like thunder and her mouth set in a grim line. He sighed inside and began to mentally review how he would deal with this latest outcome. At the very least, someone, somehow, was going to have to teach Anjo how to deal with partnering a starcat. He sighed again, his gaze settling on young Kaidan, the beginnings of a plan forming in his mind.

Chapter 14

SHANNA crouched behind a rock and carefully inched her face around its side. The granite was rough where her cheek leant against it. They were back at the site where they had rescued Anjo and Semba, all those weeks ago. The ground was disturbed and several holes were evident. The vehicle had left deep ruts towards both the mini plateau and the trail that Allad and Shanna had led it on. The fence poles still stood, and the remains of the scaly beasts that had attacked the fence lay strewn about the perimeter, bones now cleaned to whiteness by Below's scavengers. There was no sign of any Garsal, and Shanna flicked a quick hand signal to Storm and Twister to circle around the area. Faintly through the vegetation she could see the outline of Allad's large form, mostly concealed behind a large frondan tree. She eased the pack on her shoulders slightly and continued to watch. Shanna felt slightly unsettled to be back at the place where her planet's future had changed so suddenly. Where her life had changed so suddenly, she corrected herself. Storm and Twister both returned and she relaxed as she realised that their tidemarks were cycling in patterns of unconcern.

On Allad's hand signal she slowly moved out from behind the cover of the rock, signalling behind her in turn and inching forwards carefully. She skirted a barbed palm that she remembered from the previous visit, and directed her attention towards the now silent line of fence posts. There were no ruby lines connecting them any more, and she ran a tentative hand down the unfamiliar material. It was hard yet felt oddly light to her touch.

Fractus, Radiant and Teacher fanned out in the open area, and the rest of the Patrol spread itself about the rock spires and the edge of the vegetation. Their starcats began circling quietly around the area. Little Nosey bounced her way into the centre of the rock area and began batting her paws at a waving seedhead. She had spent the days of trekking either padding along behind Arad, or snoring gently on the top of his pack. Shanna had been impressed at the Scout's strength. A growing starcat was no easy burden. As a cub, Nosey only weighed ten to twelve kilos, but on top of Arad's pack she almost doubled the weight he carried. He hadn't complained, simply kept up the easy gliding stride of the trained Scout kilometre after kilometre.

Surprisingly, Nosey hadn't put a paw out of line the whole time. She'd obeyed every command given by her partner, stayed strictly in the centre of the patrol, and spent part of each evening snuggled up to one of the Starlynes coiled in their campsite before tucking herself against Arad and falling asleep. The Scouts had maintained their standard watch pattern with the assistance of their Starlyne allies, which meant that each night, fully half of the group was able to sleep the full night. Shanna had appreciated the extra sleep time.

Spiron conferred briefly with Fractus, and then signalled the group to begin setting up for the night. The sheltered spot was a logical place to overnight before climbing up and over the plateau and venturing further into Below. Shanna realised that by this time the next night, she would be further Below than she had ever been before. A small frisson of excitement tickled the back of her neck. Despite the dangers of Below and the presence of the alien Garsal, every moment she spent Below was becoming more and more precious to her. The abundance of plant and animal life, so like that above on the plateau yet always and ever so slightly different, fascinated her. The ever present smells of greenery wafted on the breeze as she called Twister and Storm in and sent them out to hunt their dinner.

The Patrol sat quietly around the fire that evening. There was a subdued atmosphere that had been lacking in the preceding evenings. The cadets were all seated on one side of the fire, starcats lounging around them, while Barron and Hunter sat the watch above on the rock spires. The sky was faintly visible through the overhanging canopy, the great spiral of The Compass winking its myriad stars as the trees swayed in the soft breeze. The night was cool, signalling the beginning of Autumn and the end of the storm season.

"Tomorrow you will need to begin aerial surveillance," said Fractus. His thoughts had practical overtones. "It is important that we locate the most direct path to their ship and that you learn to fly smoothly, while we are yet far from their location."

"I was thinking that the southern edge of the mini plateau might be a good launching spot," Spiron said thoughtfully. "It's high, both for launching and for sighting in flight, so it shouldn't be too difficult to locate from a distance in the air." Shanna sat back quietly in the group of cadets, still embarrassed by her awkward landing, while next to her Amma leaned forward eagerly.

"How far were you thinking that we should fly, Spiron?" she asked.

"Fractus and I were considering a two-hour flight – an hour south followed by a return to the launch site – while the rest of us check for any further Garsal campsites in the vicinity. It appears that they may have been looking for minerals on their way to the plateau, and any information is better than no information. We'll take samples from any hole we find dug in the ground. Fractus assures me that the Starlynes can analyse them when we return."

"And you all need to practice your new skills every evening when we stop," broke in Teacher. "You must be ready for anything when we arrive at the Garsal encampment."

There was a mutter from Taya. "And how am I to practice stopping mechanicals out here?"

"You will practice your other skills, Taya," came the tart thought. "There are still more things for you to accomplish. It would be useful if all of you manage to fade by yourselves. Whether that is achievable is still to be seen." She shifted herself to coil more comfortably by the fireside. "And feeling your way through the dark – you all need practice in this." Shanna wondered if she'd imagined the faint overtones of worry she could feel in Teacher's thoughts.

Communicating with their Starlyne friends had been a strange process. Hearing someone else's voice inside your head but not with your ears took some getting used to. And feeling their emotions was sometimes overwhelming. For the first few days it had been completely overpowering but now Shanna felt that she had somehow managed to buffer the emotions somewhat – not exclude them but filter them a bit, so that the experience was a little less intense. She replayed Teacher's words in her head again. Yes, there was an undertone of worry, and Shanna looked quizzically at the normally composed and confident Starlyne on the other side of the fire. No one else appeared to have noticed, or at least no one else was showing any concern that Shanna could detect. Perhaps she had imagined it.

She shelved the thought and began worrying about the next day's activities. She was expected to fly again – and land! She hoped fervently that this time she'd be able to land without crashing. She had the final watch of the night, so she decided to get to sleep early. She called Storm and Twister, rolled herself up in her blanket, and went to sleep.

The southern side of the little plateau provided a spectacular view to the south. The huge expanse of country lay spread out in front of the Patrol. It was densely vegetated with several meandering watercourses. It was not flat, but undulating and dotted with large rocky outcrops, seemingly rising for no reason at all, their flat tops rearing up out of the vegetation at irregular intervals. There was a faint breeze stirring the treetops in ripples of green as the rest of the Patrol emerged from the tree line, and sent their cats spiralling out around them. Fractus and Radiant perched themselves on the edge of the rocky outcrop to the west, while Teacher positioned herself at the rear of the group.

Spiron quickly detailed Karri, Perri and Challon to proceed down the slope to that night's encampment while he sent Barron, Nelson, Verren, Kalli and Zandany to search out any signs of Garsal activity. They were to parallel the vehicle tracks for two hours and then return.

"Taya," Spiron said, "you, Ragar and your cats will guard this area so that the rest of us can prepare for flight. Arad, you'll do the final checks." Setting Fury to watch the region directly below the outcrop, he shed his pack and began to don his own flight suit.

With a degree of trepidation, Shanna pulled her wingsuit out of her pack and donned it. Storm nudged her gently as if to reassure her, before returning his attention to the tree line behind them. Twister was up one of the larger trees, perched high in its branches, nose turned to the breeze. He hummed contentedly. The four fliers spent several minutes double-checking each other, then one after another turned themselves into the wind and launched.

Again, Shanna felt the first swooping drop deep in the pit of her stomach. She concentrated, located the nearest thermal, and followed Amma's graceful spiral upwards. To her right she could see Allad, on her left, Spiron. Her flight wavered briefly until she concentrated harder and 'saw' the air currents as if overlaid on her normal vision, which allowed her to steady herself in the air. Once airborne, Spiron had suggested that they attempt to assume a triangular formation with Amma at the apex, and the other three spread out like the base of the triangle. Finding herself in the middle, Shanna had to work hard to keep herself evenly spaced from Allad and Spiron. Faintly through the rushing wind, she heard Amma's voice trailing back to her.

"I can see the vehicle track below us!"

Shanna risked a look down and immediately wished she hadn't as the ground seemed to be rushing past at a ridiculous speed. Momentarily nauseous she swallowed, and had to reorient herself in the flight group again. Her glimpse of the ground had shown the vehicle track like the slash of a knife through the vegetation. Carefully she looked back down again, more in control this time, and managed to keep her eyes on the ground for a couple of minutes. The track wound tortuously through the bush, seemingly meandering all over the terrain. Shanna wondered at the waste of time taken for the vehicle to traverse the countryside but then realised that the cumbersome vehicles would have needed to find the path with the easiest terrain for its wheeled convenience. Turning her eyes back towards Amma, she rechecked her position in the air against Spiron and Allad, and realised that she was flying easily. The sensation of sailing through the air was intoxicating, and for a moment she was hard pressed to stop herself from swooping and diving like an exuberant bird.

Amma continued to lead them south following the slash of damaged vegetation, occasionally banking sideways and circling around an area for a closer look, until the four of them could see four individual tracks converging into one, and realised that the four vehicles that had assaulted the plateau had come from four different directions.

Following Amma in a circle around the convergence, she saw Amma give the little swoop in the air that meant it was time to turn for home. Beside her, Spiron indicated his agreement, and signalled that they should spread out and fly abreast on the return trip.

They followed Amma's lead into a large thermal, spread themselves out, and headed back northward towards their origin. Shanna was glad to see that the mini plateau was still easy to see from the air, but as they flew back towards the southern edge she was disconcerted to realise that she couldn't remember what the landmarks around their take off point looked like. Everything looked subtly different from the air. She looked to either side, to see complete unconcern on Allad and Spiron's faces, though Amma's mirrored her uncertainty. She hoped the two older Scouts knew where they were heading. She tried a shout against the wind of their flight.

"Where's the landing point?" The wind whipped the words from her, but Allad on her right smiled and nodded, and signalled that she should drop behind him. Gladly she dropped back, wobbling a little in the turbulence from his passage, until she'd dropped back far enough to fly in relatively clear air.

She could see that Amma and Spiron were following suit on her other side. Allad zigged and zagged, then settled on a straight line approach. As the rock face became more evident, Shanna realised she could see the slope downwards into the bush with the outcrop to one side, and the tiny dots of human and starcat figures spaced around it.

Once sighted, she was completely reoriented, but with a rush of nervous energy realised that she still had to land. Standing off from the outcrop to allow Allad room, Shanna realised that she was tired. That same all encompassing tiredness she'd experienced on the valley navigation exercise. Suddenly, she wasn't sure she had enough energy to land safely. Her arms and legs were beginning to tremble, and her smooth flight became slightly wobbly again. As Allad touched down safely, she took a deep breath, tried to still the trembling, and began her approach. This time she remembered to stay high enough, but almost forgot to turn into the wind for the final touchdown. Awkwardly she turned at the last moment and wobbled to a bumpy halt, stumbling to her knees. She dropped her arms and pulled in her extenders before resting her hands on the ground.

"Shan, move!" She turned her head tiredly at Ragar's voice uncomprehendingly, and realised that Spiron was circling in. She grabbed Taya's outstretched hand and staggered out of the way, as Spiron turned into the wind and dropped neatly out of the sky. She half fell as Taya pulled her further away from the edge so that Amma could land.

Amma swooped lightly onto the rock, almost seeming to defy gravity as she landed. Exhausted, Shanna fumbled some dried fruit into her mouth before the tiredness became so overwhelming she fell off the rock, and felt the fatigue slowly drain away as she chewed.

Finally more aware of her surroundings, she could see that Spiron and Allad were also looking very tired, while Amma still seemed elated. Obviously the effort required for her to fly was significantly less. On the other hand, Shanna had seen her exhausted after attempting to route find. It seemed that inherent skills were easier to maintain than those that had to be awakened through simple hard work. Shanna wondered how she would be able to keep up with the demands that practicing all of the new skills would make on her body, while walking all day carrying a heavy pack. She swallowed the last of her fruit and began to remove her flight suit.

"There are four converging tracks," she heard Allad say to Radiant, "I'd say they're about two days' walk from here, Spiron? By my reckoning, I reckon that they converge near that cave site where we sat out the big storm last year."

"I'd agree," replied Spiron. "The question is, what do we do then? Amma, how long do you think you could fly for?" Amma looked up at him, surprise all over her face.

"Well, I don't feel too fatigued right now, so I think that I could probably fly for twice as long, perhaps longer with practice. It's more my arms and legs than the rest of me ... " she broke off uncertainly, looking at the other three fliers.

"Well, I couldn't fly for that long," replied Shanna., "I only just made it down today. Perhaps I'll get better with practice." She took a swallow from her water bottle, wondering where Spiron's line of thought was taking him.

"I'm pretty tired too," said Allad. Satin strolled up to him and ducked her head against his shoulder, emerald tidemarks twinkling. "I could probably have flown for about another thirty minutes, but that'd be all. It's not the arms and legs with me, just the effort required to concentrate on the air currents."

Spiron, lowered his eyebrows slightly in concentration. "I'm about as fatigued as Allad and Shanna. That means that at the moment, the three of us are only useful for short range reconnaissance. Perhaps we'll have to rethink our plans. I'm concerned that we may need to divide into smaller groups to backtrack each individual vehicle."

"But surely they'll all lead back to the Garsal ship?" asked Arad.

"I'm sure they will eventually," replied Spiron. "But how far does each vehicle track meander? It's possible that if we follow the wrong track, then it will take a lot longer than it could have to locate the ship, and every day extra increases the chance that the Garsal will attempt to bring in reinforcements from off world."

Fractus glided towards the humans. "You are correct, Spiron. Every day saved is one less for the Garsal to contact their fellows. It is essential that we determine the fastest route to the Garsal ship. We must consider the best use of our resources. It may be that we need to divide into four groups, each with a flier, to determine the fastest route to take. Or perhaps we simply need to locate another elevated position, then we can send out our fliers in different directions to follow the four different vehicle tracks. It is a problem that we need to ponder." He turned and moved off down the side of the plateau towards that night's campsite.

Shanna finished packing her wingsuit away with Taya's help. It felt strange to be working so companionably with the other girl after so many months of antagonism. Since her confession, the change in Taya had been remarkable. She retained her prickly nature and was still hesitant when talking to Shanna, and occasionally Shanna would see a reflection of her previous antagonism in the other girl's eyes, but then Taya would set her mouth in a determined line and simply get on with whatever task they were working at. Shanna's respect for the older girl grew every day. She couldn't imagine how she'd have coped if her own father had rejected her.

With their cats around them, the group descended the slope to a pungo grove. A small creek provided a welcome fresh water supply, and Shanna happily refilled her water bottles before arranging her bedding under one of the overhanging trees. Amma and Taya spread their bedding near hers, then together they sent their cats out to hunt. Storm and Twister twinkled their tidemarks at her before vanishing into the bush.

Challon had already begun the evening meal. Despite the dried fruit she'd just eaten, Shanna's stomach rumbled enthusiastically as he lifted a lid off one of the pots sitting over a bed of embers and gave it a stir. In the relative safety of the pungo grove, it was safe to cook something hot. Add the mediating presence of the Starlynes, and Shanna felt almost uncomfortably secure at this stage of the trip.

The conversation around the fire was again focused on locating the Garsal ship, along with the best use of the four fliers. Amma participated animatedly in the discussion, but Shanna felt apprehensive about the idea of flying alone then navigating back to the start point accurately, given her recent experience. She was now comfortable navigating on the ground, but the complexities of flying and navigating at the same time, while attempting to be vigilant enough to discover the Garsal location and tracking them back to their ship, seemed to be just too much to consider doing all at once.

Her two cats seemed unperturbed. They were sitting on either side of her, both completely relaxed. She wished she had their perspective. She also worried about them. Each time she donned the flight suit, she flew away from them. What if she was unable to navigate back accurately? What would Storm and Twister do? If she became lost Below, how would they find her? As if to reassure her, Storm nudged her hand gently with his head. She looked down at him surprised, and found his great violet eyes regarding her steadily.

She realised that he and Twister had now come to their full growth — sleek, black coats rippling over muscled frames and huge paws. Both of them were large cats, easily Fury and Hunter's size, and both now slightly larger than Satin. She reflexively slid her hand down Storm's sleek neck and ran her eyes over Twister. He was also watching her, violet eyes showing no apprehension, just simple reassurance, and his ear tip tidemarks twinkled in measured patterns of security.

She stared back into the fire, thoughts wandering aimlessly around her head, suddenly disturbed again by images of her family. She wondered what they were doing, and loneliness welled up inside her so strongly that it was almost physical pain. Both cats leaned more firmly against her, sandwiching her lovingly. She put a hand on each neck and hugged them tightly, and the pain of missing her family eased slightly. She felt faintly in her mind the warm presence of Fractus projecting a sense of compassion, and was there an echo of sadness as well? The Starlyne's presence vanished, however, leaving her feeling slightly comforted.

Shanna drew her attention back to the discussion. The talk was quiet despite the reassuring presence of their Starlyne companions – long held habits of years inhibiting the experienced Scouts from being anything but careful while Below. She realised that she had missed a significant portion of the discussion during her bout of homesickness and self-doubt.

"So we'll break into four groups then?" asked Challon.

"Yes, when we reach the four converging tracks," replied Spiron. His face was creased in thought. "We'll make a base camp in the cave – it's easily big enough for our Starlyne friends, and Arad and Perri can set up a base camp while the rest of us divide and attempt to locate the most direct track to the Garsal base. Arad, you'll stay there because of Nosey. And Perri, you've hidden the limp well, but it's obvious you could do with a few days' rest." Perri gave a wry grin and eased her leg slightly.

"You're right, Spiron. It's fine, but the muscles are still recovering and I'd appreciate a break for a few days. Spangles and I can hunt, and Spangles can give Nosey a few pointers."

"We'll keep a look out for high ground as well. Any time we can get a couple of fliers in the air, we will. There's not a lot of scope between here and that cave, but we all need the practice, and any clues we can pick up about the Garsal are invaluable." Spiron nodded decisively, satisfied that his plan was viable. "Teacher, Fractus and Radiant, it would be advantageous to have one of you at the cave, I would think?"

"Yes. We can communicate over some distance, as you have obviously divined." Radiant's though was clear. "However, there will be a limit to that distance. If you go too far then we will be unable to hear each other. Or you."

"You mean you can 'hear' us over distance as well?" asked Ragar incredulously.

"We can hear you at some distance, but not as far as we hear each other. We will need to decide just how far each group might go before turning back. Locating a high point for our fliers must be a priority. Fractus and I will accompany two of the groups, and Teacher will remain at the cave." Spiron nodded his thanks.

"Barron will go with Shanna, Verren and Kalli. I'll go with Taya, Karri and Challon. Allad will go with Zandany and Nelson. Karri will take Sandar, Ragar and Amma. If Fractus would go with Barron's group and Radiant with Allad's, then we'll have a good mix of experience and talents. We'll leave here early tomorrow. We have two days' travelling before reaching the cave, so I'd like to make the most of the daylight hours. Normal watch schedule." He emptied the dregs out of his mug. "The rest of us need to turn in." The fire was extinguished and Shanna pushed herself slowly to her feet. Tiredly she and the two cats made their way to underneath the drooping pungo branch where Shanna had left her pack. After carefully checking the ground, Shanna rolled herself in her bedding and tucked herself into her two cats. Their purrs were soothing and she drifted off slowly to sleep.

***

The Overlord surveyed the troops arrayed for his inspection. They were smaller than the average trooper and stood neatly in a row before their small vehicles. He stalked back and forth for some minutes as they stared impassively ahead, their manipulator arms still and controlled. He motioned, and they boarded the small vehicles in pairs. He signalled to the fence controller and the red beams of light around the hive and ship winked out briefly. The four vehicles moved quickly to exit the compound, nimbly dodging around the large predators pacing around the perimeter. They bounced over the ruts left by the larger vehicles and vanished slowly into the thick greenness, followed by several of the smaller, more agile predators. The fence line blinked back into existence and the Overlord watched the last vehicle vanish into the vegetation. He stood watching until the tree limbs ceased their swaying, and the sound of their engines had been swallowed up by distance.

The aircraft frames were progressing, but the Matriarch's displeasure was niggling away at his mind. He was torn. Conquest. The opportunity for offspring. The chance to become the preeminent Overlord in this part of the galaxy. The possibility of disgrace and failure. The sun had set before he moved back inside the ship.

Chapter 15

ANJO wriggled, then wriggled again. He was still uncomfortable, so he rolled over. Right out of bed onto the hard stone floor. The impact jerked him fully awake and he opened his eyes, to come face to face with Ember. The black starcat regarded him quizzically from the bed. His eyes seemed to be saying: why on earth are you on the floor? Anjo groaned softly and levered himself to his feet. Fortunately the weeks since his rescue from the Garsal had included enough good food to put a bit of padding on his bones.

"You took all of the bed again!" he grumbled at Ember. Ember had the grace to look slightly abashed, ducking his face down under one paw before peeking out and looking up at Anjo from under his lashes. His whiskers twitched slightly and Anjo gave in, sat on the bed, and rubbed the cat's head, marvelling at the silkiness under his hand. Every time he thought he was becoming used to this planet, it turned his world upside down.

This time, his world had developed paws and whiskers, and apparently, overwhelming love. He ran his hands down Ember's coat, admiring the satiny texture of the cat's fur and the gem-toned tidemarks, flickering now in patterns of relaxation and contentment. He was unsure how he knew that that was what they meant, but he knew that he knew.

The last two days had been a flurry of new things. Anjo had initially tried to give Ember back to Josen, assuming that the cat was playing a joke. He'd seen enough of Master Cerren's Socks now to know that the big cats enjoyed pranks. Josen had smiled back at him, shaken his head, and explained that once a starcat had made a choice, that choice was final. Kaidan had backed the breeder up, and his parents had agreed with him - before suggesting that Kaidan spend the afternoon with Anjo, giving him some pointers.

Anjo was more and more grateful for those few hours. The Masters and Scouts in Scout Compound had also been helpful. Anjo now knew where to find food and a food bowl for Ember, had relocated to one of the downstairs cadet rooms so that Ember could come and go outside as he required, and had a basic understanding of the commands used to work with a starcat.

He was still getting used to sharing his bed with one. Delicata had been a beautiful world, but Anjo's experience of life had been urban. Some of his contemporaries had had pets. But he'd very quickly come to the realisation that a starcat was not a pet. No one he knew had shared their bed with a pet, and starcats apparently liked beds. And he'd not yet figured out how to get Ember to share his equally. Ember liked body contact. Lots of it. And he purred. Very loudly when he was comfortable. And he also kneaded the bed clothes.

All of this was unfamiliar to Anjo. He'd slept in many uncomfortable places as a Garsal slave and on occasion he'd huddled together with other slaves for warmth, but never before had he had to share a bed with an enormous, loving feline who insisted on being comfortable and leaning on him. And sharing the bed was only the beginning. He pushed himself up, and decided to wash and get breakfast. His stomach rumbled as he pulled on his socks and began to lace up his boots.

There was a tap at the door. When he opened it, Master Peron was waiting outside, little Thunder sitting neatly at his feet. "Anjo, walk with me to breakfast, we have a few things to discuss." Anjo nodded, called Ember, remembered to ask him to walk at heel, and walked with Peron towards the dining hall. Thunder padded neatly at the Master's heel, occasionally bouncing sideways when he spied a piece of fluff on the ground. Anjo was conscious of Ember pacing just behind him as he and Master Peron entered the dining hall. They fed their cats first then Anjo followed the tall Master to a table set slightly to one side of the room. Master Peron sat, stirred his cereal contemplatively with a spoon and took a sip of his tea. "Anjo, we'd like to place you in a class here at Scout Compound."

Anjo looked up, startled, and opened his mouth.

"Let me finish and then you can ask questions," Peron said, placing his mug back on the table. "You now have a starcat, and you will need to learn to care for him and how to continue his training. Although Ember is a readytrained cat, you are completely unfamiliar with starcats, and have no idea how to maintain what he's already learnt or how to expand it. And despite your work with Kaidan, you remain unaware of many of the simplest things that anyone on Frontier grows up knowing." He took another sip from his mug. "We think that this might be the most effective way for you to learn. At the same time, you'll learn more about Frontier than you could possibly learn anywhere else. Skills that may well keep you alive someday." He looked at Anjo, and raised his eyebrows at him. "So, what do you think?"

Anjo played with his cereal. It was some sort of porridge that was served every day. It often had chunks of dried fruit in it, and he'd become very fond of it during his stay with the Scouts. He wasn't sure what to say and uncertain about the plan. To give himself a little more time, he took a spoonful of porridge and swallowed. "I've enjoyed the sessions with Kaidan, but am I ready for a class here? I mean, are you talking about placing me with your cadets?"

"Not as a cadet as such, but with a group of students who are the children of our starcat breeders, or youngsters whose parents or grandparents are Scout Personnel. They will be younger than you but we plan to adopt the cadet program syllabus, simply stepped down a bit to their level. With the current emergency their schooling has been completely disrupted, so for those children who are residing here with their parents, we will be running classes. In our cadet program, all of our cadets take turns teaching in their areas of expertise – things their families are particularly good at, and in this you will be no different, except that you will teach the students and our cadets about the Garsal, and what it was like to live as one of their slaves. In turn, you will learn about starcats and how to properly care for one along with the skills to survive here. There will be advantages for all."

Anjo was doubtful. His sessions with Kaidan had demonstrated his ignorance of life on a rural planet very effectively, and his formal schooling had ceased when the Garsal invaded Delicata. "But Master Peron, there's every chance that I'll be so far below the standard of even the youngest student that I'll handicap them."

Peron looked at him, sympathy in his eyes. "Anjo, it will be very good for our youngsters to teach you the things they take for granted, and to help you learn what you need to know." He paused and sipped from his mug before continuing. "Of course it won't be easy, and you will have to work hard, but I'm sure that you have the ability to adapt to Frontier. Since Ember decided that he needed you, we've had a fair few discussions about the two of you." Anjo felt slightly awkward, but Peron continued. "It's not just about you – there are many advantages for the children too."

"What about Semba?" asked Anjo. He'd barely seen her since Ember had joined him.

"Semba is still very fragile, and not yet ready to learn anything more than that she is safe."

"Will I still be able to see her?"

"Of course, Anjo. Most of the instruction will take place here in the Compound and around Watchtower. Young Kaidan will continue to tutor you after classes in the subjects you are lacking most. If you are willing to do this, and have finished your breakfast, we'll outfit you appropriately and introduce you to your fellow students." Master Peron pushed his cereal bowl away and Anjo hastened to finish his last few spoonfuls, suddenly excited about the prospect of finding a real place on Frontier.

***

"So, Anjo will join the students then?" asked Erilla.

"Yes, and Kaidan, and Josen's two. I believe there will be another half dozen as well once all the recalls have occurred," replied Peron.

"And their parents are in agreement?"

"Yes, none of them are happy about the enforced move to Watchtower, so they're happy to cooperate in any way they can if their children can stay with them. The youngsters may make other profession choices when they're older, but at least during this emergency they'll be able to remain close to their families and still receive some education – unlike those who've been evacuated from Watchtower." He sighed heavily, shaking his head.

"Those are advantages, of course," said Cerren. Socks purred loudly, startling him slightly, and he looked down at her. She was resting her head on his leg and the whole limb was vibrating. "Hopefully we'll be able to assist the breeders to settle in properly, and help their cats to feel that this place is home." He sighed. "I still wish Tamazine would see reason. Since the choosing, she's been even more intractable."

Peron nodded, frowning. "I'd hoped that she'd see some kind of reason once she realised that starcats are not so easily fitted into her plans. Unfortunately she's decided that her rejection was a personal affront, and possibly a plot by the Scout Corps. Her irrationality grows by the hour."

Cerren nodded, idly stroking Socks' head. "She's more and more difficult to deal with, and few of the Councillors are willing to stand against her. Payne and I are struggling through every meeting. At the moment, even our simplest suggestions seem to find little favour with her."

The three Masters sat silently, lost in anxious thought.

***

"Anjo!" Kaidan's voice echoed down the hall as one of the exterior doors slammed. Anjo turned around, almost treading on Ember's tail as Kaidan hurried down the hall towards him. Like Anjo he was attired in a basic, unadorned cadet uniform, and he was followed by a very large, very black cat. The uniform was comfortable, but he felt slightly out of place and hoped that no one would mistake him for a proper cadet.

"Kaidan! How are you?"

" Good. Hi, Ember! So, you're going to be in the class here at Scout Compound?"

"Yes," replied Anjo. "We're meant to be starting very soon, apparently. I was just on my way. Who's your cat?" Ember and the large black cat were touching noses.

"This is Boots," replied Kaidan. "Apparently we're going to be working with starcats as part of our classes, and Dad lent me Boots." He laughed. "Actually, Boots lent himself. I think he's hoping that Satin might be around here somewhere."

"Satin? Allad's cat?" asked Anjo, puzzled.

"Yes. She's his mate, and he hasn't seen her for weeks," replied Kaidan, rubbing his hand down Boots' head. "He's missing her." As if to emphasise Kaidan's statement, Boots hummed plaintively. "She's not here, Bootsy. I keep telling you that she's somewhere Below. Probably with Shanna." Kaidan's face suddenly fell, and once again Anjo was reminded that despite his apparent maturity, Kaidan was still very young and obviously missed his sister.

"Come on," he said in an effort to distract the youngster. "We'd better get moving or we'll be late."

Kaidan nodded in agreement, and together they climbed the stairs to the first floor.

Several hours later, Anjo collapsed thankfully into the hot bathing pool in the mens' change room. Kaidan and the three other young men from his class were already reclining in the hot water. Anjo ran their names through his mind again. Jareth, the tall one and Josen's youngest; Balto, Kaidan's former archery classmate and apparently Master Yendy's son; and Hadder, who was Erilla's eldest child.

He stretched his aching muscles slightly and allowed the warmth of the water to slowly ease his discomfort. The last few hours had been a revelation. One of the retired Scouts had run the group through the expected timetable, then he'd sent the group off for two hours of written tests, followed by a physical assessment that had astounded Anjo in its depth. He'd run, jumped and climbed, and then he'd been put through a series of strength tests that had left him exhausted and trembling.

Ember and the group's other starcats had sat by the side of the arena, watching the activity with great interest. The cats had ranged in age from cubs, up to a venerable cat who had come along with one of the girls, apparently a granddaughter of one of the recalled Scouts. The old cat had sat several tiers up in the arena seating, presiding over the other cats. Even Boots had paid his respects to the oldster. If Anjo hadn't been so exhausted, he'd have been fascinated by the interactions between the different cats.

There was a sudden splash and the water in front of Anjo fountained violently. Anjo was swamped by a wave that rushed over him and splashed out of the bathing pool, puddling the dry flooring. As he spluttered and coughed and pushed his sopping hair out of his eyes to try and clear his vision, the water exploded with another two heavy splashes and Kaidan's infectious laugh.

"Anjo, you forgot to tell Ember not to hop in!"

"What?" Anjo could barely get the word past the mouthful of water.

"I suppose you didn't know and of course no one told you," Kaidan giggled. "But the cats love water! If you don't specifically tell them not to hop in, they do. And of course as soon as Ember hopped in, the little ones did too. Only Boots and Stomper stayed out. You need to tell Ember to get out, then we'll be able to get the cubs out."

Anjo stood and the water finally cleared from his eyes. Ember was happily swimming in the pool, tail trailing behind him, with the two cubs who'd come with Jareth and Balto paddling after him. He called Ember and the cat looked at him, flickering his tidemarks with enjoyment, and paddled over, swiping his soggy body heavily against Anjo. "Anjo, you have to tell him to get out," prompted Kaidan.

"Oh," replied Anjo, "Ember, out!" The cat gave him a reproachful look, but dutifully paddled over to the edge and hoisted himself out. He shook violently, spraying water everywhere. Boots grumbled slightly and backed fastidiously out of the way, and Balto and Jareth waded over to the happily swimming cubs and grabbed each of them around the belly, interrupting the happy paddling. The wriggling cubs were deposited, squirming, on the pool edge. Each shook itself, and at Boots' grumbling hum, toddled away from the edge, sat and began to wash.

"Come on, we'd better finish washing up," said Jareth. "The dining hall will be closed if we don't hurry, and I'm starving." Anjo shared a companionable smile with the three boys and passed over several soapleaves. As he lathered his hair, he contemplated the pain he'd be experiencing from his sore muscles over the next few weeks. He'd been surprised how much he'd enjoyed the company of the youngsters during the testing. They were all very accustomed to starcats and seemed to enjoy giving him pointers. Kaidan, Jareth and his two sisters, Ella and Marn were all the children of breeders. Their knowledge was extensive, and they enjoyed showing off their cats's skills. Even the other youngsters were comfortable handling their loaned starcats – obviously familiar with their parents' and grandparents' partners.

Anjo levered himself out of the steaming water reluctantly, and after dressing, the group headed off to the dining hall, starcats and cubs following or bouncing as their ages and natures allowed. Anjo's stomach rumbled vigorously as the savoury smells wafted from the dining hall, and he hurried in to sit with the other students, feeling stupidly tall in stature but short in knowledge. It also felt like coming home. Some of the grief he'd felt when losing all that he'd held dear had somehow eased during the day. As if sensing his feelings, Ember leaned into Anjo's leg, ruby tidemarks flickering gently, and his violet eyes fixed on Anjo. He felt a rush of emotion and leant down to hug the cat's warm softness to his chest. He felt a hand on his shoulder and looked up to see Kaidan looking down at him, understanding clear in his vividly blue eyes.

***

Peron, Erilla and Cerren sat at the far end of the dining hall at a table set slightly behind a partition. Their cats were reclining in a group together. Thunder had tucked himself into a ball, leaning on Nimbus, and the adult cat had a slightly resigned expression on his face. Socks was looking slightly amused.

"How did Anjo cope today?" Cerren asked Peron.

Peron smiled at the other two Scouts. "Rather well, actually. He was weak in the areas that we expected – his ability to identify animals and plants was limited and his ability to navigate was extremely rudimentary, but he scored surprisingly well in mathematics. It appears that his previous education, despite its interruption by the Garsal, was reasonably advanced."

"How did he cope with the physical testing?" asked Erilla curiously.

"He struggled, but persevered. Obviously his captivity with the Garsal has left him undernourished, but the physical labour has left him reasonably strong. He needs conditioning, but there is promise. More importantly, he and Ember are getting along well. He is knowledge poor, but not unwilling to learn." He laughed. "No one told him about starcats and water — the bathing room was a swamp after he and the three youngsters had bathed and changed. Madder looked in briefly when he heard some over vigorous splashing. Ember, followed by the cubs, had taken a flying leap." Cerren and Erilla chuckled appreciatively. "It's good to see that there is still time for enjoyment despite the gravity of the situation we find ourselves in. There has been too little of it lately."

"On a more depressing note," Cerren said. "Today's meetings with Tamazine and Starfall's council were another round of stalemates. We suggest, and they say no. Payne has managed to talk some sense into them regarding the militia deployments, but they refuse to move on this centralisation of control." Cerren's brows lowered and he tapped the table in frustration. "I fear that when the Garsal locate us and attack - something that is inevitable - if all of our resources are so easily discoverable, located as they are in one area, it may be our downfall."

"You're right," replied Erilla. "There is no flexibility in her thinking. We are relatively few. If the Garsal manage to find their way onto this plateau, our settlements will be easy to locate. If we concentrate all of our resources in our settlements, then defeating us will not be difficult."

"We're much more suited to guerrilla tactics," replied Peron. "We Scouts can easily survive outside a settlement, and most of the population in Watchtower is at least basically competent. With enough time we can prepare safe sites for small groups to take refuge in, and if we take up our Starlyne friends' offers, we can place the small children with them." He shook his head. "There's so much we could do if Tamazine and her councillors would just think." He pushed his chair back and ran his hands through his hair tiredly.

"All we can do at this point is to keep nibbling away at them," replied Cerren.

"Toman has those contingencies in hand at least," said Erilla. "They'll be a buffer of sorts. And the recall continues. We have more resources than we thought." The three Master Scouts continued their meal in silence for some time. Days of frustration were taking a heavy toll, but the Masters' mood was lightened by the laughter coming from Anjo and Kaidan's table. The sounds of happiness echoed through the dining hall as the boys recounted Ember's entry into the bathing pool and the subsequent tsunami. There was the sound of purring from the three cats next to the Masters. Thunder had woken and was sitting attentively with Nimbus and Socks.

"It helps to remember why we're doing this," Erilla said, gesturing towards the group of youngsters. "And there is still hope. The Garsal have not yet located us. And Patrol Ten and the first-years are on their way to locate the Garsal – we're not waiting passively to be overrun, but taking the first steps to ensure our safety." She pushed her chair back decisively. "We will continue and somehow, some way, we will bring reason back to the table."

Chapter 16

AFTER two days of silently moving through Below, Patrol Ten and its Starlyne allies were climbing a small rise when Satin appeared from under a particularly thick shrub, winked her tidemarks, then turned and vanished. Allad held up one hand and signalled the all clear to those behind him, then he and Shanna ducked under the shrub and followed the starcat. The vegetation was extraordinarily thick, and after carefully ducking around a barbed palm, Shanna was startled to emerge into a sunny clearing in front of a limestone cave. A small creek trickled musically out of the cave mouth, and a family of iridescent bluehawks winged up from their perch on a rock outcropping into the air above the dell. They circled several times, sun glinting off their sapphire blue wings, before gliding down into the trees.

After a glance at Allad, Shanna sent Storm into the cave to flush out any current inhabitants. Several minutes later he appeared, completely unperturbed, and returned to Shanna. Allad signalled her forward, and she pulled her glowstone out of her shirt and quietly entered the cave with Storm by her side. Despite Storm's reassurance, Shanna's heart rate increased as she stepped through the entrance. The floor was rocky, and as she held the glowstone up she could see spectacular limestone formations scattered across the cave. Once inside the cavern, she could see that the underground haven was enormous, extending back beyond the pool of light emitted by the glowstone.

Storm hummed reassuringly and paced forward, and the two of them walked further into the cave. Shanna was astounded as the light from the glowstone illuminated more and more fanciful rock features. Giant shawls of thin limestone glowed in the light, huge stalactites and stalagmites hung from the roof, or stretched upwards from the floor. Some had joined into immense columns of translucent rock that appeared to be supporting the roof.

Distracted by the spectacular rock formations, Shanna almost stumbled into the creek. Storm flickered his tidemarks in amusement and she hurriedly took her attention off the beautiful stone and put it where it belonged — making sure that none of Below's predators had decided that the cave was a suitable residence.

There was no sign of animal tracks or dung anywhere although there was an old abandoned harroth nest in one corner, but there were no signs of the toothy carnivores anywhere about, and the nest had only ancient egg shell fragments scattered around.

Finally reaching the back of the cave, Shanna and Storm circled around the perimeter. The myriad formations meant that their progress was meandering, but by the time they had circled in both directions, Shanna was happy that the cave held no lethal surprises and rejoined Allad and the rest of the group. Barron set Hunter circling around the dell, and the group began to settle into the cave for the night.

In the morning, the group assembled two kilometres from the cave where four paths of devastation met in an area of toppled trees and crushed plant life. There was a large staureg skeleton, already gnawed to stark whiteness by the lower order carnivores of the area. As the three Starlynes and their human companions moved into the devastated region, the starcats flushed a number of small beasts from the staureg skeleton. Each of the four Garsal vehicles had left an easy path to follow. The starcats slunk around the area, muted tidemarks flickering in patterns of displeasure and distaste, and Shanna was again saddened by the devastation the creatures seemed to always leave in their wake.

Spiron motioned them into a circle. "We'll divide here. Barron, your group will take the most southerly track. Allad, you'll take the track west of Barron's. Karri, you'll take the eastern one, and I'll take my group on the final one. Groups without a Starlyne will send a starcat with a message back to the cave if they locate anything significant. While Radiant and Fractus can stay in touch with Teacher, we'll use that form of communication, otherwise it's cats with messages for all of us. We'll proceed for a maximum of four days down each track, utilising the wingsuits whenever possible. After four days everyone is to return to the cave."

There were no questions. The four groups filed away, gliding through the bush near their assigned vehicle tracks. Shanna and her cats took the front at Barron's request, as the four humans and Fractus began the search for more signs of the Garsal invaders. Sending Twister leaping ahead into the trees, and Storm ranging from side to side, Shanna settled into the rhythm of a steady stride, her attention focused on moving smoothly and silently, carefully avoiding dangerous plants and ever watchful for signs of inimical wildlife or signs of the Garsal.

The first day and night were uneventful. The track made by the Garsal vehicle remained steadily southward. Halfway through the morning of the second day, a tall knoll came into view slightly south of the vehicle track. As they climbed the knoll, carefully skirting several carnivorous plants, Shanna felt her apprehension about flying rise almost uncontrollably.

On the way to the cave site, they had made several practice flights. She had returned safely and landed in a controlled fashion each time, but this would be her first solo flight Below. She asked Storm to circle the group while she offloaded her pack onto the ground. The knoll wasn't ideal, but it was the best launching point they'd seen since beginning to follow the vehicle track.

The further south they'd progressed, the more vegetative recovery they'd seen. It had been obvious that the Garsal had struggled to manoeuvre their heavy vehicle over Below's largely untouched terrain. They had already passed at least two campsites in less than two days. Each had been ringed by the bony remains of frustrated predators. They had found nothing of use to collect. Shanna wondered what those on the plateau had made of the equipment they had brought back from that first eventful contact, and whether they'd managed to extract any useful information from the fourteen Garsal who had survived the vehicle assault.

As she shook her wingsuit out of its folds, Verren hurried forward to help her. "You'll be OK, Shan," he whispered, and Shanna realised she must have let some of her worry appear on her face. She grimaced slightly and nodded. There were so many things everyone expected of her. Fading, flying, machinery stopping, weather sensing, seeing in the dark, navigating. The memory of the Starlyne's first contact, with the image of herself, Storm and Twister kept intruding on her dreams and waking thoughts. Why should she be the one that everyone believed was so special? So special she couldn't even be sure of her own abilities.

She pulled the wingsuit up and fastened it securely, then turned around so that Verren could double check everything. He finished with a pat on her shoulder and a look of sympathy on his face so plain that Shanna almost wondered if he could read her mind.

"You ready, Shan?" asked Barron. "Try and follow the vehicle track if you can — see how long it still goes south and if there are any obvious landmarks. If you can describe them well enough, Karri and I might be able to figure out exactly where they are. We've travelled Below enough times in this area, and our maps are quite detailed."

"And myself also," came Fractus' voice. "There are no Starlyne habitations in this particular area, as we have preferred to remain in the warmer, more northern reaches of this continent, but I have travelled widely. There may be some feature that you can image for me." Shanna nodded to both and perched herself on the edge of the knoll, then took a step away from the edge and turned to Barron.

"I'd like to see whether a starcat can keep up with me, Barron." She went on before the Patrol Second could interrupt. "We know they're fast, but not really how fast. And if someone had to land unexpectedly, it might be advantageous to have a cat around." Barron tapped a finger on his cheek in thought. The strongly built, dark haired Scout was not given to snap decisions.

"It is a good idea, Barron," said Fractus. "If Storm can keep up with a flyer, it would mean an amazing advantage. And Shanna is unlikely to fly out of my range today, so if need be I can call Storm back here."

Fractus could call Storm? Shanna was startled. She knew that the Starlynes could talk across some distance, but call her starcat? There was another feeling of amusement from the Starlyne. Barron looked at her thoughtfully, and then nodded.

"Any possible advantage against the Garsal must be explored. Do it, Shanna." Shanna nodded and called Storm over. He flickered his ear tips at her in eagerness, almost as if he'd known what she'd ask of him. She used a variation of her seeking command, then placed her silent whistle in her mouth. He vanished into the vegetation, and she prepared to launch herself off the knoll. She checked that there was enough room to land, relaxed deliberately and 'saw' the air currents, then simultaneously jumped and flicked her wingsuit extensions to their full length.

Shanna soared, almost lost the whistle, and clamped her teeth and lips more firmly around it. She circled in a thermal to gain height before she blew her signal to Storm. Far below, she saw the rustle of a tree top and a faint blue flicker. She smiled in relief and almost lost the whistle again. Hurriedly she checked her bearings, located the group on the knoll and turned her attention to the track below.

It snaked southward, and from her elevated position she could see that it vanished into a range of rugged hills. She followed its path, trying to memorise the shapes of some of the more unique peaks in the hope that one of the others might recognise a landmark from her description. She couldn't see Storm, but hoped that he was keeping pace with her. That blurring speed starcats could exhibit might be another advantage in their fight against the Garsal. She concentrated harder and began to glide southwards, carefully locating and catching appropriate air currents.

As she approached the range of hills, Shanna could see that there was a watercourse meandering its way around their base. It was quite wide, and the vehicle track emerged from the river at a wide spot that had apparently provided a shallow ford. The track was then seen to be following the river for some time to the east before plunging into a deep valley between two of the hills.

Shanna spent several minutes circling, trying to decide whether she could safely cross the range of hills. She was still feeling strong, and decided that she would at least try and climb to a height far enough above them to get an idea of the direction the vehicle had come from. She spotted a likely thermal and turned into it, feeling the strain in her arms and legs as she climbed rapidly. She hoped that somewhere below, Storm was nearby.

She remembered the 'feel' of her cats' presence that she always experienced when she faded, and as she spiralled higher, attempted to extend that 'feel,' pushing it away from her in the bubble she imagined when extending the fade. Abruptly she could 'feel' Storm, and, very faintly, Twister far behind her. Storm was directly below her.

A smile came involuntarily. If she could 'feel' her cats, she'd never be lost. Reassured, she climbed higher in the thermal and was suddenly above the summits of the range below. Her breath came quickly as she saw the vast expanse of Below beyond the range. A sea of endless green seemed to extend forever in all directions. As her arms and legs began to feel the strain of pushing so high, Shanna searched hurriedly for signs of the Garsal vehicle track. The temptation to soar further southwards then survey the other side of the range was very strong, but Shanna finally turned back and began to reduce her height. She was tiring, and she still needed to get back safely to her companions.

She felt for Storm, and using his location as a beacon, lost altitude. The whistle between her lips was becoming harder to hold, but she kept it there until she was just above the treetops, and signalled Storm to climb the nearest tree. There was a flash of blue and she signalled him to follow her back, homing in on Twister's presence.

An hour later, she dropped exhaustedly out of the sky onto the knoll just as Storm appeared out of the vegetation. She sat tiredly with her arms on her knees as Verren slapped an energy patch onto her arm and shoved some of the fruit concentrate into her mouth. She chewed mechanically, feeling the exhaustion fade, before standing and beginning to strip off the wingsuit.

"Where did the vehicle track go?" asked Kalli, curiously. "Fractus said that he could see the Southern Short Range in your thoughts." Shanna looked up, surprised.

"Fractus could hear me that far away?"

"Only just. He said that if you'd gone any further he would have lost your thoughts completely."

"I could see the image because you were concentrating so hard on memorising it. Shanna. With you here, I can now share the picture with Barron and Kalli, and Verren." Shanna's mind was suddenly filled with the image of the range she'd memorised so carefully. It was a very strange sensation. Deliberately, she thought back to the images of the track vanishing between the two hills, and the view from above the range. There were surprised gasps from the others as Fractus shared the images with them. Storm and Twister hummed at her, and Shanna suddenly realised that Storm was almost as tired as she had been. He sat himself at her feet and leaned heavily against her legs, and she busied herself running her hands through his soft fur to make sure that he was just tired, not injured as well.

Above her head she could hear the conversation continuing. "Definitely the Southern Short Range," Kalli's voice was confident. "You remember when we were down there last year Barron? Allad found that variant of plybrush – you know, the one with the sticky coating. Took him ages to get it off his hands."

"Yes, I do, you're right Kalli." Barron looked over at Shanna. "Is Storm OK? And do you know if he was able to follow you?"

"I think he's just extremely tired, and yes, he did follow me." As she ran her hands over Storm, Shanna related how she had used her ability to 'feel' Storm and Twister to navigate and know where Storm was.

"So it's like when we're 'feeling' our way in the darkness?" asked Verren.

Shanna nodded. "It's just like that although a lot easier, at least for me. Whether we'll all be able to do it at a distance or not, who knows? Time for some more experimenting perhaps, if we're able. Fractus, would an energy patch work for Storm too?" There was a feeling of pondering from the Starlyne as he considered Shanna's question.

"Perhaps. Try one of the fast-acting ones. There is nothing in the patches that could harm him, but I'm not sure if the small injectors will penetrate his fur. It's more likely that he'll appreciate something a bit more meaty in a short while. Perhaps Twister could oblige." There was a smile in Fractus' voice and Twister vanished immediately at Shanna's signal.

She pulled the backing off one of her fast-acting patches and looked for somewhere to put it on the furry body. Storm gave her a sceptical look and she replaced the backing and put it back in her pocket. He lay back down, and turned a sad pair of violet eyes on her. Smiling she gave in, and pulled a small piece of cheese from her pack.

"Twister will be back soon, Storm." He took the piece of cheese delicately from her hand and wolfed it down, purring in appreciation. Putting his head in her lap he closed his eyes.

"Well, I think we'll camp nearby. It's early, but we need to plan – it's another two days' travel to the range, which will take us to our four-day limit." Barron quickly detailed Verren and Kalli to locate a suitable campsite, while he and Hunter foraged. Fractus remained on watch with Shanna while they waited for Twister to return with a suitable food offering for Storm. Shanna was suspicious that Storm was sneakily playing his tiredness up slightly, in order to receive a little more attention. As if sensing her thoughts, he snuggled a little more into her lap, rolled onto his back and opened one eye to look lovingly up at her. She scratched his cheek and his eyelid slowly lowered.

The next morning, the group began the trek southwards towards the range. They had spent some time discussing their prospective route. Barron had finally decided that taking a direct route to the point where the Garsal vehicle entered the range would be more profitable. The lack of any debris at any Garsal campsite so far surveyed suggested that there would be little value in following the vehicle track closely, when their main objective was to locate the Garsal ship. Storm had recovered completely after Twister's provision of a pair of marmals, and was pacing beside her as she sent Twister out in front of their small group.

She practiced 'feeling' her cat, and those of her fellow Scouts. It was strange to be doing so in broad daylight, but in the end Shanna decided it was simply an extension of the ability that allowed her to see air currents or find her way amongst the vegetation in complete darkness. It would take more practice though. She was able to 'feel' her own cats easily, but those of others were more difficult to keep track of. For some reason though, when she faded herself it was easier to 'feel' everything.

Barron's route took them as directly as possible to a river crossing known to himself and Kalli from previous explorations Below. He estimated that travelling by the most direct route would take only one of their two days, and give them the opportunity to explore the route taken through the valley between the two hills. Few patrols had gone beyond the Southern Short Range, and the last time that Patrol Ten had ventured in that direction had been several years previous. Barron had explained that the Patrol had been on a mapping and survey mission, attempting to map the course of the river along with possible fords or places to construct bridges in the future, should the human population attempt to expand off the plateau.

Once again, Shanna was struck by the forward planning of the Scout Patrol. Not only were they astoundingly organised and skilled, but were planning for a day when the human population of Frontier could expand its horizons. That is, she amended drily to herself, *if we can get past the threat of an invading alien species that has already conquered the entire known galaxy.*

Gliding forward, she asked Storm to range around the group and sent Twister up into the canopy ahead. There were still hours of travel to get through before the river crossing, and the group needed to make good time. Shanna was conscious of the ever present need to locate the Garsal ship. She hoped and prayed that there would be no setbacks to their travel. Fractus' presence appeared to be effective in keeping the larger predators at bay, but she wondered what might happen should a slider swarm eventuate, or another tornado serpent appear. She carefully avoided a cluster of spikeblooms and followed Storm's path through a small grove of pungo trees.

***

The four small Garsal vehicles with their tracks, wheels and extensible servo arms, proved adept at manoeuvring through the verdant greenness of the planet. The eight Garsal troopers travelled in a convoy following the tracks left by the larger vehicles, easily evading the larger carnivores and moving quickly through the ruts that marred the area around the hive site and ship. When the sun began to lower, the smaller vehicles tucked themselves into a rocky niche to provide security for the night, and the Senior Trooper initiated communication with the colony ship.

"We have made good progress. As expected, the climbers are much more efficient in this terrain. Please notify the--" The vehicle shuddered violently and roaring sounds reverberated through the metal walls. The Senior Trooper hastily dropped the communicator. "Tell the ship that I will resume contact shortly." He left the cockpit hurriedly. The sound of weapon pulses began to colour the air. Several hours later, he finally completed his report.

"One of our vehicles is severely damaged. We will abandon it here and proceed with the other three. We have one fatality – a trooper perished when he brushed against an innocuous looking plant. It has poisonous barbs. I am forwarding an image to you." He hesitated slightly. "We have disposed of the body and the other trooper joins my vehicle."

The Overlord spoke, overtones of displeasure evident in his voice. "You will ensure the other vehicles are well protected each night. Our resources are not endless."

"Yes, Overlord. We will separate as planned, following the crawler tracks. I will take the most northerly track myself."

"You will locate a route onto that plateau." The Overlord's tone was flat.

"I will, Overlord. We will leave at first light." The Senior Trooper hurried to placate the Overlord. The thought of a successful mission spurred him on. It might mean the chance of offspring, or at the very least an audience with the Matriarch.

Chapter 17

SHANNA peered carefully over the edge of the rocks surrounding the valley mouth. The previous day's travel had brought them over the river with plenty of daylight left, so Barron had pushed as far as possible towards the foot of the range. An hour's journey from their campsite had brought them to the cleft between the hills. The vehicle tracks were clearly visible, but again Frontier's resilient vegetation was beginning to re-establish itself. The valley was extremely narrow, more of a gorge than a valley. The sides shot steeply upwards, and the rock walls were dotted with small trees whose roots clawed footholds into the bare stone. It was dim and there were signs that a variety of Below's predators used the gorge as a thoroughfare along the creek that pooled into waterholes along its length.

At Barron's nod, she sent both Twister and Storm into the gorge, watching their tidemarks fade silently into the green of the dense undergrowth. Several soothall berry bushes were scattered to one side of the dark slot, and Shanna carefully marked their locations on her map as she crouched behind the rocky facade. Beside her, Kalli signalled to Flyer to continue his sweeps around the group, while Verren sent Cirrus up to a rocky perch above them. Fractus coiled his length into a surprisingly compact space and dimmed his tidemarks. He blended quietly into the background. The group settled in to wait for Storm and Twister to return.

Shanna found herself musing on the trip. It came as a surprise to realise she now felt comfortable navigating Below, and no longer doubted her ability to find her way back to the plateau. The bond with her two cats seemed to become stronger every day. Even now if she concentrated, she could 'feel' their presence ahead, moving rapidly towards the bottom of the gorge at the blurring speed that starcats preferred when they travelled alone. She wondered just how fast a starcat could move when urgency required it. Certainly they were much faster than a human being. Idly, she wondered if anyone had actually measured starcat speed.

Her thoughts drifted as she waited. She could hear the sounds of Below, and rather than finding them threatening, she found them reassuring. Even the sudden cry from a spikebill relaxed her, when once, not understanding the sound, she would have felt a sudden racing of her heart. Now she knew that the spikebill was simply calling its chicks home. The wailing sound was their homing signal, not the danger alarm it sounded like. The normal clicks, whistles and rustles signalled that there were no sliders, tornado serpents, or indeed Garsal, in the vicinity.

As she waited for her cats to return, Shanna ran her mind over her companions. Barron reminded her of Allad more every day. He was competent and steadfast. Hunter, his cat, seemed to reflect the same qualities, and her two cats accorded him significant respect. On the other hand, Kalli's ability to move unseen through the bush was enviable, and Flyer complemented her perfectly. She had alternated with Shanna at the front of the group, moving easily and silently from cover to cover, and she had an uncanny ability to spot potential danger. It was while watching Kalli deal with a harroth just that day that Shanna had realised how much she still had to learn. If at the end of her period as a cadet she ended up with just half the skills Kalli had so calmly demonstrated, Shanna didn't think anyone would fault her.

There was no question that Fractus was intriguing. He reminded Shanna of Keeper in many ways. She sensed that he was younger than Keeper, but he seemed to hold a slightly unusual place in the Starlyne hierarchy. The other Starlynes held him in respect and sometimes there had even been a sense of awe when he entered the room. She wondered what it was that set him apart. Storm and Twister adored him, taking every opportunity to rub against his glowing sides. She wondered at the way he moved through the vegetation. It was hard to believe that such a large creature could move so silently, leaving so little indication of his presence. No wonder the human settlers of Frontier had regarded the Starlyne as rare and wondrous creatures when they had first seen them.

And Verren, presently sitting quietly behind Shanna. He was perched on a rock and sitting so still that he had almost faded into the background. His caring nature warmed her and everyone around him. She found herself remembering the last time that Cirrus had leapt into his arms and flattened him, and her lips twitched slightly.

She let herself 'feel' for her cats again. She could tell that they were heading back towards the group, and dropped back towards Barron. "They're on their way back, shouldn't be long now." He nodded and she glided back to the rocky cover. Storm appeared from the gorge, a collection of vegetation in his mouth, and she looked behind him for Twister. She could tell he was close, but he didn't appear. Storm started up the rocky slope towards her, and her heart nearly popped out of her chest with a thud when Twister's head appeared, upside down directly in front of her. He was hanging from the tree above, and his indigo tidemarks twinkled with amusement as she started. "Twister!" she gasped, shaking a finger at him.

There was a muffled snort from Kalli beside her, then Storm was dropping his mouthful of twigs at her feet. Twister dropped out of the tree and sat at her feet. She could have sworn he was laughing. She felt a sense of amusement from Fractus, and as she sorted through the vegetation she saw amused smiles on both Verren and Barron's faces. "If they're playing jokes, I'd say that the halfway point of the gorge looks to be safe," Barron said quietly.

"And there's water, three different types of nut trees, and two tuber plants," replied Shanna. She raised an eyebrow at Barron. "How far down do you think we should go? There are a lot of tracks going down there. It's obviously fine at the moment, but what will happen at night?"

The stocky Scout fingered the selection of vegetation that Storm had brought back and pondered. "We'll travel until mid-afternoon. Fractus, can you still contact Radiant and Teacher?"

"Yes, just," replied the Starlyne. "But I'm likely to lose touch when I'm surrounded by the rock walls of the gorge."

"Let them know what we're about and see where they're up to, and then we'll go through. If we find a likely spot by mid-afternoon we'll stop there and spend the night. If there's nowhere safe enough to camp, then we'll come out again and make for where we were last night. I'm hopeful that we'll find something concrete to report, or that one of the others has. Otherwise, we'll be faced with the decision of continuing in our small groups, or concentrating on one path only." He sighed. "I'd really hoped to know a little more by this stage." There were nods of agreement around the group.

"Do you think we'll make it through the gorge today?" asked Verren. "Perhaps Shan will be able to find a spot on the other side to launch from and see a little further ahead."

"It's possible," Barron said. "It's rare that we go much further than this range. I believe a couple of the other Patrols have explored the Eastern end of it, but it's quite extensive, so we've concentrated our efforts on the country on this side." He motioned to the group. "Let's move. Kalli you take the point, let Shanna have a break for a while."

They moved off, and the vegetation swallowed them almost immediately. The light dimmed, reduced by the towering stone walls and the thick undergrowth. Kalli guided them to one side of the gorge, staying several metres from the deep wheel ruts left by the alien vehicle, hugging the rock wall where possible and skirting the barbed palms that seemed to flourish in the partial twilight. The floor of gorge stayed relatively flat and after thirty minutes of careful gliding, Shanna began to hear the splashing sounds of a waterfall somewhere faintly in the distance ahead. Storm and Twister were moving easily, and she concentrated on avoiding loose rocks and dry, crackling twigs.

Two hours of travel later, and the group paused at the foot of an astounding waterfall. It plummeted from an unseen source far above, into a deep bowl pool. The gorge had suddenly widened, and a patch of sunlight illuminated the spray misting the air above the water thundering into the pool. The area was pristine. The Garsal vehicle had hugged the other side of the gorge where the going was easy, while the Scouts, unhampered by wheels and heavy metal, had climbed over the uneven, broken ground and ghosted their way through the thick trees that surrounded the bottom of the waterfall. Ferns crowded around the pool and dripped from the rock walls, and a grove of nut trees flourished to one side.

The starcats spread out in a circle around their human friends as they stood, stunned by the majesty of the spot. "Imagine this place in a cyclone," whispered Verren in a hushed voice.

"Imagining would be the only thing to do, I'd say," replied Kalli. "The water would be thundering down from above and funnelling through here as well. Look at the debris lines." She gestured above, and Shanna saw that there were piles of storm debris ten metres above them, caught on protrusions and stuck on the trees clinging to the walls.

"I wonder how this all survives so well, when it must flood several times a year," wondered Shanna.

"The nuts are scoopers," replied Kalli, "you don't see many of them on the plateau, because they need so much water." She strode quickly to the nearest nut tree, pulled several nuts off them, and showed Verren and Shanna. "See, you pull off the outer casing, then carefully cut this end off." She pulled out her knife and sliced the top of the nut off, just as she'd remove the top of a boiled egg. Inside, they could all see the juicy purple interior. "Then you can scoop out the soft part." She deftly ran her knife around the nut and popped the jelly-like interior out intact. "Taste it." She cut it into two glistening halves. Verren took one and Shanna the other. Shanna tentatively nibbled the purple softness, then as a rush of sweetness rolled over her tongue popped the rest into her mouth.

"Mmm," Verren's voice indicated his approval, and Shanna nodded her agreement.

"And then you run your knife just under the skin and pull out the firmer flesh." She demonstrated, and a hollow sphere of whiter flesh, fading to pink where the juicy part had sat, popped into her palm. She divided it again, and gave each cadet a half. Shanna had no hesitation this time. She popped the half sphere into her mouth and chewed. The firm flesh crunched pleasingly, and its sweet nutty flavour spread throughout her mouth.

"It's delicious!" she mumbled through her mouthful.

"It is!" replied Kalli with a smile. "But two or three is enough, or you'll spend the rest of the day squatting behind a tree." She dropped the empty skin, handed Barron and Fractus a nut each, then began to shell one for herself. "This is a good spot to mark, Barron. I think there are caves closer to the waterfall, and it looks like there's a few pungos over there." Barron nodded and pulled out his map.

Shanna realised that the Starlyne was suddenly absent from the group, and looked around puzzled to see him amongst the scooper nut trees, harvesting a large bounty. She caught his amused glance. "We Starlyne do not have the same digestive issues that you humans have. And we consider these nuts a delicacy – we call them paradise nuts! The dried rations are good, but a belly of nuts is much better!" He tucked the nuts into the large pouch he carried around his neck. He sounded smug to Shanna, and she giggled slightly before turning her attention back to Barron.

Three hours later after a steep climb, they exited the gorge. It had gradually widened as they moved further south, and the Garsal vehicle track had
begun to meander from side to side as the vehicle had sought the easiest path.
There was an obvious campsite tucked into a rocky niche in the western wall
that again had been empty of useful debris, and they had decided to see
whether the southern end of the gorge would provide Shanna with a perch
from which to fly.

As Shanna approached the top of the rise, she sent Storm ahead to survey
the countryside before dropping to her belly and beginning to crawl. Her hair
itched, and she really wanted a bath. The last few hours had been hot, sweaty,
and constantly upwards. Twister, crawling just in front, was unworried, and
she concentrated, signalled him, then faded before popping her head over the
summit. And almost gasped. The gorge through the range had exited at the
top of a long slope down to the plain below. The countryside she'd seen
spread out when she had been gliding above the range stretched for kilometres in front of her, broken here and there by knolls and steep sided hills
seemingly popping out of nowhere. It was very different to the terrain north
of the range. The vegetation seemed similar, but the land forms were star-
tlingly different.

Directly in front of her, further down the slope, she could see a line of
frondan trees neatly marking what was probably a watercourse. Storm returned, ducking his head against her and appearing completely relaxed. He
dropped a selection of vegetation in front of her including, she noted, a
frondan twig. She ran her hands over him in appreciation, and the big cat
purred. Dropping below the skyline she moved back to re-join the group.

"So, is it high enough to use as a launch platform, Shanna ?" Barron asked
after she had reported on what she had seen. Shanna took her time answering,
weighing up a number of variables. She was tired, and the sun was low in the
sky. Already the spot they were standing in was darkening prematurely, closed
in as it was by the rock walls to either side.

"I could, but it would have to be a short flight. I'm pretty tired already,
and there's not a lot of light left. I'd rather try for an hour or so in the morning – leave at dawn and then fly for an hour. The elevation's pretty good, so I
should be able to fly and see a fair way, and then maybe we'll have something
else to report." Barron tapped his chin thoughtfully with one finger tip.

"We should have no trouble making it back to the cave within four days if
we're not stopping to fly on the way, so an hour or two in the morning is more
likely to yield results than rushing tonight, particularly if you're tired. Let's
spend the next hour or two locating a decent spot for the night and surveying
the immediate area. If it turns out that this is the quickest way to the ship, then
knowing the terrain might be the difference between making it home or not."

He directed the group to fan out as they came over the top of the rise,
cautioned the cadets against touching anything they were unfamiliar with, and

asked Shanna to fade the entire group. She obliged, extending her 'bubble' around them as her faded cats slipped into the bush below them. Again she was awed by the scope of the land, extending as far as she could see to the south, east and west. As they followed the cats into the protection offered by the vegetation, Shanna allowed her 'bubble' to collapse and concentrated on ensuring that she gave a wide berth to any unfamiliar plants, noting their location mentally so that she could point them out to either Barron, Kalli, or Fractus later.

The following morning, Shanna watched an edge of gold glimmer on the horizon as the sun prepared to rise. A low grey haze fogged into golden fluff as the sun inched its way upwards. She perched on an outcropping to the west of the gorge mouth. She detailed Twister to follow her and flung herself into the air. Catching a thermal, she spiralled upwards as fast as she could then arrowed south along the line of the vehicle track. She could see the toppled trees marking the path the vehicle had taken, and was able to see that the track continued almost due south. She swooped into another air current, almost flying by instinct now, and extended her senses to locate her two cats. Storm was stationary, north of her, and she could feel Twister blurring with speed almost directly below.

She checked the angle of the sunlight and drove herself to more speed, hoping yet dreading to see the end of the track and the Garsal ship. She wondered what it might look like. Her mind imagined all kinds of spiky protrusions and a matt-black hull, squatting hunched and possessive on the ground amongst the devastation of its landing, and she mentally smiled at the stereotyped image in her mind.

There was a lull in her smooth flight, and she dropped like a stone. Frantically Shanna tried to regain her sense of the air currents, shoving her panic down as the air whistled past her face. She finally regained control of her flight, arms and legs trembling, and swooped into a climb, scanning the air around her. She realised that she'd become so preoccupied with thoughts of the Garsal ship that she'd neglected to keep an eye on the weather conditions. The grey haze on the horizon had solidified into a pile of towering, dark grey clouds, and as she concentrated, her weather sense began to prickle. She hastily checked the clouds and took another look below her. She could feel Twister pacing her still, and Storm's presence to the north. The scar through the vegetation seemed to go on as far as she could see. She was certain that there was nothing like a Garsal ship evident for at least two or three days' walk. After another glance at the rapidly piling clouds she decided to return to the others, signalling Twister with her whistle and gliding in a wide turn, scanning the ground for any extra signs of the Garsal. There was nothing, so she arrowed north as fast as she was able. This time she focused her whole attention on flying, mindful that there might be some more unpredictable air pockets.

***

The small nimble Garsal troop carrier climbed one last rise onto the top of a small knoll. After several days of hard travel, the troop carrier had suffered quite a bit of damage. Since separating from the other two vehicles, they had struggled to find safe havens each night. The outside was scarred and dented, and the Senior Trooper knew that they needed to stop for repairs in the next few hours. His major concern was to find somewhere safe enough to stop. It seemed that there were few safe places on this planet. Each day brought a new predator prowling around or attacking the vehicle, or another piece of vegetation with spines, or spikes, or marauding tentacles. He surveyed the terrain ahead and noticed the clouds on the horizon to the east. They were large and menacing, and growing by the second. He remembered the titanic storms that had rocked the ship and looked ahead with growing uneasiness. There were several rocky outcroppings slightly off their projected track, and he decided to plot a course for them, hoping to find a safe hollow in which they might secrete themselves for the duration of the bad weather. Far ahead, he noted a large bird wheeling a wide arc in the sky.

***

Shanna glided around into the wind and settled lightly to the ground where the others waited. "No sign of the ship or anything else," she reported. "But the weather looks like it's worsening in a big hurry." There were murmurs of agreement.

"It isn't a cyclone," stated Fractus. "But I think there will be a lot of rain. We will not be able to return through the gorge."

Barron shook his head. "We'll be late returning to the others, but there's nothing to be done about it. Amma's group is probably already on its way back, but Fractus is still unable to make contact with either Radiant or Teacher, so they may worry. Hopefully they'll realise that the weather is the reason for our delay though. We'll need to locate some kind of shelter away from the gorge."

Ever wary of the weather, the small group began to trek obliquely down the slope, angling slightly eastward as they glided from one piece of cover to the next. There had been few marauding predators on their travels. The Starlyne's presence had kept them at a distance, but there were still many dangerous plants to avoid and Shanna was sure that nothing would keep a slider swarm at bay.

An hour later, as the first fat drops began to fall, the group tucked themselves into a shallow hollow underneath an overhang. It was high enough to keep them out of any flowing water, but not as good as a dry cave. Verren was seated towards the front of the hollow with Cirrus keeping a steady watch outwards. Fractus had coiled himself into as small a space as possible, and the others were compressed together trying to stay as dry as possible. Shanna carefully tended a small, smokeless fire, feeding it judiciously from dry wood hurriedly stowed at the very back of the hollow.

The rain escalated rapidly into a heavy downpour, and the clouds darkened the sky into a kind of twilight. The starcats tucked themselves into dry niches, as comfortable as only cats could be under the circumstances. Their tidemarks glowed softly, adding to the illumination generated by the fire as Barron turned from looking out over the dripping foliage of the trees below the hollow. The panorama vanished into invisibility as the rain grew even more heavy.

"We'll be in for a long wait," came Fractus' voice. "I think the rain will remain heavy for most of the day." Storm and Twister rose and joined Shanna near the fire, watching with eager eyes as she placed the billy carefully over the heat. Earlier, they'd each brought in a large greyfowl - a plump, tasty game bird - which Shanna had plucked and then wrapped in tuber leaves. She shovelled a pile of coals over them, and sat back with the others to wait out the rain. Her two cats took the opportunity to snuggle closer to her and she ran her hands lovingly across their soft heads, and began to think about what might happen when they finally located the Garsal. The emotional roller coaster ride began again.

***

From his seat inside the vehicle, the Senior trooper watched the water cascade down the windows. Thunder rumbled and rolled, and the rocky walls had sheets of water pouring down them. He and the other two troopers had finally managed to erect the portable barrier to enclose the vehicle in a triangle of safety formed by two angular rock walls and the fence. There was a variety of unfamiliar flora inside the triangle, but the three Garsal were content to sit inside the vehicle and wait for the rain to stop. The Senior trooper took the opportunity to report in some detail to the colony ship, before beginning to plan how to perform the maintenance required by the vehicle if the weather didn't improve. He pulled up the partial log that had been transmitted by the original vehicle and began to study it in some detail, planning how he might avoid the pitfalls experienced by the overly arrogant vehicle commander.

***

In the cave four days to the north, Teacher prowled in circles while Arad and Perri watched Nosey bounce around the cave, hiding behind stalagmites and leaping out to chase imaginary playmates around and through the cave formations.

"Still no word from Fractus," came Teacher's thought, overlaid with a small tinge of anxiety.

"They're probably just holed up waiting for the weather to ease." Arad indicated the rain pouring down outside the cave. Spangles sat patiently on guard at the entrance, carefully out of range of the flowing water.

"Radiant says that they're only three days out, but they're waiting for the rain to stop. Their track seemed to be heading for the eastern end of the Southern Short Range. No sign of the ship," said Teacher. She was unusually perturbed and kept circling around the cave, demonstrating the first sign of impatience that the humans had seen from the normally composed Starlyne.

"Why are you so worried?" asked Perri, easing her leg out in front of her, and propping it up on a convenient flat rock. She bent forward to stretch the muscles.

The Starlyne's thought was muddled. "Fractus said they were entering a deep gorge in the Southern Short Range. I'm concerned that this rain might cut them off. He anticipated regaining contact with me tomorrow, but if there's a range in the way contact may be impossible."

"Well there's nothing we can do about it for the moment," Arad said calmly, indicating the grey sheet of rain. "We'll just have to sit tight here until the weather settles."

***

Barron surveyed the downpour sourly. "I'm worried that the gorge we came through will be flooded for a few days. If the rain continues overnight as I expect, then there's no question we'll be stuck on this side of the range for a while." He picked up another piece of roast greyfowl. "What's your weather sense telling you Shanna?"

Shanna pondered for some moments, listening to the rain as she tried to extend her senses as she'd seen Amma do. Fractus had told them all that the ability to detect the weather patterns was similar to that that allowed them to fly. Shanna hoped that it had nothing to do with the ability to land.

"It's hard to tell, I'm nowhere near as good at this as Amma is, but I think you're right, Barron. I think the rain will continue for at least the night, and possibly tomorrow as well. Anyone else feel any different?" She looked around the group. There were shaken heads, and a sense of agreement from Fractus.

"In that case," said Barron, "I think we can plan on being stuck on this side of the range for up to three or four days. You've tried to contact the others again, Fractus?"

"Yes," came the Starlyne's voice. "It's too far with the range in between us."

"So what do we do?" asked Verren.

"The others will figure out what's happened," replied Kalli. "When the rain settles, I'd suggest we continue to explore south for at least another day."

"I agree,"Barron replied. "Our message got through before the storm, so the others will understand why we can't send a cat. Even for them, going up and over the range is too far." He stared at the coals of the fire for a few minutes. Shanna savoured the last juicy mouthful of her greyfowl, before licking her fingers appreciatively. It had been a long day, and she'd been very hungry. She was still tired from flying, and looked forward to getting a few hours sleep before her watch.

"We're going to be stuck on this side for at least two days, possibly four, so we'll plan on one or two days of exploration along the vehicle track. Shan, did you see anywhere ahead that you might be able to launch off?"

"Perhaps," Shanna replied. "But I think they might be too far to reach in the time we have."

"We'll just see how we go then," Barron said. "At the very least, we can survey the flora and fauna in the immediate area. You never know, maybe the Garsal have left some clues for us." He held out his cup for some tea. "Normal watches tonight."

An hour later, Shanna curled herself up in her bedding with a sigh of relief. Storm tucked himself in on one side, and with Twister on the other their warm comfort quickly lulled her to sleep.

Chapter 18

THE rain finally stopped at the end of the following day, although it was almost dark before the deluge reduced to a misty sprinkle. From their shelter beneath the overhang, the four humans sat huddled around the glowing embers of their fire while Fractus took the watch. Shanna always enjoyed watching Fractus at these times; he became so still and quiet that he almost appeared to merge into the rock.

Slightly west of them was the entrance to the gorge, and from its depths the thundering rush of water could be heard. For Shanna, the wait until the rain had eased had seemed much longer than it actually had been, and with nothing to do she had had too much time to think. Much of the time she'd spent worrying about her family, wondering how they were, what Kaidan might be up to, and how her parents were coping. It seemed such a long time since she'd last seen them. As she'd sat on watch with Storm and Twister, watching the grey sky blend into the grey rain, she'd been hard pressed to push back the tears that threatened to flood her eyes. Her eyes had felt hot and full, and her throat ached. She'd remained facing outwards, staring resolutely into the watery day, while her emotions pushed unbearably at her.

Storm and Twister had sensed her distress, and had taken turns to tuck themselves under her arms. Their warm love had allowed her to regain her self-possession. Then the fear of the unknown had struck. What on earth was she doing, trekking through an unknown area of Below in search of an alien ship? She imagined her cats injured or killed by the Garsal, her friends vanishing one by one as the alien marauders attacked them, and she worried that she would be found wanting when they finally located the ship. They had talked quietly when not on watch, but the constant rain had seemed to affect them all, and the mood was sombre and quieter than normal. The enforced idleness in a time of need was frustrating, and Shanna was very glad when the rain lessened and the prospect of doing something – anything – was a reality again.

Barron laid out the plan of travel for the next day – a solid day's travel southward, paralleling the Garsal track, while keeping an eye out for something high enough for Shanna to launch from. They sent their cats out to hunt in pairs, and with Cirrus providing a pair of marmals for roasting, the group made a good meal. "If we're to make as much time as possible, we'll need to work hard tomorrow," said Barron. "But a day and a half's rest isn't a bad thing really. We'll move faster and be more alert."

"I wonder just how far we'll end up going," mused Verren. He took another piece of marmal and chewed contemplatively.

"Who knows, really," replied Kalli. "Normally when we're Below, we spend most of our time exploring thoroughly, so that we have a really good idea of the terrain and its flora and fauna. There's not usually a lot of time spent travelling in direct lines." She grinned suddenly. "At least we've finally gone beyond the range. I've wanted to do that for years!"

"Pity we don't have time for a proper look, though," said Barron, "I've already seen several variations on the standard vegetation." Hunter purred appreciatively and nudged his hand. Shanna had slowly realised that although all of the Scouts had an encyclopaedic knowledge of plants and animals, most of them were experts in one or two fields. Barron had proved to be fond of discovering and recording new plant species.

She'd seen his field journal, full of finely drawn pictures of plants and seeds, along with descriptions of their habitats and companion plants. It was a fascinating insight into Spiron's Patrol second. At their first meeting, Shanna would never have believed the strong, decisive and competent Scout had an artist's flair with a pencil, or a love of plants and trees for that matter. While they'd been camped, she'd seen him carefully notating in his field journal, concentrating on the fine details of some of the carefully saved pieces of vegetation that the cats had brought to him.

"And of course, there's our small problem of locating a dangerous alien species," said Verren. "Without being located ourselves, or stumbling onto some previously unknown predator or plant, or becoming completely stuck on this side of the range." He rolled his eyes and made a face, and Shanna joined in the quiet amusement. It made her feel a little better to know that her companions were just as apprehensive as herself.

The next morning dawned clear and fresh. There were no clouds to be seen, and Shanna's weather sense remained quiet. The thundering from the gorge was now titanic, and Shanna wondered just how much water was flowing down the chasm. There was substantial run-off from the surrounding hills trickling in transient cascades around the group as they began their trek, carefully moving through the sopping bush, trying to remain as dry as possible while still moving safely and as fast as possible.

***

The Senior Trooper surveyed his vehicle. It was dented and scratched in places, and there were a number of repairs needed before he would be able to leave the safe spot. He signalled to one of the others to operate the climbing and manipulating arms, and hurried back into the vehicle. A moment later, the climbing arms extruded themselves from the vehicle's undercarriage and lifted it off its combined wheels and tracks.

At the Senior Trooper's signal, the vehicle pivoted and sidestepped on its arms, allowing him to inspect the underside. The repairs beneath were not as extensive as he'd first believed. It would be only a few hours until they were able to get underway. He signalled again, and the vehicle lowered itself until the underside was easily accessible. A few curt sentences, and the other trooper began the repair job, carefully skirting one of the spiky plants they'd learned were deadly.

Striding to the fence line, the Senior Trooper looked northwards. A day's travel and they would be at the barrier range. The logs from the original expedition indicated that they had located a deep pass between the tall hills. He expected that it would be flooded by now. No matter. He dismissed the pass as an option. Climbing the range would be good practice if they were to scale the plateau. The original vehicles had lacked climbing arms. His did not. Even if he was unable to locate an easy wheeled access up onto the plateau, there would be no problems. They would simply climb. The range ahead beckoned and the thought of his introduction to the Matriarch, as the first to bring reliable intelligence from the plateau, made his thoughts even sweeter.

***

Travelling after the rain had been relatively smooth, but very soggy. Shanna, Twister and Storm peered out from behind a fan palm, its huge size dwarfing them, at a herd of weldens. They'd seen a number of such herds over the course of the day. She signalled back to the others, and the group halted as the herd slowly grazed its way past them. Shanna was about to move out of concealment, when Twister and Storm suddenly tensed and the leading welden threw its head up. She sent Storm ahead and signalling to the others to drop back, held herself to absolute stillness. She considered fading, but decided that the fan palm was cover enough.

Twister hummed quietly at her, and she signalled for him to sweep around the rear of the welden herd. He vanished silently and she squatted behind the huge fan-like leaf, carefully parting the fronds in front of her to look ahead. There was the sound of snapping vegetation and the welden herd stampeded frantically away. Twister reappeared by her side and urged her further into the cover afforded by the palm. She signalled silently with one hand behind her, and waited to see what was coming. A spiky nightmare shouldered its way through the trees to her left. The two metre high quadruped was covered in dark quills and armoured in spiky plates down each of its legs. Its small head swung from side to side as it scented the air with its protruding and flexible nose. This much larger relative of the cavechidna was rarely seen on the plateau. Shanna had only seen drawings and pictures of the sharpback, but she knew that they tracked and hunted by scent. She hoped fervently that the pungo leaves she'd rubbed on herself earlier in the day were still pungent enough to hide her human smell from the creature.

This was one of the first larger creatures that had approached them since they had begun travelling with their Starlyne companions. Shanna wondered why the sharpback didn't shy away, as many of the other predators had when they were on the other side of the ranges. She thought a query towards Fractus. "Our influence is small here," came the reply, "Closer to our habitats, the creatures of Below know not to tangle with us. They have been conditioned over many years. We rarely venture this far south. These creatures will have little or no knowledge of myself or any other Starlyne. I have long wondered how far our influence extends. Now I know." His tone was wry. "We will need to be even more careful now."

The sharpback stalked past Shanna, almost close enough for her to reach out and touch one of its huge quills. There was a panicked rustle ahead of it and she caught a glimpse of blue tidemarks through the trees. Two weldens appeared, saw the sharpback, and vanished as fast as they could move. The sharpback uttered a snorting grunt and thundered after them, its quills raised in an offensive posture. As the creatures vanished, Storm reappeared looking inordinately pleased with himself, almost dusting his paws as he strolled nonchalantly towards Shanna. She extended her hand to him, suppressing a giggle at his expression and rubbed his head appreciatively, before returning her attention back to where it should have been - locating a safe path forward for the group.

As she ducked under the palm frond, the tree branches above rustled in a brief breeze, raining drops down onto Shanna. She sent Twister sweeping forward and wiped the water out of her eyes, feeling the drops seep coldly down her collar.

So far the half day of walking had shown no signs of any Garsal presence, exactly as Shanna's earlier flight had suggested. Each of them had carefully noted their travel direction and distance in their field logs, so much more important now that they were heading into relatively unknown territory. Shanna felt reassured that Verren with his now unerring sense of direction was part of her group. The dark haired cadet had become more and more confident with his ability to always know where he was, in relation to places he'd been. It was a pity, she thought, that he was unable to know what was ahead, before dismissing the thought as ridiculous.

She followed her two cats as they padded noiselessly ahead, keeping the Garsal track just to their west. According to Barron's plan, they needed to head a bit further west shortly so that she could scope out one of the abutments she'd spied from the air on her previous flight. She hoped that this time she might be able to see something that would give them a clue to the location of the Garsal ship.

***

The Senior Trooper ordered the vehicle to drop back onto its wheels and tracks. The climber arms lowered it and then retracted, slotting neatly into their protective sheaths. The repairs had gone well. The trooper stowed the last few pieces of fencing, then swung into the cab as a large reptilian predator, realising that the laser fencing was down, began to stalk towards the vehicle. The vehicle roared into life and the driver swung it expertly around the oncoming predator and out of its rocky niche.

"Follow a path back east towards the original track, then after we strike the track be on the lookout for a likely route up the range." The other trooper acquiesced and directed the vehicle along the indicated route.

***

Verren dropped from the last branch of the tree onto the ground. "We need to head that way," he said, pointing with his hand. "There's a tall rock face that should be high enough." Shanna, along with the others, took a bearing on his indicated direction and noted it carefully. Although Verren would be able to unerringly retrace their steps, there was always the possibility of becoming separated from the group.

At some point, Shanna's field journal would become part of the greater depository kept in the archives at Scout Compound. From the exploratory journals, master mapmakers would then carefully construct new additions to the maps of Frontier. Each time she made a notation in her field journal she had a sense of satisfaction. Even though she was hunting for an alien ship, she was still doing what a Scout was meant to do. She was extending their knowledge of Frontier and preparing for the future of her people. She firmly ignored the nagging thought that they might not have a future.

Kalli took the lead and began moving forward carefully, Flyer ranging ahead. For two hours they headed east away from the track, before the ground began to rise steadily. It became rockier then suddenly began to climb steeply. They scrambled higher and higher up the slope, then cautiously emerged from the tree line. Above them a square rock face towered, while below them a sea of green spread out in all directions, broken only by the range in the north, gradually sloping away in undulations to the south. To both the east and west the greenery stretched unbroken except for other islands of rock like the one above them, thrusting upwards from the trees.

"Fractus, you remain with Kalli and Flyer here," said Barron. "We'll go higher, to where Shanna can launch."

Verren, Shanna and Barron began the scramble up towards the top of the outcrop. Mindful of her previous experience with the fire lichen, Shanna kept her eyes carefully peeled for any signs of dangerous or unknown plants. Small rodents skittered and rustled away, and Cirrus scattered a group of fluffers as she forged ahead of the group to the top of the butte.

The rock face was nicely flat at the top and largely bare of vegetation. A few basking lizards scuttled into crevices as Shanna arrived at the top. Twister and Storm perched themselves on the very edge, surveying the country laid out below. She took a couple of deep breaths, then dropped her pack to remove the flight suit.

Some moments later as she soared above the trees, Shanna spotted a thermal and spiralled as high as she was able, before arrowing south. To her right, in the west, she could see the Garsal vehicle track. She angled towards it and began to follow it as fast as she could fly. The green sea of trees seemed to extend endlessly southwards, with the scored track clearly visible through the vegetation like a scar. She followed the track steadily for an hour, easily gliding through the air and feeling the presence of her two cats, steadfastly waiting behind her on the butte.

Again there was no sign of the Garsal ship, or even the end of the track. She decided to keep on flying south for a few more minutes.

***

The Garsal vehicle bounced and swayed as it headed on its path back towards the original track. Every now and then its passing would disturb the limbs of the trees it dodged around. They struck the track as predicted and began to follow it towards the range. The Senior Trooper clicked his jaw in satisfaction. They would strike the range by mid-afternoon at this speed.

***

Shanna turned in a wide arc towards the north, preparing to return to the butte. She was disappointed to find nothing helpful yet again. The trail south seemed to be going on forever. She aligned her flight with the butte, but continued to survey the ground below as she flew. Far ahead, a metallic glint drew her attention. She veered back towards the slice in the vegetation, and focused forward again. Nothing. She shook her head slightly, as the wind rushed past. *Must have been my imagination.* Nevertheless, she followed the damaged vegetation a little further, scanning diligently. As she turned her head to the east in preparation to angle back towards her friends, another glint sparkled through the vegetation far ahead. Her heart began to race. She turned her attention back to the spot where she'd seen the metallic flash and carefully checked the air currents ahead, intent on getting as close as possible to see what might be up ahead.

She could see flashes of metal coming frequently through the trees, and now that she was closer, could see some swaying of vegetation. The metallic glints were moving rapidly. Its speed was almost as fast as hers, faster probably given that she was moving in a straight line, and the metallic object was following the variations of the original Garsal track. She narrowed her eyes and increased her speed as much as she was able, arms and legs quivering with the strain. She drew closer and closer, and then she saw it. A tracked and wheeled vehicle, smaller and much faster than the massive vehicles that she had battled at the base of the plateau, moving along the rutted track towards the range of hills they'd left that morning. She dropped lower, trying to see more details of the vehicle, but her arms and legs were trembling as she tried to maintain the speed required, and she was forced to pull up and spiral slowly upwards to regain enough height to return to the group on the square rock, now some way behind her.

Conscious of her fatigue, she plotted her course to be as straight as possible towards the butte, her mind in turmoil and heart racing. Small though the vehicle was, it was another threat to her family and her friends, and she knew that somehow they needed to stop the vehicle or get some kind of message to the plateau.

She finally glided down to the flat topped rock and landed, trying to gasp out her news as fast as possible before she collapsed in exhaustion. Storm and Twister pushed their way through to her, tidemarks flickering with concern, and nosed her gently. Verren began to undo the buckles of her flight suit as she stammered out what she'd seen to Barron, at the same time trying to keep the images clear in her mind so that Fractus would have a clear picture.

"So they are heading towards the plateau again, perhaps," said Barron, thoughtfully. "But you say that this vehicle is different? Smaller?" Shanna nodded, and sipped from her water bottle. "I wonder what their purpose is this time." Shanna was confused, she'd thought that Barron would be in a hurry to get moving, to track the new threat closely. Yet he'd perched himself on a rock and was tapping his jaw thoughtfully, as Verren helped her out of her suit and stowed it neatly in her pack. He noticed Shanna's quizzical look and smiled. "There's no way they can make it through that gorge yet, Shanna. They're as stuck on this side of the range as we are." Realisation dawned on Shanna and she relaxed slightly, finally taking the deep breaths she needed and fishing for one of the patches in her thigh pocket. She fumbled one onto her arm, and felt renewed energy course through her body.

"Then what shall we do, Barron?" asked Verren.

"First of all, we'll get off the top of this rock and get back to Kalli and Fractus. Then we'll take a few moments to plan before we set off after them. They shouldn't be too hard to track, if last time is any indication." Shanna pushed herself to her feet and hoisted her pack, settling it into place with a grunt and began the climb back down to the other two.

"How fast do you think they were travelling, Shan?" asked Kalli.

"As fast as I could fly, and more. I was going in a straight line and they were following the old track."

"The question is," came Fractus' thoughts, "where are they actually going, and should we follow them?"

"I didn't think there was any question," replied Barron. "We need to follow them, to find out what they're doing."

"But do we?" asked Fractus. "Our mission is to find the ship and destroy its communication facilities." There was silence after Fractus' last statement as the group digested it. Shanna was confused. Her immediate thought on sighting the Garsal vehicle had been the necessity to pursue it, to prevent any of the alien marauders from getting anywhere near her family and friends. In short, she realised that she had lost sight of the bigger picture. Her heart continued to pull her towards eliminating the immediate threat, but her head worried that in doing so they might lose the chance to prevent the aliens from reinforcing their numbers on her world.

Barron sighed heavily. "You're right to remind us of our purpose, Fractus, but the fact remains that we need to rendezvous with the others at the cave, and the Garsal are going in the same direction at this point. We'll follow them as far as our paths head in the same direction. If we can stop them then we will. But our priority must be the ship. One small vehicle offers little threat to the plateau, but a colony ship with communication ability is a huge one."

"Are you sure, Barron?" asked Verren.

"Yes, I am. The colony ship is our priority. It may be that Spiron will decide to divide us, but for now our primary mission is to locate that ship. Fractus, is there anything else you wish to add?"

The Starlyne was silent for a moment. "If Shanna is correct about the speed that vehicle was travelling at, then the Garsal will be at the range far in advance of us. Hopefully they'll have to wait until the flooding drops, just as we will. If that's the case, then perhaps we will have an opportunity to sabotage their vehicle or prevent them from travelling on in some way."

"Then we travel now. We can't match the speed of that vehicle, but they should be stopped by the flooding long enough for us to catch them." Barron signalled, and they began to retrace their steps.

***

The Garsal vehicle followed the track to the gorge mouth and then stopped. While the troopers kept a careful eye out for any of the many dangers that lurked everywhere on this planet, the Senior Trooper surveyed the steepness of the entry point. Even through the vehicle shell, he could hear the deep thundering of torrents of water pouring through its depths somewhere out of sight.

"We will go over." He directed the other two troopers, and the vehicle turned slightly to the west and began to traverse the slope. "Look for an ascent point." He was quietly pleased. The vehicle's capabilities would be tested thoroughly before he had to tackle the walls of the plateau.

***

Five long hours of fast but nerve wracking travel later, Shanna signalled that she had located a suitable campsite for the night. They were within two hours' walk of their storm hideaway, but the sun had set an hour previously and all of them were exhausted. Shanna had been forced to use another of the energy patches simply to keep going, and for the last hour had been tempted to pull out her glowstone to help light her way. Instead, mindful of the hazards of Below, she had concentrated on extending her senses to avoid the pitfalls, but again it increased her fatigue levels. Never had she been so glad to locate a tiny pungo grove. Somewhere relatively safe to hole up for the night, to collapse in exhaustion and to somehow try and prepare for whatever might happen the next day.

Chapter 19

VERREN had taken point as the first, early light began to brighten the sky. His unerring sense of direction ensured the fastest route back to their campsite near the deep pass through the range. Shanna asked Storm to range ahead on Verren's request, to assist Cirrus to provide advance notice of any contact with the Garsal. She and Twister guarded the left flank, and for once Shanna was glad to have a less stressful position.

She was still tired. Her thoughts kept wandering in circles. She half hoped that they would locate the Garsal vehicle and be able to eliminate another threat to her people, but the rational part of her mind kept wondering how they'd do that if they found it. Fractus' reminder that their primary goal was to locate the Garsal colony ship continued to intrude on her thoughts. If they were unable to knock out the communication systems, it was possible that thousands - maybe tens of thousands - of the insectoid invaders might converge on her home world. Their best hope was to isolate the Garsal already on Frontier, and hope their demise would pass unnoticed. With enough time to prepare, and the alliance with the Starlynes, perhaps her world could begin the fight to free the Federation of Races.

She skirted a tanglefoot and 'felt' for Storm and Twister. She could 'feel' Storm ranging ahead of them and if she concentrated hard, Cirrus off to his right and Twister pacing through the bush on her left. Verren was moving smoothly through the bush ahead; she could just see the back of his shirt through the thick vegetation and she hoped that their choices would become clear, unmuddied by diversions.

Two hours later, she peered carefully through the leaves of a frondan tree towards the gorge mouth. The tracks from the Garsal vehicle were clearly visible, going up the slope towards the slot between the hills. She could still hear the water thundering deep inside the gorge. Slowly, foot by foot, they advanced. With the end of their chase in sight, Barron had placed both Shanna and Kalli at the head of the group, their three cats ranging from side to side as they moved forwards. Fractus, with his large bulk, kept the rear guard, while Verren and Barron watched to each side. At the top of the rise the tracks turned abruptly to the west, paralleling the range; Shanna sent Twister up the nearest tree to move through the treetops, and she and Kalli advanced cautiously along the vegetation lining the deeply scored tracks pressed deeply into the rain-softened earth. This high on the slope it was more difficult to remain concealed, as the trees thinned the higher they went.

An hour later, they had still not sighted the Garsal vehicle. The track had meandered along the foot of the range, almost as though the alien invaders were out for an afternoon stroll. They had located an obvious overnight camp, but the track continued westwards after that. Barron signalled them in for a quiet conference.

"I'd say they're looking for another way through," he said quietly, as Hunter circled them.

"I think you're right," replied Fractus. "We probably need to decide how far we'll follow their track today."

Barron nodded at the Starlyne. "Again you are correct, Fractus. In addition, I think we need to investigate how flooded that gorge is. If our estimates are wrong and we end up trapped on this side of the range for some days, then I would suggest that we continue south, attempting to locate the colony ship."

"But the others ... " said Verren.

"Spiron and I have patrolled for many years together, and we know each other's minds. He will expect us to move forward rather than remain stuck in one place." replied Barron. "If we're caught on this side of the range, unable to make contact, then he will follow as he sees fit, assuming none of the other groups have located signs of the Garsal ship. I've given this much thought, and the constant southwards path of this track suggests that the ship will be on this side of the range. Fractus and I have discussed this while we've travelled this morning."

"Barron is correct. All of the vehicle tracks went effectively southwards, and this track has not deviated much at all. Our surmise is that the ship is still further south. I believe that when the others meet back at the cave, their conclusions will be similar. Radiant, Teacher and I have known each other for many years, just as Spiron and Barron have. We understand each other well. I believe that this is the right decision."

Kalli was nodding slowly in agreement. "So then, how much further should we pursue this vehicle? Or should we turn back now, and attempt to ascertain how much longer we'll be stranded on this side of the gorge?"

"We'll follow the tracks for another four hours," said Barron. "If they continue west, then we'll return to the gorge and see what the water level's like. If they stop or turn northwards, then we'll revise our choices."

Shanna had remained quiet for the whole discussion, until then. "And if they turn northwards, how do we warn the plateau? Or the others?"

"Shanna, if that happens we'll see what we can do, but at this time, Fractus has no contact with the others, our only known access north is blocked, and we know of no others. We'll make the decisions as we can, when we can. In the meantime, I want you and Kalli to continue on point together for the next few hours. Let's move."

Shanna and Kalli nodded and signalling their cats, moved off into the vegetation.

An hour later, the vehicle track turned northwards, and the vegetation became even sparser as the group began to work its way up the now sloping ground. Shanna signalled Twister out of the trees. They were too far apart for him to progress efficiently, so she sent him in a sweeping run forwards. Kalli, who was slightly ahead, signalled suddenly, and Shanna automatically dropped behind the nearest rock, remaining motionless for several minutes. Both cats appeared, tidemarks muted.

"Shan," came the barest whisper, "Come here." Shanna slid from behind her rock and glided forwards, carefully keeping as low as possible. Kalli was positioned behind a large tree trunk. It had low lying limbs, and she'd managed to lean around it to look up towards the top of the slope. Shanna followed her pointing finger. In the distance, a metallic glint tickled her vision. Trying to focus on the top of the slope, she became confused. The glint failed to resolve into a vehicle. Kalli tapped her arm. "I think it's on the hill."

Surprised, Shanna looked again, squinting slightly, and peered past the top of the slope. Further - much further than she'd thought - she saw it again, and found she could just make out the lines of the alien vehicle she'd seen from the sky. For a confused moment she thought the vehicle was hanging in mid air, then she realised that it had sprouted arms and legs and was jerkily ascending the sheer rock face in front of it. It looked eerily like a mechanical spooner spider. Storm hummed angrily and she turned to him in surprise. His hackles were raised, and both he and Twister were crouched as if to attack. Flyer returned to Kalli, and she was mirroring Storm and Twister's reactions. The three starcats were angry. Every line of their sleek bodies radiated anger.

"Well, that's a surprise," said Shanna quietly. "There's no way we can follow them now."

Kalli shook her head. "I'd hoped that when we encountered them, you and I might have been able to stop them." Shanna turned to her in surprise. "They are a mechanical vehicle you know."

Of course, Shanna thought, they are a mechanical vehicle — and that's what Kalli does — like Taya, she stops mechanisms. And so do I. She sighed. "You're right. I hadn't thought of that. And now we're not going to have the opportunity."

"No," replied Kalli, "but we'd better bring the others up here. They need to see this and then we need to decide our next move. I don't think anyone factored climbing vehicles into their equations." Shanna was oddly relieved, but at the same time regretful. The threat to her people was climbing steadily northwards, but she reminded herself that it was only one small vehicle despite its agility, and not a spaceship, complete with long-range communications gear.

The discussion had been short but to the point, and within a few minutes they were on their way back to the gorge. If they could, they'd cross the water when they came to it, but if all else failed and the water remained high, they would head south and continue to search for the Garsal ship.

Twister tucked his head under her hand comfortingly, twinkling the violet tidemarks on the tips of his ears, before ranging at her request.

Several hours later, Shanna and Kalli emerged together from behind a line of boulders onto a scene of thundering grandeur. The noise of the waterfall was deafening as torrents of water poured endlessly from above into the bowl below, overflowing its distant edge in a violent swirl of muddy water, and pouring through the gorge towards the river on the other side of the range. Shanna imagined the water rising further and further through the narrow parts of the gorge they'd traversed only a few days before, and shuddered at the thought of being caught in its raging currents. Shanna and Kalli were perched at the top of a slope, looking down towards the pool. The scooper grove was completely submerged, and the delicate beauty that had so entranced them on the way through was replaced with ear-splitting noise and humid spray from below.

"There's no way through for several days," sighed Kalli. "Even after the waterfall calms down, it will take another day or two for the narrow parts to be fordable or swimmable." Shanna nodded her agreement as the others joined them. Storm, Twister and Flyer bounded towards them, dark coats sparkling with spray, and Shanna sent Twister circling back behind them, making sure that nothing would take them by surprise as they discussed their next move. Storm and Flyer positioned themselves on convenient boulders on either side, overlooking the maelstrom.

"Well, that's our answer," said Barron, gesturing at the impassable water. "We'll leave a message here in a cairn along with the standard markers, and begin moving south. Fractus, you still have no contact with the others?" He raised an eyebrow at the Starlyne.

"Nothing." The Starlyne's tone was frustrated. "The narrowness of the gorge and the width of the range have blocked all my attempts to contact them. The only option I can offer is to wait here, and hope that the others move closer. Whether that's actually useful is doubtful. There is little to gain when we can simply leave a message. Time is passing and we have yet to locate the ship."

Barron nodded his agreement. "We move south. Kalli, you and Shanna build the cairn. I'll leave a message. We'll travel short days to allow the others to catch up, and leave messages each night with our plans for the next day. It's unlikely that the Garsal will locate them or even notice a pile of rock, for that matter, given what we know of them."

***

The small vehicle ground its way steadily up the side of the range. The Senior Trooper was satisfied with the steady progress made, but as they tucked the vehicle into a crevice and deployed its anchor bolts, he expressed his desire for faster progress the next day. The faster they crossed the range, the faster they would approach the plateau. He hungered for the chance of offspring.

***

They made camp that evening where they'd sheltered during the downpour, and the next day began the trek southwards, careful to remain hidden from sight should another Garsal vehicle be following the original track. Shanna noticed that the vigorous vegetation was already beginning to re-establish itself in the wheel ruts left behind, although some of the new growth was bent and trampled from the smaller vehicle's path. The going was slow, as they took the time to assess new or slightly different plants and animals that they encountered. The Starlyne's presence no longer deterred the larger predators, and they spent significant periods of time concealed from them, trusting their camouflage skills along with the abilities of their starcats to keep them safe. Shanna became more and more impressed with Barron's leadership skills. It was obvious he was a natural leader, and years as Spiron's second had not dulled his own skills.

After three steady days of travel, they reached the extent of Shanna's aerial surveillance. As Twister and Storm circled, they made a secure camp in a small pungo grove. Shanna was tired as she took first watch at the edge of the grove, positioning herself on a rock under the overhanging pungo branches. Absently, she rubbed yet another handful of crushed pungo leaves over face and clothing. She was dirty and sweaty, and her hair felt greasy and tangled. For the last three days they had carefully navigated their way stealthily through the endless green of Below. As they moved further and further south, the subtle changes in the vegetation became more pronounced. Even Fractus had moved with greater caution, although his size would be a deterrent to most predators.

She was also feeling very small. Despite all the preparations with the Starlynes, despite the planning and training and the knowledge of her expanding skills, she was there Below, hunting for alien invaders with only three other humans, five starcats and a Starlyne. Twister and Storm were a great comfort but the long days without her family, and now the isolation from the larger group, were taking their toll. The light faded gradually and Shanna kept her attention directed outwards, allowing her vision to adjust to the encroaching darkness. Behind her, she could hear the others moving around quietly. The occasional hushed murmur reached her ears, and a slight smell of smoke wafted past her. Hints of reflected firelight slipped through the foliage and coloured some of the leaves in front of her.

She tensed slightly as something rustled in the undergrowth, then settled back as Twister reappeared beside her. His tidemarks were twinkling in patterns of unconcern, so she relaxed slightly and dropped her hand to his soft coat. She could feel Storm circling in towards them. A hint of blue and he was at her side, sliding his head under her hand. She decided to send them out alternately to circle around the camp. That way she maximised the protection the three of them could offer, while still being able to give each cat some individual attention.

With a pang, she felt a sudden longing for the fire lit warmth of her family home. She imagined her parents and Kaidan sharing an evening cup of tea in front of the fire, while the family cats lounged on the rug in front of it, bathing in its warmth. There was a tightness in her throat and an ache in her chest. For the second time in only a few days her doubts came streaming back, and she struggled to keep steady watch whilst trying to push back the ache that threatened to crawl its way out through her ribs.

An hour later, Verren relieved her. Instead of moving back to the fire straight away, she sat beside him for a few moments. "Do you miss your family, Verren?" she asked quietly.

"Of course," he replied quietly. "So much sometimes that I ache with it. It's been so long since I've seen them. I worry about them too. I worry that I'll never see them again, and that they'll never know what's happened to me or where I am. We all do, I'm sure." The pain in his voice was audible and Shanna nodded quietly in the darkness.

"Me too."

She stood, called her cats in and took her time moving towards the fire, composing herself before she moved into the dim light of the embers deep in the pit. Kalli handed her several pieces of marmal on twig skewers and a mug of tea, as Shanna sat cross legged on the ground. There was little conversation. Everyone seemed in a quiet mood; even the cats were subdued. Kalli was rubbing Flyer's belly as he lay sprawled on his side with his back arched. Hunter was curved around Barron's back, and Storm and Twister had positioned their heads in easy reach of Shanna's hands. She realised that neither had hunted, and sent Twister off with a hand signal.

Barron looked up from his notebook, and tucked his pencil into the crease. "All quiet?"

Shanna nodded and pulled a piece of meat off the first skewer with her teeth.

"Good," Barron said, and picking his pencil up began sketching again. Shanna noticed that there was an unfamiliar plant carefully positioned in front of him. The slight hiss that Shanna had learnt to associate with Starlyne movement sounded just behind her, and Fractus' voice sounded quietly in her head. "When you've finished, Shanna, please join me for few moments."

Shanna jerked her head up slightly, and then nodded. "I won't be long."

"Take your time, you must be hungry."

She nodded. She was. The Starlyne glided silently to the edge of the dim firelight and coiled himself to wait, while Shanna returned her attention to the savoury meat and her cup of tea. The warm cup helped to ease the aching slightly. As Twister returned, she sent Storm out to hunt. He twinkled his ears at her and vanished rapidly.

Several minutes later, Shanna placed her mug neatly back into her pack pocket and walked over to the Starlyne. He was coiled comfortably and showed no signs of impatience. "Thank you, Shanna." There was a moment of silence, and Shanna stood awkwardly next to the creature. His tidemarks spiralled in subtle tones of violet as he looked at her. There was a faint feeling of sadness emanating from the creature which segued into compassion so seamlessly that Shanna was unsure she had felt the first emotion. "You are struggling," came the thought, and this time there was so much compassion in the statement that Shanna was almost overwhelmed.

Choked by emotion so strong that she almost staggered, she was unable to reply and simply nodded mutely. Twister leaned his long length lovingly on her legs, then Storm was there as well adding his warmth to her other side. The Starlyne moved suddenly, and she and her cats were enveloped in his warm coils, silkily soft and smelling faintly of something subtly warm and comforting.

She was wrapped not only in his warmth, but in affection, compassion and love. Faintly underlying those emotions, she could feel his regret that she and her fellows had been swept up into a conflict so desperate that their two races' survival depended on a mission that might now only consist of the five of them. She buried her head in his warmth, an arm around each of her cats. Their reassuring purring vibrated through her body, and the thoughts of the Starlyne turned into one of those dizzying spirals of images that poured into her mind.

She was swept up in Fractus' memories of his family. His mate, a sleek and graceful female, and several Starlyne younglings, frolicking in a sunlit glade. There was a sequence of images so fast that Shanna almost lost her breath trying to follow them. His mate, perishing in a fiery explosion that Shanna realised must have been her ancestors' ship, and then the image of the Starlyne youngling, the human child, and the tiny cat.

Fractus' memories lingered on the Starlyne youngling; most vivid was the feeling of love as the group played together, bouncing and running, gliding and pouncing. There was joy as the images ended, mixed with sadness — sadness that Promise would never see the fruition of the bond their child had formed with the human beings, who had so sadly caused her death. Shanna's mind finally made the connection.

The youngling was the child of Fractus, and it was Fractus who had come upon the trio playing in the bush together unheeding of any danger or prejudice. It was Fractus who had taken the possibility of an alliance to Keeper, requesting the elder's support for a venture fraught with danger for both species, and Fractus who had first proposed the modification of the human settlers of Frontier. There was guilt, apology, sadness, and regret, all spiralling round Shanna, but as well there was love — endless love that asked for forgiveness and promised as much security as could be found in the trackless expanse of Below. Shanna was overwhelmed. The new revelations from the Starlyne were so personal, and so private, that although she knew that on one level she should be disturbed that he had meddled with her species' genetic destiny, on another she felt privileged to have been allowed to share his most precious memories.

Images and feelings whirled and she felt tossed about, yet cradled and most of all loved. Loved in a way that was the best of how she'd felt when last she'd been home. It felt like so long ago now. The sorrow she felt at missing her family was gently soothed and affirmed by the Starlyne as a good and proper way to feel, but his gentle concern allowed her to put it into perspective; to know that her parents loved her, there was nothing that would ever cause them to love her less, and that they missed her as much as she missed them. But to know that despite their separation, she had things to do, things that would hopefully allow her family to live in peace and safety so that one day they might be reunited. With a pang, she realised that Fractus would never see Promise again. She treasured the knowledge of his mate's full name — Promise of Hope — and tucked it away carefully to treasure. His reassurance rolled over her then. His sons and daughter still lived and all had younglings of their own now, and his promise hung in her mind — he would take her to meet his daughter, the now grown youngling, when all was safe again.

Enfolded in his love and in the warm comfort of her cats, Shanna relaxed and allowed her eyes to close. For the first time in days she slept without dreams.

Chapter 20

MASTER Cerren sat, pencil in hand, pondering the information in the leather bound book. Once again he perused the figures supplied by Toman, nodding at some and shaking his head as his eyes travelled over others. Socks rolled onto her back near his feet and presented her belly for a rub, and he absently used the socked toe of one foot to oblige her. Purring rumbled through his foot as she stretched a little further.

He jotted a few notes, then penned a brief note to Toman on a fresh piece of paper. He sealed the note, and rising to his socked feet opened the door. "Kaidan!" Shanna's brother appeared from his seat further along the hallway. "Please take this to Master Toman, with my compliments." One of the after-hours duties that the new class had was messenger duty. In this time of potential hostilities, there was no time for anyone to be idle. Almost every moment of every day was taken up with a variety of tasks – small things that a youngster could achieve easily, leaving more experienced heads for other duties. Kaidan nodded and jogged away.

Returning to his desk, Cerren shut the book with a snap and carefully locked it away in his bottom drawer, pocketing the key. He sat for a moment and pondered the Garsal in the cells under the storm shelter. There had been no progress made at all, and Cerren was reluctant to use what Tamazine had called 'stronger methods'. It was an affront to his deeper morals, but there seemed to be no easier solution. He sighed.

There was a querying hum from Socks, and he fished his boots out from under the desk and began to lace them back on. "Time to go and talk to Tamazine again, Socks." The grey cat dimmed her tidemarks and hummed deep in her throat. She'd developed a strong antipathy to the Senior Councillor after Tamazine's abortive attempt to attract a starcat. "You behave, young lady!" he cautioned, though his tone was tinged with amusement. The cat's dislike of Tamazine, combined with her penchant for tricks and her ability to disappear and move soundlessly, had resulted in several episodes where Tamazine's dignity had been compromised.

Somehow, she'd never caught on to the idea that the incident might have been starcat-generated. Cerren had felt somewhat childish to be caught trying to hide a snort of laughter as the Senior Councillor had fallen flat on her very dignified face as she stepped over the threshold of Scout Headquarters two days previously.

A brief twinkle of blue had betrayed the 'obstacle's' identity to him, and he'd spent a few minutes chastising his completely unrepentant cat after

Tamazine's visit had concluded. He made a mental note to insist on her being welded to his heel during the upcoming discussion.

"Come on Socks," he signalled the grey cat, and she rolled to her feet, stretched, and followed him obediently out the door, tidemarks twinkling in tones of blue innocence. Peron joined him as he exited Scout Compound, and they made their way slowly through Watchtower to the Council Chambers.

"How's the new class, Peron?" he asked.

Master Peron smiled, "A rousing success, I'd say. The youngsters are learning a lot, and Anjo is learning more. He'll make a fair Scout should he wish to one day. There's still a lot of hardening up to do of course, but he's bright, learns quickly and of course has Ember. It's something we might keep in mind for when this emergency is over."

"Emergency? Is that what we're calling this?" asked Cerren, incredulously.

"Well, it's what Tamazine's calling it currently," replied Peron, his mouth turning down in distaste. "Obviously we've had no contact with the Garsal since the battle Below, and the quiet is allowing her to settle into an attitude of complacency. Her initial fear has subsided, and now she's begun to suggest that this alien incursion is limited, and that the lack of contact means reduced risk." Cerren's eyebrows almost disappeared into his hairline and a low growl sounded from Socks. Little Thunder skittered sideways, then popped back behind Master Peron determinedly. "Then there's her issues with our agreement with the Starlyne."

"I've been working with Toman most of the last few days, and it appears I've missed a few things." sighed Cerren. "So this is how she's decided to play it." He shook his head in disgust. "Our Starlyne allies tell me that the group looking for the Garsal vessel is now out of contact range with them. It will be some time until we know where the vessel is, how big it is, and whether they've been able to disable the communications. The lack of contact makes me edgy. I wish we knew more about what might be going on down below."

"While up here on the plateau, Tamazine dithers, insists on surrounding herself with our forces, avoids our allies, and has begun to deny that there's a problem, 'just 'an emergency', while all the time we are little closer to a workable plan."

"Well, Toman has the buffer well under way. She's already managed to stock the waystations, and she has all of the retirees working on the final stages of its preparations. All of the physically able have been recalled, while those oldsters whose condition precludes them from fieldwork are reporting directly to Toman. The old communication network has been reactivated, and the signal lights are ready." Cerren paced steadily forward as he ticked the points off on his hand.

"The standard signals?" asked Peron.

"Yes, it's unlikely the Garsal will understand them even if they manage to establish a presence here on the plateau. Our allies have cautioned us against the use of any more sophisticated systems. They're telepathic themselves as you know, which negates the need for short range communication devices, but apparently one of the Garsal's strengths has been the detection and destruction of more sophisticated technology. They've shut down most of the their higher level equipment in the hope of avoiding detection for as long as possible. They fear that premature discovery of their presence here would mean that the Garsal would call for assistance immediately, then our hopes of defeating them on this world would be in ruins."

Peron nodded soberly. "Our allies have technology beyond our dreams, and yet they still fear the Garsal and believe that our alliance is their only hope. I still wonder why they think that our contribution is so important."

"Well, obviously they feel that it is. Somehow, the meddling they've done with our genetic codes and that of our feline friends, is more significant than we think. That 'spark' we've fostered in the Scout Corps for so long appears to be the key. Young Shanna's unprecedented ability to disappear is only the beginning I suspect."

Peron nodded his agreement. "Speaker has requested that we try and spare more of our people to begin learning what they have to teach us. I've suggested that they begin with the oldsters in the Waystations and our newest cadets. I know it should be a priority, but we have so little time available! Perhaps we could suggest the youngsters as well?"

"Perhaps," said Cerren. "Obviously young Kaidan has the spark, given his ability to fade, but we haven't tested any of the others. Is there any indication that some might look to join the Corps?"

"There are," replied Peron, "They're all children of breeders or Scouts. Jareth, perhaps – he's Josen's youngest – and Erilla's Hadder. Then there's Toman's granddaughter Mira, and possibly young Kaidan, although with his ability with mathematics ... " he broke off as they reached Watchtower's central square.

The two Scout Masters paused in the shadow of the council building. The upper level was well lit, and they could see shadows moving at the windows above. Cerren spoke again. "Well, here we are. Let's hope that we can make Tamazine see reason. Payne will take the lead tonight?"

"Yes, he's managed to remain in Tamazine's confidence, despite her intractable attitude about the disposition of Watchtower's population. I'm just glad he's with us, or there'd be no hope for us." Cerren nodded in agreement. Payne had been the Senior Councillor for Watchtower for a decade. The tall, bearded man was a master diplomat, and during his years leading the council Watchtower had prospered greatly. Cerren imagined the dark skinned man, forehead creased in concentration, carefully manoeuvring Tamazine towards the desired outcome, and a small flame of hope flared to light.

"Well, are we ready?" he asked Peron.

"As ready as we'll be tonight. Payne will begin, and hopefully all we'll need to do is provide the necessary information at the right time." The two Scouts began walking again, and a few moments later entered the council building as the dusk deepened into the darkness of night.

The upper level council room was full. There were reflective lanterns on all sides bathing the room in light. Aides bustled from desks at the sides of the room to provide information to the Councillors and Guild Heads on request. Peron and Cerren slid into the two seats left vacant. Beyond a normal greeting, the two Scouts were careful to keep themselves from paying extra attention to Payne. They knew that Tamazine was aware of their long association, but they'd all agreed that a reminder of this relationship would not help their cause.

Tamazine looked up as the men took their seats. "Good of you to join us, gentlemen." She looked down at her leather jotter and the room quieted. "Latest updates on the Garsal please. Payne, you begin."

Watchtower's first citizen began to run through his report. One by one, the leaders around the table delivered theirs. There were no new contacts to report from any of the individual leaders. Tamazine began the round table run through of the list of preparations. All the groups were on schedule, and the reports were short and to the point. As Tamazine began to expound on the current situation, Payne's assistants quietly deposited paper copies of the pertinent reports in front of each of the leaders seated around the table. Cerren smiled at the careful efficiency of Watchtower's leader, and began to flick through the figures in front of him.

There were food supply lists, lists of available personnel, of available weapon supplies and locations, available resources, and of procedures designated to spread the alarm and disseminate information. It was efficient and organised, but completely centralised, relying on the ongoing existence of Watchtower. Cerren was a Scout, and had been for his entire adult life. Accustomed to independent thought and action, he could see the potential folly of completely centralising the command and defence structures. Human settlement on Frontier had been tenuous, and the early years of survival had been dependent on decentralisation. Building multiple small havens had kept humanity alive on this planet, and he wasn't about to throw three hundred years of struggle and striving away for the complacency and fear of one woman.

He tapped his pencil on the top of the pile and exchanged a resigned glance with Peron. The other Master shook his head minimally, more a twitch than anything else, and signalled under the table to Thunder. The small starcat obediently vanished under the table and poked Payne with his paw. Cerren caught the small start as the Councillor felt the cub's paw on his leg, and dropped his eyes to the paperwork again. Tamazine's voice droned on, and Cerren struggled to keep his attention on what she was saying, distracted by Payne's upcoming attempt to challenge the Senior Councillor's desire to centralise.

As the drone of Tamazine's voice finally ceased, Cerren heard Payne's chair scrape back, and lifted his eyes off the papers in front of him. He leant back and prepared to listen.

"Senior Councillor, I'd like us to revisit the current organisational structure." Payne took a couple of steps to one side, one hand smoothing his beard. "I've had a map and table prepared." There was a flurry of activity at one of the side tables, and two of his administrative assistants hurried forwards while another pulled a pin board over. At Cerren's feet, Socks relaxed, and he settled into his chair more comfortably to listen to Payne.

"When we first arrived on Frontier, we were few. Every year, on the Day of Remembrance, we honour the memory of their struggle to survive." He paused and Tamazine opened her mouth. "Bear with me, Tamazine, I have a point to make." The Senior Councillor subsided, but Cerren noticed that she was eyeing Payne with a degree of suspicion. "The early years were an enormous struggle. In the midst of the destruction of our arrival, we fought simply to preserve our lives and to protect our families from the death that so often stalked us. We remember them with honour, and we have vowed to make this planet a better place for our descendants."

He took a sip of water from the glass in front of him. "Our successes came from small steps," he took several across the front of the room, "the establishment of our underground shelters, the building of the first walls, and the multiple, small, well-defended farming centres." He gestured briefly and one of the assistants carefully attached a map to the pin board. It was mounted on a backing board, and from its shine Cerren realised that the map was impregnated with frondan resin, which made it one of the originals from the archives. He was impressed with Payne's thoroughness. The use of an original emphasised the gravity of Payne's message. Spread out before them was Starfall, ringed by small, fortified farming communities. The lettering was square and regular – printed, Cerren realised, most likely by one of the now unavailable technologies of his ancestors – and clearly designated each small settlement, detailing its strengths, vulnerabilities and structure.

"When we began to live here on Frontier, an overtly hostile planet, we knew that to group everyone together was to invite disaster. As we gained a foothold, we wisely spread our resources and our population, so that one catastrophe did not spell the complete end to our population. Slowly we built secure settlements, each one walled and storm proof, and so we spread across this plateau." Cerren glanced quickly towards Tamazine. Her face was showing obvious displeasure as she began to realise where Payne's speech was going. Her right hand had picked up her pencil, and she had begun to tap the blunt end on the edge of the table. Payne gestured again, and a trio of assistants tacked three more maps to the pin board – one large one and two smaller, less detailed ones.

"If you would look at the large map, you'll notice that our resources are now pooled in one place – Watchtower. There are no markers in any outlying settlements, because those settlements have been stripped of their personnel and resources. You'll notice that the population markers at the southern end of the plateau are now all concentrated here, and at Starfall." He pointed to the two larger markers, then motioned to his assistants again. One hurried forward with a list and a handful of small coloured pins in her hand. She began pinning, intermittently consulting her list. "The violet pins are our Starlyne allies' settlements."

There was an audible gasp as she continued to add pins. The Starlyne peoples' habitations were all over the plateau. Most were at a distance from any human habitation, but several of the pins were almost on top of the inked markings that designated a human settlement. There were many Below, but all were scattered and there were few further south than the plateau. Cerren marvelled at the effort Payne had gone to, to get the Starlyne liaison, Speaker, to provide those details. It gave him a renewed sense of trust in their large allies. He hoped their human counterparts proved worthy of it. "And if you'd note the smaller maps, you'll see the old beacon hill stations on the top one, and the wilderness storm shelters on the other." There was surprised murmuring around the table. Cerren sat back and listened. Some of the others began to call questions to Payne, but Tamazine stood, shoving her chair back so hard that it overturned. The crash resounded across the room, and the questions came to a sudden halt. The silence was loud in its suddenness.

"And what are you suggesting, Payne?" Watchtower's Councillor turned towards Tamazine, with his eyebrows raised, polite astonishment in every line of his tall leanness.

"Suggesting, Tamazine?" he asked. "I'm suggesting that perhaps our history as a people tells us that we should rethink our placement of resources." He pulled the pin board closer to the table, pointing to the pinned maps. "History has much to tell us, as do our Starlyne allies. Perhaps we should listen both to history and to Speaker." There was a sudden murmuring from those seated around the table, and a number of heads turned as the unmistakeable glow of Starlyne tidemarks illuminated the room as Speaker swept in. Cerren wished he knew how the creatures moved so silently. And how Speaker had climbed the stairs. He shelved the puzzle for another, more appropriate time, mentally congratulating Payne on his inspired presentation.

"Good evening, allies," came the silent voice. "Thank you for inviting me to join your deliberations tonight." Cerren schooled his face to stillness, as he knew that Tamazine had avoided inviting their allies into their closest councils. The Starlyne's presence was Payne's work. He wondered how much Speaker actually knew about the situation. "Almost all." The quiet voice echoed in his mind and Cerren looked around, startled. Surely everyone head heard that comment. There was a feeling of amusement. "Only you, Master Cerren. We can speak to as many or as few as we wish." The Starlyne finished sliding his length into the room and coiled himself neatly at the end of the table closest to Payne.

"I hope that the information about our locations has been useful." This time Cerren was sure that the whole room had heard the Starlyne's voice.

"Senior Councillor, Councillors, Guild Seniors, I'm glad and honoured to be here with you tonight." He inclined his head graciously, and his tidemarks glowed brightly for a moment.

"Yes, very helpful," replied Payne. The tall man gestured to the pin board behind him, and the Starlyne turned his head to view it.

"Ah yes. Since the escape from our home world, we have been wary of putting all of our 'eggs in one basket' as you humans like to say. We learnt the hard way." There was a strong wave of sorrow from the creature, and his tidemarks dimmed. A flash of shared memory brushed Cerren's mind. Flames falling in gouts from the sky as he fled with his family, only to see the youngest turned to smoking ruin in front of his eyes. Tears prickled unexpectedly as the smell of smoke, flames, heat, and the scent of a burning homeland ignited his senses.

Determinedly, Cerren pulled himself back from the raw emotion and swept a slightly blurred gaze around the room. The humans were sitting stunned into silence, and there were tears tracking down more than one face. Even Tamazine was silent, eyes fixed on the Starlyne. Alone of the humans, Payne was aware of Cerren's gaze. He nodded slightly although his dark skin was abnormally pale. It was hard to draw back from the wash of emotions being generated by the Starlyne.

"He asked me to tell some of my story," whispered Speaker's voice inside his mind. "And I am unable to do so without the emotion spilling over into my images and voice. I am sorry."

Inside his head, Cerren replied, "No apology is necessary. You have my thanks." He turned his gaze around the room once more. Tamazine was rigid now as the Starlyne's emotions continued to wash over the group. At the back of his mind, Cerren continued to experience the story. Pain, death, fire, blood and despair. The pain of families separated, the desperate rush to launch the vessels that might take the few survivors into space. Somewhere, anywhere, free of the Garsal menace.

Visions of the planet from space showed great glowing gouts of red marring its surface, and the knowledge that those left behind were no doubt dead. Distance had brought separation from the minds of loved ones, torn holes through wedded links, and sundered family thoughts until all that was left was the memory of the love and the beauty that had been the Starlyne home.

There was a shocked silence as the Starlyne's thoughts ceased. The images and voice of the creature before him slowly melted away, and Cerren's own thoughts were at last the only ones inside his head. Beside him, he heard Peron sigh and ease himself in his chair. He was certain that no-one would be able to miss the point that Payne had made. He allowed himself to hope that Tamazine might finally see reason. At the head of the table, Payne stood again.

"Our allies knew the folly of locating all their resources in one place. I would hope that we can learn from this." He sat down and yielded the floor.

Tamazine got slowly to her feet, and as he saw the expression on her face he was filled with foreboding. Her face was closed, controlled and set. He saw the muscles around her jaw tighten, and her eyes harden. Surely not, he thought, surely even Tamazine can see what happened to the Starlyne, surely she can finally understand that we cannot, must not, completely centralise. Surely she has realised that our strength is in our flexibility!

But the Senior Councillor's tone was grim as she began to speak. "You think to manipulate us with emotion? You think that I will bow to a medley of concocted images? Do you really think I'm that stupid?" Her voice was almost a sneer, and for the first time Cerren looked at the Senior Councillor with her professional veneer stripped away, and what he saw he did not like.

Several of her fellow Councillors were nodding in agreement, expressions of distaste on their faces, while others sat stunned and aghast around the table. There was no movement or sound from the aides at the edges of the room. Cerren felt his heart lurch as he realised that Tamazine was not about to bow to good sense, or to change her mind about anything. A quick glance towards Payne, and Cerren knew that the man had come to the same conclusion. Speaker's tidemarks began to cycle more rapidly, and Cerren could feel the resignation radiating from him.

"I see you do not believe the truth then, Tamazine," came Speaker's voice. "If you choose to place your people at risk in this way, then the loss of life should the Garsal attack will be catastrophic. And attack they will, there is no doubt about that."

"Tamazine, the Starlyne is not fabricating! Please, you need to reconsider!" Payne had left any pretence at quiet reasoning behind and was standing, leaning forward with his hands on the table. "Surely the rest of you must see that our current plans are folly!" He turned with a sweeping gesture to the maps on the pin board. "We have gathered all our resources in three major locations – Watchtower, Starfall and Northaven. It would take only one airborne attack against us to lose almost everything!"

"You are out of order!" thundered Tamazine. "They've had plenty of time to launch that kind of assault and what, nothing? Do you really think they're here in force? If they are, then why haven't we seen them?"

Beside Cerren, Peron pushed his chair back and stood in one fluid movement. "Tamazine, do you doubt the intelligence gleaned from the two human offworlders? Or the presence of our Garsal captives? What does that tell you?"

"Intelligence from whom? A snivelling idiot who can't string two words together, and a young man barely older than your final year cadets? I have no doubt that they've exaggerated their information in order to gain our trust and allow them to stay here in comfort. And as for your captives, well, I have yet to see any valuable intelligence wrung from that source." Her tone was disdainful and dismissive.

"Are you mad?" Peron almost shouted, and Cerren reached up to try and calm his friend slightly while attempting to quell his own anger. "Even a fool must be able to see the danger!"

"A fool would see that these Starlyne are attempting to manipulate us!" shouted Tamazine. "They want us to bow to their control!" Cerren got to his feet.

"Tamazine, there is no reason for the Starlynes to want to control us. Their dealings with us have been fair and even handed." He tried to keep his tone reasonable while his hands urged Peron to sit. Beside him, he felt Socks get to her feet, and as she brushed his hand he realised that her hackles had risen, and she was on the verge of hissing at the Senior Councillor. He flicked an admonitory finger at her. She remained standing but eased her stance slightly, although he could tell from the blue reflections on the polished timber in front of him that her tidemarks were intensifying their glow. He tried to keep his eyes from the grey cat. "They want to defeat the Garsal on this planet, just as we do, and hopefully together we can achieve this, but not if you continue to distrust them!"

Tamazine's face and voice sneered her reply. "You might have been deceived by their smooth manipulation, Cerren, but fortunately you are not the only councillor here. The Starlyne will leave and then we will vote. Vote to end this dissension now and for the duration of the emergency. I have no doubt that there are Garsal on this planet, but they are not the threat you and the Starlyne have made them out to be." She dropped one hand to the table and looked around at the assembled leaders. Cerren sat slowly, all of his worry coalescing into thoughts of desperation. If Tamazine was to win the vote, then the future of his people would be at enormous risk. He thought with a pang of Patrol Ten and the first year cadets, even now searching for the Garsal ship, somewhere Below. What would happen to them if Tamazine remained in control?

Peron leaned towards him. "It will be close," he whispered, "Starfall's Councillors are known to vote in blocs, and they have been too sheltered for too long. I'm sorry I lost my temper, but she is truly delusional, not just fearful."

"You're right, we cannot avoid this vote. It's lawful. Payne will vote with us and most of Watchtower's Councillors, but I'm not certain about the Guild Heads. The only thing we have in our favour is the laws of Frontier. We need Erilla – her expertise is essential at this point. I'll send Socks with a message."

"I will leave now," came the Starlyne's thought. "You must resolve this issue. We are ever your allies - you have but to call. We must face this threat together and united." He turned and a final thought wafted to Cerren. "And if the vote goes the wrong way, you must still call, Master Cerren." Reassurance accompanied the Starlyne's voice and Cerren relaxed slightly. He wondered how much information the Starlyne might have picked from his brain. The thought was slightly unsettling but reassuring all the same.

"We will break for thirty minutes, refresh ourselves, then vote," said Tamazine, and a buzz of conversation whirled around the room.

Cerren tucked a note into Socks' harness and sent her off with an entreaty to be fast. Her form blurred as she exited the room, then he and Peron stood, walked over to Payne and began to plan. It looked like a long night ahead.

Two hours later, the voting was deadlocked. Tamazine had set a formal proposal in front of the group under the emergency laws written into Frontier's charter of governance. Although each major centre was effectively autonomous in its decision making, there had been a provision in the first charter for centralisation of government should the need arise. Instead of good sense and a coordinated response to the potential disaster now facing them, Tamazine had sidetracked the discussion into a hair-splitting interpretation of the law. A trained legalist herself, she was an expert when it came to twisting words and phrases.

Cerren was enormously glad that he'd sent for Erilla. The Scout Master was an expert on Frontier's charter in her own right. Her ability to read character and nuance had also proved invaluable. Every effort to redirect the meeting's direction back to their response to the Garsal incursion had been met by Tamazine's tactic of sending the discussion off into tangents based around interpretation of the intent of the original charter. Erilla had provided Cerren with clever points to pull the discussion back to where it should have been.

Never in the three hundred year history of Frontier, had the settlers found it necessary to hand over complete control of the human settlements to one governing council, let alone the Senior Councillor of Starfall. Tamazine's interpretation of the law aimed to provide her with complete control and oversight of all of the governing structures on the plateau.

Cerren and his faction argued that the original settlers had never intended the charter to be read in that way. Government on Frontier was designed to be forever and always by consensus, and never by dictatorship. Cerren had so far resisted using the word 'dictator' but it was there, sitting in the back of his mind. Tamazine had reverted to her shrewd, smooth diplomatic manner. If Cerren hadn't seen her lapse into self-serving delusion, he might have been deceived into allowing her silver tongued oration to sway him. He stretched as Tamazine called a short break.

"You have to admire her ability to spin," whispered Erilla. "If you hadn't told me what she'd actually said, I might not have believed her capable of such duplicity. I hope the others remember what she was like, and are not swayed by what they see now."

"The question is, though," replied Peron. "How do we stop control devolving to her?"

"We keep canvassing," said Cerren. "Erilla, I want you to try and persuade some of Starfall's Councillors to see sense."

Erilla sighed. "They're so used to toeing the line that some of them appear to have forgotten that they have opinions of their own." She pushed herself tiredly to her feet. "But I'll see what I can do with Welton and Nampi. When we last discussed this subject, they seemed somewhat amenable to change. It's a pity we don't have any further information from Spiron." She shook her head, but resolutely walked over to the two mentioned Councillors and began to talk to them. Cerren could see Welton shaking his head but Nampi seemed slightly more inclined to listen, inclining her head to Erilla and nodding thoughtfully.

Socks nudged Cerren gently. He looked down to see her curled neatly at his feet, and extended a toe to scratch her cheek. She hummed a query, looking pointedly towards Tamazine, and flickered her tidemarks slightly. "No!" he said, and she shook herself slightly and dimmed her tidemarks in disappointment. "That's all we'd need, lady cat!" He couldn't say that he hadn't been tempted though.

There was a tap from the other side of the council table, and he dragged his attention back to the matter in hand. Erilla scooted around the table to her chair just behind him and leaned in. Cerren tilted his head back. "Nampi's promised to consider carefully, but no luck with Welton." Cerren nodded resignedly. With Nampi's possible support, they stood a chance of voting complete control away from Tamazine. The Starfall council might still hold the balance of power, but Tamazine would not have complete control, and at this stage that was all that Cerren was hopeful of. Two of Watchtower's guildsmen had jumped ship and voted with Tamazine's bloc, seeking profit rather than sense. Peron had simply shaken his head, and during the break had attempted to change their minds. Cerren tapped him on the shoulder and raised an eyebrow. He wobbled his hand from side to side and twisted his mouth. At his feet, Thunder snored gently.

Tamazine called for the proposal, and one of her sycophants rose and began to read the two motions before the meeting. The first proposed that the Senior Councillor be granted emergency powers for the duration of the Garsal threat. The second motion proposed that the three councils - Starfall, Watchtower and Northaven – merge for the duration of the Garsal threat. Although Cerren hoped desperately that both motions would be defeated, he was certain the second one would not be. The best that they could hope for was to avoid complete control devolving to Tamazine.

He filled in his ballot neatly, folded it, then dropped it through the slot of the ballot box handed around by Payne's senior aide. The grey haired man looked exhausted and dispirited. His eloquent and well-researched argument had been completely scorned by Tamazine and now they were sitting in an unprecedented council, wasting precious moments of preparation time, when their planet and their very lives were in danger. He looked like Cerren felt.

There was a lull while the votes were counted. Next to Cerron, Peron was tapping a foot, his only outward display of agitation. The tapping woke Thunder who gave him a grumpy look, and rolled over to lean on Socks. The grey cat looked up at Peron in a resigned fashion and allowed the young cat to stay where he was. It was late, he was tired, and it kept him out of trouble. It had been a long day.

Payne's senior aide returned with the tally, and Cerren sat up straighter in his seat.

"The votes have indicated that two decisions have been made. In the first instance, for motion one." There were mixed sounds around the room, some sounded like sighs of relief. Cerren held his breath and the room seemed to stop as the aide paused. The moment stretched out longer and longer, before he spoke. "The motion is defeated." Cerren let his breath out slowly. So far the worst had been averted, but there was still one motion to go. He drew in another breath as the aide swapped pages. "In the second instance," he paused again and Cerren felt like leaping out of his seat to implore the man to hurry. "The motion is passed. The councils will merge." There was a buzz of conversation, and the room began to break into small pockets again.

Cerren remained seated, exchanging grim glances with Peron and Erilla. "And although the greater disaster has been averted for now, there's going to be a lot of work ahead of us. I expect we'll adjourn, now that there's been a clear decision." Erilla nodded.

"And then we need to begin convincing the majority of the Councillors that we must decentralise."

Tamazine's face across the table was unhappy. She had had a small victory but not the one she'd wanted. Still, Cerren mused, she would retain most of the control she seemed to crave; that is, he amended to himself, *until we can sway enough Councillors to see sense.* As she rose to end the night's meeting, he steeled himself for the upcoming battles. Battles not only against the Garsal, but against the tenets of good sense and tactics. It would be a difficult time. Socks nudged him affectionately and he dropped a hand to her head. She was a treasure and a moment of sanity in the chaos.

Chapter 21

ANJO woke suddenly, nearly falling out of bed when he found himself confronted by a pair of large violet eyes staring lovingly into his. His heart pounded vigorously until his sleepy brain realised that it was Ember's eyes. Apparently the cat had decided to share his pillow sometime during the night. As his heart slowed he shook himself slightly, and with a sigh reached out to the suddenly upside down head to provide a scratch under the chin. Ember purred and attempted a coy, 'scratch my belly' position, paws tucked up under his chin, emitting a plaintive hum which contrasted oddly with his large size.

Unable to resist his starcat's entreaties, Anjo scratched the black belly while Ember began to purr vigorously. He wondered what his old friends on Delicata would have said if they could have seen him now. Some of the old sadness of missing friends and lost family pushed its way up from the place he'd carefully stored it.

As if sensing his feelings, Ember rolled onto his belly and swiped him gently with his head. He relaxed with his hand on Ember's soft coat, memories rolling gently through his mind. His mother's chestnut hair and the sound of her laughter; his father's earnest smile and bad puns; and the lost laughter of his school friends. Many had died in the early fighting, but others like himself had been shipped offworld on the slave ships. Despite the passing of years the sadness remained. He'd had too much time with his thoughts while the ship had been in transit, sitting alone in the slave pen, trying to honour the promise he had made to his mother to never give up.

It was a promise that the ship's arrival on Frontier had come perilously close to breaking though, heralding as it did day after day of nightmarish labour. He'd watched fellow slaves killed by the huge reptilian predators that assaulted the ship on almost an hourly basis, seen both slave and Garsal perish after contact with seemingly innocuous vegetation, then been assigned to the Garsal commander of the exploratory vehicle. He'd fully expected to die on that trip. Yet here he was, sharing his bed with an enormous starcat, living in the company of other free human beings, and learning to live in the fearsome world of Frontier. And today was another milestone. Today they were going outside Watchtower's walls for the first time since the arrival of the Senior Councillor.

The Senior Councillor had spoken with him once. He'd been introduced to her, and she'd spent an hour quizzing him about the Garsal. He'd got the impression she gave his answers little credit and he'd been taken aback by her apparent dismissal of what he'd said. A response totally unlike that shown by the Scout Council and Watchtower's Council. They had impressed him with their ability to grasp the important facts, and with their theoretical knowledge of the universe and the sciences. He might have wondered at first why the people of Frontier seemed to have so little technology but then remembering his own early days on the planet – the sheer terror of the plant and wildlife, he'd marvelled that they'd been able keep what they had. It seemed a cruel twist of fate that against all odds they'd managed to preserve the knowledge they needed to redevelop technology, and now after nearly three hundred years, just when they were finally in a position to use that knowledge, they'd been found by the Garsal and could lose everything.

Mind you, he reminded himself, given that same society had managed to rescue himself and Semba while stopping a Garsal attack dead in its tracks, the Garsal would not find it an easy task. Surprise had played a part of course, but ingenuity and clever strategy had shown the people of Frontier were a force to be reckoned with. Once again, Anjo determined to enjoy the freedom that these people had given to him for as long as possible, while doing everything he could to help them prepare to face the Garsal themselves.

He bounced out of bed and began to ready himself for the day.

***

Kaidan wondered yet again how Shanna was doing, as he and Boots left the quarters assigned to his family and their cats in Scout Compound. It seemed strange that his sister's presence was something he hadn't known he'd miss so acutely until there was no chance of seeing her, possibly ever again. He stopped that train of thought. He'd been up early, helping his parents feed and care for their breeding cats. They had several pregnant females now, including Sabre again, and one was expected to litter any day. The quarters, although adequate, were not the comfortable set-up they'd left at Hillview, and Kaidan felt resentment roll through him again. There'd been no need for them to relocate just yet, and he felt sure that his parents were equally annoyed.

Hope you're OK, Shan, he said to himself as he walked briskly up the corridor towards the arena. There had been no indication of what Patrol Ten and the cadets were up to Below. That image of his sister and her cats continued to haunt him, though. He wondered what it was the Starlynes had been teaching her.

It had been almost two months since he'd seen her and her cats, and more months since Storm and Twister had last stalked him at his sister's gleeful urging. His parents were preoccupied with their cats and the politics that so clearly bothered them, so he was pleased to have the class to occupy his time. He enjoyed doing messenger duty when he wasn't in class, tutoring Anjo, or performing the multitude of other duties that the older Scouts seemed to find for him and his classmates anytime they looked like they might sit down for a few moments.

Kaidan's stride quickened as he anticipated being outside Watchtower's walls again. The field trip would be an enjoyable distraction and he hoped that Anjo would enjoy it too. The offworlder was improving in his knowledge of Frontier's wildlife, but he still had a tendency to start if he heard an unfamiliar sound. Kaidan supposed that he'd probably be the same on a different planet. And of course, Frontier did have a large quantity of interesting wildlife.

Boots was still looking for Satin. Every time he went anywhere with Kaidan, he kept a careful eye out for the green-toned starcat, and despite his partnership with Adlan, he was almost shadowing Kaidan's every move. Everyone seemed to be missing someone, mused Kaidan. He pushed open the external door and hurried off to the arena, eager for the day to begin.

***

The Senior Trooper had decided to stay away from the track left by the original vehicle after he'd crossed the range. He was mindful that four large exploratory vehicles had vanished during their approach to the plateau. Determined to be selected to reproduce, he opted for a more cautious approach.

As a result, the three insectoid creatures forged a new path, several kilometres to the west of the original track. Maps developed from the initial flyover indicated a possible route to a more westerly portion of the plateau than the last recorded positions of the original vehicles. In some ways it was riskier, as it would take longer to get to the plateau, but the commander felt the old approaches might well be guarded by the humans now, and that stealth and a different approach were more likely to be effective. If he was able to provide detailed information of the human settlement, and perhaps some human prisoners, he might well be awarded breeding privileges .

The vehicle's climbing limbs had performed so well, that the commander was certain that the plateau would pose no major obstacle for the vehicle. In the meantime, he urged the other troopers to keep a careful lookout for safe places to pause for the evening. In order to maintain their safety, they needed to tuck their vehicle into secure rocky hideaways each night, and twice night had fallen before they had been able to locate a safe place. At night, Frontier's predators became more bold and were attracted by the lights shining from the vehicle as the Garsal attempted to find their way.

The vehicle was now battered and dented in places, and its original sheen had dulled under the lashing attacks of one of the larger reptiles. The last time, a spike-tailed beast had come close to damaging several essential systems.

As the day wore on, the search for a safe place became more urgent, and the vehicle began to deviate from its path, looking for any likely rocky outcrops.

The vehicle bucked and jostled its way north, occasionally turning east or west as the those inside looked for a safe haven for the night. They settled into a crevice underneath an overhang just before sunset, and all three troopers worked rapidly to erect the laser fencing across the mouth of the crevice. Already there were distant sounds of approach. Carefully skirting plants they had learnt were dangerous, the three troopers quickly tucked themselves back into their vehicle for the night.

***

Allad signalled a halt and the patrol sank silently into the undergrowth. The two Starlynes managed to somehow make their huge bulk almost invisible amongst the trees. Four days previously, the three smaller groups had rejoined Perri, Arad and Teacher at the cave. With no further word from Barron, Spiron had decided to take the whole group south, following in the other group's wake. He had reasoned that the rain had most likely caused a rise of the river that had prevented the other group from returning as planned. None of the three groups had discovered anything of significance, except that the Garsal appeared to be looking for deposits of minerals. The most easterly path had had many small excavations along its track. All had come from the south.

Allad sent Satin out and around, listening carefully to the thundering water, and then moved forward cautiously. All through the gorge there were signs that the river had risen enormously. Fresh debris was strewn metres above the gorge floor and the body of water was still turbulent and fast. It was ebbing rapidly now, but Allad wondered whether the noise ahead might herald a watery barrier. Several metres more of cautious progress and the gorge began to widen, allowing direct sunlight to pour down and glint off the water foaming into the pool below a waterfall. The water was cascading from the pool over its western rim, and running furiously into the riverbed that then followed the gorge north. Allad marvelled at the sheer quantity flowing past him and falling from above. Satin returned to his side, and he signalled behind to the Patrol secreted in the trees. The group joined him rapidly and they stood quietly in a ring of starcats. Even little Nosey sat on a tall rock, her attention directed alertly outward, diligently attempting to guard Arad. Allad smiled slightly to himself.

"Well, I think we know why they didn't return as planned," sighed Spiron, "This end of the gorge was probably completely impassable until just before we arrived. Even now, I'd estimate another twenty four hours before we're able to continue." Allad nodded his agreement.

"You think Barron's continued southwards then?"

"Yes." The patrol leader was definite. "There would have been no point sitting idle on the other side of the gorge. I'd guess that they waited out the heavy rain somewhere secure, checked the gorge, then decided to press on when they realised that it might be days until they could return to us. They're probably not moving fast, as they'll be Scouting out a completely new area. Am I right to assume that there's little Starlyne presence here, Teacher?"

Teacher inclined her head. "You are correct, Spiron. And I suspect we have little sway over the larger predators in this region. Our settlements are mostly much further north than this. They will not be conditioned to avoid us as their more northerly cousins are, which may well have slowed their progress even further." Her tone was contemplative. "It may be that the others have already located the ship, but that Fractus has simply been unable to contact us due to the barrier presented by the range." The patrol leader nodded.

"We camp here until the river drops, and as soon as we're able we'll be on our way. With some luck, once we exit the gorge, you or Radiant might be able to contact Fractus. Amma, what's the likelihood of further rain?" The curly haired cadet took her time replying, face creased in concentration.

"Nothing for at least four days. Cyclone season has finished, and any further rain over the next week should be minimal."

"Good," replied Spiron. "In that case, Perri, perhaps you could introduce our cadets to Scooper nuts while the rest of us make camp." He smiled. "Don't let them eat too many!"

***

Shanna placed the capstone on the small rock cairn erected at their latest campsite. Kalli had found a small cave tucked in one of the rocky outcrops, and for once they were camped in relative safety. It was even just big enough for Fractus to coil his large bulk into. She checked that the structure was stable, and that the message Barron had penned was secure in its resin treated pouch and sealed against both insects and water.

"All done, Barron," she called quietly over her shoulder. "I'll relieve Fractus now." The light was fading as she perched herself on a rock near the cave entrance.

"Thank you, Shanna," the Starlyne inclined his head as he glided silently into the cave. "Safe watching." Shanna nodded her thanks before turning her attention towards the vegetation around the cave mouth. She sent Storm out briefly in a wide half circle while Twister settled himself next to her, ears pricked and eyes alert. In the sky directly above, two of Frontier's three moons were visible, and their faint light began to cast odd shadows through the gathering dusk. The last few days of travel had been very slow. Shanna was reminded of her first trip Below with Patrol Ten. The stealth, patience and caution required had been mirrored during this trek south. She pulled a few pungo leaves off the tree overhanging her perch and began to systematically crush them and rub them over her clothes and exposed skin, the odour of the leaves masking her very edible human scent. Though given how long it had been since she'd last washed she wondered how anything could actually enjoy eating her. She longed for a hot bath with surprising intensity.

Storm returned from his circuit, tidemarks glowing softly in reassuring patterns, and settled on her other side. She dropped her hands to her cats and spent the first few moments of their combined watch simply enjoying the silence and their loving company. She pondered the changes she'd observed in them over the last few turbulent months.

Now fully grown, they were two of the largest starcats she'd ever seen, and she realised that when they got back she'd have to get an even larger bed or be prepared to sleep squished up in one corner – they were truly huge. But it wasn't just their size; they'd both matured into intelligent and reliable cats, with Twister's love of climbing echoed in Storm's love of water, and their bond with Shanna seemed to strengthen each day. Relaxing slightly, she allowed herself to 'feel' their presence, then, keeping contact with them both, allowed her senses to extend in front of her so that she could 'feel' her way through the vegetation in front of her.

Each night when on watch she practiced, trying to extend her range. It was easier when she was touching her starcats, but she seemed to have recently reached a limit. She could reliably 'feel' animal life within about fifty metres in all its myriad forms. Larger predators were relatively easy to detect, but the smaller animals were often more difficult. She relaxed a little more and 'felt' forward. A family group of weldens, several trenchers digging their way through a hillock just to her west, the earthy feel of them enabling her to identify them easily, a flotter near the small rock pool just to the east of the cave, and half a dozen stinkrats squabbling over a choice morsel. She sat back on her rock and melded herself with the environment around her. Each time she worked with Storm and Twister, she was able to 'feel' more easily. The two cats felt content. Storm was a rock of stability and strength on her left and Twister a coil of poised agility. They were different, yet complementary, and she felt complete with their companionship.

Shanna often wondered what it was that made the three of them so important to the Starlyne people. So important that each encounter with them seemed to finish with that lingering picture of her and her cats. It was as if each Starlyne used that picture as a farewell image, an image that held both hope and promise but also a tiny tinge of apprehension. The evening tucked in Fractus' coils had gone oddly unremarked by her companions. Shanna wondered if the Starlyne had simply told the others not to mention it to her. She had been so tired, so exhausted and so fearful that evening, that she'd slept completely without dreams for the first time since last leaving the plateau. It had been her first unbroken sleep for weeks. Now she felt slightly guilty that she'd had that luxury – given the need to keep rotating watches – while her friends had not.

Her watch wore on, minutes merging into an hour, then a second. The darkness was complete. During the first hour, Barron had brought her a warm mug of tea, and she'd sipped it gratefully while keeping her attention firmly on the area outside. Watching and 'feeling' while in contact with her cats allowed her to practice her technique without the debilitating fatigue she'd experienced trying to hone her other gifts. Idly, she wondered what the mechanism might be. It didn't seem to exhaust her cats at all.

She 'felt' a smugness from Storm and agreement from Twister. It startled her slightly. Each time she sat like this with her cats, it seemed that she 'felt' more from them. She'd always known that she and her fellow starcat owners knew more of what their starcats thought and meant than say, a horgal owner, no matter how devoted. But now it seemed that she was beginning to experience shared emotions, in a similar way to how she felt when talking with Fractus or Teacher.

Not for the first time, she wondered just how much her cats really understood. More than most people gave them credit for, she believed, but how much more? She sat and pondered as the watch wore on, carefully making sure that she kept her attention outwards while allowing her brain to mull over her thoughts on starcat intelligence and communication. It was an interesting puzzle.

Towards the end of her watch, a flicker of movement caught her attention just as her two cats pricked their ears, and both came to their feet in a silent, fluid rush. She strained her senses, hands on her cats, and the flicker resolved into a myriad of slithering forms, just on the periphery of her augmented vision. A silent hand signal and Storm was gone into the cave, tidemarks flickering in tones of alarm. She and Twister remained utterly still. The cat's alarm was palpable and Shanna knew precisely what those flickering, slithering forms were. Sliders. She felt a wash of chill fill her body, and faded reflexively. Beside her she could feel Twister doing the same thing, and behind her in the cave she 'felt' all the others and Storm fade as well.

There was complete silence. Nothing moved anywhere in the vegetation surrounding the mouth of the cave. The slithering stream continued to flow past on the extreme edge of Shanna's senses. They 'felt' ... odd ... thousands of individuals driven; massed together with only one desire – the desire to devour living flesh, then procreate yet again, leaving a legacy of death in their wake. Shanna sat frozen and faded, her right hand buried in Twister's fur the only thing reminding her that she was still sitting there inside her own body. The rest of her was focused on the slithering, sliding, whispering mass travelling northwest. She felt their direction like an arrow. They'd heard something in that direction, felt the vibrations that it was was leaving, and were intent on tracking it. The small group of faded humans and Starlyne (Shanna almost gasped) – Fractus was faded too – were still and silent, almost unbreathing in their desire to remain hidden.

The flickers trickled slowly to a few stragglers, then the swarm was gone from Shanna's senses. Beside her Twister slowly relaxed, and Shanna realised that his hackles, which had risen under her hand, were now subsiding. She felt him lose the fade and allowed hers to drop with a sigh of relief, only then realising that somehow she'd managed to fade not only herself and Twister but the entire entry of the cave, replacing it with a mirror image of the vegetation in front of her. Barely daring to move, she slowly removed her hand from Twister. At her signal, he faded again and moved silently off into the darkness. She 'felt' for both her cats, keeping a light touch with Twister and feeling Storm move to her side. She put a hand on the blue-toned cat, and her vision expanded suddenly. Completely disoriented, she almost fell off the rock before she realised that the augmented vision she was experiencing was somehow being relayed from Twister through Storm, to her. Her stomach swirled slightly as her eyes and brain attempted to compensate, and then she could 'see' where Twister was. The perspective was odd, slightly lower than she was accustomed to, and the dull colours of night were overlaid with subtle scents drifting across her vision.

Was this how a starcat perceived the world? She wondered even as she continued to track the slider swarm with Twister. They were safely away now and further away with every second. She 'felt' Twister's satisfaction, then her perspective swooped alarmingly and she slid off the rock, landing with a quiet thud,while the night spiralled nauseously around her. Storm poked her in a slightly puzzled manner with his cold, wet nose. Shanna blinked and her vision righted itself, resolving back into her normal, limited human senses. This time Storm poked her with his paw, encouraging her to get herself off the ground. She did so, still marvelling at what she'd just experienced.

There was a soft rustle, and Barron appeared at her side. "Sliders?"

"Gone now," she replied softly, pleased that her voice was normal, "Twister's just on his way back." Storm was nose to nose with Hunter, and Barron's cat made a pleased hum and winked his tidemarks at Shanna, then turned and nosed Barron. "And I think I've just learnt something new about my cats."

"And we've just learnt something new about Verren. You cadets are full of surprises." He stopped for a moment, and in the darkness Shanna could sense that he was pondering something. "Kalli will be out shortly – you're alright to finish up your watch?"

"Yes, but I do need to tell you what just happened."

"I know, but we also need to discuss what just happened in there." His tone was dry, and he turned and vanished into the cave, and Shanna was left wondering just what it was that Verren had done. By her best guess, she had about half an hour left of her watch, so she sat back down on the rock, resolutely turned her attention outwards again, and tried to still the shivers that suddenly overtook her.

Chapter 22

"AT THE same moment that Storm appeared, Verren gasped, 'Sliders,' then faded himself and Fractus, and the fire went out," said Barron as he handed Shanna a bowl of stew. "While we knew that he could fade easily, he'd never faded anyone else."

"His sudden ability to sense the sliders is unexpected," said Fractus. "The fire? Well, it was always possible, but more likely in Zandany, Ragar, or yourself, Shanna."

"Me? I think I've already got too much to learn. But how did you know about the sliders?" she asked turning to Verren, who was sitting quietly by the fire. He looked shaken and pale to Shanna's eyes, but looked up at her question.

"I'm ... not really sure. We were talking and finishing dinner, and then, there was something. Just on the edges of my mind — but like needles inside my head pricking closer and closer." He shivered, closed his eyes and, wrapped his arms around himself. Shanna dropped to her knees and put a hand on his shoulder.

"They were flickering on the edge of my vision, Verren, but not inside my mind, and that was bad enough." Verren shook his head.

"It was painful, Shan, and I don't know if I can do that again."

"Do what, Verren? Fade Fractus? Put out the fire? Or is it just the sliders?"

"The fading? Well that just made me tired. And I'm not sure how I put the fire out. But the sliders?" He shuddered and dropped his head again. "They were awful, Shan. I could feel them, like a swarm of monsters in my mind wanting to pull me into the abyss with them. All their minds were focused on was food; the need to devour, and to lay their eggs in the warm flesh. It was the one thing on their minds — all of their minds." His voice was muffled and Shanna thought that he sounded close to tears. Cirrus wrapped her long body around his back, her head under his hands, and he cradled her, trembling slightly. Shanna wasn't sure what else to do. She felt suddenly awkward crouched there with her hand on his shoulder, and removed it slowly. Storm hummed quietly at her, but Twister, ever the more impulsive, leaned so heavily on her leg that she overbalanced and ended up throwing her arms around Verren to avoid knocking him over. Obviously mistaking her stumble for a hug, he leaned his head on her shoulder and took a slightly ragged breath. "Thanks, Shan."

She felt even more awkward but at an almost silent hum from Storm, left her arms where they were, tightened them slightly, and cleared her throat.

"That's OK Verren, all this stuff is just so ... " She broke off, not really knowing what to say, but it had apparently been enough because he lifted his head, took another deep breath, then leaned slightly away. She relaxed her arms and tried to drop them normally. They felt odd, a bit like they were too long, so she gave them a wriggle and they seemed to shrink back to normal.

Barron looked at Verren with a slight frown. "This new ability is a gift, Verren." He nodded slowly as Verren looked up startled. "We still remember the Patrols who haven't returned. Or the vanished Scouts. It has been many years since such an occurrence, but once a year we hold our own remembrance ceremony at Scout compound to remember those of our number who have vanished here Below and on the plateau. Our group's beginnings are with the initial eradication of slider colonies from the plateau."

A slight feeling of awkwardness tinged the atmosphere, and Shanna was certain it came from Fractus. She turned her head and glanced at the Starlyne. His tidemarks were cycling in unfathomable patterns, and the last few images that Keeper had transmitted before his death slid across her mind. She shelved the half-formed thought and turned her attention back to Barron. "You may hold the key to our safety, Verren. You and Shanna, and others like you, who can detect the approach of a slider swarm and provide warning." Verren shook his head slightly.

"He's right, Verren, We both detected them at the same time as the cats today. Imagine a settlement Below – even without cats, they'd have advance warning!" Verren continued to look unconvinced, and Shanna wondered just what it was that he'd felt that had shaken him so much.

"And what did you discover, Shanna?" Barron turned his attention to Shanna with one eyebrow raised in query. She hurried to explain, and as she described looking through Twister's eyes, experienced a mild swirl of nausea at the remembered sensation.

Barron's face broke into a smile. "So our ability to see ahead has just increased! I wonder how many of us might be able to do this! Explain again how you discovered this ability, Shanna!" He and Fractus began to quiz her, extracting as many details as possible, then Barron began experimenting with Hunter. Shanna noticed that he had avoided questioning Verren any further, and hadn't requested a demonstration of Verren's skill. The dark haired young man still looked shaken, and Shanna wondered if he'd considered whether he could identify other predators in the same way. She sneaked another glance then put the thought firmly away for another time, and continued instructing Barron.

Later when Fractus had taken the watch, she sent Storm outside to assist him and began with Kalli. It appeared that the ability was linked to the individual's ability to 'see' at night with that oddly enhanced vision. The more developed the ability, the easier it was for the person to link with their cat and 'see ahead'. It was a relief to find that both Barron and Kalli experienced the same nausea that Shanna had when seeing through her cats' eyes, and that for once she was not alone in struggling with a new skill.

As they experimented, she realised that having two cats seemed to extend her ability far beyond that of her comrades. The others struggled to maintain the vision further than about fifty metres. Shanna, by keeping one cat with her and using him to link to the other, was able to push her perception out to at least twice that. She experimented briefly, sending Storm on wide sweeps while maintaining contact with Twister in the cave. She ceased the contact abruptly, when she called Storm in using her silent whistle and he blurred into top speed. She nearly emptied her stomach of its dinner and hurriedly removed her hand, as the night-time world swooped in a circle and trees began to blur past. She slumped forward, sweating and pale, swallowing convulsively as she fought to keep her stomach under control.

"You OK, Shan?" Verren's face was concerned, and despite her nausea, Shanna was glad to hear him speak. He'd been unnaturally quiet since the episode with the sliders, sitting next to the fire with his arms tucked around his legs, pale and morose. It was such a different Verren to the smiling, compassionate one she'd come to know so well, that Shanna had become more and more worried as the evening progressed.

Swallowing against her nausea, she raised one hand palm out, and said. "I'm alright, but make sure you break contact with your cat before you call them – having them run while looking through their eyes is not doing my stomach any good!" Twister nosed her gently although she had the distinct idea that he was slightly amused, and she finally sat back and pushed her hair out of her eyes. "That was not fun. I don't know if I'll ever get used to that kind of motion while looking through either of their eyes." She blew out through puffed cheeks and sipped from her bottle. The nausea subsided slowly until she was able to sit up again. "I think that's enough for tonight." She stretched her legs and wriggled a bit to get more comfortable.

"Time to turn in, I think," said Barron. "Are you right to take the early watch, Shanna?" He raised his eyebrows meaningfully at her. Surprised, Shanna was about to remind him that she'd already sat her watch, but then realised why he was asking and simply nodded.

"But that's my watch," began Verren.

"You need a full night's sleep," Barron said. "Shanna had one a few nights ago, and I need you alert and awake tomorrow."

"That's right," replied Shanna. "And I felt heaps better the next morning. It's not a problem for me tonight." She knew she'd be tired the next night, but Verren still looked shaken, and it was obvious that he'd struggle with strange noises and the possibility of sliders swarming through the night. Much better for me to take that watch tonight, she thought. And there was also the possibility of practicing with her cats. Although the thought of a running starcat sent a tiny tremble through her stomach, which she immediately repressed ruthlessly.

"I'll turn in then," she said, and pushed herself to her feet, collected her pack, and began to pull out her bedding. She yawned and rummaged through her spare clothing. After so many weeks Below, her socks and underwear were in need of a good wash. She wrinkled her nose as she removed her boots and slid into her sleepsack. Barron carefully banked the fire, and in the dim light Shanna could see the others beginning to settle down around her.

Cirrus paused by her spot as she snuggled down, and hummed a query at her cats. Storm and Twister replied with a flicker of tidemarks, and Cirrus purred and settled down next to Shanna's head near the cave wall. Shanna looked at her cats quizzically in the dim light, then nodded as Verren brought his sleepsack over. She wriggled away from the side of the cave, and patted the ground next to her. "Come and tuck in here, Verren, the ground's not too hard, and none of us will wake you if you're near the wall." He looked relieved, and Shanna realised that Cirrus had positioned him in the most secure portion of the cave; bracketed by three starcats, and next to the person he knew best.

She smiled as Verren tucked himself in beside her, and Cirrus lay between them. Storm positioned himself near her head and Twister at her feet, a barrier between Verren and any possible threat. She hoped that the security might bring him some rest and new perspective the following morning. Pretending to drift off, she watched as Cirrus carefully snuggled into Verren, her long length vibrating in a gentle purr. He tucked an arm over her and his eyes slowly closed. As exhaustion claimed him, he began to take the long slow breaths of deep sleep. Reassured, she closed her own eyes and allowed sleep to claim her.

It seemed like only a moment later when Barron woke her gently. Yawning, she shoved her way out of her sleepsack, automatically compacting it into its compression sack and stowing it in her pack by the faint light from the few remaining embers, before making her way out into the cool night air. It was the deep dark of final watch. Shanna recalled hearing someone say that it was always darkest before dawn, and she wondered who had originally coined the expression. The early watch always reminded her of that. It was often pitch dark, and as she walked silently outside to where Barron awaited her with Hunter, she was hard pressed to make out his form.

"Nothing much tonight," came his quiet voice. "A few weldens passed an hour ago, but no sign of the slider swarm returning. And thank you. Verren needed the sleep. You know him better than I do, so I'd like you to keep a close eye on him over the next few days. He was more shaken than I'd like tonight."

"Of course," she replied quietly.

After he'd left Shanna settled herself on her rock again, sending her cats to circle the camp in opposite directions before settling in to concentrate on listening and allowing her vision to adjust fully to the darkness. Knowing that there was little to bother them in the vicinity right then, she decided not to practice looking through the eyes of her cats, but instead to make sure she was blending into her surrounds, sitting so still and silent that there was nothing to distinguish her from the sounds and scents of the last few hours of night.

The last watch of the night was always the most difficult, Shanna had found. The combination of not quite enough sleep and the quiet darkness that bled slowly into grey was mesmerising. Shanna often struggled to stay properly alert when it was her turn to take the last watch, but her memory of the sliders was still vivid, and she found her mind wandering back to her first encounter with them. It seemed like such a long time ago, and she realised that it was on that trip that they'd realised that someone else had come to Frontier. She remembered the hope that had run through her. The possibility of recontact with the Federation of Races and the old dream that she'd shared with her father, the one that said that one day they'd regain the stars and soar amongst the galaxies. That hope had been sorely crushed.

The heart pounding fear she'd felt when the swarm of sliders had slithered past on that first nerve-wracking journey into the wildness of Below, woke her arms to shivers, goosebumps tickling and tingling on her bare skin. She curled her toes in her boots and pushed the memory back. Instead she turned her attention to Verren's new skill. The idea of 'feeling' the minds of creatures like the sliders made her uneasy, but she could easily understand Barron's enthusiasm for the idea.

Verren had always been so relaxed and comfortable Below that to see him so upset had shaken Shanna. As she sat on her rock staring into the darkness, part of her listening to the sounds of Below, she reminded herself of his cleverness, the joyful relationship he had with Cirrus, and the easy camaraderie he had with all their cadet group. Over the past months, Verren had grown and matured – as they had all had to Shanna reminded herself – but he had taken each new thing in his stride. Shanna knew he had a large family, but she wondered suddenly whether the sadness of missing his family was also affecting him. Perhaps he'd been masking it better than she had. She'd been so tied up in her own worries that she'd spared little time for anyone else's.

A small tsunami of guilt broke over her. Barron had a wife, she recalled, and Kalli had two sisters she often talked about. Fractus had children and grandchildren. Her other friends and colleagues had loved ones they hadn't seen for weeks, and Shanna realised that they'd largely avoided talking about those they'd left behind on the plateau. Perhaps the uncertainty had been too difficult to cope with, but she knew that she had had moments where she'd wallowed in self pity and loss herself, oblivious to her friends' needs. In the quiet of the hours before dawn, she resolved to be a better friend who looked out for the needs of others.

As the sky began to fade from darkness into the grey of early morning, she stifled a yawn and wriggled her toes in their boots against the chill. The watch had been quiet, and she was as tired as she'd ever been at the end of one. The cave behind her was still silent, and Shanna's stomach rumbled as Twister returned from a circle through the trees. There was a soft sound from behind her and Storm flicked one unconcerned ear before relaxing. Verren stepped softly into view, and handed her a mug of warm tea. She nodded her thanks and moved over on the rock so that he could sit down if he wished.

"Thanks, Shan." His voice was quiet and subdued as he perched himself on the rock beside her. He flicked a finger, and Cirrus darted off into the undergrowth, hunting for her breakfast. Shanna felt Storm twitch slightly and with a small smile, signalled him to follow Cirrus . As he vanished after his sister, she ran a consoling hand over Twister's head.

"Not long. Twister. As soon as he's eaten you can catch yours." Her voice was muted, cautious as ever to blend in while Below. She sneaked a glance at Verren, wondering how he was after the night's dramas. In the weak light of early dawn he still looked pale and drawn, but somehow more at peace than the previous night. She decided to risk a question. "How are you this morning, Verren?"

There was silence from beside her, that seemed to stretch out awkwardly. Finally she heard Verren draw a slightly ragged indrawn breath. "I'll be OK I think, but it'll take some time." His voice trailed into silence again and they sat, looking into the dense greenery, listening to the morning noises of Below begin to sound around them. Shanna idly catalogued them in her mind, then wondered whether Verren could 'hear' them, like he'd heard the sliders.

"Can you 'hear' anything but sliders, Verren?" The words were out before she could stop them, and she wondered if she'd overstepped. Shanna was acutely conscious of Verren's rigidity beside her and she was about to apologise when he spoke up. His voice was almost too quiet to hear.

"No, it's only sliders as far as I can tell," he said, "And although I can understand that it's a useful talent, I'm dreading 'hearing' them again." He shuddered slightly. "They're so alien, so cold, and so single minded, and it's like they're crawling around inside my head." Shanna shook her head and felt a shiver.

"I'm so sorry, Verren," she said quietly. "It's hard isn't it? Suddenly developing 'talents' that will help us defeat the Garsal, but that also turn you upside down and inside out at the same time." Sometimes her head buzzed with all of the things she was supposed to be able to do. Verren said nothing, just nodded, but a few minutes later he stood and returned to the cave, saying nothing but leaving her with a brief hand on her shoulder. A few moments later, Storm and Cirrus returned, each carrying several large marmals. Storm dropped one at Twister's feet, then went with Cirrus to deliver the others to the cave. He returned in a minute or two and began to eat. Shanna sipped her now lukewarm tea and continued her watch.

An hour later as Shanna breakfasted on a variety of fruits and nuts foraged by Kalli, she almost dropped her second cup of tea as Fractus uncoiled rapidly and hurtled out of the cave. Fearful of another slider swarm, she started to her feet, but after realising that her cats were completely relaxed, Shanna hurriedly finished the dregs in her cup, shovelled down a few last nuts, and got to her feet, wiping her hands on her grubby trousers. She followed Barron out of the cave.

Fractus was under a tree, head raised, and arms unfolded. His tensed coils showed concentration in every line. Barron held up one hand, signalling silence and caution, and the four humans fanned out around him, each signalling their cat to begin an overlapping guard pattern. Shanna deliberately extended her senses, swallowing against sudden nausea as she realised that she was seeing through two sets of starcat eyes. She disengaged as fast as possible and the nausea subsided.

Cautiously she reached out to her cats, and realising that Twister was ranging further out than Storm, allowed herself to see through only his eyes. He climbed a tree in a rush and Shanna nearly lost her breakfast, swallowing convulsively to keep it in her stomach. Once at the top of the tree, Twister paused and Shanna had enough time to steady herself, before he began to leap from treetop to treetop. She was better prepared after his first leap, and was able to begin to process the images seen through Twister's eyes, along with the ones coming through her own. She felt as though her brain was slightly dislocated and the images occasionally overlapped. After several minutes the strain grew too much and she let go of contact with Twister. Fortunately Barron's low call came very shortly, and she closed in on his command, assembling around Fractus with the others. The Starlyne sagged slightly and his coils relaxed.

"I have made contact with Teacher and Radiant," came his voice. "The others have just exited the gorge. They will make haste to catch up with us. In the meantime, Spiron wishes us to continue south. They will be faster, navigating from cairn to cairn, and should catch us up within the week. I have warned them about the sliders. Hopefully they won't encounter them. I will need to rest, I'm afraid, the distance was almost too far."

Uncharacteristically, the Starlyne faltered slightly, and Shanna wondered how they'd deal with an unconscious Starlyne if he collapsed. She couldn't imagine how they'd move him.

"We'll stay here for as long as required, Fractus," replied Barron. "A day's rest will do all of us some good, and we can work on replenishing our supplies. There's an abundance of fruit and nut trees here. And perhaps we can work on Verren and Shanna's new talents. It may be that others of us have further skills to add."

Shanna was relieved. An extra day for both herself and Verren to process their new skills would be very welcome, and the cave was a much more secure campsite than most of the others they'd located south of the range. She wondered just how many more skills she might develop, and how she was possibly going to hone them all. She called in Twister and Storm as Barron began to assign tasks.

Chapter 23

A WEEK later, Shanna launched herself off an escarpment overlooking a wide basin. It had been a long, slow week as they worked their way gradually further south, pausing frequently to allow inimical wildlife to move on, and roughly cataloguing the slowly increasing numbers of plants that were either unknown on the plateau, or variants on familiar ones. Fractus had reported that the other group was coming closer each day, and Shanna hoped to see them later that day.

She'd left both of her cats sitting on the edge of the dropoff. Their presence was a steady beacon in her mind, anchoring her and giving her a safe point to return to. She swept her eyes across the vista spread before her, and concentrated on maintaining steady flight across the basin. The weeks of hard travel and flying had toughened her body. She felt strong as the wind whistled around her, and soared higher on a convenient thermal. Her ability to see the wind currents while she was aloft had strengthened with repeated flights, and her fears of those first few trials had receded, and had largely been replaced by feelings of exhilaration as she rode the winds, high above the ground.

Angling her flight to the east, Shanna began a wide sweep around the perimeter of the basin. The vehicle tracks had plummeted over the edge of the escarpment and disappeared into dense vegetation, and despite the height of the ridge line it had been almost impossible to see where they were headed. Shanna hoped she'd be able to get a general sense of direction. For the first time since beginning the trek, the tracks were difficult to identify from a height. She continued following the edge of the basin, scanning along it to make sure that the vehicle hadn't simply dropped in and out of the bowl-like formation briefly. The western portion of the bowl was obscured by light, misty cloud and Shanna hoped that she would locate the track before having to plunge into its cold wetness to scout the other side of the basin. Unfortunately the cloud was so low that she would have no room to fly underneath it.

Still feeling strong after half an hour of sweeping the rim, Shanna came to the unhappy conclusion that she would have to grit her teeth and drop into the dampness. She took a quick mental bearing on her cats and flew towards the cloud. It was just as cold and wet as she'd dreaded; as chilly trickles began to dribble down her neck she had to shake her head repeatedly to clear her vision. Several minutes of discomfort later, she dropped as low as she dared, straining her eyes as much as she was able to penetrate the silvery mist, in order to scan the edge of the basin.

Gradually she was able to make out the rocky formations clothed in dense greenery that formed the escarpment to the west and south west, and began flying along it. It was cold, miserable work, and as the thickly forested slopes continued unbroken, Shanna began to wonder if they had finally come to the end of their southward trek. She flew on, gradually becoming colder and wetter, and still no scar in the ridge line indicated that the Garsal vehicle had entered the basin from the west.

Shanna suddenly realised that her limbs were rapidly tiring. She was beginning to shiver and her arms had begun to tremble. She risked a glance over the surface of her wings. Her wingsuit, although normally light and comfortable had become heavy with condensation, and the very forward edges even had small areas of frost beginning to form. With a slight sense of panic Shanna tried to estimate how far she was from her start point. Muffled by the cloud layer, it was difficult to see the sun, so she concentrated hard on Storm and Twister. To her relief, they were close by on her right, and commencing one final sweep she began to arrow towards them. As she homed in on them, she realised that during her flight, the cloud layer must have slowly drifted to the east and now covered her take off point.

She slipped in and out of her 'other' vision, desperately trying to penetrate the mist enough to be able to sight her landing. Beginning to despair she was just starting to consider flying as fast as she could to the east, hoping to fly far enough out of the cloud to land somewhere - anywhere - when Fractus' voice sounded in her mind.

"You're on target, Shanna, follow my voice and the 'feel' of your cats. Just lift a little, now." She complied, pushing back some of the panic that threatened to overwhelm her. The heaviness in her limbs was increasing very quickly now, and she hoped that the ledge she'd launched from was close.

"A little higher. That's right. Now straight to me, slow your speed a little, feel your cats ... " She focused on Fractus' voice and tried as hard as she could to keep her flight steady. The mist had thickened again, and she felt like she was flying in a cold wet cocoon far from any firm ground. "Almost there, slow down, slow down, more, more, more – now just lift slightly, slowly, you'll be landing in thirty seconds."

Shanna gulped slightly. She still couldn't see anything. She could however 'feel' her cats, and tried to concentrate on them as an anchor in the mist. "Begin to head into the wind, Shan," came the Starlyne's voice and she obeyed, even as she could feel the panic starting to overwhelm her again. "Now, pull up, then drop in 3,2,1, now!" She followed Fractus' instructions and dropped blindly through the mist.

There was a moment of suspension, then she hit the ground hard and crumpled forward, barely remembering to pull in the extensions of her suit before everything ended in a tangle. She landed on her right shoulder as she stumbled forward, feeling it hit something sharp, then finally came to rest, painfully aware that she hurt in a number of places, and that several faces were peering down at her in concern. She slumped completely and tried to ease her shoulder off the rock she'd hit. Yet again she was exhausted, and this time she was sore, cold and wet as well.

"Are you all right, Shanna?" There was concern in Verren's voice as he carefully helped her roll over.

"I'm not sure," she replied. She carefully tested her limbs as he began to help her slowly out of her flight suit. There was a fair amount of aching in her right shoulder, and the muscles of her abdomen complained bitterly as Verren heaved her to her feet. She swung her arm experimentally and winced as it twinged, then realised that she'd probably rolled her ankle as well. It was mildly uncomfortable as she leaned her weight on it. "My shoulder's pretty sore, but it seems to be more bruising than anything. And I think my ankle will be sore for a day or two. I know my stomach muscles are unhappy."

"We'll have a proper look when we make camp," said Barron. "Kalli's found us a nice little niche just under the edge of the escarpment, right in a grove of pungo trees. Apparently there's even a creek nearby. Here, lean on me and tell your cats to range ahead. I don't want to trip over them."

Shanna carefully leaned some of her weight onto Barron's outstretched arm, and with his help began to work her way carefully down to the campsite, hoping fervently she'd be all right by the next morning. Injuring herself just as it looked like they might have located the general area of the Garsal ship, would make things difficult for everyone.

After she was seated in Kalli's campsite, she began to relate what she'd seen – or more properly what she hadn't. Apparently Fractus had managed to pull quite a number of images from her mind as she flew, but after she'd dropped into the mist he'd had little to relay.

"Unfortunately most of what I found was you feeling cold and shivery," he said, with a feeling of wry amusement. "When we realised how fast that cloud bank was moving, we had to try and figure out how to get you back safely. It was Barron's idea to have me talk you in. And it was successful – mostly." There was a feeling of amusement radiating from the Starlyne.

Shanna shivered slightly; she was still cold and very tired, and she ached all over. A quick check from Verren had declared her more bruised than any-thing else, but the ankle was likely to be uncomfortable for a few days. Her boot was off, and there was some mild swelling and bruising appearing around the outside of her anklebone. She hoped her boot would go back on.

"Where are the others?" she asked, suddenly remembering that they had expected to meet up with the larger group later that day.

"They'll be here very shortly," said Fractus. "Are you sure there were no signs of the vehicle track anywhere on the rim?"

"I'm sure," said Shanna. "I think they're probably down in the basin somewhere." As she said the words, the reality of finally viewing the Garsal ship made her feel suddenly shaky – but not fearfully so – shaky in the kind of way she'd felt before exciting new challenges. Anticipatory rather than frightened. She wondered briefly if she was mad to feel that, surely she should be terrified at the prospect of confronting one of the galaxy's most dangerous species.

There were odd expressions on the faces looking at her. She could feel a grim kind of resolution emanating from the Starlyne, and Verren's face was closed and still. Kalli's expression was simply determined. It was the kind of look Shanna had seen when someone had an unpleasant task to do, but knew it needed to be done and done well. Verren broke the spell.

"Let's get this ankle strapped for the evening. You'll want to be able to put your boot on in the morning, so you're going to have to keep it elevated to-night."

"And you want to survive the experience of my dirty sock," said Shanna, attempting to lighten the mood. The first proper smile she'd seen for days crossed Verren's face as he rummaged in his pack.

"I wondered what the stench was," he replied as he pulled a roll of band-age from his pack. "This is something that I haven't tried out yet. Mum said it might come in handy months ago. I'd almost forgotten I had it." He began to strap Shanna's ankle, carefully covering the swelling, tightening the bandage gently, making sure to firm the pressure on the outside of her ankle as he pulled it upwards. "Can you pass me that water, Kalli?" He took the offered water-bottle and dripped water carefully onto the bandage. Shanna felt a cool tingle, and as she tried to move her ankle stopped, surprised.

"Is it stuck to me?" she asked.

"Yes," replied Verren. He tested the strapping and smiled as it restricted her sideways movement. "Apparently they've impregnated the cloth with some kind of adhesive that's safe for skin. You can leave it on for a few days and let the ligaments settle down. It'll make sure you don't roll it again. It'll also help stop the swelling. When it's starting to feel loose, we'll take it off and see how the ankle is."

With her ankle strapped and elevated on her pack, Shanna felt much better and managed to smile her thanks to Verren. She did notice that he handled her sock rather gingerly as he tucked it into her boot, though. "Sorry!" she said contritely, "I was hoping to have time to wash and dry them at some point, but we've been too much on the move. Hope I haven't poisoned you!" Verren snickered.

"I thought mine were going to walk away last night. I've saved one pair for a moment of need. The others? Well, better not to think about them." He swallowed slightly and went on, "Well, now that you're laid up, and we're go-ing to be here for the rest of the day, perhaps I could wash both our socks. I'll check with Barron first though."

"Now that's a statement of true friendship if ever I heard one!" comment-ed Kalli. "I can smell your socks from here Shanna!"

"You'd wash my socks, Verren?"

"Only because you can't do it yourself, and don't worry, I'll extract some suitable payment at a later date. Assuming I survive the experience – judging by the smell, they could be toxic!" He moved off quietly to where Barron sat on the perimeter of the pungo grove and Shanna relaxed, oddly reassured by the conversation. Perhaps Verren had overcome his horror of feeling the sliders inside his mind. By her side, both cats suddenly pricked their ears then relaxed, and a few moments later Satin strolled into the campsite. The others had finally arrived.

***

Cerren looked up as Peron entered his office, Thunder as always, trotting after him. The young cat was growing, he mused, and would be a very large cat one day if the promise of the size of his feet were to be believed. Socks greeted the youngster with a hum and flicked her tail in an enticement for him to play. Peron released the cub with a quick gesture, and he bounded exuberantly over to the grey starcat.

Peron collapsed tiredly into a chair and pulled another over to prop his booted feet on.

"How was your check of the old storm shelters?" asked Cerren.

"Toman has them all manned with oldsters, the signal fires have been set, and our allies have provided us with some powerful lights as well. Toman has a group working with them to devise appropriate signal codes. Where the shelters are near Starlyne habitations, there are communications set in place so that we can coordinate quickly. If all else fails, the Starlynes have agreed to take the children."

"And Tamazine still has no idea?"

"Not unless she's had someone undetectable by a starcat trailing me day and night," replied Peron. "I was fortunate enough to have the loan of Shanti, one of the breeding females from Hillview. She's a good tracker, and adept at stalking. She didn't twitch an ear the whole time I was out there. She taught Thunder a good deal too." He looked over indulgently at the playing cub. "I think she was glad to have a break from her latest litter, and Janna was keen to wean them, so the timing was perfect."

"Well that's one less worry," said Cerren. "At least if it all goes awry, we have a chance of hiding some of our people, and at least the children will be safe."

"And how is the Senior Councillor?" asked Peron.

Cerren shook his head slowly.

"No improvement at all. Some of the Councillors are beginning to come around but she remains intractable. Who knows what idiocy she might think up next?" Cerren rose, leaned across the desk and pushed the papers he'd been working on across to Peron. "These are my suggestions to streamline the emergency measures that the militia subcommittee have been working on. Unfortunately the subcommittee is mostly composed of Councillors from Northaven and Starfall. The only one with intimate knowledge of the terrain around this region is Payne, and he's only one man. The others should bow to his superior knowledge of the area, but some of Tamazine's cronies are hell-bent on following her directions. Payne asked me to add my thoughts." Peron picked up the sheaf of papers and began to flick through them. His bushy eyebrows rose higher at each page. Finally her threw them back onto the desk with disgust.

"Why can't they see simple reason?" His exasperation was obvious. "They need the simplest things explained to them in words of one syllable. How did these idiots ever get voted into office?"

Cerren nodded in sympathy. "You know, I've wondered that myself. It's been fifty years since the last real disaster. In that time, we've allowed ourselves to become complacent."

He looked up at Peron's exclamation, "Not the Scout Corps, but the populace in general. We've kept ourselves looking forward, and spent our time gathering information and exploring. But those who live in the larger centres have been removed from the immediacy of life in the outer regions. Despite our ceremonies on the Day of Remembrance, survival on Frontier has been accomplished in their eyes. Consequently, they've elected good administrators rather than visionaries, or those with an eye to expansion. It's only in Watch-tower and the smaller centres that we remember just how tenuous our hold on this world really is." He paused again. "And now when we find ourselves confronting an enemy none of us ever expected to encounter, our leadership is lacking."

"You really think this is the problem?" asked Peron seriously.

"Yes I do," replied Cerren. "How many times have you seen outward looking candidates overlooked for conservative ones?" Peron pondered his statement for some time before replying, absently rubbing Thunder's head as the cub ambled over to his partner.

"It's true. Our candidates are never inward looking conservatives, though."

"No they're not – they're Scouts, and to be a good Scout you have to be able to look beyond the end of your nose and into the future. There are other good leaders, and in normal times our leadership is adequate, but now is not a normal time." He pulled the paperwork back towards himself and began to leaf through it. "All we can do now is continue what we've begun. Our Star-lyne friends are as well prepared as possible, and we have our buffer, thanks to Toman and the oldsters." He pulled another file from the bookcase behind his desk. It was cased in leather and tied neatly with string.

"This is the full roster of Scout personnel. I've included the families and the starcat breeders as well, along with key personnel in the militia and council who must be saved at all costs should the worst occur. I'd like you to prepare an evacuation plan." Peron nodded slowly and took the folder.

"Let's hope it doesn't come to that."

***

The Garsal vehicle approached the southwestern portion of the Plateau cautiously. They had made good time as they became accustomed to manoeuvring the vehicle through the dense jungle. Trial and error had taught the Senior Trooper that caution and speed were the two things that kept them relatively unscathed. His vehicle was agile and it moved swiftly, and as the days had worn on, the three Garsal had become adept at avoiding the more dangerous predators.

He had been in contact with the Overlord on a regular basis, and was now able to report that they were within striking distance of the plateau. His instructions were to use all possible stealth to ascend then survey the plateau. He toyed with the map screen again, his manipulator arms deftly flicking through the images relayed from the colony ship. The original surveys from the flyover showed only basic definition. The plateau appeared to have three main settlements. One towards the northern edge, one centrally located, and one not far from the southern edge. He could just make out smaller satellite settlements around the larger areas. They were ill defined, noted only because they had tight congregations of life signs. He pulled up some of the images taken by colony ship as it had passed high above the plateau. They were difficult to interpret, but he was fairly certain that there was an area in the south west where he might be able to ascend the plateau undetected.

Despite their familiarity with the planet's ecology, there were no signs that these humans had high tech capabilities. That they were clever, he had no doubt, and wondered yet again how they had managed to defeat four armoured vehicles. He dismissed the tinge of apprehension that came with that thought and began to plan the ascent.

More concerning to him was the thought that to properly assess the human settlements on the plateau, he might have to leave the safety of the vehicle to scout on foot. The vehicle was simply too noticeable. Unfortunately, survival outside the vehicle was problematic. He also wondered whether having come so far, he might fail and pay the ultimate price at the last hurdle.

Having made his decision, he turned his attention to the communicator and began to contact the colony ship with his updated plans.

***

The Garsal Overlord clicked his palps with satisfaction as he scrolled through the reports from the hive builders on the screen in front of him. As he did he rolled a small stone backwards and forwards across the work surface. It was an unusual find, but his scientists had indicated that the glowing rock was safe and most likely possessed of unique qualities. It was also attractive, and he now had several in the hands of the artisans being prepared in decorative settings. They should prove fitting gifts for the Matriarch.

Despite days of inclement weather, and the setbacks caused by the discovery of the unexpected human presence on the planet, hive construction was now well under way, and he was looking forward to the next tour with the Matriarch. There was little she would be able to find fault with this time, and to present her with such a find as the glowing stone would be one more step towards the chance of offspring. One more roll across his workstation, and he placed the stone back into the carved box he'd had fashioned to display its beauty.

A chime sounded from his tablet and he tapped the two new icons on the screen. With satisfaction he read the report from Vehicle One, now located at the base of the plateau. The report was concise and well structured, and the Senior Trooper's plan sound. His success to date was all the more remarkable given that the other two surviving vehicles had limped back to the colony ship some weeks previously, heavily damaged. He tapped again, uploading a small commendation to the trooper's file, then opened the other icon.

Again he clacked his palps. After months of struggle, his tenuous grip on this planet was about to firm. The minerals needed for reconstruction of the lost aircraft had been located and refined. The equipment carried in the hold of the huge ship was set up in the hive's new manufacturing chambers. It appeared that his decision to remain in sole control was being vindicated. Production of replacement aircraft would begin almost immediately. Decisively, he tapped at the screen again.

"Prepare an offering tray for the Matriarch," he said when Zoash appeared. "Include the jewellery and some of the fruits she so likes. I will write the invitation in my own hand." Zoash inclined his head and proffered the brush pen.

"She will be pleased with the progress of the hive, Overlord."

"She cannot fail to be. All proceeds perfectly." He completed the last flowery phrase and handed the thick paper to Zoash. "And our plans are beginning to prosper." He sat back satisfied as his Sib departed.

***

"Peron, I need more messengers," said Toman, tapping her list with her pencil. "The old storm shelters are now usable again but some of the oldsters manning them are no longer agile enough to travel regularly. Although we have signal fires and those lights from the Starlynes, we need to be able to send more complex messages." Peron frowned at the old Scout Master across his desk.

"Are you sure you can't just reorganise your assignments — pair able-bodied with aged?" he asked.

"I just don't have enough able bodies," replied Toman. "And before you ask about able-bodied cats — you have to remember these are our retirees, and their cats are generally old or injured too. For heaven's sakes, I'm a retiree." She shook her head in frustration, white hair now tousled into disarray. She pushed one dark brown, weathered hand through the white strands impatiently and tapped her list again. "What about that class of yours? There's a few possibilities in there, surely."

"They're only children," said Peron. "None of them are cadets, and they only have borrowed cats."

"That young offworlder has his own cat, and he's no child," replied Toman. "What about if I paired them up?"

"They're not trained, Toman," replied Peron patiently. "We're just trying to keep their education on track really, and teach young Anjo about this world and how to survive in it. In return, those children learn about the Garsal first hand. Some of them may choose the Scout Corps perhaps, when this is over."

"When this is over? Do we really have the luxury of waiting until 'this is over' for anything?" Toman's tone was impatient. "I need messengers. You have possibilities. Let's try for a compromise. I'll take on their education along with a couple of the other oldsters, and you'll let me train them as messengers." She raised a hand as Peron opened his mouth to object. "I'll keep them safe, and those without their own cats can continue to work with the cubs under the guidance of some of our most experienced cat trainers." She flicked a calculating glance at Peron. "I've got Cally tucked away at one of the outposts and she's still got Mirror, old though she may be." She played her trump card slyly. "And they'll only be doing short trips — two to three hours at most. It's mainly routine stuff — supply lists, maps, tactical information and Starlyne liaison." She chuckled. "And I know you want to expose the youngsters to the Starlynes sooner rather than later."

Peron raised his eyebrows in surprise. "You're as devious as you always were, Toman. I don't know why I'm so surprised — you're right of course, we don't want the youngsters to learn Tamazine's xenophobia. We want them to think that contact with an alien species is right and proper and normal." He rubbed his chin thoughtfully. "You may have a point, but I'll need to canvass the parents."

"You know, Peron, most of those parents will probably be glad that their children aren't sitting in the midst of the biggest target on this edge of the plateau." Her voice was forthright. "They're not stupid. Everyone with any sense can see what Tamazine's doing, and you'd probably be surprised at how many of them have guessed at how we're trying to work around her."

"So long as Tamazine doesn't guess as well."

"I don't think you need have any worries about that. Tamazine couldn't spot a staureg in a wood pile until it was gnawing her leg off."

Peron looked soberly at the old Master. She was thin and weathered, and her starcat had jagged scars down one side and walked with a limp, but her skinny frame exuded strength. Her starcat was purring steadily. His name was Ghost, Peron recalled. Ghost's injury almost ten years ago, in defence of a small child who had strayed from her home, had been a sore loss to the scouts.

"I'll talk to Cerren and the other Masters, Toman, and let you know our decision this evening." He fished in his tray and pulled out the list Cerren had given him, now attached to his evacuation plan. "You need a copy of this as well. Make sure your core group are familiar with it. You'll be primarily responsible for carrying it out should the need arise." Toman took the list and ran her eyes down it slowly, then folded it neatly into her satchel.

"You can be sure it will be done, Peron. And think on what I've said. It's a good plan, and will take some of burden from us both." She rose easily from her chair and gestured to Ghost. He rose with less grace and carefully stretched his leg before limping to her side. She gently scratched his cheek and then the two of them left the room.

"Come, Thunder, let's see what Cerren thinks of Toman's plan." The little starcat padded obediently after him as they exited the office.

Chapter 24

SHANNA peered carefully through a screen of overhanging leaves, easing herself gently into a half-crouch. Dropping onto one knee she signalled Storm to sweep ahead with Satin, and the two cats glided out on oblique headings while she sent Twister ahead through the treetops and concentrated on staying concealed.

After the reunion with the rest of Patrol Ten, Amma, Spiron and Allad had taken to the skies early the next morning. It had been a cloudless day, and the three fliers had carefully flown a search pattern across the basin. Within two hours, they had located the Garsal ship. Images relayed by the three Starlynes had shown a squat black hemisphere surrounded by blackened vegetation, tucked into the far western portion of the basin, just where the clouds had been at their thickest the previous day. Shanna had probably flown within a kilometre of the site, but focused as she had been on the rim and handicapped by the confounding cloud, had been unable to see the ship. Amma had flown directly over it on her fifth sweep. Still the strongest and most capable of the fliers, she had swooped as low as she dared, trying to fix as many details in her mind as possible, while hoping that she was out of reach of the Garsal sensors.

And then the three Starlynes had explained why they were unable to venture any further.

"The Garsal know our body signatures," Teacher had explained. "We are large, and the Garsal are masters of technology. It was the reason that so few of our people escaped them. For many years we strove to defeat their ability to detect us, to no avail. All attempts ended in failure and death for those involved. Even now after many thousands of years on this planet, we are still no closer to being able to avoid detection. You humans, on the other hand, are more difficult to detect, particularly when paired with starcats, and when you fade you become virtually undetectable. But we are unable to go further towards the Garsal ship with you. The three of us will wait here and prepare for your escape once the communications systems have been disabled, but this is our stopping point."

Shanna could feel the frustration, shame, sadness and hope colouring Teacher's thoughts as she finished speaking.

Then Fractus had spoken. "Radiant will begin the trek back towards the southern range. He will attempt to contact our people so that they will know that we have located the ship. We ask that you send one Scout and starcat with him. They can share the watches. It is imperative that our people know the location of this ship, should our mission fail."

Shanna had been shocked, but Spiron had simply nodded, exchanged a look with Barron, and tasked Perri with accompanying Radiant. The Scout had nodded, called her cat and vanished to prepare for the journey. Objectively, Shanna could understand the reasoning behind Spiron's decision, but the idea that they might all perish in the assault on the Garsal communications systems still shocked her. It was an outcome she had never considered. From the moment they'd left the Starlyne habitation, she'd known that lives were at stake, hers, Storm's, Twister's and everyone's individually, but all of them? Her mind kept rejecting the idea.

The farewell with Perri had been particularly difficult. Perri knew that her still recovering knee was a liability for an assault on the aliens, but she also knew that she might be farewelling friends and colleagues for the last time. For Shanna, it had been the most sobering moment since the battle with the Garsal vehicles, and along with nearly all of the others she had decided to send a note to her family. It said, very simply:

Mum, Dad, Kaidan, I love you. Know that I'm where I am, by my choice alone, because I have the chance to make a difference in this fight. The boys are with me, and we'll look after each other. There's nothing more to do except to say it again. I love you all. See you when I'm home. Shan.

She'd never been much of a writer, but she'd wanted her family to know that she hadn't stopped thinking about them. Perri had taken it, hugged her, and placed it along with the others and Spiron's detailed report in her pack, carefully wrapped in waterproofing. After the last hug, she, Radiant and Spangles had left, turning resolutely northwards towards the Southern Range.

Patrol Ten and the cadets had then farewelled Fractus and Teacher, before dropping down into the basin to begin the final trek towards the alien vessel. Two days later, Verren's best estimates suggested that they were within five kilometres of its location.

Now, as Shanna peered carefully through the screen of leaves, she cautiously tested her ankle, wriggling it from side to side. The ankle was still mildly uncomfortable, but feeling better every day, and she could feel Verren's strapping beginning to loosen. She pushed her attention back to where it belonged — looking outward and listening for any sound that might be foreign to Below. Two metres to her left, Allad was mirroring her pose. It had been nice to slip back into the routine of taking point with Allad. She and Allad alternated with Kalli and Verren, and Shanna had been glad to see her friend slowly regain his confidence. She was unsure what might happen the next time he encountered a slider swarm, but he had seemed to put the experience behind him, at least for the moment. As she crouched, she realised that they'd never explored his ability to put out fires — everything had been eclipsed by the discovery of the alien vessel. She resolved to mention it next time there was an opportunity.

Failing to detect anything unusual she allowed herself to 'feel' Storm, letting herself see through his eyes. He was almost out of range. She saw

undergrowth, the flash of Satin's tidemarks through the trees, and smelt –
smelt? – an oddly pungent odour that made her sneeze. Hastily she withdrew from Storm and looked at Allad. His posture was undisturbed, so it
must have been Storm sneezing, not herself. Relieved, she touched Storm
again and looked through his eyes.

The starcat was moving fast, and she felt a touch of the nausea she'd experienced the first time she'd linked with him. Distancing herself from her
stomach, she concentrated again. Then all movement ceased and Storm's eyes
zeroed in on a glint that had escaped Shanna's attention. Something was
there, and Storm had gone to ground. She 'heard' Twister above her and his
movement ceased as well. Hoping to get a better view, Shanna switched her
perspective to Twister.

A round, metal object sat on a three metre post set into the ground. It moved,
swivelling the boulder-like silvery spheroid. Trying to estimate size through a
starcat's eyes was difficult, but Shanna's best approximation suggested that it was
at least a metre in diameter. A small red light glowed at its knobbed apex, and just
underneath the round portion a collection of angular objects sat clustered. A
small frisson of alarm flickered through her from Twister.

A family group of weldens was approaching, grazing as they went, on the far
side of the post. The calf, not quite the size of an adult starcat, gamboled happily in the sunlight slanting through the trees. It bounced towards the post with
all the unsuspecting curiosity of the very young. The post stilled, the light flickered slightly, then the angular objects detached themselves, resolving into min-
iatures of the Garsal flying machines. A moment later, they had caged the
young welden in a dizzying sphere. It stood entranced for a moment, then a red
beam lanced from each flier and the youngster screamed, sending its parents
bolting towards it, before it collapsed in a smoking heap. The post swiveled
again, the fliers formed into two groups, and the adult weldens went down in a
flurry of red beams, the smell of roasting flesh wafting nauseatingly through the
trees.

Shanna felt Storm freeze to absolute stillness as a wash of heat rolled over
him, and the flyers hovered for a moment. The metal sentinel began its survey
of the surrounds again, and after a few moments of uninterrupted swivelling,
the flyers returned to cluster below it, slotting onto it with audible clunks. Her
heart raced as she felt her cats begin to move again with more caution than
she'd ever felt from either of them. Now alerted to the danger, through their
eyes she saw the telltale scorch marks on nearby trees.

Shanna became aware she was sweating as she dropped her awareness
back into her own eyes. Pulling her whistle from her shirt she blew the recall
soundlessly and moved over to Allad, taking care to stay low. A brief explanation, he nodded, and the two of them began to move back to the others.

"We need to find out how many of these things there are," Spiron said, later
that day. It was late afternoon, and the Patrol was gathered in a small clearing a

safe distance from the alien guard post. Careful tossing of rocks had demonstrated that it appeared to be activated by motion, yet somehow it differentiated between rocks and twigs. Shanna supposed that if it went on alert every time a breeze blew a branch, everything in reach would have been incinerated. There was a delay of about ten seconds before the flying mechanicals appeared. Shanna was reminded of the device that they'd encountered on the training exercise. "We'll have to survey. Three groups – one to stay here and work on how to get past them, the other two to see how many of those things there are. I'm guessing they'll be in a circle, evenly spaced around the Garsal camp. There must be some way for them to deactivate them as they go in and out, though." He looked at his assembled Scouts consideringly. "Allad, Shanna, Ragar and Sandar, you go north, Verren, Kalli, Zandany and Karri, you'll take the south. The rest of us will stay here. When you meet up, come back by the shortest route."

Two days later, the two groups met in a pungo grove to compare notes on the barrier around the Garsal landing site. The globes were evenly spaced every fifty metres, in a circle approximately ten kilometres in diameter. The western edge abutted the edge of the basin. Shanna's group had travelled only eleven kilometres, while the other group had made just over twenty. Verren's ability to accurately position each globe had allowed them to travel and plot more quickly than the other group. Shanna's group had needed to painstakingly plot each position using known landmarks, then extrapolating in order to position the globes properly on the map. Without the need to plot map positions, the journey back to the others took less than a day.

Shanna's ankle had finally settled down, and as they sat quietly in the darkness of the evening, she carefully removed her boot and began to take off the strapping. Shielding her glowstone in her hand to direct the light onto her ankle, she was pleased to see the swelling had completely gone, and that it was moving well. For the first time in days, she had time to spend just sitting with her cats. She'd been spared the night watch on her return with her team, and was sitting on her bedding when Zandany, Ragar and Verren joined her.

"How's the foot, Shanna?" asked Verren quietly. His face was tired in the shielded light, and she remembered how she'd felt when using her gifts for extended periods.

"I'm fine – but you look like you need more sleep," she replied. She picked up her sock and pulled it back on, grimacing a little at the smell. She looked forward to the day she'd be able to pull on a clean pair. "I'd love a pair of clean socks, though," she sighed.

She sensed rather than saw Ragar's smile in the darkness. "Know what you mean. And a bath, and a soft bed."

"I'm tired," said Verren, "and worried. Even if we get in, how are we going to get out?" He said the words that were on all of their minds.

"I'm sure that Spiron has some kind of plan," replied Zandany. "They've had three days to think about it, and test the nearest globe. Spiron, Barron and Allad are discussing what we found now. No doubt it'll be some clever thing that I'd never think of if I tried for weeks."

"Amma and Taya are on dawn watches, so we thought it might be the last chance the six of us have to be together before it all gets messy," said Ragar, "Spiron suggested we take the opportunity now." His voice changed, and Shanna could hear the grimness despite the darkness masking his face. "Who knows if we'll all come out of this." Shanna gulped and nodded, then cleared her throat.

"Yes, that'd be good," She let the glowstone fall back inside her shirt. "Want to bring your stuff here, or shall I move over?"

"We'll be back — I'm just going to let Taya and Amma know," said Ragar. He got to his feet and vanished into the darkness, Verren and Zandany following slowly. Shanna sat quietly with her cats, tickling both of them in turn and allowing them to bat her gently with their paws. Storm rolled onto his back and presented his tummy for a rub, and Twister snuck his head onto her lap as she crossed her legs and rummaged in her pack for the very last two pieces of the cheese she'd stashed before leaving the Starlyne habitat. Both cats purred vigorously as she presented the cheese, delicately picking it out of her fingers. She slipped an arm around each neck and hugged them tightly.

The six cadets lay in a group together, bedding in a circle, so that their heads were together in the middle and their legs formed the spokes of a wheel. Their cats lounged by their sides as they conversed in soft tones, catching up on their individual adventures. Each attempted to see through their cat's eyes as Shanna described the technique, with varying degrees of success. Verren chilled them with his description of the sliders; and Shanna was reminded about his ability to smother the fire, and asked him about it.

"I'm not sure, actually," he replied. "I've tried it again, and there's nothing. What do you think, Ragar, Zandany?" Shanna recalled that Ragar and Zandany's abilities were with fire and heat, and felt a little stupid for not thinking of it earlier.

"I'm not sure, Verren, I don't really have to think about it now," replied Zandany. "Maybe it's just when we're stressed that we can do stuff that would normally be really difficult. You know, sometimes I struggle to fade, but when there's a staureg around it's suddenly easier." There were a number of sounds of amusement in the dark.

"And who knows how we do what we do?" replied Amma. "When I fly I feel like I'm totally free, yet when I try and know precisely where I am, it's like I'm pushing a huge rock up a hill."

"I'm worried that I won't be able to do what's needed when it's time," said Taya. She'd been quiet for most of the evening, spending most of the time tickling Spinner's ears. Shanna never ceased to marvel at the change wrought in the girl after she gave in and let Spinner love her. Her astonishing confession had eased her relationship with all of the others, most notably with Shanna.

"Tay, no one can stop mechanical stuff like you can, and we're all worried," said Ragar. "Who knows what we'll have to do tomorrow? Or even whether there's anything we can do." There was silence for some time. "But no matter what happens, we're together tonight. And when we work together, there's no end to what we can achieve. Keeper had faith in us all. He asked for us to stand with him together at the moment of his death, and he saw a future where there could be peace. He died to save us so that we might help save everyone else. He didn't guarantee we'd come out unscathed, but he believed in all of us, and even more in all of us together."

He extended a hand to Taya on his right and Verren on his left. Verren extended his hand to Shanna, and she reached out to Amma. Amma linked her other hand with Zandany, and he tucked his hand into Taya's to complete their circle. The seven starcats tucked themselves under the linked hands and Shanna felt a surge of energy run through the group which expanded into a feeling of love, echoing that of Keeper's passing. Wonderingly, she looked at the faces reflected faintly in the moonlight now slanting through the leaves of the trees. Each of her friends mirrored her expression – wonder, delight and hope, and she squeezed Verren's and Amma's hands. They stayed united like that for some time, then one by one dropped off to sleep, hands still linked. Unseen, the gentle glow that had illuminated the group slowly faded.

As the dawn light filtered through the leaves, Shanna tasked her cats to guard Taya and Spinner. Taya was seated on the ground just out of range of the globe, hands stroking Spinner's fur as she concentrated. Beside her, Shanna was poised to fade all of them at the first sign of danger. The rest of the Patrol was positioned further back, far from the range of the globe and its flying minions should anything go wrong. Spiron had postulated that taking out one globe was likely to be taken by the Garsal as a simple malfunction, but to deactivate multiple globes would be tantamount to declaring an invasion. The problem was that they knew nothing about what might be beyond the ring of globes, so the first starcats and humans through ran a significant risk.

She cast a glance at Taya. The other girl's face was screwed up in concentration, her hands resting in Spinner's fur. Her hair had begun to glow in Spinner's patterns, and Shanna looked around hurriedly to make sure that the red tones were subdued enough not to attract any of Frontier's nastier predators.

Behind her, she could see Satin poised to make the first dash when the globe deactivated. She cast around for a couple of pebbles to throw when Taya signalled. She smiled slightly, remembering Taya's easy deactivation during the training trek.

A small trickle of sweat traced a path down Taya's face, and Shanna could see her forehead crinkle in thought. Suddenly the other girl's face relaxed and the corners of her mouth lifted slightly. She opened her eyes and nodded at

Shanna. Shanna threw a pebble. Nothing. She lobbed another pebble, then each of her other missiles in a circular pattern around the globe. Still nothing.

Holding her breath, she signalled back towards Allad, and a green-toned streak blurred past her and beyond the globe in a flash. She let her breath out in a long sigh, sent Twister after Satin, and she and Allad started forward. As she passed Taya, she realised the other girl was still seated on the ground and offered a helping hand. Taya gripped Shanna's hand, then dropped behind Shanna and Allad. Keeping low, she and Allad slunk towards the globe, Storm shadowing them, while Satin and Twister ranged ahead. When they were past, both paused and signalled their cats to scout ahead. Shanna located a secure rock and ducked behind it, watching the vegetation behind her to make sure all of her fellow Scouts were through. Taya dropped into the shadow of the rock with her.

"Once I figured it out, it was easy. Hope the rest of it's that simple," Taya whispered.

Shanna smiled at the other girl, then turned her attention forward. "Can you keep an eye on the others, Tay, let me know when they're all through?" She waited for Taya's nod before transferring her attention to Twister's eyes. He was slinking through the greenery, ears pricked for any sound, each foot-fall soundless. Switching to Storm, she was reassured by the normality of the vegetation, with no sign in the vicinity of any other Garsal technology. She turned to Taya and the other girl held up two fingers, indicating that only two were left to cross. She crouched ready to begin moving, and when Taya tapped her shoulder, began to edge forward.

Three hours later, she climbed swiftly into a tree as sound heralded the approach of another mechanical contraption. Twister joined her, then Storm, and together they froze, tucked in the fork of a frondan tree, as the vehicle appeared through the trees. It seemed to be coming directly towards them and Shanna hoped that the shaking tree branches weren't evident to the approaching vehicle. Praying the others were well concealed she shrank back, fading reflexively as the vehicle ground into view. It was a small vehicle, multi-tracked and wheeled, with odd protuberances at each corner. Its size meant that it looked as though it would only hold four Garsal, perhaps five at a pinch.

The vehicle clanked by, leaving a much smaller trail of crushed vegetation than the grinding monsters that had almost reached the foot of the plateau. Shanna and her cats sat silently faded in the tree until the sounds of the vehicle disappeared into the distance. She sent Storm down first, then followed, feeling the rough bark under her hands as she swung as quietly as she could onto the leaf litter. Eyes swivelling she finally relaxed the fade. Signalling for Twister to join her she sent him to sweep around the Patrol. Dry-mouthed, she took a sip from her water bottle, absently noting that she'd need to refill it fairly shortly. Satin appeared by her side, and at the big cat's gentle tug on her sleeve, she followed her quietly to Allad's position a short distance away on her right. As she slid through the fronds of a softpalm, he signalled her to drop to her belly and crawl. She complied, heart rate beginning to elevate, and crawled silently to his side. "Tell me what you can see ahead." His voice was almost inaudible.

Shanna peered through the thick vegetation, squinting slightly to try and penetrate the emerald maze. Nothing registered, then she saw what Allad was watching as several branches rustled and moved in the slight breeze. She turned slightly and mouthed, "Sunlight!" Beyond the thick stand of trees and shrubs directly ahead of them sunlight poured down, bright shafts of light glowing through the emerald foliage. It appeared that they had reached the clearing surrounding the Garsal ship.

***

"Matriarch," The Garsal Overlord gestured for the Matriarch to precede him through the double doors into the manufactory. Nearly-assembled aircraft buzzed with workers on one side of the cavernous structure set into the ground to the side of the main hive, while on the other side of the cavern, different manufacturing equipment hummed and rumbled as workers laboured over their tasks. The Matriarch and her entourage stepped briskly through the cavern, heads swivelling and filmy robes trailing in their wake. Although she retained her haughty demeanour, he knew that she could not fail to be impressed by the huge gains made since her last tour. The thought of offspring was almost tangible.

As they exited the cavern, a group of slaves straggled past, labouring over a handcart laden with heavy stone. The mechanical tread kept bogging down in the soft ground and they had to throw their weight against the metal back to ensure that it kept moving. Behind them paced two Garsal guards, weapons held casually yet ready to punish any shirking. They were dirty and ragged, and the Overlord spared them barely a glance. The Matriarch paused for a moment and her entourage halted with her. She passed her gaze over the group, expressionless manipulator arms still. Without a word she continued her progress, sweeping into the hive as her attendants flocked after her.

***

Kaidan stood with the other students and looked slightly apprehensively at the skinny, elderly Scout before him. Her starcat sat slightly awkwardly at her side and Kaidan looked at him curiously, eyes tracing the scar that stretched down his side, marring the perfection of his glowing tidemarks.

"Eyes in front!" Toman's voice cracked loudly in his ears, startling him with its suddenness. "Those of you with cubs, make sure they behave themselves. Ghost has a keen eye for misbehaviour and he's less tolerant than he used to be, just like me. Must be our age." Kaidan looked down at the youngster his parents had decided to send with him, one of the two who hadn't found a partner when Tamazine had been ignored. It was a huge compliment to him that they'd trusted him with one of their cubs, but he hoped that Tempest wouldn't get them into any trouble.

They marched out behind Toman, following the oldster nervously. Kaidan shared a shaky grin with Anjo as Ember paced between them, and Tempest trotted to keep up.

"Remember, Kaidan," his mother had said, "If Cally says something about training, just do it, don't argue even if it sounds odd. She's the best trainer I ever met, and both you and Tempest are lucky to have the opportunity to work with her!" Janna had waggled a finger at him, then pulled him into a hug. "Look after yourself, and look after Anjo and Ember too. Times are difficult." She broke off suddenly as her eyes became suspiciously shiny.

"Yes, they are," said Adlan, "but you'll be safe with Toman and the oldsters. Safer than being here probably." He'd cleared his throat, slapped his son on the back, hugged him, and then sent him on his way. Kaidan finally had an inkling of how Shanna had felt during her repeated goodbyes. He hefted his pack and felt his cased bow, securely fastened by straps to the back of his pack. As they swung through Watchtower's gates, and for the first time Kaidan heard them clang shut behind him, he focused on the road ahead with mixed feelings of excitement and uncertainty.

Chapter 25

SHANNA inched towards the line of trees surrounding the clearing. Each step was as silent as possible. She had faded, but fading would not prevent the sound of a breaking twig echoing through the air. Just in front of her, she could 'feel' her two cats, poised at the tree line, while beside her she could 'feel' Allad's solid presence and Satin's alertness. The rest of the Patrol was hidden behind them, safely concealed across a wide area.

She held her breath and took another slow step as the line of bright sunlight, so unusual in the dense vegetation, came closer. There was no signal of alarm from Storm or Twister, just a sensation of readiness. A few more cautious steps, and she reached a large clump of boulders and tucked herself behind them. After quickly scanning for dangerous plant life, she cautiously began to scale the boulders slowly, one muscle at a time.

At the top, as she started the long crawl forward towards the light and the clearing beyond it the palm of her hand tingled as the memory of the firemoss distracted her briefly. She scanned ahead as she crawled, reminding herself sternly that the lack of water meant little chance that she would find a patch. A tiny grating noise alerted her that Allad had followed, and she inched forward to the edge of the rocks and took her first look at the Garsal ship..

The ship squatting solidly on the ground was not at all what Shanna had expected. Its blocky, ovoid shape was relatively featureless, with not a window or view port in sight. The dull black of the ship's skin seemed to absorb rather than reflect light, and a series of rods and dishes sat perched on its apex. Around it the cauterised, blackened vegetation lay like a scar on the landscape. She lay faded for a few minutes trying to made head or tail of the ship, before finally realising that what was most likely to be the back end was pointing towards them. She pulled her whistle and signalled Storm to circle around the rocks, and asked Twister to guard them from the front. She felt Allad's large form settle beside her. They watched in silence for some time.

The whole clearing was quite large and surrounded by one of the high tech fences that had guarded the vehicle carrying Anjo and Semba. Shanna could see piles of bones at some points along the fence, evidence of the deaths of some of Frontier's largest predators, and occasionally the breeze brought a whiff of decay to her nose.

To her left, vehicle tracks had left wide ruts at what was obviously a well-used entry and exit point. "Look to your right." Allad's mouth was so close to her ear that his moustache tickled her, and Shanna started slightly before turning her attention to the right side of the clearing. A group of human slaves laboured away in the sunlight to level the uneven ground. They were using a variety of mechanical tools to flatten out small hillocks and fill depressions, watched by two pacing Garsal guards. Each human had bright-orange locator bracelets locked around their ankles. Several taller creatures worked with them, lanky arms jointed oddly and seemingly capable of strangely flexible movement. With a thrill, Shanna realised that she was seeing for the first time one of the other species that had been part of the Federation of Races.

The thrill lasted only briefly before Shanna was reminded of the destruction of the peaceful alliance by the Garsal, and dropped her eyes to the anklets encircling the alien creatures' bare, grey legs. She dug in her memory for the facts — the creatures were most likely to be Orex: humanoid shaped yet taller, and possessed of extra joints in all their limbs. Anger rose inside of her. Anger at hopes dashed, at sentient species enslaved, and for the loss of freedom that now threatened her home. Shanna gritted her teeth and deliberately began to memorise the scene before her.

The ship, the fence, the humans and Orex, the great gaping entryway carved into a sheer rock face to the right of the ship. Carefully outlined in quarried rock, it was an incision into the flesh of her planet. "Where do you think the communications equipment is?" she voiced her question as quietly as possible.

"I think some of it's on the top of the spaceship," replied Allad. "But some of it is probably inside, or perhaps even embedded in the hull. Can you try your new trick with one of your cats? Get one up here and send the other around the fence?"

Shanna nodded and pulling out her whistle again called Twister. As the cat tucked himself in next to her, she put one hand on his body and sent Storm to move slowly around the fence line. Gritting her teeth against the sudden nausea, she let her eyes see through Storm's. It took a moment for her to orient herself to Storm's lower perspective. He paced steadily, occasionally pausing to look directly into the compound, and Shanna filed the images away in her memory. She wished that the Starlynes were within range to pick them out and share them with her fellow Scouts. After a few minutes of hard work, she drew back and shook her head to release the image flow.

"It's too hard at that kind of angle, Allad. I'd be better off sending him to pre-planned positions to look straight into the compound. This way I'm just getting a pile of jumbled up stuff, and sick to boot." She was unable to keep from a convulsive swallow as the memory of Storm turning too quickly, threatened to upturn her stomach. She felt Allad wriggle slightly beside her and imagined him nodding.

"We'll drop back then. We need to plan how best to scout this out." They withdrew from the edge and descended the rock, before making their way back to Spiron.

"Kalli's found a hideaway," said Spiron, and they followed the Patrol First through a maze of trees into a hidden grotto. Shanna was pleased to see a small spring welling up on one side of the hollow, and hastened to refill her water bottle. As she let the fade go she felt a small wave of fatigue trickle over her, and hurriedly pulled out a handful of the nuts she'd stowed in her pocket. She crunched them gratefully as the group gathered around Spiron, and sent her cats to join the others circling the perimeter, diligently protecting their partners from any possible danger.

She joined Amma and Verren in the circle as Spiron began to speak. "We need to find a way in so that we can locate the communications equipment. Ideas?"

"Can we dig under the fence, do you think?" asked Sandar, thoughtfully. Spiron nodded.

"An idea to explore, perhaps."

"Or is there anything we can drop down from?" said Nelson.

"There does look like a decent overhang on the other side of the clearing," said Shanna. "But I don't know whether we'd be able to get in and out undetected. I mean, surely they'd notice a dangling rope."

"A possibility for darkness, perhaps," replied Barron, frowning slightly. "Allad, what do you think is the likelihood of scouting the perimeter undetected?"

"There was little activity near the fence line. It was obvious that they're using one entrance and exit point though, and given the number of dead creatures around the edge, I'd say they keep well away from the fence. The main danger is probably the native flora and fauna, to be honest, and perhaps those prowling machines. I think that if we divide into four, we can cover the entire perimeter before nightfall." Spiron nodded his head.

"Then that's what we'll do. In these groups ... "

Two hours later, Shanna dropped to one knee behind a small hillock on the rim side of the bowl. Her elevated position allowed her to look across the clearing towards the front of the spaceship. It still seemed rather featureless from the outside, although there appeared to be some darkened view ports at the front. The entrance to the underground facility was hidden by the rising ground that extended almost to the rim. She could clearly see the activity inside the glowing fence line. The group of slaves was still labouring over the same patch of ground that from Shanna's vantage point was now clearly delineated as circular. As she watched, one of the Garsal guards raised its weapon and clubbed a man. He staggered, and Shanna's anger began to burn again. She shook her head and thrust it away. She needed all of her attention on the task at hand. She, Verren, Arad and Allad had been detailed to see if there was a viable access point from the heights, but it was looking doubtful.

"Shanna, I want you to fade and see what the edge looks like," whispered Allad. Shanna nodded, faded, then crawled forward, flanked by Storm and Twister. Although she could have walked as she was faded and invisible to watching eyes, she knew the lower she stayed, the less likely she was to leave disturbed vegetation in her wake.

As she approached the highest point above the glowing fence line, she was very conscious of the Garsal troopers patrolling in full view. She was higher than the top of the fence, and a small ridge ran along beside it about a metre from the glowing lines. Deciding to trust to her faded state, Shanna took a slightly shaky breath and stood, and taking great care, walked the ridgeline. Although the fence was probably within jumping distance for a starcat, there was nothing sufficiently overhanging to allow a human to descend on a rope. Shanna joined the others silently, relaxed her fade, and shook her head at the others.

"Well, that's that. Back to the others then. I'd say we'll be attempting to go under the fence," said Allad, "Verren, take us by the shortest route."

They began their trek back to the others, and as Shanna, Twister and Storm brought up the rear, Shanna marvelled yet again at the incongruousness of Arad's cub Nosey padding obediently at his heels, in the most dangerous place on the whole planet. Sometimes she was still bemused at the idea of a cub joining them on their dangerous mission.

Several hours later as the light dimmed, Shanna stood poised with her cats behind a large tree to one side of the fence. Twister and Storm sat on either side as she extended her bubble of fade over Taya. The other cadet began to creep forward with Spinner faded by her side. Shanna concentrated hard, hands gliding over silky fur, as Taya approached the glowing fence. She could 'feel' the other girl and her cat, but couldn't see her. There was a sensation of effort, enormous effort, Shanna thought, and the ruby lines flickered several times. Across the clearing, a loud throbbing alarm rang out and Shanna almost lost her fade. She 'felt' Taya's effort cease suddenly, there was a flurry of almost silent footsteps and she knew that Taya was returning to the trees. Her bubble was elastic and she contracted it around the other girl, as she returned to the group.

They sat frozen as a line of Garsal ran from the ship and another from the archway. Their shiny carapaces reflected the last of the sunlight as they spread out along the fence line, weapons ready and heads with their faceted eyes swivelling rapidly. Shanna's heart rate accelerated despite her faded state, and she hoped fervently that the starcats were continuing to provide protective distortion that would confuse the Garsal equipment.

The Garsal were poised and watchful rather than urgently seeking intruders, and Shanna wondered if the flicker of the fence was something they'd experienced before. One of the troopers ran quickly down the fence, directing a handheld gadget towards each of the poles as he passed. He paused at the closest one and ran the gadget up and down it, tapping it rapidly with one of the small manipulator arms at the top of his thorax.

Shanna held her breath and felt Taya give a small start beside her. The hackles on her cats' necks rose slowly, and she tightened her hands slightly as she felt the hint of a growl begin in Twister's chest. He fell silent but she could feel the tension, the desire to spring, in the set of Storm's posture and the slight quiver running through Twister.

The Garsal trooper spent a further moment bent over his gadget, then turned to the line of troopers around the fence. Another tap and the alarm ceased, then a quick gesture sent the line of troopers filing back in. The other trooper swept his glance once more around the unbroken glowing lines, pointed his device one last time at the pole, then joined the end of the line and vanished back into the ship with the others.

There was a loud rustle back in the bushes behind Shanna; and she spun quickly and sent Storm off towards it. She stared intensely into the gathering gloom, and was relieved to see the familiar colours of a welden group moving through the vegetation. She slowly relaxed the fade she'd maintained over herself and Taya. Twister flicked an ear, and Fury materialised next to her. She pulled out the note tucked into his collar. "We need to go to the secondary point, Taya," she whispered. "We'll be going under." The other girl shook her head, her frustration clear even in the dim light.

"I could have taken it down! Who was to know there'd be an alarm?"

Shanna nodded. "Looks like we'll have to do it the hard way," she said regretfully.

They backed away from the clearing as Fury vanished and set out for the designated point, carefully avoiding the welden herd. Shanna flicked a quick glance at Taya as she skirted a barbed palm, and sent Spinner ahead of them, the red-toned cat brushing Taya's leg affectionately as he surged forward, sure in his ability to protect his partner.

She was almost a friend now, Shanna realised. After such a long time dreading any encounter with the other girl, it felt odd to feel kinship with her. Taya like all of them wore clothes that showed how hard and far they'd travelled, but she moved more confidently than Shanna had ever seen her manage Below, and Spinner now worked as an extension of her — finally finding that partnership that had eluded of them for so long.

As they joined the others, Spiron set Kalli, Sandar and Challon in a staggered formation to watch the rear, while Shanna hastily slapped a long acting patch on her arm. She counted the others by feel, noting their numbers were low, and hoped she'd have enough for the night's activities. At Spiron's signal, she faded and extended her bubble over the designated diggers as they slipped towards the fence. The fence spanned a small hollow at that point and was fractionally closer to the forest than at anywhere else. It had seemed the logical point to try and go under the fence.

Unusually, she and her cats were not at the forefront of the Patrol. It felt a little odd, but Shanna knew that what she was doing was essential for their safety. The sounds of quiet digging seemed awfully loud, and Spiron sent Verren and Amma to either side with Cirrus and Spider, to see off any marauding predators. The hoots and whistles of evening began to sound through the trees, along with the far-off sounds of something larger stalking its way through the undergrowth. From the other side of the enclosed area there was a commotion and the sound of a roaring staureg. Shanna pushed her fade out a bit further, enveloping the roving Scouts and waiting diggers as well as the three digging quietly at the fence.

The wait seemed endless as they attempted to discover whether digging below the fence was possible. There was a soft flurry of movement, then Spiron's voice came softly. "Relax, Shanna." Shanna dropped the fade.

"Shanna, you, Allad, Taya, Verren, Challon and Ragar are first through. Send your cats under first, then follow. You'll penetrate the ship if you're able and escort Taya to the communications equipment. Taya, you know what you ned to do – Challon's your back up. If you can't stop it, he'll fry it. Arad, you, Kalli and Sandar will hold the line to the grotto. Arad, you'll wait in the grotto with Nosey. Make preparations for any outcome. Zandany and Karri will wait here. Barron, Amma, and I will be inside the compound. If required, we'll start something diversionary to give us all time to get out." Shanna could hear the grim smile in his voice. "Shanna, your job is keep them all hidden. Can you do it?"

"I think so, Spiron." Shanna felt slightly short of breath and her heart pounded.

"Verren, you'll make sure they're able to find their way back."

"Yes."

"Allad, you'll lead. Ragar's your second." There was silence, then Spiron's voice came one last time, softly through the darkness. "Let's do it."

"Follow me, then," said Allad, "Shan, you're through first. Send in your cats." Shanna sent Storm under the fence then Twister, before fading herself.

"I'll have Storm twinkle an ear, when I'm through and I have you all faded," she whispered, and slid silently towards the glowing lines. She dropped to her belly and wriggled under the fence, careful to keep her body well below the glowing lines. Soft damp dirt was gritty under her hands as she pulled herself into a crouch and looked around in the darkness. She listened with her whole body, willing her ears to catch the slightest sound, and when nothing but the normal sounds of Below sounded, extended her fade and signalled Storm.

Without the contact with her cats, she could feel the strain - not bad, but enough that she knew that holding it for an extended period would fatigue her. While she waited, tense in the darkness, peering towards the ship she checked her patch stock once more, sipped from her water bottle and forced a few bits of dried fruit into her mouth. She swallowed the last of it and put her whistle in her mouth, signalling Storm and Twister to cover the others as they came through the hole under the fence.

She could 'feel' the others as they joined her inside the fence line, and she deliberately extended her senses, dropping into the other vision so that she could see what might be lurking ahead in the darkness. Her heart rate began to accelerate as she felt Allad, the last one through, join her. Then she felt his hand on her shoulder as he whispered his instructions in her ear.

Calling her cats with the silent whistle, Shanna crept forward, carefully maintaining the fade around her friends as they sent their cats circling around the group. She could 'feel' Storm directing his brother and Twister's surprisingly easy acquiescence. They moved as a group toward the Garsal ship, trusting to their faded state amongst the deforestation left by the Garsal. Shanna's heart pounded so loudly that she felt it must be audible to anyone nearby.

She felt a sudden sense of alarm from Twister, and briefly saw the flick of a violet tidemark. She dropped to her belly as Storm passed in a silent flurry, and knew he was warning the others. They held still, and at the far extent of her vision Shanna saw the dark form of a Garsal trooper pace by. She held her breath then relaxed slightly, feeling stupid. Twister was pacing the trooper, and there was nearly fifty metres between them. She held motionless in the dark until she felt Storm brush past again, then rose to her feet, scanning ahead to avoid making any sound.

She skirted the back of the ship, feeling dwarfed by its size, and began to track along its side. The scorched ground was hard under her boots and she had to move extremely carefully to avoid unwanted sound. By the time they reached the area near the entrance they'd seen earlier, she was taut with tension and beginning to sweat despite the coolness of the air. She sent Storm to circle the entrance and Twister to investigate the area just past it.

"Watch and wait," Allad whispered in her ear, causing her to jump. "We need to see how to get in. You can drop the group fade now. We've called in the cats for those who need contact, and the others are running the screen. I'm going to send Satin in as soon as there's a window." Shanna nodded knowing that Allad couldn't see it, and dropped the bubble down to her own skin with a feeling of relief. After the training exercise, she knew she had to conserve her strength for moments of real need.

The wait was long as they watched the shadowy forms of Garsal pacing their measured watch. The troopers were nervy despite being inside the fence line, a legacy of their encounters with Frontier's wildlife, Shanna supposed. The fence might keep out the larger predators, but the insects, plants and smaller wildlife would still be moving through the ruby lines relatively freely, and as Shanna knew, some of the smaller wildlife was more deadly than even the largest staureg. The image of the sliders crossed her mind and she shuddered slightly. She wondered if the Garsal had encountered them yet.

Another guard passed and she counted silently. There was a pattern, and she thought she had the timing figured. Allad's moustache tickled her ear again. "Do you see the pattern?"

"Yes."

"If the door opens, I'll send Satin in. Do you think you can get close to the entrance without being seen? Near the hillock?"

"I think so. But what if Satin gets in and can't get out?"

"She'll get out." Allad's voice was quietly confident. "And we're going in just as soon as we can. Once you're past the guards, the rest of us will follow." Shanna signalled her cats and took a deep breath, counted carefully and prepared to make her move. She calculated that she had less than twenty seconds to move from where she was, to the spot Allad had indicated. She crouched, counted the last few seconds, and darted forwards.

She could hear the sound of the Garsal trooper pacing towards her and saw the dim glow of its headlight, and pushed herself to move faster. She scuttled the last few metres and dropped to her belly. She had a clear line of sight to the entrance, which was outlined by dully glowing lights.

As she watched, the darkness was split by the door opening and a new cadre of troopers exited the ship. They lined up neatly to one side of the doorway, and as the trooper Shanna had narrowly dodged arrived, he came to a halt on the other side of the door and the endmost trooper took his place, pacing in measured fashion away from the entrance. As he passed her hiding place, Shanna caught a glimpse of the heat shimmer sometimes left by a faded starcat, silhouetted at the open doorway. She assumed that Satin had entered the ship. She extended her senses, and was able to 'feel' her fellow Scouts poised ready to join her. As the next trooper vanished into the darkness, his lamp a fast-fading, dim glow, Allad's moustache tickled Shanna's ear once more. "Send in Storm, have a look through his eyes, and if it's all clear, we'll go in."

Shanna's already elevated heart rate climbed another notch, but she called Storm and sent him after Satin. Heart pounding, she stilled her nausea as he allowed her to share his vision. He was traveling fast as he went past the troopers on either side of the door, and Shanna was glad she was lying down as her vision blurred and her stomach rebelled vigorously as the linked images spun. Then he was inside and (somehow she knew) next to Satin. Her world spun as he took a look outwards into the darkness before turning his head back again. He was standing in a large square area with another open door on the far side. Storm turned slowly as if he knew that the fast movement was unhelpful.

There was one Garsal standing at the side of the doorway and another at the far side, near the other doorway. He moved steadily towards the other door, and Shanna could see that a long corridor stretched away into the ship. There were few Garsal moving around, and the corridor was lined with entry ways, some open, others closed. For the first time, Shanna wondered how on earth they'd find the communications equipment. She left Storm as he returned to the large room and took up a guard stance close to the exit point.

She relayed her findings to Allad, and she felt his hand briefly on her shoulder in the darkness, before he spoke once again. "On my signal, we'll go through. There's only three troopers left to change out. We'll go in two groups – you'll take Taya and Verren with you. I'll bring up the rear with Challon and Ragar. You'll need to cover all of us until we're inside." He was abruptly gone. Shanna watched and counted as the next trooper changed over. As he moved off into the darkness of the compound, she extended her bubble once more, feeling the strain a bit more than the last time, and wondered how long she'd have to hold it this time. As Allad settled next to her again, she 'felt' the presence of Taya and Verren just behind. She called Twister in.

Allad's hand tapped on her shoulder, and she was up and running as silently as she knew how. Halfway to the ominous entrance, she realised she was holding her breath and let it out as gently as possible, hoping that it was unheard, and that Taya and Verren were close behind.

Her bubble felt stretched as she flitted through the door, eyes struggling to adjust to the brighter light inside. Ahead of her she 'felt' the reassuring presence of Storm, and headed almost blindly in his direction. In her haste, she almost ran into the Garsal trooper she'd forgotten was standing beside the doorway. She ducked around him at the last moment, hoping he hadn't heard her, and froze to stillness against the smooth wall of the ship.

He must have felt something, because he spun suddenly, jointed arms lifting his weapon, head swivelling. Shanna almost stopped breathing as he appeared to look straight at her, faceted eyes gleaming oddly in the light, which Shanna realised was tinged just slightly red.

She felt her two cats suddenly beside her legs, one on either side, and she dropped her hands to their smooth coats as the strain of holding the fade over not only herself and the two cadets beside her but also the other three outside, became enormous. It felt like her bubble had been compressed in the middle – almost as if she was holding two connected by a thin bar between. Somehow she'd managed to avoid fading the Garsal as well.

Seeing nothing to disturb him, the Garsal guard relaxed his stance and turned back to his post by the doorway, leaning his weapon back to a rest position. Shanna stopped holding her breath, trying to draw badly needed air into her lungs as quietly as possible. As she maintained her fade, she felt first Verren, then Taya and Spinner, relax their reliance upon her. She concentrated on the other three outside, and as they began to move, drew her bubble in as they in turn slid through the doorway. She was slightly embarrassed to note that none of them came anywhere near the Garsal guard. It was a strangely odd sensation, standing in full view of the alien invaders yet unseen.

Within a few moments, the squad of troopers so recently relieved of duty filed through the door and marched through the other doorway. The guard at the doorway tapped several times on a square pad set into a pillar near the door, and the outer door closed with a solid thunk. He followed the other guard out of the room, and the far door shut behind them. They were left standing faded, in a room with two shut doors.

Chapter 26

KAIDAN tickled Tempest's tummy while he and Anjo waited for Toman to give out the next day's assignments. He enjoyed being paired with the offworlder. He shook his head; he really needed to stop thinking of Anjo as from another planet. He sneaked a look sideways as Anjo scratched Ember's head and the red-toned cat purred loudly. Dressed in the multi-toned pants and shirt supplied by the Scout Corps, he looked just like any other human on Frontier, except for his eyes, which were a rich brown. Accustomed to the greens, blues, and violets of the residents of Frontier, Anjo's deep brown eyes always surprised Kaidan. Why eye colour would surprise him, he didn't know, but he supposed that if you were used to something, then its absence in someone else stood out more. Not absence, really, he mused, just difference, and really what did it matter .... He was jerked out of his contemplations by Toman's voice.

"Kaidan and Anjo, you'll head to Cally's outpost tomorrow. I've dispatches from Peron, and a number of parcels from the Starlynes here. You'll also drop into the Starlyne habitation on the way back with her completed logs and supply registers."

"Yes Toman." Kaidan had learnt to be prompt with his replies. The old Scout Master didn't miss a trick.

"And keep an eye out — there have been a few hints of a predator in the area. Nothing large, but enough to make Cally wary. You'll spend the afternoon with her and Mirror working on some of those skills she tells me you need to develop." Kaidan repressed a sigh. Cally and Mirror might be old, but they were both hard task masters and while Cally's training methods were effective they had also been a little unusual. He'd done as his mother had suggested and had followed her instructions, no matter how surprising and, even after only one session with her, Tempest had come along amazingly.

More importantly, Anjo's understanding of starcats had skyrocketed. Both had returned from their last visit completely exhausted though. Cally's methods had involved some seriously hard physical activity, not only on the part of the starcats, but on behalf of their handlers. "And no sighing either, Kaidan. You still need to toughen up a bit."

***

The Garsal Overlord tapped his screen once more and it dropped into blackness. The aircraft were finally ready, and his last message from the trooper on the plateau was promising. His vehicle was concealed not far from the outskirts of a major human settlement. The telemetry sent back to the ship had indicated a large population with a number of satellite towns. Most of the satellite towns seemed to be empty though, a development that had taken him by surprise. There had also been some odd information contained in the electronic files. Strange patterns appeared now and then on the re-played files – oddly paired but distorted signs that his techs had suggested might be some kind of interference. However, after reviewing the files several times, he'd dismissed them as artefacts. And then there had been two large detections that while fleeting had seemed oddly familiar, despite him being confident that he'd seen nothing like it before.

He tapped the screen into life again and sent a message to the bio-archivist. Perhaps there was something in the library that matched those traces. He dismissed the puzzle with a flick of his manipulator arms and sat back in satisfaction.

The aircraft were ready, and the Matriarch had indicated her approval of the quarters being constructed for her and her attendants within the hive. The presentation of the jewellery had been met with clicks and nods of pleasure from the attendants. The Matriarch had inclined her head with gracious thanks, as he'd presented the final piece to her. One more triumph, and he'd be assured of a breeding partner. He sat forward in his chair and tapped the orders into the system. The aircraft were to be prepped and ready for flight the next morning.

He sent one burst of data to the Senior trooper on the plateau. He was to secure human slaves and return, coordinating his snatch with the aircraft as they flew over the settlement on the plateau. The humans had no idea of the destruction they had brought upon themselves. Not too much destruction though, he needed enough stock left to reinforce his workforce and to pro-vide the basis for a breeding colony. Motioning to an aide, he shut his work-station down and retired for the night.

***

Cerren looked across at Socks, who was tucked up on her couch, watching him with unblinking eyes. "Yes, I know. We've not been outside Watchtower for weeks, have we?" She stretched, poured herself off the couch, and strolled over to him, laying her head on his lap. "Well, you're in luck, young lady. We're to visit the nearest Starlyne habitation with a council delegation tomor-row."

He dropped his hands to her head, smoothing the silky grey fur as Socks slowly closed her eyes the better to enjoy the caress. Her purring rumbled through the room, and for the first time in days, Master Cerren closed his own eyes and let his thoughts drift. He was tired, bone tired from the constant battle he was being forced to wage to try to ensure Watchtower's safety. He wondered why the Garsal hadn't sent any other flying craft over the plateau. The bits of the craft they'd found after the storm suggested that the cyclone was the cause of its demise. Perhaps they'd lost them all, he thought hopefully, perhaps the human beings were safe from aerial assault. From what Anjo had told them about the Garsal assault on his own world, they'd come in force with devastating armaments and overwhelming numbers.

That this was probably only a single colony ship might be their salvation. Cerren held tight to that thought. Even now, perhaps Patrol Ten and the first year cadets had already knocked its communications out. *Did I really make the decision to send cadets to do that?* he wondered. But he knew he had and they haunted his nightmares, as did the casualties suffered in the first encounter with the Garsal. He leaned back in his old leather chair and let the warmth of Socks' love wash over him, providing some comfort for the doubt that assailed him whenever he pondered his actions. And those same first year cadets and their adult mentors, might even now be dead or dying somewhere Below. He closed his eyes and took a deep breath, released it slowly and straightened in his chair.

"Come on, Socks. It's been a while since my pack has seen any outdoor use. It's time to go and sort it out." No-one, whether they were a Scout or not, left Watchtower without being fully prepared now. Even Tamazine had seen the sense of that. *Oh yes, Tamazine, that's one thing you'll be doing tomorrow — carrying your own pack.* He smiled grimly. The habitation was only two hours' walk away, but a full pack was heavy, and Cerren suspected that Tamazine had rarely carried a pack on her own. The Starfall Council had arrived in horgal wagons accompanied by a roving Scout Patrol from Starfall, with everything necessary for their comfort. Something Foster, the Patrol First, had imparted to Cerren with a slightly snide grin. Her Patrol was now temporarily attached to Watchtower's Scout Headquarters. Cerren had found her easy to work with, and it didn't hurt that he remembered a number of her Scouts from his time in Starfall. He'd already detailed them to escort the council delegation tomorrow.

Entering his quarters, he pulled his pack from the cupboard and began to lay out the necessities. He was looking forward to shedding his robe and pulling on his uniform again. "Could be a good day tomorrow, Socks!" His mood had already improved at the prospect of a trek outside Watchtower's walls.

***

There was silence inside the Garsal ship. Shanna looked around, wondering if she'd ever see the outside world again.

"Taya, is there anything watching us?" Allad's voice was so quiet Shanna almost thought he hadn't spoken. For a few more moments there was silence again.

"I think we're alright now," came Taya's voice finally. "I've disabled what I think were devices for watching and listening."

"Let the fade go then, Shan. And Taya, be ready to restart the devices when I say; we can't leave them off, or the Garsal will become suspicious." Shanna dropped her bubble, and seven starcats and five other humans came into view around her.

"Can you open the door, Taya?" asked Allad. The dark haired girl screwed her face up in concentration.

"Yes, I think so. Shall I open it now?"

"No," replied Allad. "When I say so. Teach Challon." He turned to the others. "We have no real idea where the communications equipment is. The Starlynes think it's most likely to be forward and up. That's the best they could tell us. That means checking each room we pass, and that means staying faded for a very long time. Taya and Challon, Shanna will help, but only if you really need it. You're to keep your cats close, and the rest of us will use ours to guard you as we search each room. Ragar, you and Verren take the right, Shanna and I will take the left. We need to move as fast as possible, but we need to stay undetected. Are you ready?" He looked around and as they nodded, he said. "Let's fade then, and go. Open the door, Taya, and then turn those devices back on." The group faded from view and Shanna readied herself. The door opened suddenly, and they darted through and began to move through the ship.

It was exhausting, tedious, and terrifying. There was no time to appreciate the strangeness all around them, just a frantic search of each open room. Avoiding the occasional Garsal moving through the ship was nerve wracking. Time after time they froze into immobility, barely daring to breathe as the creatures marched past. Fortunately, most of the rooms off the corridor were open, the Garsal obviously seeing little need to seal them off with the hull protecting them from the dangers of the planet. Shanna wondered how many of them had transferred to the hole in the hill. Anjo had said they preferred to dwell in subterranean hives. Room after empty room was checked. Most appeared to be living quarters, while even more appeared to be storerooms filled to the brim with racks and rows of crates and storage. One room was filled with locked and barred cabinets, containing the weapons Shanna had seen the Garsal troopers fire. By the end of the corridor, they'd seen nothing resembling the communications equipment the Starlynes had described. How they were to move up a level, Shanna didn't know.

She was certain of one thing only: she, the cats, and the others, were in unfamiliar and fearful territory each time they slunk through a doorway or stood motionless waiting for a group of Garsal to pass. She was aware of the others via that extra sense that allowed her to 'feel' them. It seemed to be developing faster than ever, now that she'd been faded for what seemed like hours. Gradually as time passed, the Garsal activity in the ship slowed, then became only occasional as the night deepened. Suddenly she felt Allad's hand on her shoulder, and nearly exclaimed out loud. "Watch where that one goes." Shanna followed the only Garsal currently in the corridor with her eyes, and watched as it entered a small room at the end of the corridor. As the door closed, it turned around and waited, patiently facing towards the end of the corridor. When the doors opened again, it was no longer there. "I think that's a device for moving between levels," came the big Scout's whisper. "And we're going to have to use it."

"How?" Shanna's whisper was startled. "What happens if we're all in there and a pile of them try and get in. Even if they can't see us, they'll walk right into us."

"Well, we're not all going in," came the soft voice. "You and Taya will go on the first trip. The rest of us will follow in pairs."

"But what if we all end up on different levels?"

"It's a risk we have to take," replied Allad. "We have little time, and limited knowledge of where we are. It seems logical that there will be some kind of panel to control the thing. These creatures seem to like buttons. Press the top one. We'll do the same. We have to take some chances. If the others hear nothing from us, they'll do their best to destroy the external antennas." His presence left her side briefly, then returned. "Ready?" He took her hand and placed it in Taya's.

"Yes." She wasn't ready at all, but what other choice was there? She walked forward with Taya, flanked by her cats, and stood before the door to the little room. It hissed open, they took a step back and the door closed again. Nothing had exited. Shanna took a step forward again, and the door opened again. Pulling the other girl with her she entered, feeling Spinner, Storm and Twister join them. As the Garsal had, she turned to face the door as it shut behind them.

"Now what do we do?" whispered Taya uncertainly.

"Look for buttons and press the top one, apparently," Shanna whispered back, scanning the small room. Immediately to her right she found a panel covered with square impressions. She hesitantly touched the top one, and the floor lurched. There was a startled hiss from Twister, and she realised that they were moving upwards.

She experimented by trying a small jump, and the floor came up and hit the soles of her feet, hard. And then it stopped moving and the door hissed open onto a huge room with three Garsal stationed around it, working at panels covered in glowing symbols. One of them turned its head as the door opened, looked straight into the small mobile room, then very obviously dismissed the emptiness and turned straight back to its task. As Shanna watched amazed, one of them flicked the small arms at the top of its thorax across the screen in front of him and an insectoid face appeared on it, a string of odd sounding syllables sounding across the room. All activity stopped, and the three creatures focused their attention on the screen.

In the mobile room Taya grabbed Shanna by the arm and pulled her out into the workroom and the door slid shut behind them. While the sound of the creature on the screen covered any noise, Taya spoke quietly into Shanna's ear. "This must be the communication room. Cover me while I see what I can do, then get ready to run." Shanna gulped slightly, and extended her bubble over Taya. She placed her hands on Storm and Twister, and felt their raised hackles and poised alertness, and tried to 'feel' where the others were. There was nothing she could detect, so slightly worried, she continued shielding Taya, wondering what the other girl was doing. A light flickered and dimmed in the ceiling, and one of the Garsal looked up, before returning its attention to the screen. The Garsal head on the screen continued talking, and one of the three in the room was diligently flickering its small set of arms across the screen embedded in its desk.

The light returned to its normal brightness, but the sound from the screen suddenly blurred and slowed, and the picture began to look scratchy. Two of the technicians began to tap quickly at their screens, and the picture steadied. A flurry of Garsal conversation ensued, with much flicking of limbs and emphatic tapping. Shanna hoped that Taya knew what she was doing and wondered if she should assist, but couldn't imagine trying to fade, extend her bubble, 'feel', and manipulate machinery all at the same time.

The volume of sound began to vary wildly, to the consternation of the Garsal technicians. All three were now tapping their screens frantically, heads and eyes swivelling backwards and forwards from their screens to the large one in front of them. A whining sound began, vibrating deep in Shanna's bones, and she felt her cats move restlessly under her hands. The sound rose in pitch until it was an almost inaudible assault pressuring Shanna's ears, and she felt that her eardrums would burst. To her horror she felt the fade flicker and concentrated harder, feeling the strain despite her contact with her cats.

The whine built even further, then all the lights went out, followed by a series of sharp cracks that sliced through the air. A moment later, the red glow of small fires could be seen throughout the room as smoke began to rise from several locations. At the same time, the door to the mobile room opened and she heard a thud from beside her. She dropped to her knees and felt with her hands on the floor for Taya.

The girl had collapsed, and Spinner was nosing her frantically. Shanna pushed him back and felt for a pulse in her throat. It was there, throbbing slowly, and Taya's chest was rising and falling under her hands. She chanced a glance through the darkness at the empty room, hoping that its arrival meant that two of the others had arrived. The three Garsal were shouting loudly across the room at each other; one was attempting to extinguish the flames with a handheld device, while the other two were tapping even more frantically at their screens.

There was a flicker of green tidemarks across the room, and Shanna knew with relief that if Satin was in the room, so was Allad. In the darkness and chaos of the room, now filling quickly with acrid smoke, Shanna decided to try and pull Taya towards the mobile room, hoping that the others would be able to help. She sent her cats bounding towards where she thought Allad might be and, hooking her hands under Taya's armpits, began to pull her towards the open door. She hoped that the general hubbub would hide the faint sliding sounds she was making. She felt a warm starcat presence, then she felt Allad's large hands joining hers on Taya's limp body. Someone else lifted Taya's legs, and they wrestled Taya into the mobile room just as a loud klaxon sounded. A dark purple light flicked on and the room was bathed in eerie light, and Shanna realised that she could see Challon's familiar figure outlined against it. She extended her bubble to include him, but not before one of the Garsal had looked up and seen him. It leapt across the room and Shanna cried a warning, but the Garsal crashed into Challon's faded body and there was a howl of starcat anger.

"Keep the fade, Shan!" Allad's voice was urgent. "Ragar, help Challon!" Two cats suddenly flickered into view. Dipper was slashing and biting at the Garsal on top of his partner, and Sparks snarled and hissed at the other two Garsal who'd begun to move across the room toward the commotion. One went down unexpectedly, and Shanna knew that the other starcats were doing their jobs - protecting their partners. With a last surge, Taya's limp form was deposited inside the mobile room. "Verren, look after her," said Allad. "Shan, join me, we need to get Challon and leave. Don't drop the fade!" Shanna pulled her knife and ran forward, steeling herself to keep the fade constant, 'feeling' Taya and Verren behind her, and Challon, Ragar, and Allad ahead. Her two cats were circling the third Garsal, then they struck in a coordinated attack, snarling and growling as Shanna and Allad arrived by Dipper's side. The cat was still snarling and worrying the now lifeless corpse atop Challon's faded body. All the noise had ceased elsewhere in the room. "You can let it go now, Shan."

She dropped the fade, feeling tiredness wash through her body, and Challon appeared on the ground. He had a number of deep lacerations on his face, and there was blood and milky fluid staining his uniform in a number of places. He was alive though and conscious, and with the help of Allad managed to get to his feet and limp over to the mobile room. As they entered, starcats crowding around them, Shanna hit the bottom button and then dropped to her knees next to Verren and Taya.

"Is she alright?"

Verren looked up at her, concern clear in his vivid blue eyes. "I think so, but she's exhausted and unconscious, much as you were after that exercise. She must have expended an enormous amount of energy to stop all of that. Spinner seems OK though."

Shanna fumbled in her pocket for an energy patch. "Do you think this might help?"

"I've already tried one, but we'll try again. Thanks." He bent over Taya with his water bottle as the room descended. The trip down seemed to be taking longer than the one up, and Shanna looked up uneasily. Ragar was helping Challon to clean his wounds. Most seemed superficial, but Ragar was bandaging a large wound on Challon's left arm while Dipper watched closely. The room continued to descend, seemingly endlessly. There was no sound.

"We must have gone past the entrance room, surely," said Allad, "what button did you push, Shan?"

"I just assumed we'd started at the bottom," Shanna broke off, shaking her head. "Sorry."

"No matter, none of us had any idea where we started. Verren, what do you think?"

Verren looked up, face pale in the violet light, and concentrated. "It's hard to say in here. I know what direction to take towards the exit," he pointed. "But all I can tell is that we're too low by some metres." Allad pushed a button three levels above the bottom one, but the room continued its downward travel. He tried one another three levels higher with the same result.

"It looks like we're going to end up at the bottom. Maybe when we reach it, we'll be able to go up again. But just in case, Shan, fade yourself, Taya and Challon; the rest of us will look after ourselves. Verren, pick Taya up, and Ragar, you're with me. Cats on alert." Shanna prepared herself, then looked at her cats. They were crouched, waiting, tidemarks flickering in angry tones, black fur glistening oddly in the purple light. She signalled her cats to fade, faded herself, extended her bubble as requested, then waited as she felt the room start to slow.

The door slid open and a troop of Garsal marched past, as the sounds of wailing filled the air.

Chapter 27

SHANNA flattened herself reflexively against the wall of the moving room. A few of the Garsal troopers had glanced into the apparently empty room as its doors opened, but then turned their heads forward and continued marching. Shanna heard Allad tapping on the wall of the little room, but the doors remained open and the room didn't move. "Challon, are you able to do anything?" Allad's voice whispered.

"I'll try, I just don't have Taya's skill though." There was silence, and Shanna wondered if she could do anything. She knew she had some ability, but Taya's skill at ferreting out exactly what a machine did and how to stop it often eluded her. She placed a hand on the metal wall and concentrated. There was a sensation of ... something ... or rather, nothing, where something should have been. She tried nudging it and then shoving it, but the sensation of nothing remained. She surfaced just as Challon's whisper reached her.

"I think they've done something that's cut the power to this room. I can't do anything without that. We'll have to try something else."

"We'll exit and turn left then. Be alert. They obviously know we're in the ship now. We'll need to try and find our way out. Verren, you'll take the lead, so transfer Taya to Ragar." There was a flurry of hushed movement and a flicker of Ragar's form. Shanna hastily extended her bubble over him, then lifted her hands from her cats. The strain of holding the bubble over the others made itself immediately evident. She fished in her pocket for another of the energy patches and stuck it onto her arm. "Communicate by touch signals. Shanna, if you can, have a look through your cats' eyes as you're able. Exit now." Shanna sent Storm ahead, briefly contemplated looking through his eyes, then decided against it. Despite the energy patch, she could feel the drain of an extended bubble hold already. She left the room and turned left, hugging the wall.

The light was dim — even dimmer than it had been, and the wailing grew louder. She turned her head rapidly, trying to take in what might be making the sound, and almost stopped moving in shock. On the other side of the corridor was the slave quarters. Individual, barred cells extended the full length of the passageway, and in triple-storied levels above. The sounds and smells of both human and non-human misery permeated the atmosphere, and Shanna's core trembled with the horror of their desolation. Her fellow human beings and their allies were there in front of her, trapped and caged and without hope. She stopped moving and almost fell, as Ragar walked into her. He stumbled and let out a brief exclamation, and Shanna hurriedly began moving again. She didn't know where to look or what to do.

The woman in the nearest cell was huddled at the back of it, her ragged clothing draped in tatters around her thin form. As Shanna moved past concealed by her fade, guilt at leaving the woman crashed down upon her, and redoubled as the man in the next cell shook the bars of the cell door and shouted in wordless rage. She tried not to look, knowing that it was impossible to rescue them all, or even one, and hoping desperately to return one day to set all of the captives free. It was a moment she hadn't prepared herself for. Tears began to fill her eyes but she gritted her teeth, and allowed her anger at the Garsal invaders to strengthen her resolve. She heard a wordless sound from the front, and looked hurriedly forward. She caught the faint heat shimmer of a faded form, but nothing else was evident. The Garsal troop had vanished down the long corridor, and the sounds of feet in unison could still be heard marching steadily onwards.

Twister paced beside Shanna. She could 'feel' his presence by her side, and his anger. Ahead of them, Storm felt like an ominous thundercloud, and Shanna could feel that each step her cats took fed their anger. The constant sound of the alarm was beginning to irritate her, and her anger began to rebound on that of her cats. There was a low snarl from beside her and she hastily tried to damp her feelings, concentrating guiltily on shutting out the sounds of misery around her. She felt Twister subside slightly.

Ahead, there was a sudden escalation of noise, and the sound of marching Garsal filtered back to Shanna's ears. There was a fumbling grab at her arm and the tap code that meant stop, and she flattened herself against the wall, fumbling in turn for Ragar behind her. She tapped and he stopped, and heard a quiet grunt as he leaned back against the wall. She wondered how he was coping, carrying Taya. She checked her bubble, sweating as the troop of Garsal trotted past. They were moving with more urgency, and their heads were turning from side to side. They were obviously searching for intruders.

Another tap on her hand and she moved forward, simultaneously tapping Ragar's hand. The strain of holding the fade seemed to be escalating with every minute, and she reminded herself that all of them would be feeling the strain, not just herself. The signal to stop came again, and then a whisper. "Stairwell ahead. We're going up. Send Twister ahead and recall Storm."

She passed the message along and changed her cats over, sending Twister ahead with a whistle, telling him to take Allad's direction. She readied herself, then moved forward on the agreed signal. The smooth wall gave way to the cavity of the stairwell and she sidled into it. They began the climb and exited into yet another of the long corridors. This one had doorways at regular intervals, all with obvious labels written in an unknown script.

The attempt to find the exit from the ship wore on and on. They slunk past open rooms and working Garsal and up numerous stairwells, and all the time, the alarm rang constantly. Shanna hoped fervently that Verren knew what he was doing and where they were headed. Several times they'd had to backtrack from dead ends, and Shanna wondered how much longer they'd be able to remain undetected. Behind her, she could hear Ragar's breathing slowly become more audible, and she wondered how much longer he'd be able to carry Taya. The signal to stop came once more, and a whispered command came via Challon. "Allad's going to carry Taya; alert Ragar, and tell him to take the front with Verren."

No Garsal were in the current corridor, and the exchange was made quickly. A small sigh of relief had escaped Ragar as she passed the message along. As she helped transfer Taya from Ragar to Allad, she felt his sweat soaked shoulders under her hands. "Verren thinks we're on the right level now," came Allad's whisper. "Be prepared for more Garsal. Can you continue to hold the fade?" Shanna felt her stomach lurch slightly.

"I think so, Allad, but I'm tiring."

"Do your best," he said, resting his hand lightly on her shoulder. "We're all tired, but it's our best chance." She heard the worry in his whisper and steeled her resolve, unconsciously squaring her shoulders.

A few minutes later they came to a sudden halt, as the biggest squad of Garsal yet trotted past. Shanna studied the shiny blackness of their carapaces, noting the differing heights, builds, and the slight colour differences on the thorax, while she pressed her body against the wall and checked her bubble of fade. The strain was beginning to become more and more of a problem. The last time she'd put her hand in her thigh pocket, she'd found she was down to her last energy patch. There were a few more in her pack, but that pack was back in the grotto with Arad and Nosey. She hoped she'd have enough strength to see them out of the ship.

The troop passed, and the faded Scouts began to move again. Shanna began to sweat again, and checked her bubble, wishing she could place a hand on one of her cats for a moment of respite, but Twister was ahead and Storm was ranging to the side, doing his job of flanking the group. She soldiered on.

They turned a corner, and with an enormous feeling of relief Shanna realised that they'd finally returned to the corridor leading to the exit from the ship. Her relief was short lived though, as the sight of a solid mass of Garsal troopers in formation in front of the doorway sent her spirits plummeting. The fade was an enormous weight on her shoulders, and with the passing of every moment it seemed to be getting heavier. Hand pressure sent her back around the corner again, and Allad's voice came softly.

"We've run out of options. We need to get through those Garsal. Challon, if we can do that can you open the doors?"

"Yes," replied Challon. "As long as they still have power."

"Ragar, what kind of flame can you make?"

Ragar's voice was uncertain. "I think I could probably send a few rolling balls. If there was anything to burn, I could probably light it … " His whisper trailed off.

"Do what you can. Verren, you, Shanna, and your cats are to run interference. I don't care how you do it. We just need something that will move those Garsal far enough for Challon to get to the door. I'm going to try and knock the Garsal over. On my signal, we'll begin."

Shanna steeled herself, pulled her knife, checked her cats and stuck her silent whistle in her mouth. She could feel the fade with every heartbeat now. It felt as though it was beginning to siphon her energy directly from her bones. She signalled her cats, and felt them poised and ready.

"Now!" Allad's voice was just above a whisper and frightening in its intensity, and Shanna and her cats went around the corner again at a run. She tried to keep her movements as silent as possible. She, Storm, and Twister positioned themselves a few metres from the waiting Garsal troops, and flattened themselves against the wall as several fireballs erupted down the corridor. The Garsal troops reacted with confusion, stumbling over each other as they tried to avoid the burning globes, then a group in the very centre of the formation flew backwards, slamming hard into the metal wall containing the doorway. There were sickening cracking sounds and Shanna saw several of the creatures slide lifelessly to the floor, the milky Garsal equivalent of blood leaking from their bodies to puddle on the floor.

She signalled her cats and with snarls they leapt, their faded forms occasionally showing glints of violet and blue in the maelstrom. She ducked and weaved around the confusion, trying to stay to one side of the fight in case Ragar decided to launch any more fireballs. Smoke began to waft through the corridor, black and choking, and it began to tickle the back of Shanna's throat. When she concentrated she could 'feel' where the others were, but the bubble of fade began to draw even more heavily on her dwindling resources, and she hoped that Challon would open the door soon.

She sent Storm and Twister into the intensifying fight near the door. She could see the Garsal forms flailing and staggering, and knew that the faded starcats were taking their toll on the insectoid creatures. She ducked as one staggered backwards and nearly knocked her over, then saw Verren's form flicker to her right. With a shock, she realised that she could see several wavering human forms in the midst of the fight. One of the Garsal shouted, and those nearby converged on the human forms. She heard a choked cry from Verren, and an exclamation from Allad, then as another wave of fireballs erupted and the Garsal near the door were abruptly thrown to the side, she gritted her teeth, dashed for the door, and extended her bubble over everyone. There were audible snarls from the cats, and she hoped fervently that Storm and Twister would be all right. She could 'feel' Challon crouched by the door and faced away from him, knife held forwards, as a Garsal trooper ran towards their faded forms.

Her heart was pounding, and her arm shook slightly, as for the first time she was unable to duck and dodge, intent on protecting Challon as he attempted to open the door. The fade siphoned the energy from her in increasing waves. The Garsal trooper began to lift his weapon. He had obviously come to the conclusion that there was someone at the doorway, and had decided to fire blindly in the hope of hitting someone. She lunged forward, pushing her knife hand forward and up as she leapt. She felt it strike home with a horrible crunch, and the trooper let out a high pitched, vibrating cry and dropped its weapon. Its mid limbs snapped out though, and one closed around the wrist of her knife arm with a painful pressure. She struggled and flailed, before her training in unarmed combat reasserted itself, and she stepped sideways into the creature's hold, dropped her shoulder under its limb and thorax, and used her hips to throw the creature. Its grip broke as it crashed to the ground, milky fluid now pouring from its thorax. Shanna spun hastily, feeling the throb of her injured arm, and hurriedly transferred her knife to the other hand.

"I've got it!" Challon's exclamation rang through the corridor as the door slid sideways. Shanna 'felt' him run through the doorway with Dipper, and hoped that he wasn't running straight into another group of Garsal.

"Out!" shouted Allad. Shanna caught a glimpse of green tidemarks as Satin flashed past her, and whistled for her cats.

"I'll take the rear, Allad," she called. She felt the big Scout thud past her, still encumbered by the unconscious Taya, and could hear the effort in his footsteps. She took a breath and held the fade over them. all, 'feeling' desperately for her friends in the chaos. The snarls of starcats escalated and the chaos intensified as the Garsal attempted to converge on the doorway.

Ragar passed her, and she felt Sparks pause in the doorway. She counted desperately in her mind. Where was Verren? Storm and Twister were now fighting directly in front of her as she 'felt' for Verren with increasing fear, the sound of his cry echoing in her mind. "Verren!" she called, risking drawing the Garsal attention to herself.

"Coming!" Verren's voice was ragged, and she could hear the exhaustion.

"Twister! Help him!" There was another flurry of movement to one side, and finally Shanna realised that Verren was nearby. Her exhaustion was beginning to dim her senses. She felt Twister draw closer and the Garsal pressed inwards, more of the insectoid creatures now raising their weapons as they realised that the chance of hitting their fellows was now minimal and that their prey were escaping.

She struggled to hold the fade as Verren neared, and they ducked through the doorway together, followed immediately by their cats. There had been no sounds of fighting from the other side, and Shanna hoped fervently that it meant that no Garsal were in the holding room. As she cleared the doorway she felt the fade vanish of its own accord, and looked around guiltily. The door slammed behind them and she spun in place to assure herself that her cats were with her.

Challon was crouched by the doorway, hand on the metal, with his face pale and his jaw clenched. Blood seeped from a wound on his back, then Dipper slid himself under his hand and his expression of strain eased slightly.

Shanna looked around. The room was empty except for the Scouts. Allad had placed Taya near the outer doorway. Her form was very still, but Shanna could see the slow rise and fall of her chest. Her own was heaving, and sweat and other fluids were trickling stickily down various parts of her body. Her hands were shaking, and her inability to hold the fade any longer pricked her with guilt.

"Challon, can you leave that door and open this one?" asked Allad tensely.

"I think so. I think I've got it jammed." Pounding noises began to echo through the metal walls. Challon pushed himself to his feet and jogged tiredly over to the outside door, dropping to his knees again he concentrated.

"Allad, I can't do the group fade any more," Shanna panted. "I'm sorry, but I've run out of patches." She stopped as the older Scout held up a hand.

"You've done what you could. Let's just concentrate on getting out of here. I'm guessing from their actions that their local communications are probably still working, so I suspect there'll be another warm welcome on the other side of this door. If you can still fade yourself, you'll do that, just as the rest of us will. Those who need their cats will have to have them at their sides."

"But what about Taya?" asked Shanna, confused. Spinner was lying next to his partner, head on his paws. His tidemarks were dimmed, and he looked as worried as a starcat could look.

"We'll just have to do our best. If I carry, and you have a cat by your side, do you think you could fade just her?"

Shanna was doubtful, and she recoiled from the idea of experiencing the horrendous drain on her reserves again. She steeled herself, however, forcing a normal sounding voice. "Only if I'm touching, I think."

"Well, you'll just have to touch, then."

There was a soft noise from the door, and the group gathered next to Challon. "I'm ready."

"All right then, get ready to fade yourselves again. Get your cats to help. We'll make directly for the hole under the fence. Hopefully Spiron and the others are ready to help. Shanna, you'll send one of your cats ahead with a message to him." Allad handed her a small piece of paper, then looked around at the group of exhausted Scouts. His expression hardened. "No matter what happens, no one stops. You just keep going until you're at the grotto. Don't lead any Garsal there, and let your cats guide you in. You're responsible only for yourselves – no one else. Now, I'll be sending Satin out first as soon as the door's open. Ready?" There were nods, but no words, just a simple sense of readiness, as Shanna stood up from tucking the note into Storm's harness. With a grunt, Allad lifted Taya's body onto his shoulders. "Fade then. Open the door, Challon."

The door slid sideways with a hiss and Shanna saw a minute flicker of green as Satin exited, and sent Storm after the green-toned cat with a command to find Spiron and return. She placed a hand on Taya, and moved forward slowly on Allad's command. Twister's fur was soft under her other hand, and she and Allad ducked immediately to one side as they went through the door. There was a sizzling hum, and several red beams lanced into the open doorway. There was a gasping cry, and Challon's body appeared suddenly as he toppled lifelessly to the ground. The sound of an enraged starcat split the air, Dipper's form shimmered past Shanna in a blur, and the three Garsal troopers were dropped by an enraged ball of teeth and claws. The cat was a spitting, shrieking fury of destruction heedless of his own safety, and the Garsal around the doorway scattered.

Clenching her teeth against the sudden grief, Shanna stumbled forward, gripping Taya's ankle desperately as she and Twister laboured to keep the girl's unconscious form safe. Several hundred metres away, between the ship and the archway, a blossom of fire appeared, and the Garsal around the entryway were momentarily distracted.

"To the hole," Allad gasped. Shanna suddenly realised that the other Scout was maintaining his own fade with no help from his starcat, and redoubled her effort to move faster. Sweat was a steady trickle down her face, and she blinked her eyes to clear them in what she recognised was the early dimness of dawn.

There was confusion all around. Starcats were growling and hissing, and Shanna could 'feel' Twister's anger rumbling through his body. Garsal troopers were running across the area, dashing towards the doorway and the glowing firelight. Ruby lines lanced from their weapons, spraying the open doorway and lighting Challon's still figure on the ground.

Not worrying about anything except a direct line, Shanna and Allad gasped their way across the fenced area towards the hole under the fence. Even with Twister's help, Shanna was struggling to hold the fade. As they approached the glowing fence, there was a rustle of movement, and Shanna saw the dim forms of Amma and Karri on either side. She hoped that the Garsal's attention would remain on the fire and the open doorway. "Amma, take Taya." Allad's voice was hoarse with effort, and Shanna let the fade drop from the unconscious girl as Allad placed her on the ground. With a grunt, Amma began to slide Taya's form into the hole, Karri assisting from the other side to pull her through. Spinner appeared and followed his partner's body. His red tidemarks glowed slightly as he dropped to his belly to crawl underneath the ruby lines. Karri heaved Taya onto her shoulders and vanished into the greenery, Spinner pacing next to her. Her starcat, Moon, raced ahead at the flick of a hand signal.

"Where are the others?" whispered Amma.

"Coming," replied Allad. "Are Spiron and Barron still in there?"

"Yes, and Zandany as well. They needed him to set the fire."

Shanna wanted desperately to be under the fence and away with her cats. Away from the chaos and smoke and fear and death. But she held her ground, trembling with fatigue, waiting for Storm to rejoin her. There was a rush of unseen feet and Ragar's form wavered into view. Amma helped him under the fence, and he and Sparks vanished towards the grotto at a staggering run. The Garsal appeared to be in a state of complete confusion. Then there was the sound of a small explosion to one side. The flames intensified, and Shanna could hear the angry growls of enraged starcats. She whistled, hoping that Dipper might break off his attack and join them, but she knew that the starcat was more likely to fight until he was unable to fight any more, then join his partner in death.

A starcat with a deceased partner rarely chose another human companion, although they might occasionally attach themselves to the partner of their mate. She realised that she didn't know if Dipper had a mate. Her heart gave an abrupt lurch as she imagined Storm or Twister attempting to avenge her own death. She scanned the slowly brightening compound, hoping to catch a glimpse of Storm's blue-tipped ears, or any sign of the other four still inside the compound.

Beside her, Allad was scanning too, looking for Satin to appear. There was the sound of staggering steps and Verren limped into view, supporting himself on Cirrus. Amma helped the exhausted pair under the fence, then Twister hummed softly and Storm was suddenly under her other hand even as Allad stepped forward to run his hands over Satin.

The commotion near the ship intensified and more flames erupted, and as Shanna dragged her tired body under the fence, Spiron, Barron and Zandany glided silently into view. She forced her leaden legs to obey her, and she and the two starcats headed for the grotto.

*****

Kaidan and Anjo collected their messages, and Anjo stowed the packages in his backpack. Anjo's fitness had certainly come along, Kaidan thought. He had no difficulty keeping up with Kaidan now, and under Cally's strict tutelage had begun to exhibit some of the skill needed to move silently in the bush, so necessary to safe travel on Frontier. Kaidan hefted his own pack with a grimace. Every time they ventured away from Toman's base in one of the old Storm Shelters, they were required to take everything necessary for an extended stay in the wilderness. He felt as though his pack straps were wearing grooves in his shoulders.

"Ready?" he asked Anjo.

"As ready as I ever am on this planet," replied Anjo. "You'll make sure nothing eats me?"

"Ha! That's what Ember's for."

"Well, you're the one with the bow!"

Kaidan grinned in reply, wriggled slightly to settle the pack, and indicated that Anjo should precede him out of the half-buried entrance. They nodded at the old Scout sitting at the entrance with his aged starcat, and he smiled back.

"You're fine this morning. Nothing to make Splash twitch an eyelid so far."

"We'll be back this evening, Cam," said Kaidan.

"I'll pass it on, then. Good travel."

The two young men - one accompanied by a young cat, the other with one barely out of cub-hood - strode off, neither making more than a quiet whisper as they left, and the old Scout nodded approvingly. The early dawn light briefly outlined them and they vanished from his sight.

***

The Garsal Overlord stalked angrily into the smouldering communications centre on the top deck of the colony ship. Burned and damaged components were strewn everywhere, and the bodies of several of his comm techs were still sprawled in the debris. Splashes of red indicated that the humans had not come out unscathed.

"Report!" he snapped, as he tapped a manipulator arm angrily on the nearest surface. The Communications Officer ducked his head over his thorax nervously.

"They have completely destroyed our deep space communications system. The in-ship system appears repairable, and the ground to air system will be fixable within a few hours. Fortunately we have plenty of spare components. The deep space system will have to be manufactured from scratch, and every component replaced. It will take many, many months, perhaps the better part of a planetary year. How the humans managed this is still beyond me." The Overlord slapped his arm against the desktop in frustration.

"So we are currently blind and deaf?"

"Yes, Sir," replied the Officer.

"You will prioritise the ground to air system," said the Overlord. "We will launch the aircraft as soon as they are functional, and take our revenge on the humans."

***

Cerren settled his pack more comfortably on his shoulders as he paced through Watchtower's gates. He surveyed the group around him with some displeasure. Starfall's Councillors looked discomforted, and a number were openly dismayed at the weight of their packs. Foster's Scouts were stationed around the group in an efficient formation, and Cerren sent Socks ranging ahead to join Foster's cat. He moved easily to where the Patrol First was casting a trained eye across the group.

"Could be a long day, Foster," remarked Cerren as he matched her pace. She moved with the grace common to all Scouts.

"I think it'll be an interesting one," she replied, as she let her gaze linger on Tamazine, even as she sent her cat out on a circle. The Senior Councillor's form was stalking along, surrounded by her sycophants. "We're not likely to be bothered by much wildlife, but the Councillors are not used to this type of travel. At least it's only a few hours' walk." She sighed and Cerren nodded. He felt oddly invigorated by the chance to take a walk outside the stuffy confines of the endless meetings. He turned his head and breathed deeply of the crisp morning air, and allowed nothing but the feeling of the physical activity and the joy of being back on the trail to flood through him. His stride was vigorous and Socks was in her element. He decided to enjoy his brief freedom to the utmost.

Chapter 28

AS SHANNA stumbled through the thick vegetation, her customary grace lost to fatigue, she was dimly aware of the sounds of chaos behind her. Each step she took was a triumph of endurance. Trusting to the strength loaned to her by her starcats, she concentrated only on stumbling forward. Storm was a bastion of steadfastness under her right hand, keeping her upright, and Twister a guideline that beckoned her onward under her left. More than ever before she trusted her cats, allowing them to direct her steps. She was aware that the three of them remained faded, but this time she knew that the cats had faded her. Her human abilities had reached their end.

Brief thoughts of predators trickled their way through her mind, along with fleeting images of Below's deadly plant life. Each time, the thoughts were replaced with soft purple twilight and the blue glow of starlight. They washed through her mind, erasing the fear and leaving only love in their wake. Dimly through the burn of her body numbing fatigue, she knew that it was Twister and Storm. The tiny part of her mind not involved with propelling her body forward wondered and watched.

A hot line of fire lanced past her and incinerated a barbed palm on her left. She knew the Garsal couldn't possibly see her, and wondered why they'd left the chaos around the ship, yet the two cats began to zig and zag her around low drooping branches. Shanna foggily realised that her fatigue had made her so clumsy that she was leaving a trail of wobbling branches and crumpled bushes. The Garsal had begun shooting at the disturbed vegetation. Making a supreme effort, she straightened and attempted to resume her normal graceful glide. She had to slow down slightly to maintain the control required, and a few more sizzling bolts slammed into the tree she'd just passed. She felt the urgency inside her cats begin to climb, but attempted to send a feeling of reassurance to them; her brain knew that she needed to slow down and conceal her passing from any pursuing Garsal. The feeling of urgency changed to one of exasperation, and she was startled. Storm responded by striding faster, and she was forced to begin her rapid stumble again, or risk losing contact with them. Her mind reeled.

Another sudden increase in speed, and then a sudden deviation to the right, and Shanna realised what her cats were doing. They'd swung her around a clump of soothall berry bushes. She'd only seen isolated plants before, but this clump contained at least half a dozen mature bushes set closely together.

The trained Scout part of her wanted to stop and examine this oddity, wondering whether the mystery of being able to propagate the bushes might finally be solved. The fleeing-from-alien-invaders part kept her legs moving, however, and once she was around them it made her pause briefly, pick up a stick and rustle the branches directly behind the patch. The whip-like branches flailed back and forth, and she felt her cats' approval fill her mind. She turned back towards the pursuing Garsal briefly as they blundered through the bush, following her trail of disturbed vegetation. She rustled the branches again and several red beams lanced out towards her as she dropped flat on the ground.

There was a smell of burning, then the sound of heavy footfalls crunching through the undergrowth. Shanna risked another glance, and saw three black forms run straight into the soothall patch. There was a sudden ear-splitting screech and all three toppled heavily to the ground, and Shanna knew that the spooner spiders had done precisely what her cats had intended. There was a hum from Twister, and she dragged herself to her feet once more. In the distance she could hear the sounds of further pursuit. Deliberately holding her cats, she 'felt' for any other human or starcat presence. Nothing. It seemed she was alone for the moment, but probably not for long. With a sigh, she pushed her tired mind to figure out where she was, and failed miserably. The early morning sunlight had begun to slant through the trees as she looked around.

Twister hummed again, and she realised that her cats were now visible. She ran her hands over their heads. Both hummed again and urged her onwards, and once again she put her trust in their instincts. Twister ducked under her hand and Storm vanished ahead into the trees. She stood still briefly, but when his black head and blue glowing ear tips appeared from the screen of green ahead, forced herself to move again. This time slowly, quietly, and with as much attention to the dangers of Below as she could manage. It was easier without the fade. One foot ahead of the other, she dragged herself onwards.

An hour later, she took the last few steps into the concealed grotto. Arad rushed towards her, concern on his face, while Nosey gravely touched noses with Storm and Twister, suddenly more the young starcat than a gambolling cub.

"Shan, have you seen Spiron and Barron?" She shook her head exhaustedly and took the last few steps into the grotto. She looked around the small area, noting the collection of exhausted bodies collapsed onto the ground watched over by feline forms.

"Last time I saw them, they were approaching the fence line with Zandany. Is he back?"

"Yes, they sent him under the fence first." He pointed distractedly towards the rear of the grotto. "Go and rest, there've been no Garsal anywhere near here, so we should be safe for a few hours at least." Shanna could see Zandany's familiar lanky form lying exhausted on the ground. Further over she could see Amma asleep, dark curls cushioned against her pack. Spider was tucked against her. She managed to stagger over towards her, and with a last effort dragged her pack from the rock she'd stowed it near, collapsed to a sitting position, and began to rummage in the outer pocket. There were very few of the energy patches left. The demands of the long journey had depleted her supply more than she'd realised, so she left them where they were and turned her attention tiredly to her cats. Both had a variety of cuts and there were several patches of scorched fur along Storm's back. She pulled her cat kit from its outside pocket and began to soothe her friends' hurts.

With a sigh, Shanna dabbed antiseptic on the last of Twister's grazes and lay back on her pack. She was almost too tired to put the cat kit away but forced herself to do so, then cradled by two loving forms, she closed her eyes. With the last of her coherent thought, she wondered again at the depth of her cats' communication with her. A flicker of blue and purple washed across her mind, then the three of them slept.

***

The control centre was a babble of chaotic sound as the Overlord strode in. As the scurrying workers realised he was there, the confused noise slowly trailed away, and they straightened, directing their attention towards him. "Report!" His voice echoed through the sudden silence, and the communications chief scurried forwards, dipping his head anxiously.

"The local short range comms are now functioning. The ground to air system will be available in about two hours. The deep space system is as I first thought, completely non-functional. There are a number of components that will have to be manufactured from scratch." He waved his manipulator arms expressively. "Some will require rare earth elements that we have yet to locate on this continent."

There was silence from the Overlord, and he hastened on. "I have lost several of my technicians to the invaders. I will need to recruit from other technical sections – some of the computer techs perhaps, and several from engineering." The silence grew longer and the Comms chief slowly backed away, towards the console he had been working on. The taste of smoke and overheated components flavoured the air as the waiting continued.

"Carry on!" snapped the Overlord. "Report to me immediately the ground to air system is operational. We will still launch the aircraft today. As soon as you are able to contact Trooper Hoth on the plateau, notify me." He stalked from the room and the hubbub slowly resumed.

It had been a long and drawn-out night. The Overlord had been catapulted from his slumber when the alarms rang throughout the ship. He was tired, and knew that shortly the Matriarch would demand an explanation for the night-time activity. Footage from security cameras in the critical areas of the ship had shown very little. Doors had opened and closed, seemingly by themselves. There had been nothing until the chaos of smoke and flame in the communications room. Suddenly there were human figures in the room seemingly appearing from nowhere, and enormous feline creatures painted with glowing, pulsing marks.

They'd entered the lift and descended, then vanished yet again for hours, until the chaos near the ship's exit had erupted. He'd watched the footage multiple times, seeing forms waver and flicker then vanish yet again. Somehow they had technology that not only prevented them from appearing on the ship's scanners, but allowed them to vanish at will. He had a dozen troopers dead and more wounded, and all he had to show for it was one human body. One of the feline creatures had been visible for some time as it ripped and clawed its way through half a dozen Garsal troopers, before limping away and vanishing somewhere in the compound. More of his troopers had perished pursuing the invisible humans, attempting to track them by traces of movement in the vegetation.

Under Zoash's command others were, even now, attempting to scour the area within the outer perimeter after they'd located a hole dug underneath the laser fence. They were hampered by the deadly vegetation, and the flying sentinels had received no alerts from the watch globes set around the furthest extent of the encampment. Communications had been scratchy though, and the Overlord weighed the risks of losing more troopers on a risky land search. If he ceased the ground search, then the humans who'd already destroyed his deep space communication equipment might cause further havoc. But if he continued to pursue them in their own environment, his troops might well be further depleted. He stalked angrily through the ship's corridors towards his command centre. How was he to pursue invisible humans? The environment was so inimical that just the plant life alone might kill his troopers, let alone the marauding predators that continued to plague the expeditions he'd sent.

The doors to the command centre hissed open, and he strode in. There was a sudden pause in the activity that filled the room, then each of the Garsal bent with renewed industry to their tasks. He stepped into his private office and lowered himself to the chair in front of his work screens. With a sudden moment of rage, he swept the several of the mounted mineral samples to the floor. The bare desk surface mocked him. As bare as his achievements on the planet.

He pulled his tablet across the desktop and began tapping the surface impatiently. He pulled the files containing the roster of Garsal crewmen to the fore. With a much slower touch, he opened the roster of dead and disabled. And then the slave numbers. The planet had taken a huge toll on his Garsal and slave resources. The colony was still viable – each colony ship had plenty of male Garsal, and his precious female resources were completely safe, but the trooper resources had been heavily impacted and there had been large losses amongst the slaves. His anger grew. The planet was a treasure trove of mineral wealth, and it would be the source of his influence and power once he'd subdued it. His offspring might well rise to rule several systems on the back of this planet's resources.

He pushed the tablet away angrily. Dreams of rising to power in the Garsal hierarchy were only dreams, without the resources to communicate with Command. If the human threat on this planet was not neutralised, then there would be no empire to build. But how to deal with that threat? He was still angry, but the flames were damped enough for rational thought, and he began to plan. Complete annihilation would be inadequate. The proud history of his forbears was a pattern of conquer and enslave. To do any less would bring dishonour on his entire race.

Two hours. He tapped the in-ship communicator and gave orders to the pilots. Half the aircraft would go to the plateau. The other half would begin an aerial search for the humans who had so damaged his communication equipment.

***

"I'm so sore," said Anjo, as he stretched and groaned. He and Kaidan had just been put through their paces again by Cally and Mirror. Ember hummed quizzically at him, red tidemarks rippling and glowing affectionately. The red-toned cat had flowed effortlessly through Cally's obstacle course, occasionally assisting his less able partner, and Mirror had touched his nose gently with her own at the end. "It's alright for you, you were born on this rock, cat!"

Kaidan laughed and hefted his pack again. "We'd better keep moving. Have you got all those messages from Cally stowed?"

"Yes," sighed Anjo, and tightened his left shoulder strap slightly. "Are you sure you know where we're going?"

"Of course I am."

"Well then, show me again how you do it, and we'll be off."

Kaidan pulled his compass from his pocket, and the two heads bent over the map.

***

Cerren perched on a rock and Socks laid herself at his feet, a disgusted feline expression on her face. Her blue tidemarks flicked irritably in pulsing patterns as she watched the drama unfold. Cerren didn't know whether to be amused or disgusted. They'd made very slow time, and it was long after the hour that they should have arrived at the Starlyne habitation.

The sun was pleasantly warm as he watched Tamazine and her companions complain to Foster once again about the pace she'd set. He was feeling rather relaxed, the stroll of the last few hours had been easy for him to manage and, when he managed to ignore the grumblings around him, therapeutic. He mused on the changes that had taken place in the ten years since he'd left Starfall. There had been the odd message from old colleagues in the Scout Corps that had suggested growing complacency on the part of the council, but living in Watchtower, he'd forgotten what a cushioning effect a large population could have upon someone's physical and mental toughness.

Watchtower was the smallest of the three major settlements on the plateau, and the most recently established. Although secure - and Cerren thanked the creator that the likelihood of nasty wildlife being attracted by the scene playing out in front of him was minor - it was still small enough for its inhabitants to remember that Frontier was anything but an easy planet to live on.

Apparently Tamazine and her fellows had forgotten these things, despite their overland cart-assisted journey from Starfall, and had apparently avoided physical activity over the last few years. They had proved to be woefully unfit for the walk. He pulled his map from his thigh pocket, took a bearing on Foggy Top then Pyramid Hill, and did a quick resection. He looked at his map for a moment more doing the calculations, and slid off his rock.

"Tamazine!" He strode into the centre of the dispute. "At the pace you've been managing, we're only half an hour from the habitation. In the time it's taken you to complain again, we could have been there." The Senior Councillor spun on the spot, her mouth turned down with displeasure.

"So you say. You said it was only a two hour walk!"

"I did say it was a two hour walk. A two hour walk for a normal, active person, that is." He shook his head and allowed his exasperation to show. "Tamazine, this is a lot of fuss about nothing. Our allies will be waiting. We need to get moving. You can all rest when we arrive."

Tamazine opened her mouth once more, but Cerren, anticipating another round of complaints, simply raised one eyebrow and fixed Tamazine with a blunt stare. She closed her mouth and motioned to her aide to lift her pack for her.

"We will talk more of this later." She turned her back on him and went over to Foster. Cerren winked broadly at the Patrol First over Tamazine's shoulder as she reorganised their march. She caught his eye briefly, and had to stifle a grin before she could turn her attention back to the Senior Councillor.

"Come on Socks." Cerren strode to the front, flicked a hand signal to Foster, who acknowledged it and slipped away into the peaceful silence of the bush. As the sounds of the dignitaries faded behind him, he let out a sigh of pure relief and allowed himself to bathe in the tranquillity of the landscape. Socks let out a pleased hum and they increased their pace. Fifteen minutes and they'd be at the habitat. He hoped the Starlynes would understand the issues — at least he'd be able to give them some advance warning.

***

Peron rewarded Thunder with a small piece of cheese. The growing starcat was a fast learner, and obviously intent on pleasing his chosen partner.

"Time for lunch, I think," Peron said. Thunder hummed his agreement and together the two left the arena for Peron's planned lunch with the starcat breeders. Janna, Adlan and Josen were already waiting for him, their cats grouped together beside the table. Sabre and Moshi watched on as Boots and Anvil gravely greeted Thunder, who had carefully dropped to his belly to approach the adult cats. Definitely not stupid, Peron thought with a small smile as he watched Thunder join the two older male cats.

"Peron, it's good to see you," said Janna. "Is there any word from Below?" Her question was general, but Peron could hear the unspoken words behind it. Have you heard from Shanna? Is our daughter all right? When will we see her? What is she doing?

"Nothing more than I knew last week," he replied, wishing he knew the answers himself. There had been no messages from their Starlyne allies, and the silence concerning the mission to locate the alien ship and disable its communications played on his mind constantly. His thoughts wandered to the fourteen Garsal kept under guard in the tunnels below the old storm shelter. They still refused to communicate with their captors, and any suggestion that Semba might assist had been met with blank silence from the woman. It was obvious she was still severely traumatised from her time as a slave, and fearful of any contact with her previous masters.

He wished Anjo was still in Watchtower, even if he had been as unsuccessful as communicating with the Garsal as everyone else. The problem was, as Anjo had pointed out, while the Garsal spoke the common tongue – the one used on Frontier - they simply refused to speak to anyone who had attempted to question them, including the offworlder. What was frustrating was that Frontier's charter forbade any attempt at physical coercion. Although he hadn't really come close to breaking the charter, as time wore on Peron was more than willing to admit he had been tempted. This time however, he had something else he wanted to try. He'd noted that the Garsal reacted with apparent fear when in the presence of any starcats, so he planned to request the breeders to accompany him on his next visit – with all of their adult starcats. And perhaps they had a few tricks of their own up their sleeves.

Looking at the three starcat breeders, Peron took a spoonful of soup and blew gently across it to cool it. "I have a question for you."

***

Shanna woke from what seemed like the deepest sleep she'd ever experienced. Her eyes were blurry and they kept trying to shut again, all by themselves. Dimly, she was aware that something was odd. Then she realised her cats were standing, no longer tucked around her body, and she struggled to her feet and followed their gaze towards the sky. Something was wrong. There was a rumble, then a whooshing noise that grew steadily louder. She strained her eyes, trying to peer through the thick canopy above the grotto, and as the noise peaked, caught a glimpse of something large and metallic passing overhead. The noise gradually trailed off and she looked around. Everyone was on their feet. She counted quickly and was relieved to see Barron and Spiron had re-joined them. Both looked tired and were covered in dirt. She could see that Taya was still horizontal on the ground and Spinner was lying with her, his head resting on her stomach.

"What was that?" asked Verren. The other cadet was filthy and there was dried blood on his pants leg below the bulky bandage that showed through a tear in the cloth.

"It seems they've a few more of those aircraft," replied Spiron grimly. "Get yourselves ready to move out. It's past time that we left. Verren, do anything you can to get Taya conscious again. We'll need her to disable those mechanical sentinels, or at least to explain to Kalli and Karri how she did it." The group began to ready itself for travel, but as Shanna checked her pack she found numerous bruises and cuts marring her normal range of movement, and wondered how the others were coping. She could see Verren rousing Taya, and resolutely pulled her remaining patches from her pack and took them to him.

"Would these help, Verren?" He looked at her with concern.

"Are these all you have left?"

"Yes, but I'll be OK. We need Taya, and I bet we're all low on them. Take what you need." He nodded his thanks and selected a quick-acting patch, hesitated slightly, then took another long-acting one.

"Thanks." He turned back to the recumbent girl, bared her forearm and then pressed the patch firmly to her skin. Nothing happened for a moment, then Taya's eyes opened. She shut them quickly with an expression of pain, and raised her hands stiffly to her head.

"My head! Where are we?"

"It's OK Tay, we're in the grotto, but we need to move. Can you try?" Verren said.

Taya nodded slightly, and Shanna helped Verren lever her into an upright position. "Do you think you can stand?" Again she nodded, and Shanna saw her clench her jaw. At Verren's count, she heaved and Taya staggered but remained upright, wobbling slightly. Verren slapped the other patch onto her forearm, and the wobbling turned to a slow sway that gradually began to fade.

"Whose patch is that? I'm all out."

"We've pooled them," Shanna said hastily. "Most of us are running low. We'll use them for whoever needs them most." She gave Verren a firm stare as he opened his mouth.

"Spiron wants you to explain to Kalli and Karri how to turn off those sentinels," he said instead. "Are you up to it?"

"I think so, if you can lean me on that rock while I sort myself out. Can you send them over?" Shanna felt sympathy for the other girl, still a strange feeling, and jogged quietly over to the others. She decided to listen in as well. Perhaps she could assist.

***

Kaidan stopped and held up a hand. They were only a half hour's brisk walk from the Starlyne habitat by his calculations, but something seemed odd. Ember growled quietly and the two humans cupped their ears and listened attentively. Even Tempest knew that there was something different. She listened with her whole body, mirroring Ember's stance. Then both cats began to growl, hackles rising. There was a swooping roar and something dark flashed overhead. Light glinted off its metallic outer, then Kaidan's body took over before his brain knew what was happening. He pulled Anjo into the thickest patch of safe vegetation he could find, and forced the offworlder to his belly. Ember and Tempest followed them, and all four of them lay motionless as the sound receded slowly.

"Garsal aircraft!" whispered Anjo.

"And it's heading for Watchtower," replied Kaidan. "What should we do?"

"They'll have sensors on board, seeking lifeforms. We'll be OK, because of Ember and Tempest, but there aren't enough cats to hide everyone. And we'll be too late to warn them... " He broke off as he realised what he'd just said. Kaidan's family were at Watchtower.

***

Cerren had just reached the Starlyne habitation when the aircraft flew overhead. It whooshed past, then the sound changed. The Starlyne elder greeting him had stiffened, then urged Cerren into the tunnel.

"Cerren, we must go deep. If they detected us on their fly past, we may be undone."

"But the others ... " He thought of the open patches between where he'd left the council delegation and the habitat, and prayed that they were well concealed by the trees, not in one of the open glades.

"We must hide!" The Starlyne's tone was urgent. "We have children here!"

"You hide," replied the Master, "I must warn my people." He called Socks, and the two of them began to run. Ahead, he could hear ominous thudding and concussions.

***

Peron's plan had been largely successful. He'd had the Garsal brought one by one into the interview room, guarded by two of the militia. He and the three starcat breeders had been waiting with a dozen adult starcats ringing the room. The cats had begun a staggered pattern of fade and appear. Each time they appeared, they were a little closer to the Garsal captive. At a subtle hand signal they had begun to circle, weaving in and around each other, all the while fading and emitting an unnerving growl. The first Garsal had broken after only a few moments of this, and begun to babble and cower. Peron had felt almost sorry for the creature, but had steeled himself and begun to bark questions at the creature. Its thickly accented language had been hard to understand, but for the first time a Garsal captive had answered direct questions. Three Garsal in, and the answers were being verified. Peron now knew that it was definitely a colony ship that had landed on his world. That it was the only Garsal colony in this region of the galaxy, and that this part of the galaxy was only sparsely populated. Many more questions seethed in his mind, and the scribe sitting quietly at the table behind him had provided him with a larger list supplied by the Council. He'd just sent the third Garsal back to the holding cells.

"Well, it looks like this might be working. All the answers are the same so far."

"The growl was the starcats' idea," remarked Adlan. "All we asked them to do was weave and fade."

"They're angry," said Josen, with a frown. "We might have to do this with breaks. Anvil's anger mounts every time he sees a new Garsal."

"You're right," said Peron. "Even Thunder's seething." He looked down at the young cat lying at his feet. His hackles were still up, a sure sign of anger, and a subterranean rumble from him was still audible. Peron poked him with his foot, and the rumble subsided to an occasional grumble.

"We'll try one more, then take a break," began Peron, breaking off as all of the cats began to hiss and growl as the room shook, and a series of thundering impacts sounded from outside. For a moment no one spoke, there was a moment of confused silence and then Janna spoke.

"They've found us, haven't they?" she said. "What can we do, Peron?"

"Stay here," replied the Scout Master, "You and your cats are essential for our survival." He took off at a run. As he ran, he mentally checked through his list of essentials. Most of the Councillors were with Cerren, but the heads of the essential guilds were all over Watchtower. Still, the other Masters had his lists as well. Even now they would be sending some of them down through the arena tunnel, and others would be following the plans they'd made so painstakingly. His Scouts and cadets were well drilled and well trained. He wondered what he'd find when he exited the storm shelter. At least the children were well away.

***

The door slammed behind Peron, and the three starcat breeders looked blankly at each other. The twelve starcats surrounding them pressed closer, and Sabre gave a small, plaintive hum.

"We can't stay here" Josen said. "We need to make sure the cubs are all right." Anvil hummed approvingly, and the three humans moved as one, their massed starcats swarming through the door and up the stairs. Janna signalled with one hand as they ran, and six of the cats blurred into top speed. They would spearhead the rush to save the cubs, still tucked away at Scout Headquarters. Smoke began to flavour the air as they approached the upper levels of the storm shelter.

***

The two militia guarding the Garsal captive paused and listened intently as the underground shelter began to shake in time to the explosions outside. "Quickly!" the senior of the two said. "We need to move to our emergency stations." She hustled their captive quickly along the hallway towards the cells. Her counterpart remained partially distracted, with his head turned slightly to one side as alarm bells began to sound. As they opened the cell door to return their captive to his cell, the alien invader took advantage of the distracted man and slammed his body into him, knocking him off balance and into the wall. Using the steel manacles around his manipulator arms and mid arms as a bludgeon, he slammed them against the senior's head, leaving her unconscious on the floor. A quick pivot and the man was down too, blood pouring down his face from a cut in his forehead. The Garsal trooper didn't hesitate. He stooped, and the man breathed his last. Hurriedly, he pulled the keychain from the woman's belt and began to free his comrades, then the fourteen Garsal began to work their way out of their underground prison, dealing as much destruction as they were able to along the way.

Chapter 29

ADLAN, Janna, Josen, and their cats headed towards the upper levels of the Storm Shelter at the run, in the wake of the six cats already sent to Scout Compound. There was chaos as people covered in dust, dirt, and blood rushed past them. As they neared the entrance the chaos intensified, but there were the beginnings of organisation apparent as well. The militia had swung into gear and a triage operation had commenced in the vestibule at the bottom of the steps. As they rounded the last turn however, there was an enraged hiss from Sabre and Janna turned, just in time to see her husband fall to the ground with one of the aliens on top of him. Boots snarled and leapt, and the alien's lifeless corpse rolled clear as a melee of snarling starcats, aliens, and humans erupted in the centre of the room. Shouts from the militia were punctuated with snarls and growls from the starcats, and deep crunching cries from the aliens. Intense confusion reigned as the smoke and dust now shrouding the entry way added to the chaos.

Janna leapt into the fray, heedless of her lack of weapons, frantic to get to her husband's side. As she did, she was dimly aware of Josen launching himself after Anvil as the cat went for the closest Garsal's throat. There were several moments of complete bedlam then suddenly everything was still. All of the Garsal and several militia were down, and Boots was sporting a slash down one flank that was dripping blood. Janna finally reached her husband, who was easing himself to his feet with a nasty gash on his forehead .

"Are you alright?" Janna demanded.

"I think so," Adlan said shakily.

Sabre hummed urgently, and Moshi and Anvil leapt towards the entrance, followed by the still bleeding Boots, then the three humans and six cats reached the steps that led to the surface and were running as hard as possible up them.

***

Shanna dropped to her belly again as another aircraft thundered overhead. The canopy was thick enough that she wasn't too worried about being seen, and conscious of the few energy patches left in her pack she resisted fading and simply checked for the boys. Storm, ever dependable, was pacing Satin ahead while Twister took Spinner's place on the left flank.

The Patrol was moving in tight formation and much more slowly than normal, but even at that pace, Taya had been struggling to keep up. Shanna risked a glance behind her to where the dark haired girl was concealed. Faintly, through the overhanging leaves of the pungo tree, Shanna could see the pallor of her skin. Both hands were on Spinner as she knelt in concealment. Fatigue was evident in her posture and Shanna worried that the girl might collapse again, remembering how exhausted she'd been after her own collapse. Mentally, she counted her patches again. She had three left. Two of the shorter lasting ones and one of the longer.

Storm appeared ahead of her, flicked his blue tipped ears, then vanished again, and she moved silently to where his head had peered through the thick brush. She noted the plybrush strands trailing from underneath the characteristic foliage, and tucked the knowledge away in her mind for later, should she ever return to this place. Whatever Taya had managed to do to the communications equipment had obviously enraged the alien invaders.

Their progress had been slowed by frequent flyovers of Garsal aircraft. From their regularity, Shanna guessed that they were flying a search pattern. She felt grateful that ground pursuit appeared to have ceased. Perhaps the attrition had worn the Garsal down. By her calculations, they should be nearing the mechanical sentinels, so she moved with even more caution than usual. A couple of metres to her left, Allad moved with his customary grace. Despite the dirt and blood staining his clothing, the large Scout seemed to have largely thrown off his exhaustion. From the corner of her eye she caught his hand signal. She pulled her whistle and called Storm in. Satin had found the sentinel.

Shanna worked her way back to the others. "We've found it," she whispered to Taya, and the other girl nodded then grimaced.

"Karri and Kalli are going to try and disable it. If they can't, then I will. We can't risk those flying things coming after us!" She rubbed her hands through Spinner's fur and he gave her a worried look, then turned his gaze on Shanna and Storm. Storm flicked his tidemarks in reply, and Shanna knew immediately what the two cats meant. She nodded.

"If you need, I think I can help, Taya." Taya looked up at her, surprised.

"With Storm and Twister helping, I can probably support you," Shanna said quietly. "I don't have your skill, but the three of us have some raw ability. Spiron?"

The Patrol first nodded. "If the other two can't manage, then we'll do it that way." He signalled for Karri and Kalli to move forward, and Shanna put an arm around Taya as they followed, allowing the other girl to lean on her slightly. There was a moment of slight resistance, then Taya nodded, leaning heavily on Shanna.

"Thanks, Shan." She sounded a little as though the words were forced out rather than spoken, but Shanna smiled anyway. Their old antagonism had mostly faded, but every now and then there was a moment of awkwardness. Shanna was worried about Taya's exhaustion, though, remembering how long it had taken her to recover after her own collapse during the training exercise, and surreptitiously felt the pocket where she'd stored her patches, wondering if she'd need to sacrifice another one.

As they joined Allad, she could see the sentinel reflecting light through the trees. Taya whispered instructions to Karri and Kalli, and they moved forward slightly. Shanna and Allad setting their cats to guard the two as they began to concentrate. Flickers of colour began to run through their hair, and Shanna hastily scanned what she could see of the sky through the canopy, hoping that none of the aircraft were in the vicinity. She sent Twister up the nearest tree, and at Allad's nod began to climb another. It was hard work climbing without causing the branches to sway and thrash, and it took Shanna longer than she had expected.

Reaching the top, she perched herself carefully in the fork of two branches and turned her gaze skywards. Far on the horizon to her south, she could see three black dots moving across the sky in strict formation. She leaned downwards, hanging from one arm, and caught Allad's eye, signalling the all clear, then returned to her perch, hoping that the two Scouts would succeed quickly. There was silence for a long time with no signals from below, leaving Shanna time to worry about her family. The longing to see them again was like a physical ache that began somewhere deep in her chest, and the more she thought about them, the stronger it grew until she was forced to cease that train of thought before her vision was obscured by a watery veil. She blinked furiously and scanned the horizon again. The aircraft were still in their formation, scouring east-west at the southern end of the protected area. She looked briefly through Twister's eyes, but there was nothing more to be seen.

A quiver through the trunk was all the warning she had, before Satin joined her on her perch. The green-toned cat's gaze sent her scurrying down the tree to join Taya. Allad met her at the bottom. He motioned with one hand, and she joined Taya near Kalli and Karri.

"I know what to do," said Kalli, in a frustrated tone. "But I can't quite make it happen. Karri's the same. I'm sorry, but you'll have to help us." Shanna whistled her cats in.

"Shan, if you're willing, I think I can do it with just you and the boys," said Taya, "I'd rather the other two and their cats were watching over us. I haven't got a lot of run left, I'm afraid." Shanna nodded, and then before she could overthink it, pulled one of the two last fast-acting patches from her pocket.

"I think you need this as well." There was a brief hesitation, then Taya nodded her thanks and slapped the patch on her arm. Colour returned to her cheeks almost immediately. Shanna stifled her regret. If they couldn't get through the globes undetected, there was no way they were getting home. Taya's need was much more than hers. The faster she could travel, the better it would be for them all.

"Ready?" Taya asked. Shanna nodded and positioned her cats one on either side of Spinner, stepped behind the three of them with a hand on each black back, and closed her eyes.

Shanna felt Storm and Twister lean into Spinner, then she was looking inside the mechanism. It was odd. *Was this the way Taya saw things?* she wondered, as her mind attempted to process the alien workings pictured in her mind's eye. If she does, she's cleverer than me, she thought. There was a wry sense of amusement that Shanna realised had come from Taya, and she wondered whether the other girl had actually heard her thoughts. Momentarily she recoiled; the idea of another person (why was it so different to a Starlyne?) hearing what she said in the privacy of her own mind was shockingly invasive. Then the enormity of the situation thrust its way to the forefront and she was aware of a sense of waiting coming from the other girl. She tried to relax and the image sharpened. There were flickers of thought wandering through her mind as the image broke down into ordered layers. Apparently Taya was sorting through the innards of the mechanism. Shanna wondered why she hadn't decided on a career with the artificers – with her mechanical aptitude and mathematical ability, she would have been an absolute boon. And then she remembered – Taya was busily stopping an alien device– with her will and her mind. Through her closed eyelids and the flickering images, Shanna was aware of a red glow. By now, Taya's hair would be pulsing with Spinner's tidemark patterns. She was much better off in the Scout Corps.

The layered images stopped flickering, there was a sudden flare of redness deep in the centre, then Shanna's eyes flew open and she saw the red slowly fade from Taya's hair. Taya nodded and sighed heavily. "It's done." Satin bounded down the tree and went past the sentinel in a blur of green. Allad signalled back behind them and led the way forwards.

"I'm sure they'll know where we're exiting, so we need to hurry." He looked a question at Taya and she nodded, and he broke into a smooth jog. Shanna sent Twister after Satin, tasked Storm to shadow Spinner, and hurried after him.

***

The sound of heavy concussions spurred Cerren to greater efforts. Socks paced him. She was as anxious as he was to get back to Foster and the Councillors, but she kept her pace to his, making sure that her partner was as safe as she could make him. Smells of smoke began to filter through the trees, and he had to leap sideways as a family of panicked weldens stampeded past. The crackling of flames grew louder, as he ran through smoke towards splintered trees and shouts of fear.

As he and Socks skirted a burning tree, they hurtled into a scene of chaos. Flame-covered trees flared torch-like in a concentric ring while the centre of the strike area was blackened and cratered.

"Socks, search!" Cerren ordered. "Foster, Payne!" he called frantically through the smoke.

There were confused shouts from the other side of the crater and he skirted the flaming area gingerly, eyes and head swivelling as he called again. Socks reappeared and urged him forward.

"Cerren, is that you?" It was Foster's voice and Cerren stumbled slightly in relief, peering through the smoke.

"Yes, where are you? Are you alright?" He kept following his starcat, though her grey coat blended so well with the smoke that he was forced to track her by her tidemarks. But even their blue was dimmed by the smoke that filled the air.

"Keep coming." Even in his hurry, Cerren realised that Foster had not answered his second question. Ahead of him a form became visible in the smoke. It waved its arm and he redoubled his pace, as his pack bounced heavily on his back. "Cerren, quickly." Foster took his arm and guided him through the smoke and past the line of flaming trees. She was stained with soot and he realised that she was limping as her cat ranged to one side, scanning the undergrowth for threats.

In an opening under the trees a small group of scouts were tending to the wounded, and his heart sank as he counted the number of bodies lying on the ground. "The aircraft sent a beam of red light into the bulk of the group," said Foster. She pulled her arm across her face. "The Patrol was on the periphery, with the Councillors in the centre ... we've done what we could, but there were some we couldn't find." She broke off. The Patrol's starcats ringed the area, their posture indicating a willingness to attack any threat. Wordlessly Foster pulled Cerren towards the nearest row of recumbent forms.

Payne was propped against a tree. One of his legs was clearly broken and blood seeped from a number of wounds down one side of his torso. He motioned to the form next to him. Tamazine lay there. One side of her body was blackened and seared, and she was struggling for every breath. Cerren realised with horror that she was conscious and watching him with her one remaining eye. She drew a groaning breath. "Cerren." The sound of her voice was a strained croak.

"Tamazine ... " He fell to his knees and dropped his pack onto the ground. He always carried the basic Scout medical kit. But for this it would be completely inadequate.

"You were right," she took another breath, dragging the air into her lungs by force of will. "You need to undo what I've done." She stiffened and her eye closed then opened once more. "I'm sorry. If they've killed everyone in Watchtower, it will be my fault." Cerren opened his mouth to reply but she forestalled him with a slight headshake and rasped another breath. "It's my fault alone. You must promise me that you will do everything in your power to stop them."

"I promise that, Tamazine." Cerren's voice was ragged as he watched Tamazine fight for each breath.

"You were always a better man than me ... " her voice trailed off and her eye closed for the final time. Unexpectedly Cerren felt tears prick his eyes, and he slowly put the medical kit on the ground. Foster's eyes met his as he pushed himself off the ground and walked his hands up his legs. Socks leaned into his leg comfortingly.

"I need to get to Watchtower," Cerren said simply.

Foster flicked her hand and two of her scouts appeared as if by magic. "You two will go with Master Cerren to Watchtower. We'll cope here, Cerren. The Starlyne habitation is only a short distance. Send word when you can." He nodded, grateful for her calm in the chaos of the moment.

"Let me know who the surviving Councillors are. Payne can take control in the interim." He pulled his pack back onto his shoulders, but left the medical kit on the ground. Foster needed it more. Decisively, he turned his eyes towards Watchtower. Faintly in the distance he could hear the sounds of destruction. He hoped that Peron had had enough time to implement his plans. Or there might be nothing left to return to.

***

Peron reached the entrance to the Storm shelter, forcing his way upward against the swarms of people descending the stairs in panic. The ground shook again as the building across the street collapsed in a pile of rubble and a gust of wind brought choking smoke swirling into the entrance. The decorative archway was scarred from flying debris and a large crack snaked its way through the old stonework. Human figures were swarming into the street and there were sounds of urgency everywhere. The militia guards at the entrance pulled two injured people from the street as he leapt the last few steps.

"Master Peron, it's chaos! They're burning everything!"

"What do you mean?" Peron demanded. "And how?"

"From the sky," called another of the guards. "There's a lance of red, then an explosion. We're trying to get as many people as possible in here. Hopefully it will be safer." He looked doubtfully at the cracked arch. "It's not safe up there."

"Keep doing what you're doing. I'm going to try and get to Scout Compound. If you see any Scouts, tell them that I said 'Plan Green'." He looked right and left, then left the building at a run, eyes towards the sky. He felt a pang of fear as Thunder followed. The starcat was really too young for this, but there would be no leaving the youngster behind. He was almost spun about as six starcats blurred past him out of the storm shelter and vanished towards Scout Compound. The three starcat breeders had obviously decided to disobey his orders. He shook his head. There was no time to think about that now. He followed in the wake of the cats, Thunder shadowing his every move, as for the first time in his life he put the skills he'd learnt as a Scout venturing Below into practice inside the walls of Watchtower. Using every piece of cover he could find, he began to make his way towards Scout Head-quarters.

People were spilling out of every still intact building he passed. For the most part they were dazed and confused, woefully unprepared for the de-struction raining on them from above. There was a sudden sound like a cy-clone in full strength, and one of the aircraft howled past seemingly just above his head. Peron flattened himself behind a fallen piece of masonry and watched disbelievingly as a thick red line lanced from it, leaving a trail of ex-plosions in its wake as it burnt across several residential buildings the next street over.

"Get to cover!" he shouted as several of the dazed people in the street stopped to watch. One woman turned blankly towards him and he exploded out of his own cover as the aircraft circled back. He leapt, crushing her to the ground and rolling towards a wall on the other side of the street. He felt the wind rush from her body as they hit the ground and mentally apologised, but as soon as they were hidden again, he pushed off the ground and urged her to hide in either the storm shelter or one of the basements so common to the early Watchtower dwellings. Hopefully something strong enough to withstand a cyclone might be strong enough to protect her from the aerial bombard-ment.

Thunder pressed close to his legs. Peron was glad to feel that the young cat wasn't trembling, but spent a precious moment running his hand over the starcat's smooth fur before vaulting over the low wall, and beginning his run down the road towards Scout Compound. Scanning the sky, he saw three of the aircraft circling high above.

They swung around and in an arrowhead formation began another pass across the town. Red beams burned their way across roofs and scored deeply into walls, and explosions followed in their wake. Peron was at a loss to know what they might do against such power. He scrambled over bricks and debris, momentarily closing his eyes each time he saw a body collapsed lifelessly in the street, trying to block out the sounds of pain and devastation as he and Thunder ran towards the arena gate.

He finally ducked into the arena just as one of the aircraft began a pass above the blocky strength of Scout Compound. One of the oldest buildings in Watchtower, Scout compound was a sturdy construction. The early settlers had laboured hard to form the huge stone blocks from which it was con-structed. As the aircraft hurtled towards the compound, and one of the red beams began to burn its way through the buildings nearby, Peron saw the squat, familiar figure of Master Dinian from Scholar's precinct on the roof of the building. He was flanked by several others, and Peron realised that he had a squad of archers mustered on the roof. They raised their bows, bulbous arrow heads pointing skyward. He shook his head. It was hopeless — bows and arrows against metal would only lead to the death of the archers, surely they'd learnt that from the battle Below! The aircraft noise was deafening, a thundering whine building to an ear-splitting pitch as it bore down on the building.

Master Dinian and his archers didn't flinch. Peron heard a shout from the Master and the bows snapped, arrows leaping forwards as one. They all struck the same place on the aircraft. As if in slow motion, Peron saw the arrows impact the aircraft. The bulbous arrowheads burst, spraying liquid everywhere across the front of the craft. For a moment, nothing else happened. And then one more arrow, glowing red at the tip, followed them, striking the same place. It appeared that they were trying a different strategy this time. The front of the aircraft burst into flame and suddenly veered southwards. The red beam burnt its way towards the front of Scout Compound before abruptly cutting out as the aircraft tilted crazily in the sky. The aircraft vanished over the horizon, then the earth shook once more to announce its meeting with the ground. Peron hoped fervently that it had crashed far from any human or Starlyne habitation. On the roof, Dinian's archers could be seen slapping each other on the back and jumping about.

Peron turned and looked behind him. There were two aircraft still circling above Watchtower, but as he watched he saw them break off their circling and head southwards. They accelerated, and there was a sudden boom and within a few moments they were rapidly dwindling specks. Smoke hung heavily over Watchtower. Fires raged in some areas, and belatedly the Storm Siren began to wail, its sound rising steeply above the sounds of human tragedy.

Strangely, the thing that stuck most in his mind at that moment was the sight of six fully grown starcats herding a dozen cubs out of Scout Compound and into the arena tunnel. The cubs needed no urging to move. They followed the lead cat obediently into the darkness, while the other five patrolled around them. Behind him Peron heard the sound of running footsteps, then Sabre rushed past him and he realised the three starcat breeders had arrived on his tail. Adlan was covered in dirt and had a heavily bleeding wound down one side of his face, while Janna and Josen appeared relatively unscathed. Moshi, Boots and Anvil spread themselves out around the gateway, guarding their partners. Peron noticed absently that Boots had a bleeding wound.

"The Garsal attempted an escape, Peron," said Janna, eyes flashing furiously. "We won't have to worry about them again, though."

Peron nodded slowly, regret for the lost intelligence warring with satisfaction at the demise of the alien invaders who had just wreaked so much destruction on his home.

Chapter 30

THE Overlord lifted his head as the Senior Communications Technician appeared on his screen. "Yes?"

"One of the sentinels has just ceased functioning."

"Send a ground crawler. It will be the humans." He opened the communications screen with one manipulator arm and opened a channel to the aircraft at the plateau. "Report."

"We've lost Air Three and are currently returning to base." There was a staticky hiss from the speaker. "I'm transmitting visual recordings of our assault."

"What happened to Air Three?" barked the Overlord. The visual feed from the aircraft showed concern on the pilot's face.

"The humans appeared to use some kind of primitive projectile weapon. It apparently carried an inflammable liquid. After contact, Air Three burnt then crashed, and we lost all telemetry."

"Do you have any visual feeds from Air Three?" asked the Overlord.

"No," replied the pilot. "We were recording telemetry only." The Overlord clicked his manipulator arms in displeasure. He opened the channel to the Comm Tech again.

"All vehicles and aircraft are to be on live feed at all times." The Comm Tech acknowledged the order and his image vanished. The screen blinked again and the Archivist's face appeared in front of him.

"I have found the unknown pattern in the archives, my lord." He hesitated and the Overlord motioned irritably. The Archivist dipped his head awkwardly, and his voice was fearful. "It is impossible. It is simply impossible." His normally imperturbable tones had overtones of terror, and he tapped at his own screen with quivering manipulator arms. "I will show you, but it is still impossible." The Overlord was irritated.

"Quickly then," he growled, wondering what had the old male so perturbed. Then the picture appeared on his screen. The Great Enemy sat coiled on its tail looking down on him from the screen, glowing in those odd patterns that still sent fear into the hatchling Garsal when they listened to the evening tales. He felt a faint quiver of fear strike deep into his own viscera. As the Archivist had said, it was impossible. There was no chance that their old Enemy was here on this planet. The Archivist must have been mistaken. "Are you certain?"

"I've run the patterns again and again, and there is no mistake. I do not understand though; they were exterminated millennia ago."

"You will speak to no one of this," commanded the Overlord. "You will re-run the files, and you will cross check every scan we have on file since landing on this planet." The Archivist bowed his head silently.

The Overlord tapped again and opened a channel to the Senior Trooper on the plateau. "You are well positioned?"

"Yes."

"You will stay concealed, and you will look for this pattern on your scanners." He sent the pattern and the image. "And you will notify me immediately with live visuals if you find it."

"Immediately." The screen blanked, and the Overlord folded his manipulator arms briefly in thought. He opened another channel to the crawler.

"Report." The channel crackled and hissed as he waited.

"We are within a few hundred metres of the breach, no sign of the humans on visual or scan."

"You will continue to search. The aircraft will be tasked to join you immediately. I want them found and either brought back here for interrogation, or killed if that proves impossible." The crawler commander acquiesced. The Overlord sat for several moments in silence. The possibility of the Great Enemy being on this planet was remote – they had been exterminated centuries ago. Surely it had been just an unfortunate combination of interference on the screen. He pushed the frisson of trepidation away and resumed pondering. The absence of deep-space communications meant little in the scheme of things. He'd decided long ago that this was his own fight – one that would mean offspring and the expansion of his own empire. A planetary year without deep space communications would give him the perfect opportunity to secure his own position without meddling from other systems. By the time communications were restored, he would be secure and ready to launch his own bid for ownership of this region of space. The humans were proving quite ingenious but he was certain of Garsal supremacy, and the technology that the humans had used so far would make a worthwhile addition to his own arsenal. The climb to the Overlordship had been one of challenges overcome. This was simply another. Any thought of the Great Enemy was pushed to the back of his mind.

A chime sounded. Stifling an involuntary tic of annoyance, the Overlord rose to obey the Matriarch's summons. It would be only a short time until he had more human slaves to present to her. He would take her the good news about the likelihood of the new supply.

***

Anjo grabbed Kaidan's arm. The young man's body radiated his urgency. "No, Kaidan, we can't just go straight to Watchtower. It's too far, still several hours' walk away at least."

"But Anjo! Mum and Dad are there!"

"Yes they are," Anjo saw no point denying it. "But we're meant to be going elsewhere, and if we don't turn up, someone who needs to be doing something else will be sent to find us. We need to complete our task."

"That's easy for you to say!" Kaidan said, rounding on him angrily. "They're not your parents!"

"That's right, Kaidan, they're not. I no longer have any parents," replied Anjo. "The Garsal took them from me years ago. I'm certain that your parents will be in a protected place." He wasn't, but there was no need to add to Kaidan's distress. From the corner of his eye, he saw Ember's tidemarks flicker in approval. "We need to continue on, deliver our messages and wait for re-tasking." He kept his voice level. "More than anyone I understand how you feel Kaidan, but running into the unknown won't help. If we were medics, then yes, I'd agree we should go straight to Watchtower, but we're not. And our job is to first do as we were tasked." He kept his hands on Kaidan's arms. Tempest was doing her best to stay out of the way, but looked confused.

"But what if they're hurt?" Tears glistened in Kaidan's eyes. "What if they're ... "

"Dead?" said Anjo, finishing off the sentence Kaidan had been unable to articulate. "Kaidan, if they're dead, there's nothing to do but mourn and then get on with it." Inwardly, he stifled his own past pain. "Running in now will change nothing. If they're hurt, then they'll be in the best of care long before we arrive, and we'll know about it as soon as someone can send word." He gave Kaidan a small shake. "Listen to me. What would you actually do in Watchtower?"

"I'd fight back!" replied the boy. "I'd stop the Garsal hurting anyone else!"

"And how would you do that? One bow against a flying aircraft? What if there are more crawlers? What's one bow going to do against that?" He turned Kaidan's face gently towards him. "We need to do our job as messengers. Stop arguing and let's get moving. We can help best by being somewhere they need us." Kaidan's face was still angry, but he was biting his bottom lip now and Anjo hoped that the boy would listen to reason.

All of a sudden the fight went out of him. "All right then. We'll get to the habitation first, but I'm going to volunteer to go to Watchtower when we get there."

"I wouldn't expect anything else," Anjo said genuinely, although at that point he would have agreed to anything to get Kaidan moving in the right direction. Kaidan consulted his map and Anjo did the same, wishing he had the youngster's ease with navigation, and they set off as fast as was safe though the vegetation.

Thirty minutes later, they walked into a smoking scene of devastation. A makeshift field hospital bordered a smoking crater ringed by still burning trees. Bodies were laid out on one side, and with a shock Anjo recognised the Senior Councillor's still form.

"Anjo! Kaidan!" Payne's voice was hoarse, coming from somewhere across the small clearing.

"Payne! Are you all right sir?" Anjo asked anxiously, hastening to where Payne was propped up against a tree, one splinted leg stretched out in front of him. His normally dark brown skin was pale, and there were blood-stained dressings down one side of the man's chest. Despite his obvious injuries, he had been jotting notes onto a small pad propped on a rock beside him.

"I'll heal with time. At least I'm alive. Which is more than can be said for so many others today." Payne's tone was tired and he grimaced as he spoke. "You have messages from Cally?"

"Yes, Sir," replied Anjo, "We were to deliver them to you and Master Cerren at the Starlyne habitation."

"You can leave them with me here," said Payne. "You need to continue on to Watchtower to find Cerren. He's on his way already, but there are things he needs to know – most of all the casualty list here, and he'll have more messages to send back." Anjo pulled the sealed missives from his pack and handed them to Payne. Payne leafed through them quickly and separated two out of the pile, which he handed back to Anjo. "They're for Cerren. Take this with you and give it only into his hand. Kaidan? Are you all right?"

Anjo looked around. Kaidan was standing, eyes fixed on the line of injured laid out beneath the trees. He was extremely pale, and as Payne spoke Anjo realised that the reality of the death and suffering that followed the Garsal was suddenly real to Kaidan in a way that it hadn't been before, even after that first battle against the Garsal. Anjo had spent the years of his teens as a guerrilla fighter in a war, and the last five as a slave of the Garsal. He was accustomed to death and destruction, so much so that his mind had acknowledged the lines of dead and injured but continued to function. Unlike the first battle Kaidan had participated in, all of these people had been doing nothing but walking through the bush. None had been actively seeking out the Garsal. It was his first experience of the Garsal way of war – collateral damage was nothing to the insectoid conquerors; as long as there was a population large enough to breed slaves, that was all that mattered.

Why did they do this?" Kaidan demanded. "We haven't hurt them."

Anjo stepped to Kaidan's side and placed his hands on the boy's shoulders. Tears had run tracks down the dust that stilll clung to his face after their dive into the bushes. Little Tempest was tucked against his legs, and Ember hummed deep in his throat and ducked his head against Kaidan's hand. Anjo looked deeply into the boy's eyes.

"This is how the Garsal wage war, Kaidan. This is what they do. Thanks to Payne, and Master Cerren, and people like your sister, we have a chance, and we have allies. The Garsal still don't know that we have Starlyne friends.

This is not the end, it's just a beginning." Kaidan's expression was still desolate. "We need to pull ourselves together. Payne's given us a job. We need to get to Watchtower as fast as possible, and I can't get there alone. You need to navigate. Can you do that?" Kaidan nodded, and swallowed. "Remember, half an hour ago you couldn't be there fast enough." Anjo felt ashamed as he used the boy's love for his parents to manipulate him into activity.

"Tell Cerren that once we leave the Starlyne habitation, we'll comply with Plan Green," Payne said.

Anjo thought briefly about asking what Plan Green was, but decided he probably didn't need to know. "Come on," he told Kaidan briskly. "We need to move as fast as possible. Point us in the right direction and we'll be off." Kaidan pulled himself together and indicated with a fingertip, and the two of them moved off, by unspoken agreement, immediately into thick cover.

An hour and a half later, they emerged from the vegetation not far from Watchtower's gates. For some time, a pall of smoke had been visible on the horizon and they'd moved in silence as fast as possible. Neither had spoken, both fearful of what they might find when they arrived. A short time before they had arrived, the sounds of distant explosions had ceased and there were no further signs of aircraft in the sky, leaving Anjo uncertain of what they might find.

The town gates had suffered direct hits from the aircraft, and one pillar was completely demolished. Anjo was glad to see several of the local militia on duty at the gates.

"You're both to go directly to Scout Compound," said the woman in charge.

"My parents – are they alright?" asked Kaidan urgently.

"I don't know," she said, shaking her head sadly. "We've only just received orders from Master Cerren that anyone attached to the Scouts is to go straight to the Compound. They'll know there, I'm sure." Kaidan nodded, and Anjo hoped for his sake that there would be good news when they arrived. His young companion's face was tight with distress.

They moved into Watchtower's streets. It took a long time to get to Scout Compound. The once beautiful town was battered. Some streets were so damaged that they were impassable, while others seemed untouched. Scholars Precinct was almost unrecognisable. Everywhere there were people in the streets, some sitting dazed, others moving with desperate purpose. Many wore dressings of some sort, but there were so many still forms, most laid out with some dignity, while here and there others laboured, still trying to pull the injured from the wreckage of their homes and businesses. Anjo placed a hand on Kaidan's arm. The boy was dazed, almost staggering at what he was witnessing.

"Come on, Kaidan, we're almost there." The boy nodded and followed Anjo as he detoured around what had once been someone's house, but was now a scattered pile of burned stone that had fallen across the street. Thick dust was settling everywhere and smoke spiralled into the sky. Occasionally they passed a burning building, with firefighters working frantically to extinguish the flames. Everywhere were the sounds, smells and images of disaster. Anjo pulled Kaidan along as he skirted pieces of rubble, and they finally arrived at the Arena. The destruction seemed to have reached a pinnacle just outside the walls of Scout Compound, with a line of burning, gutted buildings that led almost to its wall, then broke off abruptly. The solid building sat almost untouched in front of them.

At the arena gate, Kaidan rushed forward with a glad cry. Boots sat there on guard, his glowing blue tidemarks bright and untarnished, and Kaidan threw himself into his father's arms as Adlan's battered face broke into a smile.

"Dad! You're OK, where's Mum?" Tears poured down Kaidan's face, and his voice was muffled in his father's shirt. Anjo stood to one side, feeling slightly awkward during the reunion.

"She's fine, she's with the others inside. They're finalising the evacuation plans. Do you have messages for Master Cerren?"

"Yes sir," replied Anjo, as Kaidan continued to hold onto his father's tall frame. "I'll take them straight away. Do you know if Semba's all right?"

"She's in the arena tunnel, in one of the anterooms, Anjo. I'm sure you'll be able to see her when you've delivered your messages." He looked at Anjo and Ember. "When you're done, if Cerren hasn't assigned you elsewhere, you can stay in our billet tonight. Just come and find me."

"Thank you, Adlan," replied Anjo. "I'll let Master Cerren know. There's no need for Kaidan to come with me, I have all of the messages in my pack. I'll be back shortly." He turned and moved off. There was no need to pull Kaidan away from his family. He was startled to feel tears pricking his eyes as he strode off. The memory of his own father had slowly begun to fade, but every now and then something refreshed the images he still treasured, and the sight of Adlan and his son was one of them. He cleared his throat slightly and felt Ember brush comfortingly against his hand. The black starcat looked up at him with loving eyes, and his grief at his own loss lessened slightly.

Despite Scout Compound's relative wholeness, the whole complex reeked of the smoke that hung over Watchtower. Everywhere through the long corridors were dirty forms hastening from task to task. He wondered at their fortitude — to stay in the building when the risk of the aircraft returning had to be high. He climbed the stairs two at a time to the council room and deposited his pack by the door. He pulled Cally, Toman and Payne's messages from it, and knocked on the door.

"Enter." He recognised Peron's voice.

"Messages, sir."

"Ah, thank you Anjo. Just wait a moment." Peron strode over to Master Cerren, and Anjo stood unobtrusively to one side of the doorway. The room was a hive of activity. There were schedules and lists attached to all of the walls, and a good proportion of the Patrol Firsts and Masters were gathered in the room. Cerren presided at the main table, and Anjo recognised members of Watchtower's Council and a few from Starfall with him as Peron bent and placed the messages in front of him. Suddenly, he wondered what the death of so many of Starfall's Councillors would do to the plans for resistance. He gritted his teeth. It didn't matter. These were his people now, and he'd do whatever it took to help them stay free of the Garsal. He wondered how Semba was, whether the bombing of Watchtower had pushed her even further into her fear. As soon as he was dismissed he'd have to check on her.

He whiled away the waiting by stroking Ember. The young starcat had become part of him. He remembered how fearful he'd been of the creatures when he'd first been rescued. They'd been so huge, and their teeth and claws so large and sharp, that the first few weeks on Frontier had been peppered with nightmares about being saved from the Garsal only to end up as a starcat's dinner. He remembered the first time he'd touched one – Shanna's Storm – and now he had one of his own gazing lovingly into his eyes. Ember appeared slightly amused, he thought, as if he knew what Anjo was thinking. The starcat's red tidemarks twinkled slightly and Anjo wondered again.

***

Senior Trooper Hoth sat quietly in his vehicle. Unlike the crawlers, the climbers were small and relatively agile. He was old as troopers went, and as he looked at the pattern and picture that the Overlord had sent, his normally canny nature quailed. It was surely impossible. The pattern on its own had initially meant nothing, but when combined with the picture ... He replayed the tales he'd heard as a juvenile. They were tales only whispered where none could hear. Tales that suggested that some had escaped and settled elsewhere in the galaxy. Official histories told only the story of the conquering and destruction of the Great Enemy. He'd seen the old images during his years of schooling, preserved in the archives and trotted out yearly when the Garsal commemorated their greatest victories. Surely it was impossible.

In the cab's confines he looked at the other two Garsal. One was working with great industry to expand the map of the human settlements, while the other sat with his eyes fixed on the screen in front of him, poised alertly for any sign of life near the climber. At least the plateau was relatively safe compared to the country they'd traversed on their journey from the ship. But he'd had to brief both troopers on the pattern sent by the Overlord, and all of them knew that they'd seen it before, ghosting past the scanners, usually late at night.

He sat and pondered, faceted eyes unreadable. Dreams of bringing back slaves paled against the moment he would present the Overlord with actual evidence that the Great Enemy – the Starlyne – still existed. His hope of off-spring now seemed insignificant, compared to the survival of all Garsal on this planet should they incur the wrath of the Great Enemy.

Chapter 31

SHANNA faded again as an aircraft roared overhead. The aircraft had been constantly in the air since their escape from inside the ring of sentinels. They'd heard one of the Garsal crawler vehicles somewhere behind them as well, and several of the smaller vehicles had been sighted through the trees. Most of the Patrol were still exhausted from the foray into the Garsal ship, and despite Shanna's donated patches Taya was on the edge of collapse again. Shanna could sense the worry plaguing Spiron and Barron. She and Allad were in their normal place at the head of the Patrol, their three starcats spearheading the escape bid. She ducked under a low hanging tree branch, and let her fade go. Storm appeared by her side, tidemarks flashing in warning patterns. Shanna signalled behind her and went to ground near a fallen log. Storm vanished again and she deliberately looked through his eyes, gritting her teeth as the nausea generated by his rapid movement shook her briefly. Directly ahead was a staureg, the first they'd seen in the bowl. It was approaching rapidly, obviously attracted by the noise made by the Garsal. She closed her eyes and switched to Twister. He was stationary and his gaze was fixed on one of the smaller Garsal vehicles moving through the trees ahead of them.

She looked through the overhanging branches and signalled Allad. He nodded and she dropped back to Spiron with the information. He pondered briefly and came to a decision. "We need to separate. Send a cat to Fractus. He and Teacher are to leave immediately – put this into your cat's harness for him." He handed her a folded piece of paper. "We'll divide into three groups. You, Allad, and the other cadets will take Taya, and do your best to avoid the Garsal. If you have to, some of you will have to decoy the Garsal while the others help Taya to move faster. Barron will take Karri, Sandar and Nelson east – they'll try and distract the staureg briefly then lay a second trail. I'll take Kalli and Arad with me. We'll go directly north and will try to divert the Garsal vehicle. Arad assures me that Nosey will keep up." He pursed his lips slightly. "It's likely that we'll be separated for some time. Once you're sure you're not being followed, head directly for the plateau and the Starlyne habitation. Leave messages at the secure sites we found on the way here. We'll do the same."

Shanna looked quizzically at Spiron as he spoke, and as she tucked the note into her trouser pocket he spoke again, his tone definite. "Frontier needs all of you to survive. You need to get back to our people because your combined gifts may well be their salvation." She looked at him, surprised, and he held her gaze until she dropped hers, feeling a mixture of embarrassment and worry. She didn't really know what to think, but as Fury trotted in towards Spiron, he flicked his tidemarks in a complex pattern that indicated absolute agreement with his partner.

Shanna was slightly bemused, and awkwardly ducked her head and nodded. If nothing else, it was essential that they protect Taya. Her ability to plumb the depths of the alien technology astounded Shanna. She was sure that she would be unable to replicate it. She was good for raw strength perhaps, but that level of finesse? She mentally shook her head as she ghosted through the vegetation to Allad, simultaneously calling Twister in. She tucked the message into his harness, rubbed his head, and sent him off to Fractus with instructions to find her when the message was delivered. She felt his determination as he blurred into top speed and vanished into the thick greenery. The others arrived within a few moments, and Allad organised them quickly into two subgroups. He, Shanna, Amma and Ragar would hold themselves ready to distract and delay the Garsal, while Verren and Zandany each put an arm around Taya to assist her through the thick undergrowth. There was a slight commotion as Barron's group deliberately attracted the attention of the staureg and moved off towards the east. The beast roared, and the sound of snapping vegetation came clearly through the trees.

Allad flicked a finger, and Shanna, taking a deep breath, led them to the west with Storm ranging ahead. Allad dropped back to the Patrol First's position in the formation, directing the cadets around him. They moved as a smoothly integrated unit.

For two hours their escape was relatively trouble free. The distractions provided by the other two groups had been very effective, but Shanna hoped fervently that they had escaped unscathed. Every now and then the sound of distant commotion still came on the breeze.

As they neared the western rim of the bowl, the terrain began to roughen and Shanna was hard pressed to find an accessible route. Storm ranged ahead, but even he had to choose his route with care. Another aircraft screamed overhead, and as Shanna dropped into the relative cover of a frondan tree, Storm came to a sudden halt as she spied a metallic glint directly ahead. She held up one hand to stop the others, then crept forward cautiously, listening as hard as possible. Two of the small Garsal vehicles were sitting stationary directly ahead. Around them, several troopers prowled cautiously. Their heads swept ceaselessly from side to side and they started at every sound. Shanna surveyed the area carefully. A tumbled mass of boulders boxed them in on her right, and further to her left the sound of tumbling water warned of a creek bed scattered with boulders. There were only two options – retrace their steps and go back the way they had come, hoping to find an alternate route, or take a chance and hope to sneak past the Garsal. She left Storm on guard and dropped back to Allad.

"Garsal ahead."

"Can you fade us all and still have enough strength to move fast?"

Shanna considered briefly. "No, I don't think so. I have one patch left, Allad – should I use it?" The big Scout frowned then shook his head.

"No. We may need it for someone else, and it appears the rest of us are out as well." His gaze strayed to where Verren and Zandany supported Taya. She was white-faced and clearly struggling. With only a brief hesitation, Shanna pulled the patch from her pocket and handed it to Allad, trying not to think about what might happen if she needed to fade the whole group. "Thank you," he replied. "I'll give it to Verren to use if and when he thinks it's necessary." His expressive eyebrows quivered slightly. "The four of us will begin by distracting the Garsal. If we move fast, do you think there'll be enough space for Verren and Zandany to slip Taya past?" Shanna gulped, but nodded.

"Yes."

"In that case, be ready to move on my signal." Shanna slid back to the waiting Storm. She felt briefly for Twister – he was still far to the north, and ran her hands nervously over Storm's head. Without diverting his eyes from the Garsal, he managed to lean into her comfortingly and she pulled herself together, taking a deep breath.

She looked backwards to the moustached Scout, caught his nod, and led the four out into the open, straight towards the waiting vehicles. For a moment it seemed the Garsal wouldn't notice them, but then one of the troopers caught sight of her and raised the alarm. His weapon rose towards her and a turret on the top of the vehicle swivelled, a red beam spearing out from it towards them, and Shanna threw herself sideways into cover. As she picked herself up and began to run she prayed fervently that their ruse would work, and Verren and Zandany would manage to get Taya safely past the alien invaders. Storm ran ahead of her, and dimly to her right she could 'feel' Twister moving further and further away from them.

Pungo leaves whipped her in the face, and she put her attention firmly back in front of her and continued her run. She was reminded of that first run which now seemed so long ago, trying to keep the attention of the lumbering Garsal vehicle. This vehicle was much more nimble and it ducked and weaved through the trees easily, making it more difficult to stay ahead. It would have been quite easy to vanish into the undergrowth or to fade to lose the vehicle, but to keep enticing it on? It was going to be extremely risky. Fortunately the sounds of the vehicle enabled her to keep track of its location easily, but Shanna found the combination of fast and visible movement terrifyingly difficult. Storm was making sure he was visible to her and Shanna saw glimpses of Satin as well, as they ducked and weaved through the trees.

Shanna scanned ahead of herself frantically, hoping to avoid any pitfalls or dangerous plants, and she kept her movement as quiet as possible, relying on providing flashes of appearance to keep the Garsal pursuing, while hoping that none of Frontier's predators would be attracted by the commotion. The hot red lance shaved a small branch off a tree just to her right and she ducked reflexively, nearly tripping over a rock. She regained her balance and swerved enough to put a few trees between herself and the Garsal vehicle. There was a whistle from Allad behind, and Shanna wondered how the Scout could possibly whistle while running. Obediently, she began to run a staggered pattern with the other three. The chase began to take on a rhythm of its own, and Shanna kept pace with a kind of tune inside her mind. Run, two three four, show myself, two three four, leap, two three four, watch for Storm, two three four ... The Garsal vehicle was firing its weapon wildly at any sight of a human form, fortunately inaccurately for the most part.

Sweat began to run freely down Shanna's back, and her pack began to rub as she maintained the pace. She wondered just how long they would need to keep leading the Garsal away. It wasn't a question she'd thought to ask. There was another whistled signal from Allad. *How could he possibly have enough breath for that?* wondered Shanna again, and she dropped back to let Amma lead.

She slowed to the rear of the group, and began the cycle of run, show, leap, watch, again. Being at the back brought her closer to the vehicle and when she showed herself, the shots from the Garsal vehicle came much closer than they had when she was leading. It did give her a chance to catch her breath slightly, though. She used the respite to 'feel' for Twister again. He was still moving rapidly away, and she wondered again just how fast a starcat could really move. Resolutely she took her mind away from her absent cat, and focused on the job at hand. It was much easier than normal to see the others, and slightly disorienting. Amma was about fifty metres ahead and appeared to be moving easily, while Spider glided ahead. Ragar was just ahead of Shanna with Allad directly to his right, both following Amma. Sparks paced Allad and Ragar, while Satin roved ahead with Spider. Shanna could see the sense of having two cats out in front clearing the way for their friends, as they moved so much more rapidly than normal through the thick vegetation of Below. She ducked under a tree branch, dodged a small barbed palm, and ran into a clear space to show herself to the vehicle. A red beam incinerated the leaves by her head, and she cringed away from the smell of burning but insisted her legs keep her moving forwards. It was a crazy chase. Her pack bounced and jostled, and every now and then it caught on protruding branches, momentarily wrenching her to one side.

Amma dropped backwards as Allad whistled again, and Ragar and Sparks surged to the front. Shanna accelerated slightly to allow Amma to slip in just behind her as Storm steered her around a clump of carnivorous plants, and the run continued.

Two hours later, Shanna was tired. They'd been jogging steadily the whole time, ducking, weaving, and enticing the vehicle on as the terrain had forced them onto one narrow route. The two vehicles had been joined by the dim, distant sound of one of the huge vehicles that they'd encountered previously. She estimated that they'd covered about ten kilometres at best, but the rim of the bowl was now towering above them. The smaller Garsal vehicles were quite nimble, and much harder to evade than the original ones.

Allad whistled again and she changed direction, now pushing towards higher ground and the rim of the bowl. She began to labour slightly as the ground rose. It was rockier though, and Shanna had to weave around larger boulders and jump the smaller ones. Just ahead of her, Storm showed himself completely as he led her around an even larger outcropping. Behind it the ground rose steeply, toward the western rim. Shanna's breath came more harshly, and her quads began to feel the strain as she climbed. She hoped that Storm knew where he was going. She showed herself briefly and heard the engine notes of the pursuing vehicles change as they began the climb.

Storm flicked his tidemarks at her and she pushed slightly harder, scrambling up the increasingly rocky ground. The large rocks gave way to the beginnings of a scree slope. Shanna followed Storm to the side of it, and began to scrabble her way up it. She looked upwards and realised that they were ascending the rim of the bowl. She hoped fervently that there was a way up and over the edge. Allad called his directions now, his voice slightly ragged with his need to breathe. Shanna moved backward through the group again, and let Amma lead. Storm paced by her side now, his coat still sleek despite the exertions of the last hours. The two small vehicles were clearly visible behind them, and they began to traverse the bottom of the scree slope. The growl from the larger vehicle was more audible. She'd lost sight of Verren, Taya and Zandany about an hour and a half into the run, and with no energy to spare, she'd had to trust that they were still nearby and safe. The fact that the Garsal were continuing to chase the four visible humans was slightly reassuring, and seemed to suggest that the other three were still undetected.

Shanna pushed herself harder as the the incline steepened. Sweat trickled into her eyes, momentarily blurring her vision, and she frantically wiped a grubby sleeve across her face. Her breath was now rasping loudly and her throat burned with the need for a drink. "Ready yourselves to fade," came Allad's voice. Shanna prepared herself but kept scrambling, waiting for Allad's command. The slope steepened again, almost becoming a climb. Storm guided Shanna off the side of the scree slope and into the scrub bordering it. She began to use some of the smaller tree trunks to help her in her climb. Her eyes darted from side to side as she scanned the handholds, the memory of the firemoss ever present in her mind.

Red beams from the vehicles spattered the rocks to her right, and the smell of burning began to sting her nostrils. Shanna climbed faster, arms and legs quivering, and her ears listening for the slightest sound from Allad. The barrage of red began to thicken and Shanna knew it was just a matter of time until one of them was hurt. Surely Allad would send them off the scree slope faded any moment now.

Storm's reassuring presence was the only thing that kept her climbing, and slowly Shanna realised that the beams coming from the vehicles were striking the scree slope well below her position. She risked a quick look backwards. The smaller vehicles had stopped moving, elevating their turrets as far as they could, but the steepness of the slope had defeated them. Shanna slowed slightly to try and allow herself to catch her breath, but Storm urged her on with an urgent hum. Puzzled, she looked back again to see the two machines beginning to sprout limbs. Remembering the vehicle they'd seen scaling the mountains, she redoubled her efforts. As soon as they began to climb, they'd have enough range to strike the climbing Scouts.

A crunching grind echoed behind them, and Shanna knew that at least one of the vehicles had begun to ascend the slope behind her. There was a rattle as rocks bounced and fell, then there was a sudden stench of acrid smoke that caught in her lungs and burned her chest. She coughed involuntarily, and finally Allad's voice rang out. "Fade and left! Follow your cats!" Gratefully, Shanna faded then immediately bore left into the scrub lining the rocky slope. Storm twinkled an ear tip at her, and she left herself 'feel' where he was and followed him. He continued to lead her upwards.

The grinding of the Garsal climbing resounded through the bowl and the echo of the bouncing and jostling rocks rose in volume as she climbed. The burning smell was still strong, and despite all her efforts coughs ripped from her throat. She desperately wanted a drink. Storm led her obliquely across the steep slope now, away from the noise behind her, and steadily upwards. Finally he led her over the rocky rim of the bowl. The last few metres were almost beyond her, but she gritted her teeth and persevered. Satin was waiting at the top, and as Storm and Shanna collapsed into the small pungo grove she winked her tidemarks at Storm.

Shanna's pack had rubbed her shoulders raw in patches, and she winced as she propped herself against a convenient rock, glad for the momentary respite, but she reminded herself that the Garsal vehicles were still climbing. She pulled her water bottle and shook it; fortunately it was still three-quarters full. She trickled it slowly into her palm, allowing Storm to lap from her hand. His pink tongue was slightly scratchy and he purred gratefully. As he lifted his head from her hand, Shanna took her first sip from the bottle, feeling the coolness slide into her mouth and slowly down her throat. It was like sipping the finest nectar. She restrained herself from emptying the bottle in one long gulp, knowing that she needed to drink slowly and save some for later.

The others pulled themselves exhaustedly over the rim, and as Allad arrived he gestured urgently. "I need your help to start the scree slope sliding!"

"What?" Shanna was confused.

"Like you did with Taya and the sentinel. I don't have the energy to do it by myself."

Shanna nodded, remembering Allad's ability to move objects. "I'm not sure, but I suppose we can only try." As Shanna pushed herself tiredly to her feet, she felt her legs nearly give way. "Can we get the others to help?"

"How far away is Twister?" asked Allad. Shanna thought for a moment, allowing herself to home in on her other cat.

"Too far for this," she replied.

"Then we'll all work together, and trust that we'll be safe for the few moments it should take. Follow me."

Shanna followed the other Scout to the edge of the bowl. One of the vehicles was steadily grinding its way upwards towards the rim, while the other had veered slightly to one side, and was very obviously searching the scrub for signs of human beings. There was a soft rustle and the others appeared. All looked exhausted, battered and sweaty. Dirt and scratches formed random patterns on their faces, and Verren and Zandany almost carried Taya into position. There were no questions, just silent agreement as Allad explained what they needed to do.

As they had the night before their foray into the Garsal ship, the cadets arranged themselves into a circle, hands linked over their cats. This time, Allad was one with them and Satin's cool greenness flavoured the mix. Via Storm, Shanna could feel the determination inside Allad's mind. There was a moment of disorientation, then it was like she and the others were pouring energy into Allad's body. The world spun despite her closed eyes but Storm was there with her, his cool blueness surrounding her and slowing the drain. She felt and saw Allad begin to agitate several large boulders on the very edge of the scree slope. She felt Storm's approval, and together they joined Satin and Allad, adding their strengths to his effort. Their closed eyes didn't see the blue, green, ruby and violet glow that rose softly around them. They didn't see the animal life settle to stillness, or the carnivorous plants that pulled in their tendrils. Not one of them saw the glow rise to a crescendo of scintillating colour before it exploded into sparkles of light in an effervescent shower. The boulders rocked and wobbled, and the cadets heaved with Allad one last time, then all of the boulders moved. Suddenly spent, Shanna attempted to open her eyes as the sound of roaring rocks slammed into her ears. Dizziness struck hard and she closed them again, then darkness descended and Shanna lost consciousness. Before her awareness faded, she felt Storms blueness surround her lovingly.

As she unglued her eyes, Shanna became conscious of an overwhelming thirst. She struggled to the top of a mountain of fatigue and willed her eyes to open.

"Are you awake?" Amma's voice sounded far away, but Shanna opened her dry mouth and rasped a dry reply.

"Of course not, I'm just pretending."

"Sorry! Stay there, I'll get you a drink." There was a faint rustle as Amma moved, and Shanna occupied herself with slowly attempting to stretch each limb. She was almost as tired as she had been after that first exercise. As she tightened and relaxed each protesting muscle, she ran her tongue over her lips, and found them dry and cracked. Amma returned and Shanna again resisted the urge to gulp the water.

"Where are we?"

"After you, Taya and Allad exhausted yourselves, Ragar found this spot and we carried you here," replied Amma. "Allad woke several hours ago, but you and Taya've been out for ages. She's still asleep and I think we need to let her keep sleeping. How are you feeling?"

"Like I've been trampled by half a dozen horgals," sighed Shanna. She lay back down with a stifled groan. "So, I assume we lost the Garsal?"

Amma was silent in the darkness for several moments. "There were no Garsal left to follow us. We dropped half the cliff face on them."

"We dropped a few boulders, and then the scree slope went," corrected Shanna, slightly disconcerted.

"After the scree slope went, so did the rim. We barely had time to drag the three of you back."

"How?"

"We're guessing it was a combination of an unstable slope and the removal of a few key rocks. It doesn't really matter how. We did it." Amma sounded half choked and close to tears.

Shanna lay quietly in the darkness, feeling slightly shaky. Shaky because they had visited so much destruction on the alien invaders, but not shaky because of regret. She remembered the guilt she'd felt that first time, when she'd killed the Garsal. This was different. This time she felt almost numb, distanced from the damage she'd caused. She tried to feel compassion for the creatures inside the vehicle and failed. They'd been intent on killing her friends, and by extension her family. This time she was in awe of the destruction she'd helped to cause, and slightly fearful of her potential for appalling acts, but not guilty for killing someone intent on killing her. She didn't know what to think, so she just lay there in silence. Amma sat quietly beside her and Shanna knew that the other girl was probably grappling with similar thoughts.

"I had no idea," she said finally. Storm made a small noise and rested his head on her belly, and she occupied her hands by stroking his head.

"No," replied Amma. "This is not what I expected to be doing. When I fly, I'm free. When I can feel the weather, it's helpful. When I fade, I'm safe, but what we all just did - well, it frightens me." Shanna could see Amma's head turn towards her in the darkness. "But at the same time, I'm glad. Glad they're dead and we're safe. The problem is I don't know what kind of person that makes me ... " Her voice trailed off and they stayed there in silence in the faint starlight, until Amma was called to her watch.

Allad took a seat next to Shanna. She'd managed to bring some semblance of normal movement back to her limbs by slowly stretching her muscles, gradually warming them up until she was able to push herself into a sitting position.

"How are you?"

"Well, the herd of horgals appears to have left a fair few hoof prints on me," she replied.

"Did Amma tell you what we did?"

"Yes."

"Are you alright with that?" Allad's voice was quietly worried.

Shanna sighed. "Not really, but I don't regret it, if that's what you mean."

"I'd only planned to set the scree slope off, but there must have been some inherent instability in the whole formation."

"Well, it gives us a bit of breathing space," said Shanna.

"That it does," replied Allad in the darkness.

***

Inside the sequestered portion of the colony ship, the Matriarch paced in her work chamber. She turned to one of her attendants. "You are sure?"

"I am sure. This is the pattern that the Overlord transmitted, and this is the match from the files."

"You know what this means then?"

"I do." The attendant, second only to the Matriarch in seniority, was privy to her deepest secrets. "This is the moment that we have awaited, and the one that we have planned for."

"It is. Who would have believed that it would be us who must bring it to fruition?" The Matriarch paced back and forth, measuring her steps across the chamber. "And there is the added complication of the humans as well."

She positioned herself next to her second. "Pull up all of the information we have. We will need everything we know about the Starlyne race, and everything we can guess about these humans"

The attendant bowed her head, manipulator arms tapping swiftly across the screens. They filled rapidly with pictures and links. "This will take some time," she said.

"It will," replied the Matriarch, "and we must tread very carefully. The presence of the humans is an unforeseen complication." She tapped the screen in front of her pensively, enlarging the picture of the glowing creature until it filled the whole screen. "We will need to factor this in before proceeding. I will also need the list of initiates. Our approach must be doubly careful. We must ensure that all who must know are trustworthy. You are sure our program taps are undetectable?"

"I am." The attendant was highly skilled, and the Matriarch nodded at the definite tone. She pulled the screen closer and studied the picture carefully. With a few quick taps, she pulled another picture to the fore. The communications centre, shrouded in smoke, appeared. Even with their forms partially obscured by smoke, the humans were still intriguing. They were not what she had expected. She enlarged the image. A tall, young, human female with striking green eyes had been captured in the images, crouching over another human on the ground. The picture showed her face as she'd turned to look at the lift area. Not far from her, two huge felines watched her protectively, their sleek blackness patterned in glowing violet and blue. The Matriarch enlarged the picture again and centred it on the girl's face.

"The humans here seem different. They have brought the fight to us, and we are unable to tell anyone about it. Our task is made even more difficult, and our sisters will remain unwarned. I must think on this. Bring me the list when you have it." As the attendant bent to her tasks, the Matriarch entered her private chamber to think further on the actions she would need to take.

***

On the plateau, Master Cerren surveyed the damage reports, then ran his eyes one more time down the lists of injured and killed. By his side, Socks made a comforting sound deep in her throat, and as he looked down at her she placed her large head in his lap and closed her eyes. He laid his hand on her grey head, and its warmth imparted some comfort to him. His eyes stung with the remnants of smoke and unshed tears. All he wanted to do was to forget the sounds and smells of the disaster visited upon Watchtower, but each time he closed his eyes he saw Tamazine's flame ravaged face and heard her plea to save her people.

Fortunately Peron's evacuation plans had saved many key personnel, but the loss of life had still been heavy. He sat in his second story office and looked out of his window. Faint glowing trails marked lines of refugees now following groups of his Scouts out of the arena, to more secure refuges in the old storm shelters. As he watched the lanterns were extinguished, the better to protect the precious human resources. If he turned his head slightly, he could see the faint glow of fires still burning in the town proper. He deliberately turned back to where the lanterns had vanished. The old shelters would be full to bursting, until the people could be redistributed to the welcoming Starlyne enclaves.

He pondered the messages he'd sent inland to Starfall with Foster's fastest two Patrol members. They were all he could spare, but they were experts and as soon as they were able, they'd deliver their messages and hopefully Starfall's remaining Council would take urgent action. The Starlynes were sending the same messages in their own fashion. Those messages would most likely reach Starfall far in advance of his own, but Cerren knew from bitter experience with Tamazine that it was unlikely that action would take place on Starlyne intelligence alone. He sighed and shook his head.

With a groan, he pushed Socks' head gently out of his lap and levered himself to his feet. "Time to sleep, my lady." He slung his pack over one shoulder and descended to the ground floor. At the bottom of the stairwell, Peron waited.

"The remnants of the Council are awaiting us in the basement conference room," Peron said. "They voted an hour ago. You're now the interim Senior Councillor. And there are more plans to make. I'll fill you in on the rest on the way down."

Cerren nodded resignedly. "Well, there's a lot to do. Kaidan and Anjo have gone with the breeders to Hillview?"

"It's a safe location, and the facilities are ideal. They will return once the breeders are settled. We will have need of as many messengers as possible."

"And Semba remains here with us?"

"Yes. She's terrified, but she's less apathetic than she was. It may be that the attack has achieved something good in that regard."

Master Cerren nodded thoughtfully. "We'd best be at it, then. I'm assuming that Toman has everything else well under control?"

"Yes, fortunately everyone's too happy to be offered some kind of safe haven to wonder how we've managed to ready them in such a short period of time. Hopefully it's something we'll never have to explain." Peron paused, and for a few moments they walked in silence.

"One more thing, Cerren," he said finally. "We've had word from Below."

Cerren drew a sharp breath. "And?"

Peron stopped and faced him. "It came in via the Starlyne network. Unfortunately it was fairly brief. All we know is that Patrol 10 had located the ship and planned to destroy its communication facilities. I've marked the location on one of the maps in the conference room. It's a fair way Below, beyond the Southern Barrier Range. That's the gist of it really."

"I'd hazard a guess that they're the reason behind this attack then. It seems to suggest that something's happened." He clicked his mouth in frustration. "I wish we had more information and that our communications were faster."

"Apparently the location is beyond the Starlyne network as well. Radiant sent the message as soon as he and Perri were within range."

"Well, we'll plan for as many contingencies as possible, then. It may be time to consider sending another patrol or two Below."

"I'd thought so too," replied Peron. "I have Patrol Four on standby."

The two men resumed their walk towards the arena door.

***

As the sun rose, the Garsal Overlord pounded his console with frustration. He still had only one human body to show for all of his efforts. Reports from several of his pursuing vehicles had ceased abruptly as the sun set the previous day, and the roar of collapsing rock had echoed around the bowl. Something had happened, but information was still sketchy. His pursuing vehicles had reported injury to several of the humans as they pursued them, but as night fell they had seemed to vanish into the darkness like ghosts. He'd grounded the aircraft for the night, hesitant to risk them in the darkness. There would be more repercussions for the upstart humans on this planet. Further reconnaissance was necessary, and careful planning. He sent for Zoash. His sib would have insights that he would have need of. Ambition as well, but at this juncture, it would only spur both of them to greater effort.

Still, no matter how hard they fought, like all humans before them they would be defeated. His hope of offspring depended upon it.

***

As the sun climbed slowly into the sky, Twister appeared by Shanna's side. He was obviously tired and a note was tucked into his harness. He sniffed her all over as she ran her hands over him, making sure that he was alright. Amma chuckled suddenly.

"I'm not sure who's more anxious, you or Twister."

Shanna smiled back. "I'm just making sure he's OK." She hugged the violet-toned cat to her, snuggling into his softness in the relief of having him back again. Storm sideswiped him enthusiastically as well.

"Time to move along," came Allad's voice, after he'd finished reading the note. "We've a long way to go, and the sooner we get there the better." Twister hummed plaintively. "And we'll be travelling much slower than you did, Twister – you can rest on the way." The violet-toned cat twinkled his tidemarks in mock sadness, but turned his head towards the plateau.

They formed up – Allad in charge, Ragar as his second, Shanna at the front, and Taya in the middle. Verren took up his position directly behind Shanna, while Amma and Zandany took flank. As they moved off they thought of their families and friends who awaited them further north. The first part of their fight against the Garsal was over but Shanna steeled herself as she contemplated the next days, weeks and months. The real fight had just begun.

List of Characters

Scout Cadets
Shanna – Storm and Twister
Amma – Spider
Ragar – Sparks
Zandany – Punch
Taya – Spinner
Verren – Cirrus

Patrol 10
Spiron (Team Leader) – Fury
Barron (Team Second) – Hunter
Allad – Satin
Nelson – Glutton
Karri - Moon
Kalli – Flyer
Sandar – Gryphon
Arad – Breeze/Nosey
Challon – Dipper
Perri – Spangles

Patrol 4
Farron (Team Leader) – Mist
Other Scouts
Feeny – Gem
Damar
Toman (senior Scout Master – retired) – Ghost
Cally – (Senior Scout/starcat trainer – retired) Mirror
Cam – Splash
Manda – (retired)
Romon (Senior Scout – retired)

Masters
Master Cerren (Teacher/Council) – Socks
Master Peron (Scout) – Thunder
Master Lonish (Scout) – Samson
Master Yendy (Scout)
Master Vandon (Scout)
Master Kenwell (Scout)
Master Erilla (Council) – Nimbus
Master Dinian (Archery)

Archers
Kaidan (Student, Shanna's brother)
Camid
Gwen
Horden
Tasha

Others
Adlan (Shanna and Kaidan's father) – Boots and Moshi
Janna (Shanna and Kaidan's mother) – Sabre
Anjo (Garsal slave) – Ember
Semba (Garsal slave)
Hodan (Horgal wagoneer)
Josen (Starcat Breeder) – Anvil
Payne (Watchtower's senior councillor)
Tamazine (Skyfall senior councillor – The Senior Councilor of Frontier)
Jareth (Student, Josen's son)
Balto (Student, Yendy's son)
Hadder (Student, Erilla's son)
Ella (Student, Josen's daughter)
Drest (Student, Old Scout's granddaughter)
Beren

Garsal
The Overlord
Zoash (The Overlord's Hatching sib)
Hoth (Senior trooper)
The Matriarch
Laretai (First Senior to the Matriarch)
Estei (Initiate female)
Hirtoi (Initiate female)

Starlynes
Keeper of the Knowledge
Fractus
Radiant
Teacher
Speaker for Law (liaison with the council)
Promise of Hope (Fractus' mate)
Dreamer (Fractus' daughter)

About The Author

GROWING up in Western Australia, Leonie Rogers was an avid reader from an early age. Her mother vividly recalls her stating "I can read faster with my eyes than you can with your mouth, Mum..." at around the age of six. Her parents and great aunt encouraged her interest in literature, providing her with books of many different genres. She began writing during high school, placing in the Western Australian Young Writers Award in 1980, and she fondly remembers several of her English teachers, who encouraged her to write, both fiction and poetry.

Leonie trained at Curtin University as a physiotherapist and moved to the remote north west of Western Australia, as a new graduate, in late 1986. She continued to write poetry for herself and for friends. Living in the remote northwest, she had the opportunity to work with camels, fight fires as a volunteer fire fighter, and develop vertical rescue and cyclone operation skills with the State Emergency Service.

After relocating to NSW with her husband and two children, Leonie continued to work as a physiotherapist while still dabbling with writing. Finally deciding to stop procrastinating, Leonie decided to write the novel she'd had sitting in the back of her head for the last twenty years. Her husband and two teenage children have been extremely tolerant of the amount of time she has devoted to writing in the last few years.

Thank you for reading Frontier Resistance. We hope you enjoyed it. If you would like to be kept informed of the further adventures of Shanna, the Scouts of Frontier, and their starcats, or other new releases from Hague Publishing, why not subscribe to our newsletter at:

www.HaguePublishing.com/subscribe.php

And if you loved the book and have a moment to spare we would really appreciate a short review. Your help in spreading the word is gratefully received.

Hague

Publishing

www.HaguePublishing.com

PO Box 451 Bassendean
Western Australia 6934